lashley

30p.

Please return/renew this item by the last date
above. You can renew on-line at

www.lbhf.gov.uk/libraries

or by phone
0207 361 3610

putting residents first

Hammersmith & Fulham Libraries

LIZ DE JAGER

Banished

The Blackhart Legacy: Book One

TOR

First published 2014 by Tor
an imprint of Pan Macmillan, a division of Macmillan Publishers Limited
Pan Macmillan, 20 New Wharf Road, London N1 9RR
Basingstoke and Oxford
Associated companies throughout the world
www.panmacmillan.com

ISBN 978-1-4472-4765-4

1 3 5 7 9 8 6 4 2

A CIP catalogue record for this book is available from the British Library.

Typeset by Palimpsest Book Production Limited, Falkirk, Stirlingshire
Printed and bound by CPI Group (UK) Ltd, Croydon, CR0 4YY

Visit www.panmacmillan.com to read more about all our books
and to buy them. You will also find features, author interviews and
news of any author events, and you can sign up for e-newsletters
so that you're always first to hear about our new releases.

This book is dedicated to

my husband, Mark.

I blame you for all of this.

Thank you for asking *what if*.

Acknowledgements

A huge debt of gratitude to my best friend Sarah Bryars who has an overabundance of enthusiasm for Kit and who helped me make sense of this world I've created. With Sarah, the third aspect to our triptych is Sharon Jones who helped me with esoteric Merrily questions and found me research books that would make a vicar go pale. And high-fives to Jenni Nock who stood by the core characters and told me things would work out: you are wise!

A big thanks to Sue Hyams, Mo O'Hara and Paolo Romeo (all whom I met through SCBWI British Isles), for all those late nights at the Southbank and for pushing me to write Kit's story. Where would I be without you all bossing me around?!

A huge debt of thanks goes to Juliet Mushens, my agent, who decided that she loved Kit's voice enough to take a chance on me and worked so hard with me to sell The Blackhart Legacy. An equal measure of thanks goes to Bella Pagan, my editor, who's held my hand, kept me sane and explained the intricacies of 'what's next?' in the publishing process.

There's a swathe of other people to acknowledge, too; authors and fellow bloggers I've known through blogging and

Twitter and who gave constant and great advice, specifically Zoe Marriott and Luisa Playa, amongst so many others. I truly get the impression that debut authors in genre have the opportunity to stand on the shoulders of giants; my deepest gratitude to those authors who keep playing it forward. A shout out, too, to Tanya Byrne and her circle of trust; a girl couldn't ask for a more kick-ass advice-giver.

A huge thanks to my family in South Africa who were so excited when I told them about the book deal. You guys may all be very far away but I carry you in my heart every day. Thank you for believing and for being smug and saying: we told you so.

And last but not least, a huge thanks to Mark who started all of this in the middle of a bookshop with that damn question: *what if?* Your support means so much to me; I can't express it in words. I hope the dedication at the front of the book goes some way towards that!

The woods are lovely, dark and deep,
But I have promises to keep,
And miles to go before I sleep,
And miles to go before I sleep.

Robert Frost,
'Stopping by Woods on
a Snowy Evening'

Chapter One

Blackhart Family: Rumoured to be the descendants of the original Hansel and Gretel made famous by the Brothers Grimm in their *Kinder- und Hausmärchen* collection from 1812, the family has been in residence in the United Kingdom since the late sixteenth century. It is unclear if the rumours about their heritage are based on fact; no evidence to prove or disprove the rumour has been found.

More information about the existing family members can be found in Archive Boxes: Blackhart/1875–present.

From an archived report filed in HMDSDI HQ, 1978

Sitting on one of the swings in the park opposite the school, my watch tells me I'm forty minutes early for the start of my schoolday and I wonder how much longer this assignment will last.

A sixth-form girl walks up to the gates and leaves a single cream rose on the pavement, placing it carefully next to an open photo album. The rose is only one of many offerings that's been left since the news broke last night. Teddy bears, photos, candles, flowers. A silent outpouring of grief.

A friend helps the girl stand and they walk through the gates. I watch them move away, leaning into each other, every line of their linked bodies speaking of the shock and horror at another friend and schoolmate taking her own life.

I sigh wearily and let my hair drop forward. It tickles my cheeks but I don't shake it back. I've not worn my hair long for – I try to think – maybe a year and half now. Back then I was a different girl, untouched by the really bad things in life. Unaware that crazy things existed. I shudder to think how fearless I was, the risks I took, going out with my friends, staying out late, dancing till dawn at clubs, kissing boys. How I planned my future in long mad emails to my best friend Karina, who lives in Germany, speculating about when we would get to see one another again and how we'd be spending our gap year travelling around Europe and Asia. But that was then, and this is now and that girl from long ago is unrecognizable in now-me.

I puff out my breath and focus on the cars pulling up in front of the school, kids saying goodbye to their parents, life going on. Today I'm all about being prey and luring David Gardner to notice me and talk to me for longer than five minutes, away from his mates and hangers-on. I've spent two weeks researching, and my plans are simple but well laid. I know he cuts through the park on his way to school in the mornings. I know he likes his girls pretty and shy and a bit dreamy – so I'm giving him a shy, arty girl secretly crying out to be noticed.

I dig a tissue out of my pocket and wipe my nose and

dab at my eyes, suppressing an inward groan at the acting. I'm not a dishonest person and I'm not good at lying, but if it helps with the overall story the mark sees, then that's what I'll do.

I kick off with one foot, letting the swing move beneath me and I lean far back and stare up at the blue sky, watching the clouds coast by. I like the feeling of being suspended and I float there quietly for a few minutes, just being. There is a soft noise by my side and the swing next to mine creaks a bit as a weight settles into it.

I sit up with a jerk and stare at the boy sitting next to me. My surprise isn't feigned. I didn't hear him walk up. I didn't see him either. I know it should bother me as my hearing is good and my sight is excellent but my thoughts are clearly drifting a bit too much. I focus on staying completely in the role here, so I dash my sleeve across my eyes and give him a tremulous smile.

'Hey,' he says, smiling a wide friendly smile. 'Are you okay?'

I begin to nod but then shake my head. 'Not so much. I'll be fine, though.' I look over to the school gates. 'It's going to be a tough day.'

'Did you know Chloe?' he asks, his eyes shifting from me to the front of the school, where more people are leaving flowers and small items, mostly little teddy bears holding hearts. 'I'm David Gardner, by the way. My friends call me Dave.'

You would never think it, but it's actually really hard to lie about your own name. I swallow against the constriction in my throat and hold out my hand. 'Kelley,' I say, shaking his hand, blushing wildly. His hand lingers for a moment longer than necessary in mine before he curls his fingers around the chain that suspends the swing. The look he gives me is slow and hot. Score one to me. 'I'm new,' I say, brushing my hair back before continuing. 'But I had art class with Chloe for about a week before – you know.' I let my eyes drift to the scene in front of the school, before looking back at him. 'We spoke a few times. She seemed a bit quiet, but friendly. I liked her art.'

I've watched Dave for two weeks now. I know he's popular and charismatic. He has a wide circle of friends he hangs out with. His grades remain good regardless of how much partying he does and he's currently not in any relationship, although there is a group of around six girls who would dearly love to change that. Nothing about him is too remarkable. He's just handsome enough to draw the attention of all the girls and just clever enough to get decent grades. He is ordinary in every way, or so it would seem, but I know better.

'I knew Chloe,' he says, staring at me. 'She was a nice girl. Always friendly, up for a laugh. I really liked her. Full of energy and she liked to try out mad things. Like, this one time we hung out, she decided she was going to do a Banksy on some of the walls in town.' He laughs at the memory. 'Good times.'

I recall the photos I'd seen of Chloe before I started school here and I remember what she looked like before she fell in with Dave Gardner. They offered up two very different images of the same girl. The Chloe I knew was thin, pale, miserable, a bad photocopy of the real vibrant

girl her parents tried to hold on to. After they had spoken
with the school's principal for help, the job got handed to
me as my first solo mission.

I draw a breath and smile at Dave. 'It's so sad, you know.
I wonder what made her . . . ?' I shake my head and my
hair irritates my cheeks. I brush it back. 'Her parents must
be devastated.'

We exchange sad expressions, but I know he's looking
at me, watching my every move. His hot eyes rake my hair,
my face, my hands, my legs. Finally he notices my school
bag and portfolio. 'You draw?' he asks, nodding his head
to the portfolio resting on the grass.

My hand flutters to my face and I nod nervously. 'But
I'm not really any good. Not like Chloe.' Which is another
blatant lie, but he can't know that.

'Can I see?'

I reach down and hand the portfolio to him. I stare at
my hands, not wanting to see his reaction to the art in my
portfolio.

'These are really cool,' he says after a few minutes of
quiet where the only sound was him paging through the
sketchbook. His voice has taken on this weird timbre,
making the hair on my arms stand up. 'Are you studying
art when you go to uni?'

I flush prettily, shake my head and smile. 'No. I'll have
to do something sensible, like become a doctor or something.
My parents'll never let me do an art degree.'

He taps one of the sketches and I look over. It is one of
my favourites. It's of a girl sitting up in bed, staring at her
window. It's night-time so the sketch is full of dark shadows

but a moon is shining through the glass and you can just see the hint of a monstrous shape outside the window. The girl's expression is one of curiosity.

Dave looks at me and there is a hunger in his eyes. 'This is incredible. You're crazy good.'

I smile lightly and take the portfolio from him. 'You are being sweet, thanks.' I hold it in front of myself, like a shield. 'I have to get going. Start the day for real.'

He stands up and walks with me as far as the gate to the park. 'Kelley. Some of us meet after school as part of the drama group. There's a place we use, behind the assembly hall. If I give you directions, do you want to come and hang out with me?'

'Today?' I did not expect this so soon and I bite back the triumphant grin I feel hovering around my mouth.

'Yeah, why not? Of course, you don't have to. But it would be nice.' His smile is full of boyish charm and sweet eagerness, as if my 'yes' answer would mean the world to him. I hold on to that image hard as he leans closer and I try not to gag as the smell of his breath hits me. It smells like rotting vegetation and stagnant water. 'Say you'll come?'

For a brief second I feel a compulsion to punch him in the head, but I get a grip on myself and smile a smile that says I'm flattered that he'd even think I'm cool enough to hang out with him.

'Okay, it sounds like fun. I'll see you after school.' My smile probably looks dazzled and I keep it there as Dave digs out a notebook from his bag and draws a rough outline of the assembly hall and shows me where the green room is. Of course I know where it is. I've prowled the school at all hours and know every single nook and hiding place. I take the piece of paper and fold it into my bag, keeping my smile a bit stunned.

We walk to the school gates, where he spots some of his mates and lifts a hand to them. He turns back to me as we near them. 'You possibly made my day. I'll see you later.'

I nod and turn away before the group of girls standing by the gates can see the look of triumph on my face. They immediately form a huddle and start whispering, slanting sly looks at me.

I touch the knife resting against my hip in its custom-made sheath and take courage from it. The trap has been laid, now all I have to do is spring it.

Chapter Two

Banshee: Commonly found in Celtic countries, the female banshee or bean sí is an omen of death and a messenger from the World of the Dead. She portends death by wailing when someone is about to die. Contrarily, male banshees are far rarer than female banshees and are dangerous to humans. They are captured by human beauty and artistic ability and, once obsessed with a human, they will stalk the human, devouring their essence through psychic draining. In most cases, the human will die or commit suicide in an attempt to get away from the banshee.

From *The Blackhart Bestiarum*

'Kelley?'

I jerk with fright when Dave's voice echoes through the room. It's just after four and I've been here for a long time, waiting for him to show up. I know it looks as if I've been sleeping because my hair is mussed and I look out of it, so I yawn widely and grin at him in an embarrassed way.

'Hey,' I say. 'I must have fallen asleep.'

'You look cute,' he says.

I know what he sees, a girl with raggedly cut chin-length dark curls that refuse to stay out of her eyes, a slightly upturned nose and a smattering of freckles that no concealer can hide. Green eyes, a wide mouth. All of it forms a pretty enough picture aimed at attracting his attention and keeping it. I'm the pretty girl next door whom boys are best friends with and never fall in love with. His smile is big and open and friendly and it belies the hunger in his eyes. I see it only for a moment, peering out at me, before he's Dave again: just a normal boy meeting a pretty girl after school.

'All soft and dreamy.'

'Ha, wait till you see me bust some awesome ninja moves,' I quip in an effort to hide my growing nervousness.

He walks further into the room, glancing around. Everything is exactly the way it's always been. The couch, the jumble of random bits of furniture and odd bits of theatre props. His eye falls on my sketchpad, lying open next to me. It shows a half-finished portrait of his face, a close-up full of shadows, his eyes dark and enigmatic.

He hesitates for a few seconds only, but it's long enough for me to see that the portrait has really pleased him. His smile, when he turns to me, is slow and languorous and I can tell he thinks he's already won me over.

'I can't wait to see your moves.' He sits down on the couch and I shift my legs so he can sit close to me. 'You really are very pretty, did you know that?'

His hand reaches out to tuck a curl of hair behind my ear. The look I give him is all big eyes and a shy, flattered smile.

I focus on the small wooden pendant hanging around my neck, beneath my clothes, taking comfort from feeling its weight against my skin. It feels a little warmer than usual and I touch it through my school shirt, only briefly, before I drop my hand. I call my magic up and let the tiniest sliver surface, just a little bit, below my skin. It enhances the way I look, the way I shine, making me more appealing, softening my hard edges, making him believe the glamour I'm projecting of the shy, awkward, flattered girl. I will him to see me as the type of girl he wants to see and I hate myself for it, just a bit, but then I know what he is and what he's done and I don't feel sorry any more.

'Thanks,' I say. 'You're not half bad yourself.'

He laughs softly. 'I'm glad you decided to come and meet me. I think we have a lot in common.'

'Oh, really?' I try not to move my head away from his hand. He's stroking my cheek and neck as if I'm a cat. I really hate being touched by strangers. 'And what is that?'

'Well, I like you. I'm pretty sure you like me. You're talented and pretty. I'm . . . well, me.' His smile is cheeky, self-deprecating. 'I'm glad we spoke today. I'm glad you're here. I'd like to get to know you better.' His eyes are bottomless pits and his voice has thickened, his tongue slurring against his teeth. His head is close to mine now and I hold my breath, waiting, suspecting, hoping for what's coming next. 'Also, you shine so brightly.'

Which is exactly the kind of thing I hoped he'd say.

The telescopic iron baton slides out from under my sleeve and into my palm and with a satisfying snick I whip it at his face, hard. It connects with his cheek, making a meaty *thwap* sound. I'm off the couch and away from him in the space of a heartbeat but he's even faster.

He runs at me and shoulders me in the stomach, driving me into the small table where countless aspiring Arlington student actors and actresses have put on their make-up. We land on the floor but I'm already moving, doing my best to ignore the pain in my back and ribs. His hands reach for my throat and I punch him in the side of the head. He jerks back with surprise, and I follow it up with another swipe of my baton across the face. As he grabs for his face, I buck him off and scrabble backwards. I suck in a breath when the movement sends flares of pain throughout my body. I'm hurt but there is no blood and I can still breathe without sobbing, so it isn't serious.

'You know,' he says, not bothering to hide his surprise or annoyance. 'You played me.'

I shrug and smile, swinging the iron rod in front of me like a slender cricket bat. 'You fell for it,' I say, not bothering to hide the smugness in my voice. 'You could have chosen anyone else, but you chose me. Pretty stupid of you.'

He snarls at me and I grimace at the smell of his rancid breath in the confined space.

'You know what else is stupid?' I say, backing away from him, luring him further into the small room. 'Hunting in the same school for over a year. You must have been desperate. Desperate and stupid. Your clan must be so relieved I'm sending you back. Your antics in the Frontier have been a true embarrassment to them.'

It's this final insult that makes David Gardner transform into a monster. In the space of a heartbeat I've come to share the room with a creature no human should face. Gone is the teenager with the bright future. In his place is a monster from an ugly nightmare. Raw-boned and big, he easily tops seven feet. Sickly grey skin ripples across his narrow, hunched shoulders and his long sinewy neck flexes as he swings his head to try and keep track of me. His face has a wide flat nose and curving thin mouth. His eyes, still impossibly human, blink at me before the pupil dilates and narrows into a vertical stripe. The silver claws at the ends of his muscled arms are a good three inches long – being cut by them would mean a course of antibiotics and a few days in the infirmary at the Manor.

The thing about banshees is that there are very few of them and they work hard to keep the equilibrium within their small matrilineal clans. There are even fewer male banshees, and once a male's appetite for human girls quickens there is no way that female banshees will stand being around him, even if it means losing a mate. It is about politics too, and the banshee clans would rather lose one of their strong male partners than face the displeasure of the Unseelie ruler, the Queen of Air and Darkness, Suola.

The banshee in front of me has no reason to be here and no permission from his clan mother or the Unseelie Queen. He is a rogue and knows that I am here to send him back.

I keep my iron baton in my hand and focus on the creature. Long thin teeth slide from engorged gums and, as he lunges for me, I run past him, somersault over the couch and come up behind it. There's an audible *whump* on the other side of the couch as he runs fully into the magic circle it had taken me most of the day to set up.

I peer over the back of the couch and see him standing in the middle of a gently glowing circle, holding his head, making confused clicking noises in the back of his throat. The air is filled with the sickening smell of singed skin and I swallow against the bile rising in my throat.

I cast an eye at the wooden floor covered by the threadbare carpet he's standing on, noticing with relief how strongly the sigils I had so painstakingly crafted with phoenix-blood ink shimmer all around him. Because I didn't know how strong he would be, I had layered two magic circles, one within the other, hoping that if he got through the first one the second one would stop him. It was extra work and time consuming, but because this is my first solo gig I do not want to screw up.

I stand up on shaky legs and walk around the couch to stand in front of him.

'By the authority of the High King of Alba and by the trust placed in the Blackhart family, you are sentenced to return to the Unseelie Court, where you will face punishment in accordance to the treaties signed by the Queen of Air and Darkness. You are guilty of unlawfully accessing a gateway, of killing a human boy and impersonating him for the duration of your unauthorized visit to the human realm and by direct interference, causing the death of three young women. You will have no chance to plead your innocence as the Court found you guilty in your absence. Your sentence will be carried out when you arrive at the Unseelie Court.'

I'm relieved that my voice quivers only slightly as I speak.

I keep my eyes on the creature in the magical circle at all times. He's raging, testing the strength of the walls by hammering on them. Each time he does, bright sparks of energy singe his hands and forearms.

'I see you now, girl.' His voice thrums low in his throat. 'There is so much darkness around you.' He pauses, waiting for me to say something else, but I bite my lip and give him my best Clint Eastwood glare. 'I can taste your future, Blackhart. It's filled with pain and anguish. The Dark Gods hunger and no one else will be there to help you. Do you think you can survive what's coming, all by yourself?'

I am standing in front of him now. And once more he looks like Dave Gardner but there is nothing in his eyes that looks even remotely human. I know he's playing mind-games but I can't shake the feeling that there's a grain of truth in what he's saying. Banshees are weird at the best of times and the males are especially touched, more likely to go off the rails in puberty because of their hormones, which is why so few of them outlast any of the females in their clans.

Their gift of foretelling usually manifests during times of great distress. And right now would definitely count as him being in distress. He knows I'm ready to send him back to Suola's Court, right into the waiting jaws of her Beast. I've heard stories about her famous executioner and the delight he takes in torturing all those who oppose the Dark Queen, and it's given me nightmares for a week, so, in a way, I don't blame him for trying to rattle me.

'Feel free to tell your queen all you see, monster. I'm interested to hear what she has to say about this mess you've left behind for us to clean up.'

'Best to watch your back, Blackhart. Most of Alba would like to see you and your family burn.'

I'm unimpressed by his threat. 'I've heard that before, monster. We all have. And as much as the Fae dislike us, we do what's necessary to prevent monsters like you killing humans.'

He gives a low rasping laugh and licks his lips with a disturbingly pink tongue. 'Never go to the Otherwhere by yourself, Blackhart. I'll find you. I'll tell my friends about you. Maybe we'll even come back here and find you. Imagine the fun we'd have.'

'Tell your friends "hi" from me when you see them. Before you die, that is. Or maybe you won't even see them. I hear that Suola's kept her Beast on a short leash lately and he's hungry.'

I'm lying through my teeth but he can't know that. A distressed whine rises from him and I cover my nose with my shirt as the room is suddenly drenched in the smell of fear and something else unpleasant I try not to identify.

I hold up the small carved wooden token that's been hanging around my neck for the past two weeks. It takes a few moments for him to stop pacing so he can focus on what I'm holding. When he does, he stands up straight and a look of alarm crosses his reptilian features.

'No,' he says. 'Don't . . .'

'Shut up.' I let the token dangle off its chain and I watch his eyes follow it as it swings. 'You didn't give Chloe or Sandra or Jo a chance. I don't see why I should give you the option of travelling back to the Otherwhere on an easy ride.'

I walk towards the door. Just as I reach it I turn around and snap the little piece of wood neatly in half between my fingers. The sound it makes is a subsonic boom that shakes your bones and makes you feel a bit funny in the head.

I watch as the walls I had created so painstakingly with my own magic flash downwards, not unlike a laser scanning a document. The lower it gets, the faster it flashes, taking the banshee – aka a boy called Dave – with it, basically slicing him to bits before my eyes. I stand there and watch it happen. I don't really want to, but I make myself. I owe it to lovely Chloe, who fell in love with the wrong guy and who paid for it with her life.

When the beam reaches the floor where the sigils are inscribed, it runs along the ground widdershins, in reverse, taking the ink with it. Within seconds there is nothing left in the room that shouldn't be there. Unless you count the stench of singed skin, fear and urine, none of which I can do anything about.

I close the door behind me with shaking hands and turn the lock, pocketing the key. Time to go and report to Principal Williams that Arlington Secondary School will now no longer be plagued by supernaturally motivated suicides.

Chapter Three

The graveyard at dusk is still. I jump over the fence a few metres away from the locked iron gate and make my way along the tumbled stones and ancient yew trees standing guard among the graves. I ignore the long shadows snaking their way across the ground as night falls. I've been here so often that I could find my nan's grave while wearing a blindfold.

The gravestone isn't ostentatious. Above Nan's birth date and the date that she died, the simple lines read:

MIRABELLE BLACKHART

GRANDMOTHER, SISTER, AUNT, FRIEND.

'EVERYTHING YOU CAN IMAGINE IS REAL.'

I sit down next to the gravestone and lay the bright spray of yellow flowers on the ground. Someone's been keeping a good eye on her grave and it looks neater and tidier than some of the others.

I hug my knees to my chest and only find my voice after a few minutes.

'First solo job, Nan. It went okay, I think. I sent the banshee back and I was tempted just to burn him and the whole building to the ground, but that would have been messy and I think Uncle Jamie would have been really annoyed with me.'

I clear my throat and touch the petals of the flowers. 'I brought you some sunny flowers. I thought they'd cheer you up a bit.'

The silence in the graveyard acts as a balm to my frayed nerves and I watch as something, a beetle of some sort, pushes its way along the grass on the far side of the grave.

'Please tell me you're not planning to turn into a creepy Goth and hang out in graveyards.'

I try not to show my fright and twist towards my uncle Jamie's voice. How a six-foot-three guy weighing two hundred and fifty pounds can move as quietly as he does is a skill he's yet to share. The knife in my hand is a reassuring presence and I don't slide it back into its sheath in the small of my back when he sits down on the ground opposite to me.

He leaves a single white rose on the ground next to my yellow flowers.

'What are you doing here?' I ask him. His features are difficult to make out in the darkness but his silhouette is something I'll recognize anywhere.

'Catching up with you before I head to Hawaii. I'm training some US government people down there.'

'Nice. Do I get to come along?'

His chuckle is low and charming. 'Oho, a good try, but

18

no. You get to go home and sleep and eat. You look like you're made from candyfloss, like you'll drift away on the breeze any second.' He waves his hand in the air to show me exactly how wafty I look.

I scowl at him in the dim light. 'I'm fine.'

'You used a lot of magic. You need to rest. Do the paperwork to close the case and just relax. You'll be off on more adventures pretty soon.'

'I'm ready now,' I say.

'What are you doing here?' he asks me, blatantly ignoring my comment.

'Just wondering about stuff,' I say. 'How different my life would have been had she lived and the house not been burned to the ground.'

He sits quietly next to me for a bit before he drags out his dented pack of cigarettes and fiddles with it between his fingers.

'Did you ever wonder why Mirabelle made you do boxing?' he asks me. 'Or why she insisted you learn karate?'

I look at him in confusion. 'She never made me do anything,' I reply. 'I chose to do those things.'

'Do you remember her prompting you?'

I hate to admit it, but I remember her showing me the karate pamphlets. It took a few weeks but I eventually told her I'd be interested in taking classes. The boxing happened later, when we moved to the village and the local gym advertised classes after school. I liked the idea of learning how to defend myself, especially as the karate instructor I had in Germany had me compete in my age group and I enjoyed the competition.

'What are you saying, Jamie?'

'Mirabelle's been training you how to look after yourself all your life, Kit. You may not have realized that, but she knew a time would come when you would be drawn back into the family. And she wanted to make sure you wouldn't be at a disadvantage.'

I want to argue with him, but I can't because I suspect he's telling the truth.

'Why did she run from the family? If she knew about my gift, about the magic, she should have stayed.'

'Mirabelle wanted to give you a chance to grow up as yourself. She knew that your life as a Blackhart would mean one of constant training and learning about the Otherwhere. She saw your parents' death as a chance to give you the opportunity to have the normal childhood that none of us had. Then, when you were older, she would tell you about the family and you could make the decision to join us or walk away. We thought we'd tell you on your eighteenth birthday. But things changed when she was threatened; when she called me.'

I grunt. 'Too late.'

He sighs and shifts uncomfortably.

'Are you going to sit here the whole night, feeling sorry for yourself?' Jamie's voice isn't as harsh as it could be. 'I'm heading to the airport and if I don't leave soon I'll miss my flight.'

'I'm done,' I say and stand up smoothly, keeping the knife by my side. It was night-time in a graveyard. You just never know what might lurk in the dark.

'I'll walk you to your car,' he says to me and drops an arm around my shoulders, giving me a quick squeeze. 'I'm proud of you. You did really well sorting out the mess at that school.'

I beam a smile at that but pretend to watch my feet, not wanting him to see how much his compliment mattered to me.

'And I'm being serious, Kit. Go back to the Manor, do your paperwork and just relax. Mrs Evans is away at her niece's wedding so you'll have the whole place to yourself. Brownie weddings go on for at least a week, if not more if all the clan turns up.'

'But I'm fine,' I tell him. 'A bit sore and bruised, but I'm okay.' I hold my hand out and my magic shimmers around my skin. 'See? If I was as tired as you're making out, I wouldn't be able to do that. And are you sure I can't come with you? I'll be no bother, I promise.'

Jamie lets out a long-suffering sigh. 'I pity the man you decide to marry one day,' he tells me as he vaults over the fence. He waits for me to do the same. 'You just don't know how to listen.'

I shrug, used to this. 'It's okay, we'll be having so much sexy times there won't be any listening.'

'Oh, that is uncalled for,' Jamie laughs, pushing me away. 'You teenagers are just gross.'

I laugh as he climbs into his jeep.

'I'm proud of you, Sparky. You've done well on this mission. Now, go home.' He kisses my forehead before shutting the door.

I lift my hand in farewell as he spins the wheel and drives away into the night. I walk back to my own rental car, a small Fiat, and climb in. I'm soon back on the main motorway heading for the Manor and at least a week of solitude.

Chapter Four

Blackhart Manor: Blackhart Manor is built on an important confluence of leylines* (commonly known as a nexus or node) within the Devon countryside. Unsubstantiated reports claim that a gateway to the Otherwhere is located within the forest that borders the property.
Leylines: lines of earth energy, similar to a highway, that criss-cross the earth, making it possible for those who have the ability to tap into it, to renew body, mind and spirit.

From an archived report filed in HMDSDI HQ, 1984

It's weird waking up in the Manor to find myself alone. I came in during the small hours of the morning, expecting at least one or two of my cousins to be around, but the rambling old house is empty. I walk through the house, my footsteps echoing down the long passageways, through majestic rooms with high ceilings, wood panelling and chandeliers and furniture that would give apoplexy to all the hosts of the *Antiques Roadshow*.

I make my way to the kitchen with some reluctance. The place is sparkling and nothing is out of place. I'm about to rummage in the cupboards when I spot a note addressed to me stuck to the industrial-sized fridge, in a neat printed hand:

Breakfast is ready in the conservatory. Jeremy and I will be back first thing on Sunday after Gwendolyn's handfasting. Dinner is in the fridge.

And it is signed by our house brownie with a rather elaborate and dramatic E.

I make myself a cup of tea and carry it through to the conservatory. It's a Victorian affair with lots of plants and a big glass table in the centre; it makes me feel as if I'm having breakfast in the jungle.

Mrs Evans is as good as her word. The elaborate breakfasts she plans when all the cousins and uncles and aunties are in town has been scaled down enough to feed a mere five of me. She's not subtle and clearly thinks I need fattening up. I agree with her. It's easier than arguing with the Blackhart brownie who runs the domestic life of the Manor with an iron fist sheathed in a Laura Ashley oven glove.

I dish myself bacon, eggs, toast, grilled tomatoes and a glass of ice-cold orange juice. This I carry to the table and fall to with gusto. It tastes as if it's just been made and I don't know how brownie magic works, only that it does, and I love Mrs Evans with all my heart.

Using my magic tires me out; it makes me hungry and I can sleep for a week after completing a tough ritual. But

I know that, if I push myself, I can go on for longer, and will just need extra sleep and to nurse a bad head for a few days. Judging by Jamie's mothering comments at the grave-yard early last night, I must have looked really bad. I didn't actually feel it then, and the only real hint of how exhausted I was came later last night as I slept like the dead until hunger woke me. Although I feel more human now, all I can think about is food and feeding this ravening maw that's opened inside me. Yet another reason not to date: I can out-eat most competitive eaters any time of the day without blinking.

I have a second course (warm fresh pastries) and coffee before I get up and wander back through the empty house to the library, where I sit down with a sigh and start on the paperwork the closure of the case necessitates. There are seven forms to fill in. In triplicate. The wording has to be in Latin and, in some rare instances, Greek.

Up until a year ago I was a normal sixteen-year-old girl, doing average everyday things, going to a normal school, enjoying art and dreaming about becoming a prop designer in Hollywood. I didn't have to know Latin or Greek or Arabic. Yet now, here I am, a Blackhart claimed and trained, and I'm expected to be able to know stuff no sane person in modern times should know. Aunt Letitia (She Who Must Be Obeyed, according to, well, all my cousins) has, however, given me some leeway as I was brought up as a norm. So instead of expecting the forms turned around within twenty-four hours of completing a case, I have forty-eight. Thanks, Aunt Letty, you're my hero.

I've done the first set of papers by lunchtime and decide to check my emails and go for a swim. It is a gloriously sunny day and I stretch out on a lounger next to the outside pool for a few minutes, letting the sun warm me, shaking off the chill from the dark library.

I swim a few laps and clamber back out again, feeling better for the exercise and getting rid of some of the stiffness from yesterday's fight. I choose not to notice the bruises along my side: a side-effect from my brush with the violent banshee. I move a bit slower than I'd like, but a few days of rest and I should be up to running the obstacle course Jamie's set up behind the house.

The sense of isolation is distracting. It doesn't bother me, not really, but I'm a bit put out by my cousins not even bothering to ring or text me to congratulate me on the successful completion of my first solo mission. It's maybe not a big thing for them, but for me it feels as if I've graduated, as if I've got my wings. And where are they? I check my phone. No text messages, no notes, no phone calls. I sigh and mutter to myself. Woe is me.

I move my sword to the side, so it can rest next to my lounger, and I pull my laptop towards me. My emails are very few. There is one from Karina in Germany and she's sent photos of her new boyfriend – he's not as hot as she seems to think he is – and tells me they're planning to backpack around Greece for the summer holidays. She sends me a photo of her brother Udo, whom I've had a crush on since I was seven. He's looking at the camera in an angry way and his scowl makes him look badass. He's dark haired, like Karina, and has the same dark melty eyes as his sister. I kiss my laptop screen and send her an email back. I tell her about school, about a random boy I like, about how different things are now that Nan's gone. I keep it light and it's all lies and I feel so bad about it. Telling Karina about any of the real Blackhart stuff isn't something I can even consider. Apart from it being dangerous to her, she'd think I've gone nuts, believing in faeries and ogres. She's the most sober and logical person I know and would never understand about monsters lurking in the darkness trying to eat your face off.

As I press 'send' on my email filled with lies and deceit, my email pings again. It's from my cousin, Megan.

The subject line says: Find it, and it's yours.

And that's it. No further message.

I grin. It's a challenge and one Megan sets for us occasionally, sending us on various quests around the estate. The victor always comes away with either a new techy gadget she's designed or, as the younger lot call it: Meganized. Jamie got his flashy new Ducati Monster that way. My cousin Marc still sulks about that, saying that Jamie cheated and that the bike was meant for him, but Megan sets the rules: finders keepers, losers weepers.

I check and notice that I'm the only recipient. This challenge is for me only.

Okay. I'm up for a bit of questing.

I pull a pair of surf shorts and a T-shirt on over my bathing suit and start my hunt. An hour of wandering around the house finding little notes hidden in obvious and not-so-obvious places, and I'm directed to the basement garage.

A cherry-red Mini Cooper sits proudly in the middle of a strategically placed spotlight, keeping the rest of the garage in darkness. An envelope's trapped beneath the windscreen wiper with my full name written on it. Katherine Gabrielle Blackhart. It's in Megan's handwriting.

It holds two pieces of paper. The first is a note that simply reads:

Congratulations on your success! We are very proud of you.
Welcome to the madness. Now, just keep staying alive!
Lots of love,
Team Blackhart – sorry, Marc made me write that,
Megan xx

The second note is the ownership papers of the Mini. It's in my name.

I lay my hand on the bonnet and grin. I can't believe it. I've seen Megan tinkering with the car for months now, restoring it, finding bits and pieces here and there and taking the already cool car and making it into a souped-up red monster that growls and purrs when the engine turns over.

And she's given it to me. It feels amazing.

My phone buzzes in my pocket and I take it out, knowing immediately that it's Megan without even looking at the display.

'Kit Blackhart!' she's yelling, sounding a bit hysterical. 'You find your toy yet?'

'I just did! Oh my God, Meg, I love her.'

'Have you taken her out for a spin?'

'No, not yet. I literally just found the note and I'm walking around her and she's the most stunning thing I've ever seen.'

'Good, I'm glad you like her. Her name is Lolita.' I

become aware of the fact that the voice is no longer in my ear, but next to me. I turn and find myself staring at all three of my nearest cousins, the twins Megan and Marc and their younger brother, Kyle. The door to the armoury's swinging shut behind them on silent hinges and I realize that they have been lurking in there.

Marc's carrying a huge platter of cakes and Kyle looks embarrassed hanging on to a forest of colourful balloons that spell out: 'Congratulations!!'

'Did you seriously think we'd miss celebrating your first lone mission?' Megan asks me as she walks into me and wraps me in a huge hug, lifting me off the ground and swinging me around. No mean feat for a girl the same height and weight as me. 'I can't believe it took you so long to check your emails! We've been down here for like a million years.'

I can't stop laughing at her exaggeration. Marc, Megan's twin, holds open his arm and balances the tray of cakes to one side.

'You kicked ass yesterday. Well done. We're super proud of you.' He pushes a kiss on my forehead and hugs me. I rest there a moment, loving how I fit in with this little trio.

The youngest of the Blackharts at fifteen, Kyle is even taller than Marc and gangly. With his glasses and serious features he looks like a version of Harry Potter who just happens to know the best way to kill a Yaksha without breaking a sweat.

'She's not kidding,' Kyle says. 'We've been hiding down here since about twelve, waiting for you to stop working. You know Aunt Letitia doesn't really mind if you're late with the paperwork, right?'

'Wrong,' Marc says, shoving a plate in my direction and a glass of something fizzy. 'Letitia gets extremely pissed off if we're late with reports. It's you she coddles, as you're the baby.'

Kyle scowls at his elder brother. 'She doesn't coddle.'

'She does. She pinches your cheeks,' Megan says with her mouth full of pastry.

'That's abuse,' Kyle counters. 'I've told her to stop.'

'It will never stop, face it. Even when you're forty, she'll still pinch your cheeks.'

He frowns at me in disapproval. 'Not you too, Kit, really?'

I grin. 'I can do and say whatever I like. This is my party.' And I push a handful of cake into his startled face.

Chapter Five

Redcaps: A type of goblin variant (berserker)
renowned for their fearlessness (some say stupidity) in
battle. Both Seelie and Unseelie Courts have bands of
redcaps in their armies and use them as kill-squads.

From *The Blackhart Bestiarum*

'I cannot believe we made this much mess,' Megan says to me as we scrape the last bit of cake into a black bag. 'It was fun, though.'

'Less moaning and more cleaning,' Marc says, throwing an empty bottle into the recycling bin. 'Dad said he was going to call tonight with a new gig for us. He'll expect us to travel immediately.'

'Not you, though,' Megan says to me as I straighten to look at them in surprise. Her face is serious as she tucks a loose blonde curl behind her ear. 'He'll make you stay behind.'

I scowl while wiping my hands free of frosting on a serviette. Who knew that frosting and icing could splatter quite that much?

'What? Why? I aced my gig. Why don't I get to go along on the new adventure?'

'You need rest.' Kyle is perched on the barstool in the games room that we took over to celebrate further the success of my solo gig. 'Look at you, you can barely stand.'

I snort in derision. 'I'm fine, nothing a good night's sleep won't cure.'

All three of them turn to look at me, the same expression on their faces. It's an expression I recognize because my nan excelled at wearing it.

'What? You know it's true. I just need a bit of rest and I'll be as right as rain.'

'A bit of rest? Kit Blackhart, the amount of magic you put out at Arlington School blazed for hours. We fielded calls from the Spook Squad who wanted to know what we were up to. Every creature in a hundred-mile radius knows what you did. You're still probably a bit high on it all but, trust me, tomorrow you're going to crash and it's going to be bad. You have to rest.'

I purse my lips in annoyance and turn away from Marc's worried look. It bothered me that even the Spook Squad had registered my activities. They were a task force set up to investigate the weird goings-on that the average citizen reported to the average police officer. A large number of unusual and peculiar crimes were reported to the police but, as they don't have the manpower or inclination to investigate, these things are usually passed on to the Spook Squad or, more formally, Her Majesty's Department of Supernatural Defence and Intervention. For example those cases where a drunken homeless person babbles on about faeries dancing under a streetlight in Hackney? Sometimes it really is faeries dancing under a streetlight in Hackney. I've never met a Spook, but I've heard plenty about how they've managed to screw up investigations for my family with their blundering ways. We are the scalpels, Jamie was fond of saying. They are the fire-axes.

But then the rest of Marc's words hit home. Yes, I am tired, more tired than I've been in as long as I can remember – but it really doesn't mean that I need to be coddled like some child. I'm seventeen, for heaven's sake. Almost eighteen if I survive the next few months.

The atmosphere is tense after that. Kyle, always the peacemaker, puts on some chill-out music and makes me dance with him but my smile is strained. They banter among themselves, like they always do, letting me wrap myself in my cloak of misery.

I feel like the newbie and the party they threw on my behalf now seems a bit patronizing. I help for as long as I can bear it before I excuse myself and go upstairs to shower and go to bed.

I'm propped up in bed, the Edwardian travel journal by one Helena Blackhart propped open on my knees. Helena had been friends with a high-ranking Fae noble, a blue-blooded Sidhe, who gave her permission to visit the Northern Wastes in Alba. The travel journal is partly about her intimate thoughts on the Sidhe noble she was travelling with and partly a study in anthropology and the mythology and legends relating to the Elder Gods that still suffused that area of the Otherwhere. I like Helena. She was also the only other Blackhart born with magic, like me. None of her journals I've managed to dig up in the library mentions how she learned to use her magic. It was just there, seemingly, all the time and she knew instinctively how to use it. It's frustrating and intriguing. She hardly ever mentions her abilities in any of her journals. But the fact remains that she was a gutsy lady, unconventional and clearly hopelessly in love with the wrong guy. I'm not entirely sure about the legends she was collecting for the Blackhart library archive. They really do sound like the hallucinations of a mentally unstable person.

The knock on my door startles me, but before I can say anything Megan's bum edges its way into my room. She's carrying a tray of Mrs Evans' finest china. She brings it over and nudges one of the small (in my opinion useless) tables with her foot. When she's satisfied it's near enough to the bed, she puts the tray down.

'I brought hot chocolate and cookies,' she says. 'I found some hidden in Mrs E's pantry.'

'I'm not in the mood, Megan,' I say, not really caring how petulant I sound. I feel genuinely annoyed at them. 'I just want to read and sleep.'

'Rubbish. You're feeling left out. I would too.' She hands me a cup full of deliciously thick hot chocolate that has a hint of chilli in it. 'Dad just rang and spoke to the boys. Apparently we're being sent to Scotland. There are reports of cattle mutilations and he wants us to investigate. He's not given us much, but he's called in the wolves.'

I can't help it: the surprise registers on my face and Megan nods, looking sombre. 'If he's involving the Garrett wolf pack it means big trouble. We'll still be up there in about a week, I'm sure. Plenty of time for you to rest and follow us up there.'

'Did he say anything about me going with you guys immediately?'

Megan's dark grey eyes fill with sympathy. 'He said you are to stay behind and to rest. He heard from Suola that she is extremely pleased with the way you handled the banshee.' She did air quotes. '"A minimum of fuss and a positive result." You really did us proud.'

I grimace. 'Yeah, but I still get to hang around at home, kicking my heels while you get to go gallivanting off.'

'Listen, Kit.' Megan stares at me and I feel uncomfortable suddenly, not used to her being this serious. 'You are the first proper magic-user we've had in the family for years. You know how big that is for us. We can't risk you getting hurt because we've not followed the bits of advice we've managed to scrounge from a batch of mouldy books.' She sips some of her own hot chocolate. 'Rest up until you no longer feel you want to eat all the food in the world, then come and join us. Three days minimum. It's nothing.' She snaps her fingers. 'You know it will be over just like that.'

Of course I know she's right but it doesn't mean I have to: a) agree, or b) like it.

'Fine. Just don't expect me to throw you guys a party if you come back before three days.'

Megan gives a snort. 'From the way the boys are packing you'd think we're going on a month-long expedition into the Mountains of the Moon.'

That makes me grin against my will. I know Kyle and

Marc pack enough gear for any job to make it look as if they're moving to another country. Compared to Megan, who packs a toolkit, undies, her iPod and a change of clothes, the boys really do overdo it. 'It'll be fun. You get to run with the Garrett wolf pack.'

Megan's eyes widen. 'You know, I actually forgot about that. Do you think we're too used to crazy being part of our lives? Faeries, werewolves.' She gestures wildly.

Against my will, my mood lifts as I'm drawn into her false dramatics. 'The infernal, monsters from beyond the grave.' I echo her flamboyant gesture but with less gusto. 'Nothing can stand in our way.'

'We are pretty badass.'

I laugh and shake my head. Megan enjoys making a fuss about what the Blackharts do, but I've come to realize that it's just a way for her to stay in control. If she can laugh at the monsters we send back to the Otherwhere, they become slightly less scary.

'We are so badass, monsters run when they know we're coming.'

She grabs another cookie before I can finish the lot, but clearly has something more serious to say. 'Listen, I spoke to Jamie yesterday. He's got Kyle digitizing what we know about your magic, putting it into an app for you. Aunt Letitia is helping on her side too, looking through older records we have in storage at the lighthouse. So far we only have the stuff you've read about from Helena, but we're hoping to find more.' She looks earnest. 'You're an asset we can't afford to lose, Kit. Not when we've just found you. There are so few of us, you know? We have to look out for one another.'

I nod, my smile fading. 'I know, Meg, I know. I just can't help but feel like I'm being coddled by you guys.' I tug my fringe out of my eyes, frustrated. 'I just want to help, show you guys I can do this.'

'We know you can, sprocket.' Marc's voice interrupts, and then he's through the half-open door. 'We just want you to be fighting fit.'

'Oy!' Megan throws a cushion at his head. 'Get out. Girly time here, no boys allowed!'

Marc lets out a very unmanly squeal and shuts the door quickly before more missiles appear.

My laughter breaks the tension and I lean forward, hugging her. 'Tell Kyle thanks for even thinking of putting all the magic info stuff together. And thanks to you for being so sweet.'

Megan extracts herself after a few seconds. 'Okay, enough, enough. I have to go get some sleep. Have a good few days' rest. See you later, Kit Solo Mission Blackhart. Sleep tight and if the bedbugs bite, bite back.'

I sit upright in my bed. My alarm clock tells me it's quarter past three in the morning. The house lies quiet around me but I'm wide awake and my body is alert. It's been twenty-four hours since Megan, Marc and Kyle flew to Scotland. They haven't been in touch to say they're coming back, so the vibration that's in the air isn't the house alerting me to their presence.

There's a static sound that's as loud as any clarion bell in my ears. This happened once before around four months ago when a group of juvenile goblins thought it would be fun to try and break into the Manor to raid Mrs Evans' fabled blackberry preserves. They didn't get very much further than the standing stones at the edge of the park surrounding the Manor and in the end, after we got them to agree to act as scouts for us on an ongoing job, we paid them with five jars.

This time, though, it feels different. The air is charged with static and the incessant hum, like an insect buzzing in my ear, is disconcerting, putting me on edge.

Drawing a deep breath and calming my stuttering heart, I carefully pull tendrils of slumbering magic to me and focus it, holding it lightly, and close my eyes, letting the magic be my eyes, allowing it to show me what my eyes can't see in the dark. My magic propels my vision forward and immediately it's as if I'm looking at the world through a soft green haze. The wards carved into the walls, doors and windows of the house glow jade. No sign of an intruder, or any physical damage to the house. With my sight, I easily pick out the muted glow of my sword resting against my vanity table.

I slide out of bed and pull on my discarded jeans and a rumpled T-shirt and slip my feet into a pair of trainers. My hand slides beneath my pillow and finds the knife Jamie gave me the night the redcaps burned down my home and killed my nan. It was the same night I found out about my heritage and who I was. The night my life changed forever.

The knife fits my palm as perfectly now as it did that night. But the difference between that awful night and now is that I now know how to use it, and I'm getting rather good at punching holes in things that attack me.

I keep the knife by my side as I cross the room to the

windows overlooking the wide expanse of back garden. The tall standing stones keep their quiet vigil at the edge of the forest, demarcating where the cultured parkland and formal gardens of Blackhart Manor begin – or end, if you are a glass-half-empty kind of person.

I push open the French doors leading to the small balcony outside my second-storey window and lean forward, narrowing my eyes. My magic responds startlingly quickly and I'm awash in colour and smell and sound. It races up to the warding stones and stays there, allowing me a better view of the thick forest that stretches for miles into the lush Devon countryside.

The protective barrier that the nine menhir, or standing stones, spaced around the garden throw up around the house is both a curse and relief. It stops bad things from getting to the house but it also prevents me from seeing further into the forest. I decide I need a closer look, knowing that there's no way I'll be able to go back to bed if I think something is out there.

Running without socks in trainers is not fun so before I leave the room I pull those on. I add the dark blue hoodie Jamie gave me after Marc accidentally knifed me in the shoulder, when I didn't move away from his attack fast enough. The fabric is stab-proof and it gives me a better chance against opponents; although I'm getting better at defending and attacking, I'm not that good yet and I can do with any bit of help.

My sword gets slung across my back, ninja-style, the knife goes into its sheath that hangs down my leg and I secure the ties around my thigh. My hiking torch stays in my hand and my mobile phone slips into my other pocket. Out of habit I slide my credit card into my front pocket. You never know how things are going to work out or where you're going to end up once you start running around following your gut instinct.

I leave the house through the back door and bypass the empty stables. The security lights are triggered by my movement as I cross the yard and I curse myself for not thinking and turning them off before leaving the house. I lengthen my stride and soon leave the tidy yard and stables behind me.

The Milky Way blazes above me in a cold clear sky and there is a sense of waiting, of breathlessness and of anticipation that makes the hair stand up on my arms and bare neck.

Two thirds of the way to the tall standing stone I crouch low as a wild ululating cry goes up, coming from the depths of the dark expanse ahead of me. *What the hell?* The silence that falls after the cry is flat, anticipatory. It lasts mere seconds, before a savage howl slices the night, painting it with chaos, accompanied by the thunder of hooves.

I fling myself forward and run flat out to the nearest stone, where I press myself against the surface, my heart shuddering in fear. A herd of around thirty deer led by an antlered stag bursts from between the trees in a confusion of speed, rolling white eyes and musk. They flash past me, shaking the earth with their passing, fleeing whatever's in the forest. I watch them speed across the lawns, disappearing into the darkness behind me, heading in the direction of the lake.

I turn my attention back to the forest, my sword in hand. Like the knife, the sword's become an extension of myself. I write reports with it to hand, I have it propped up against the table when I have breakfast, I have my showers with it leaning against the toilet and I sleep with it next to the bed. Not quite the kind of thing you tell your date – if you are the kind of normal girl who goes on dates, of course.

Now the sword rests in my hand, tip down. I creep towards the larger standing stone a few metres away and press up against it, taking comfort from its solidity. The stone, the one we refer to as the Sentinel, is taller than me by a good two feet and carved with intricate knotwork spirals that look somewhat Celtic. I touch the stone with my free hand and murmur a greeting to it. A sharp ping of magic nips the palm of my hand in answer, telling me that I'm safe here, right now, regardless of what's out there in the forest.

For a few seconds I close my eyes and allow myself to stand there in the darkness, letting the magic keeping Blackhart Manor safe wash over me. I ride the current for a few moments, enjoying the sensation it brings, how it lifts the tiredness gnawing at me.

I pull away from the stream of magic and stretch my magic towards the forest, a small tendril only. Quietly, softly, I let it snake forward, ready to pull it back as soon as I encounter any trouble. I sense there are no small creatures about; they have probably gone to ground in the wake of the deer's abrupt escape from the forest.

I follow the tendril as it makes its stealthy way into the depths of the forest, seeking, prying. It feels like an age, but when it finds the trespassers and I have the chance to take the information in, I lean back against the ward stone and rub my eyes, unsure if I'm really seeing what I'm seeing.

I've found a squad of redcap goblins carousing in our part of the forest and it looks as if they've got someone trapped and are having a grand old time toying with him. I press my fingers to my forehead and wonder how the hell I'm supposed to sort this out.

My knowledge of redcaps isn't encyclopedic. They are a particularly nasty subgroup of goblin that both the Seelie and Unseelie Courts use as foot soldiers in their ongoing squabbles for territory and political shenanigans. The name redcap comes from the legends that these goblins soak their caps in the blood of their victims. Goblins aren't ever pleasant, but the redcaps are dirtier and more evil by far than most of them. The older they are, the more gnarled and twisted they become, the warts and scarring on their faces making them outlandishly unpleasant to look at. From the look of this group there are four young ones and two older redcaps. None is taller than me but they are bulky and muscled, and as usual they carry a variety of pikes and serrated knives. They also like to play with fire. Three of the troop hold burning torches aloft, the flames flickering and throwing capering shadows against the thick trunks of the trees in the clearing.

I focus on the person they have at bay. Dusty blond hair and fine featured with the tell-tale look of something inhuman that I've come to associate with high-born Sidhe Fae, he looks maybe eighteen, no older than twenty. Dressed in plain battle-stained armour, he appears tired and angry as the redcaps do their usual trick of rushing up at him, swinging their weapons, jeering and then backing off. He holds his sword confidently in his left hand while his right arm hangs uselessly by his side, blood dripping from beneath the shirt, along his hand and fingers, onto a pennant trampled in the dirt beneath his feet. A jagged cut has parted the chainmail, showing a deep gash on his upper arm. The wound looks inflamed and his breathing is fast and ragged. There are various smaller cuts on his hands and, as he turns to snarl something in their guttural tongue, I notice blood down the side of his face, along with an impressive bruise the length of his jaw.

The stylized carved griffin rampant on the sculpted pectoral of his cuirass, the breastplate, tells me I'm dealing with someone from High King Aelfric's household. He may be a minor noble or a bodyguard, and I wonder who he was protecting, and why he's now in our forest surrounded by the thugs of the Fae world, who obviously want to kill him or eat him, and not necessarily in that order either.

Act now, think later, I tell myself. How to approach this? Six redcaps means I must take out at least three, and hope that elf boy gets at least one. Redcaps lack courage, so if we gain the upper hand, the rest *should* flee. Then I figure out what a bloody Sidhe warrior is doing in our forest, a world away from where he should be.

I draw a deep breath and step through the wall of magic keeping me safe from the creatures of the night.

Chapter Six

Seventh Son: A rather old and dated piece of folklore pertains to the seventh son of the seventh son. It was generally thought that such a person would be luckier than his siblings and would be blessed with impressive magical powers, invariably that of healing powers. The gift of prophecy is also tied in with the person's magical abilities.

From an archived report filed in HMDSDI HQ, 1942

I slink through the forest on quiet feet, stepping over tree roots, and manage to not fall on my face. The redcaps are making so much noise I wonder if they are doing it on purpose and if I'm walking into a trap. But then they are redcaps and are generally challenged in the brains department.

They are laughing and talking loudly, taunting the young man. I don't understand half of what they're saying; the large tusks that jut from their bottom jaws make conversation with them nearly impossible. There is a lot of grunting and snorting.

I hear the sound of metal against metal a few times and

I reckon that the wounded young man is bravely fending them off as they toy with him.

I don't bother taking time to think out my attack. I'm not a strategist, as Jamie wryly enjoys pointing out whenever I barge face-first into an attack. I tend to favour the 'I see my enemy, I bash him over the head' tactic which, admittedly, has worked for me in the past.

I'm twenty metres from them when I pick up speed. I run at them, a wild battle cry tearing from my throat the last few metres. I burst out of the undergrowth screaming like a demon, throwing the redcaps into confusion. I leap at the nearest one, propelling myself forward by pushing down on a tree stump with one foot, and swipe at his exposed neck in mid-air as I fly by. It's chaos around me. The first redcap I cut lets out a warbling moan and clutches the deep cut in his neck. Arterial blood sprays the clearing and the smell of the blood drives his cronies crazy.

I land with my back to the young man, then spin and deliver a kick to the head of a redcap who tries to rush me; I shoot the Fae a quick look to check he's helping out, not paralysed by my insane arrival. But he's right there, sword flashing against an opponent, focused on the fight.

I'm lucky that I've always been fast. Karate and boxing training helped but, with Jamie's rigorous training, I'm faster still. The blade in my hand dances in the pale starlight and I strike and slice my enemies with precision but little showmanship. Another redcap keels over under my onslaught and I leap over him to launch an attack on the one nearest to me.

The young man seems startled at my lack of battle tactics

but then throws himself into the fray with a great deal more grace than I can ever display. Together we take out two more redcaps each and face the final one with raised swords, our chests heaving.

The redcap growls at us, his shark-black eyes flickering between us. A serrated knife, more the size of a short sword, wavers in his hand and he takes a cautious step back. We advance on him simultaneously, as if we've practised the move. He doesn't like it. With a final snarl he turns and flees into the darkness, leaving his dead and dying cronies behind.

I turn and look at the bodies strewn around the clearing, blood and adrenalin raging through me. All five bodies are wearing the same colour armband tied high on their biceps. I nudge one over with my toe and grimace at the blood staining my trainer. I kneel down beside the body and tug at the armband, unrolling it. It's a rune, white painted on a black background. It's not a sigil from one of the twelve houses of the Fae that I recognize. My hands are shaking when I turn to look at the young man.

He leans against one of the trees and carefully wipes his blade on a piece of cloth before sheathing his sword clumsily. He's pale and dark circles have gathered beneath his eyes but when he looks at me directly, I'm struck by how solid he seems in the midst of the carnage. It's an odd thought, a disjointed reflection I realize, but there's no other way of describing his presence. There's nothing about this Fae that's whimsical or fey, rather he gives off a vibrancy that belies how tired he looks. I take a second to appreciate him, even if he smells like blood and gore, and offer him a cautious nod.

'I'm Kit Blackhart,' I say, catching my breath, and in a smooth move flick the blood off my sword and slide it home. I do it with far more style than I've ever done it before and I feel a bit swaggery. 'Nice fighting.'

His eyes are very dark in the flickering light of the dying torches the redcaps have dumped. I see him swallow against a dry throat, but then he draws himself up and executes a perfect courtly bow as if we're meeting at a royal ball, in a glittering room with perfumed courtiers, and I'm dressed in an exquisite gown, rather than ratty jeans covered in redcap blood and bits.

'A pleasure to meet you, Miss Blackhart. Prince Thorn, the seventh son of the House of Alba, at your service.' His voice is pleasant and deep and his accent is a bit foreign. A neat package, until he tries to smile and his eyes roll back in his head and I have to catch him before he hits the ground.

I'm a tall girl, and strong, but I know it's going to be hellish to try and get him back to the Manor before dawn.

I make it to the patio doors before I completely run out of energy. I carefully dump the unconscious prince on the ground and straighten my aching back. I'm still sore from my encounter with the banshee and after tonight's, no, this morning's shenanigans, I don't think I'll be able to move without doing a lot of groaning.

Behind me are the snarls and curses of the dark creatures that have hounded us through the forest, flocking to the standing stones that circle the Manor. Casting a look over my shoulder, I see a variety of dark shapes battering themselves against the wall of magic. One of them, bigger than the redcaps, maybe an ogre, is heaving at one of the marker stones, doing his utmost to shift it. Some of them start digging, trying to tunnel beneath the protective wall, and I have to give them five out of five for thinking outside the box. But, unless they have drilling equipment, I doubt they'll be able to get through. The protection spells safeguarding Blackhart Manor and the estate are centuries old and they are renewed at each equinox. Nothing is going to get through the stone circle. Nothing I've heard of, anyway.

I open the patio doors and heave the armoured young man into the informal lounge and with much swearing I lay him down on the longest couch before I run and lock the doors. I take out my knife and snick my finger lightly so that a droplet of blood wells from the cut; I press it into the elaborate carving around the doorjamb and watch as my blood sinks into the wood, leaving no trace. The effect of the safeguarding spell is instantaneous and I close my eyes hastily against the bright flare that lights up the Manor. I can feel the ripple of it go through the house and know that if anyone was watching the Manor from the Otherwhere the place just lit up like a beacon. The spell tells whoever's watching that we've gone into lockdown and that nothing will be able to get through the doors unless I let them. Sometimes you just needed more security than your average lock on the door.

Knowing that I've basically just sent off a flare for help in both worlds, to be seen by anyone with the slightest bit of magical potential, makes me feel vulnerable. There are very few places of significance in our world that exist in the Otherwhere too, and the Manor is one of them. It makes it easier for high-born Sidhe to pay visits to us, and it's easier for us to nip across than to traipse into the forest to activate the gate hidden there.

The young man on the couch moans something in a language I'm sure I should know and he struggles to grasp for his sword in his half-conscious state. I rush over and remove the sword from his side to prevent him from hurting himself. The sword feels very heavy in my hands. It makes my plain sword, with its leather-wrapped hilt, feel like a piece of scrap metal. I notice the elaborately carved hilt and the deep green stone set in the pommel. A single large stylized dragon is etched along the blade and I wonder what Jamie would make of it. He was fond of saying that weapons were meant to look like weapons, not toys. I lay it on one of the side tables and rub my bloodstained hands down my thighs.

At the sight of my hands, my heart accelerates and my knees go rubbery and weak, as if they can't support my weight one second more. I lean pathetically against the table for a few seconds, trying to get a grip on myself. I practise some of the breathing techniques Jamie's taught me for use when it feels as if my magic's about to burn free. The breathing eventually helps and I turn to survey the unconscious prince.

First things first. He has to be cleaned up and I have to see if I can sort out the cut on his arm and we both need some rest. The carriage clock above the fireplace tells me it's just after five. Dawn should arrive soon, sending the redcaps and whatever nightmares they had with them scurrying for the darkest recesses of the forest, where they'll hide till night-time before coming at the house again.

I move as fast as I can to the kitchen and down a can of full-fat Coke for my nerves. As I wait for the sugar to hit my bloodstream I gather my wits. In the utility drawer I find several scissors, which I pocket, and under the sink I find the overlarge and very well-stocked first-aid kit Mrs Evans keeps there. I grab a stack of clean bed sheets from the linen cupboard and carry them into the lounge.

He's still unconscious on the couch where I left him, thank the stars. I watch his chest move beneath his armour and wonder what the hell he was doing in my forest in the small hours of the morning. I need to rest and recoup so that I can go join my cousins up in Scotland; I don't need this. Whatever this is.

It takes some doing, but I wrestle the prince's breastplate off and dump it on the carpet to the side of the room. Next, I find the hooks of his chainmail shirt and manage to get that off without aggravating his wound too much, I think.

Two pairs of scissors later I give up in my attempts to cut the padded undershirt off him and in the end I use my knife. His soft cotton shirt is a mess of blood and I easily get rid of that and dump it with the rest.

I wince when I see how deep the cut is that goes from the top of his shoulder down the length of his upper arm. It looks painful and I wonder if I'll be able to help or if my ministrations will make it worse. I bite my lips in an effort not to walk away and throw up in Aunt Jessica's plants. I'm okay with most first-aid things, but stitching wounds is not my forte. Surprisingly, Kyle was the one for such delicate operations. I'm just the one that either gets wounded or delivers woundings.

The prince lets out a short sharp cry and he grabs at my wrist. His eyes are open and a look of panic flickers across his undoubtedly handsome face. 'Please,' he rasps. 'Help.' He falls back against the cushions, out like a light.

I prise his fingers away and sit back, hoping that someone else will turn up soon to tell me what to do next. My eyes roam over the rest of him to see if I can find any other cuts and in the process I get an eyeful of the sculpted smooth muscles on his chest. I flame bright red but I bend myself to the task I set myself. I'm relieved he's not awake to see me hesitate or how my hands shake as I start the process of cleaning the injury and sewing it up. It takes ages but the stitches look neat and tidy and my hands have lost most of their hesitation. The rest of me, though, is shaking with fatigue. I sit back on my heels and wonder about giving him a shot of antibiotics. Will I give him some kind of illness if I do? I don't know enough about Fae metabolism and decide that if he gets sick I'll give him an injection. At the moment he's got a bit of a temperature but nothing too serious. I hold my hand over his mouth and his breathing feels regular.

I bandage the wound and carry the dirty water and bits of cloth to the kitchen and mentally apologize to Mrs Evans for destroying the tidiness of her kitchen. I find a shirt in the folded laundry that belongs to either Kyle or Marc and carry it with me into the small lounge.

I start on his face, washing off the dirt and the blood. A cut seeps blood just above his eyebrow and I clean that out too, disinfecting it. It's not deep and it should heal well, so I use small butterfly plasters to keep the cut together. I pull the shirt on over him, taking care not to jostle his arm too much.

After I've done as much as I can, I manoeuvre him into a more comfortable position on the couch, using the bed linen I took from the cupboard earlier as extra padding and make sure the pillows support his head before I sigh deeply and sink down on the floor next to him. I am so tired, all I want to do is sleep for a week. My reserves are low and there's a hollow ache in my stomach that I always connect to my tiny store of magic being depleted. The thought of trying to send emails to everyone, to let them know what's going on – that the house is under siege by beasties and that I have the High King of Alba's youngest son unconscious on our couch – is just a step too far. None of this seems real. The night stretches behind me like a surreal nightmare. Even after a year and a half, all of this still feels new, and insane, and impossible. I know I have to get in touch with my family. I haul my phone out. The screen's cracked from where I sat down on it too hard. I leave my phone on the small table next to me. I lean my head back and close my eyes, intending only to rest them for a few minutes, but sleep folds me to her chest and I let her.

The Citadel, Kingdom Of Alba, Otherwhere

'Where is the boy?'

As he spoke, the duke turned his gaze to the shadows crowding the map chamber. The coals in the brazier gave off only slightly more warmth than light. The room held an ornate bookcase; most of the contents of the shelves were spread across the monumental desk. Suspended against the wall behind the desk was a tapestry depicting all the lands of Alba, the rivers, forests, cities and larger towns and army garrisons.

The duke stood before the map. He was a tall man with patrician features, a carefully trimmed goatee and neatly tied-back hair. His clothes were plain, but clearly no expense had been spared.

A cluster of sputtering stubby candles bravely fought the gloom in the room, lighting the amber liquid in the glass he carefully placed back on the desk beside him. A moonstone ring, cunningly carved to resemble a lion, glinted in the sparse light as he turned to regard his visitor.

'My troops are hunting him as we speak.' The man's voice was deep yet unpleasant. 'There were complications.'

The newcomer was not quite as tall as the duke and moved with a swordsman's grace. Like the duke he wore no visible weapons but he carried a slender silver-topped cane that seemed more an affectation than a necessity.

The duke turned to look at the man, taking no care to hide his surprise. 'Complications? What kind of complications could possibly prevent your troops from bringing a pampered princeling to heel?'

The stranger hid his annoyance at being questioned, but poorly. And as he shifted his weight under scrutiny, shadows seemed to cling somehow to his form, blurring his outline.

'The boy received helped from one of the Blackharts.'

'I thought we'd taken care of the Blackharts.' The duke's tone was unforgiving. 'Istvan, this is no longer a chess game to be played into the night. It has progressed from a game of "what ifs". There is a price for failure.'

'My lord, the girl . . . we don't know why she is at the Manor. She was supposed to be with the rest of her family in Scotia.'

'Destroy the Manor.' The duke made a small gesture. 'Do everything in your power to stop her helping the prince. Bring him here.'

'Everything in my power, my lord?' Istvan's dark voice held both amusement and threat. 'The consequences of what you're asking will alarm everyone not already with us.'

'I no longer care, sorcerer. Do as you are told. Bring him to me.'

Istvan bowed his dark head, once more the servant. 'As you wish, my lord.'

The duke was suddenly alone in the map chamber. He drew a deep uneven breath and reached for his drink, shuddering as it burned its way down into his stomach. But even after the third glass a chill remained. He moved unsteadily from the tapestry, his ears tuned to voices only he could hear.

Chapter Seven

Alba: The part of the Fae Realm in the Otherwhere
that geographically covers the UK, Europe and
Eastern Europe. Ruled by High King Aelfric the Wise,
Alba has long been renowned for fostering ties
between Fae and humans, not always to great success.
 From an archived report filed in HMDSDI HQ, 1994

I wake up with a start and, after a quick check on the still-breathing prince, I move to stand in front of the windows. The forest lies quiet and enigmatic at the edge of the park and there is no sign of the redcaps or their cronies from earlier.

I check my watch and mutter a curse under my breath. It looks as if it stopped just after four, probably taking a blow during my frisky fight with the redcaps. I undo the strap and pocket it, wondering what else I'm going to lose of Kit's Life As It Once Was. The watch belonged to my mum, and my nan gave it to me when I turned twelve, shortly after we moved back to the UK. It's literally the only thing, apart from me, that survived the fire that night.

Feeling irritable, I swing around to check on my guest, only to find that he's standing a few paces behind me, looking uncertain on his feet and keeping a steadying hand on the back of one of the over-plush leather chairs. Although he's pale, he looks better than he did when I half-carried, half-dragged him in here a few hours ago. His damp hair has dried out and instead of a dusty dark blond-brown it now looks a rich honey blond and it's come loose from its leather tie and rests on his shoulders. His features are strong, masculine, with a firm jaw and great cheekbones, but it's his eyes that hold your attention. Framed by ridiculously long lashes, they are a deep midnight blue and seem fathomless. For a few seconds I stare at him, allowing myself to think that he is utterly deliciously lovely, but then my common sense takes over and I catch myself before I gurn at him like an idiot.

I mentally shake my head to clear the fanciful imagery. The house is in peril, we're surrounded by gribblies (a non-technical term we use in the family to denote any kind of creature) and yet here I am, making moon-eyes at the person who is no doubt the cause of the current mess. I pull myself together and offer him a rather stiff smile.

'Prince Thorn, how are you feeling this morning?'

He clears his throat and inclines his head a bit, almost like a small bow in my direction. 'I've felt better. Like when my horse threw me and dragged me several yards through a lot of undergrowth and a hedge before it stopped to eat some moon meadow grass,' comes the frank answer. His accent is definitely foreign, making me think that English is not the language he learned growing up in Alba.

His voice is lovely and deep and I find myself fascinated

by his mouth with its slightly fuller lower lip. How is it possible that he can look so attractive, even when wearing bruises and cuts from the battle just a few hours before? I find myself leaning closer to him. Is it my imagination, or does he smell ever so slightly of cookies?

I pull back and tut under my breath in annoyance. What the hell is wrong with me? I'm as susceptible to a pretty boy as any warm-blooded heterosexual girl my age, but something about the warm feeling I can feel blossoming inside me is not natural. I feel my magic twist uneasily in my core in answer to my anxiety.

Another wave of warmth and the smell of cookies hits me full force and I can imagine us kissing under moonlit skies with a soft breeze lifting my hair from my neck. The imagery is so strong and real that I jerk backwards while pulling my attention back to the here and now. I palm my knife and hold it up, between the two of us.

I press my fingers to the bridge of my nose in an attempt to stop smelling him so vividly. And, as I stand away from him, the knife still between us, I ignore the shocked expression on his face and let my magic surface inside me. It happily dances along the edge of my blade and shoots across the small distance between me and the Fae prince.

It takes seconds for the pulse of magic to flicker back to me after it has done a brief inventory of the young prince. He has something on him, a piece of jewellery that compels people to like him and help him, deflecting negative energy away from him. It's a small thing, usually overlooked by his enemies, and I spot it when I focus on what to look for. It's a slender gold ring on the pinkie of his left hand.

It pretty much sucks as a magic item because I vividly remember having to rescue his butt from being eaten earlier this morning.

'Your ring,' I say, gesturing with my blade. 'Take it off. I'm sure you're breaking a host of hospitality rules by wearing it in my presence,' I tell him, keeping my voice cool. His eyes, dear heavens, who has eyes like that in real life? 'Please, don't argue. Just take it off.'

Thorn holds up both his hands towards me in a gesture of surrender and hastily wiggles the ring from his finger. He drops it onto the small table that holds some of the bandages I used the night before.

'I apologize, Blackhart. It was a token from my mother, to keep me safe. I did not realize you would react to it so strongly.'

As soon as the ring breaks contact with his skin and drops onto the table I feel the compulsion to fling myself at him fade.

'That was really not the way we do things here,' I tell him, flushing to my roots at the thought of my own emotions being toyed with. I have never lost my cool like that over anyone. 'Dangerous too. And rude. Let's not forget rude. The laws are clear, Prince Thorn. No magic, persuasive or antagonistic, is to be used in your host's home unless the host first uses magic against you.' I make a show of looking around the room and gesture with my blade. 'No magic aimed at you! You broke that rule. I have a right to throw you out on your ear and let you fight those redcaps and ogres all by yourself.'

The prince has the decency to look embarrassed enough

at my tirade and I know I'm laying it on thick but, dammit, I just saved his butt and he's not playing by the rules. I know the Fae rarely do toe the line but there are just some things that count as important enough to cause a fuss about.

I draw a deep breath and exhale, and with it I let go of my annoyance. I give him another once-over to see if I'm free of the silly glamour and I'm unlucky enough to notice that, yes, he's as pretty as before, except now I see the state we're both in.

'I am grateful to you for coming to my rescue. It was a generous gesture and one I appreciate.' His look is wry as he glances at me, his gaze taking me in. I stand my ground, refusing to blush or to drop to the floor and crawl behind a couch to hide from his frank inspection. 'Do you often attack parties of goblins and rescue people from imminent death?'

I favour him with a small smile that doesn't quite reach my eyes.

'Only when I'm bored. Last night I was bored.'

His own grin is real now, and he has laughter lines that crinkle at the corners of his eyes. It makes him look mischievous and I wonder if he is my age or older. I know there are some Sidhe Fae, nobles, who have rituals to keep them looking in their late teens to early twenties.

'I doubt anyone else in Alba has the skill to frighten away an entire pack of redcaps by yelling at them.'

He's being charming, reminding me I saved him last night so that I don't toss him out as I promised earlier. He plays a good game. But I'm filthy and I'm starving and I'm keen to get hold of my cousins.

'It's a Blackhart skill. One we get paid for very well by those from the Otherwhere.'

'I'll try and remember that.' His face suddenly looks grave. 'I owe you a life debt, Kit Blackhart.'

I force my jaw not to drop. A life debt for a Fae was serious business. It was like being handed an IOU slip that can be used to cover any eventuality. Not sure how to respond to this massive open promise, I wave my hand to show it was okay and edge past him carefully, picking up the mess of first-aid stuff from the floor.

'I think we could both do with some breakfast,' I say. 'Then we can try and figure out how to get you back to your travel party. Where are your bodyguards?' I ask him as I stuff everything I'd left lying out into a bin bag. 'I didn't see any sign of them in the clearing. They didn't leave you to cope on your own?'

As soon as the words are out of my mouth I know I've hit on a delicate point. Even without looking at him, I sense the congenial repartee we have going disappearing.

'I had a patrol of soldiers with me. We were attacked when we came through the gateway.'

I frown at him.

'I saw no other bodies,' I say as I turn to look at him. 'Why were you out there by yourself?'

Uncertainty spreads across his face. 'I'm not sure. So much happened, so quickly.' He touches his eyebrow, his fingers sliding across the cut I've bandaged, and frowns at me. 'We were heading for the gateway, all of us, ready to ride through. We kept tight formation the entire time we were being chased. Within sight of the gateway my horse threw me. I was flung to the ground and, the next thing, the men with me had me surrounded.'

'They turned on you?'

Thorn's nod is brief. 'There was something, though – something as we came near the gateway.'

'What?' I forget what I'm doing and watch him. The bandages and first-aid kit I have been gathering lie abandoned for a moment.

'A darkness. Thick black shadows and so much noise. We raced to get to the clearing and, although the noise was that of a huge battle, we found no one in the darkness. What did change were my men. I looked up at them and they were no longer the people I knew. They were different. Their faces . . .' His gaze becomes distant. 'They had turned into ravening beasts fighting each other and then they seemed to become aware of me. I had to defend myself against my friends.'

'That can't have been pleasant.' I realize it's an inane thing to say, but – really – what else can I say? I rub my face and stand up with the black bag in my hand. I think my expression reflects the horror he must feel because he nods to himself.

'The magic I felt in the air, in the shadows all around me, was unlike anything I've ever experienced. It was cloying, sickening. It smelled like something dying. I don't know how many of my soldiers fell to my blade. I lost count. When I got through the gateway alive I couldn't believe it. I looked up but found myself surrounded by the redcap welcoming committee, who looked as surprised to see me as I was to see them.'

'You weren't supposed to make it through,' I say and he nods. 'That's very interesting. Who would want you dead?' I ask him.

The look he throws me is dark and I hold up my hands. 'Sorry. Just thinking out loud.'

'No,' Thorn says and his voice is very tired. 'You're right. Something is definitely going on and we have to figure out what it is.'

'We?' I say, feeling my mouth twist into a grin. 'You're asking a Blackhart to help you sort out Alba problems?'

The smile he gives me is bleak. 'Perhaps we can talk about that after breakfast.'

In answer I can feel my stomach rumble. 'Of course,' I say, gesturing with my hands full of bandages. 'The kitchen is just through here.'

Chapter Eight

He follows me as I lead him through the quiet house. We get to the kitchen and I install him at the well-scrubbed farm table that can seat a dozen people. I dump all my mess in the bin and go into the utility room to wash my hands. I'm aware of the state I'm in so I rummage in the clean washing that's not been sent up to our rooms yet. I find a T-shirt and pull that on. There will be time for a shower later on, so I scrub my hands thoroughly and agonize for a moment over what looks like a spot coming out on my chin.

In the kitchen I busy myself with the cups and kettle.

As the water boils, I pop my mobile out of my pocket, desperately sending Megan and Marc a text to call me ASAP. Where was Jamie again? Hawaii? If he was training government people it meant that he would be out of contact for the duration of his assignment. It was part and parcel of how he operated.

I try ringing the twins and Kyle's dad, Uncle Andrew, who lives for part of the year in New York and runs a big part of the family business from there. He commutes between

New York and London as the need arises. Their mum, my aunt Jessica, works closely with him as she's a trained lawyer and is adept at both human and Fae law and lore. She welcomed me with open arms when Jamie brought me here after my nan's death. She sat with me through nightmares and fevers that racked my body as my magic tore through me. Hers is the face I now associate with coming through that ordeal alive. There's no answer at their brownstone in Boston or on either of their mobiles.

The kettle whistles and I jerk with fright, looking up from my mobile phone screen. 'Would you like coffee or tea?' I ask Thorn as I lay my phone on the counter next to me.

Thorn grimaces. 'Tea,' he says firmly. 'Coffee doesn't agree with me.'

I raise my eyebrows in question but he looks uncomfortable so I drop my initial reaction to ask him about it. I pour the water and as I wait for the tea to brew, I ring Aunt Letitia but there's no answer; that worries me a bit. She never leaves her tower or her library, not even for big family shindigs. She trusts no one to care for the archives she's in charge of and has more security and alarm systems set up in and around her land and in the tower than MI5 or the Bank of England combined.

I walk into the pantry and bring out eggs and fresh bread. 'Are you vegetarian?' I ask him. 'Would you like bacon with your scrambled eggs?'

'Bacon is good, thanks,' he says. He sees the bread and smiles. 'Your brownie, what does she call herself again? Mrs Evans? Her preserves are legendary in Alba. You must be very fond of her.'

'About as fond of her as she is of us.' I don't tell him about sweet Mrs Evans, who is a royal terror to live with. She bosses us all around and guards her preserves and cakes more fiercely than a dragon does his treasure. Whenever she leaves the house I get to unpick her spells so we can feast on the stuff she's left behind.

However, the best thing, in my opinion, about having a house brownie look after your home is that you have a practically unlimited supply of baked goods in the house. I glimpsed scones and a double-layered chocolate cake in the pantry as I rummaged for the bread and eggs.

'Do you visit the human world . . . I mean the Frontier often?' I ask him over my shoulder. 'You don't look as unfamiliar with things as I thought you'd be.' I don't tell him that I'm utterly clueless about what the Fae world is like. Do they even have electricity in Alba?

'I spent a year here, staying with one of my father's friends. We lived in a place, far from here. Canada, I think it's called.' When I nod he continues. 'I was only young, maybe eleven. My father's friend, he had a human job, working for the human authorities, looking after a nature reserve.'

'That sounds cool,' I say. 'Did you learn much?'

Thorn shrugs and winces when he pulls the stitches in his shoulder. 'I think not. It wasn't very different from being on a really long fishing and hunting trip with my brothers. Gregor lives an isolated life and he didn't really approve of me wanting to visit town and making friends.'

'But you did, though? Did you go to school?'

'No. I didn't attend school, not here, anyway. I had tutors in Alba.'

'Teaching you how to be a prince?'

'Something along those lines.'

I scramble the eggs and toast the bread – only lightly burning two of the slices. The bacon's a dream and I try not to drool on myself as I put our laden plates down on the table.

I sit down and devour half of my breakfast before I come up for air and see Thorn doing the same. We trade crumbly smiles, happy enough to be just stuffing our faces. After my fourth slice of toast I start feeling alive again and lean back in my chair. The tail-end of the headache I've had since I woke up the day before has eased up and my head feels clear.

I lean forward and grip my cup of coffee.

'So, do you have any idea what's going on? Why were redcaps waiting for you in the forest here, in the Frontier?'

I get a small smile at my clarification about using the word 'here'. While he considers his answer and drinks more tea, I can't shake the feeling of pretend. Using the words 'the Frontier' to describe the human world while the faerie realm is the Otherwhere still feels awkward. Who came up with the names anyway? They don't really trip off the tongue.

'I'm not sure it has anything to do with Suola or the Sun King,' Thorn says, taking a deep drink of his tea. The Sun King was the title for the Seelie ruler and his Court is also known as the Sun Court. Suola is Queen of the Unseelie and not someone I've ever actually met in real life, and I'm not keen to, either. Thorn's dad, King Aelfric of Alba, one of the large countries within the Otherwhere, is Alba's high king and both Suola and the Sun King bend their knee to him. 'I've been on the road for several months, running dispatches for my father. I've been backwards and forwards between the two Courts and they could have taken me any time they wanted.' He rubs his brow. 'We've had skirmishes with some bandits and a tribe of goblins, but nothing serious. Nothing out of the ordinary. Not until maybe two weeks ago. We were camping near Mikkeli, getting ready to meet a band of ogres to sign a treaty with a bunch of farmers. The night before the meeting, a stranger rode into the camp. She identified herself as a King's Rider.'

He's too distracted to notice my blank look so I sigh and ask him. 'What is a King's Rider?'

Thorn turns to look directly at me and I notice how his bleak expression intensifies during his explanation. 'A King's Rider is dispatched only during state emergencies. They are messengers, directly from the king. Their word is the king's word.'

'What was the message this one carried?'

'That the Citadel had been attacked. That the king and my mother had escaped through the quick thinking of their chamberlain, Istvan. They've gone into hiding, with three of my brothers and some of the Privy Council. Part of the Citadel was destroyed in the attack and one of my brothers, Kieran, has been confirmed captured. Two of my other brothers were on patrol in the North with their regiment when the attack happened. No one's heard of them. They could be alive, or dead.'

What do you say to that? I open my mouth but he cuts me short, holding up a hand. 'The Rider gave me a sealed message. The ring you had me take off was the only thing

I could use to open it. It was a note from my eldest brother, Petur, urging me to leave Alba with all speed, to find help here, at Blackhart Manor.'

'So you took your bodyguard and travelled to the nearest gateway . . .'

'And we got attacked by a group of outcasts and redcaps. We rode for days, from one gateway to the next. Every gateway we visited had been destroyed. We were hounded by group after group of goblins and redcaps. Finally, we found the gateway I used last night. The rest you know.'

'Do you know who attacked the Citadel? Do you know who the enemy is?'

The brief shake of his head makes me want to shout in annoyance.

'Do you know what happened to your friends? What changed them?'

'Dark magic.' His gaze meets mine. 'I don't know how the magic they used on my guards works, but it's not anything I've heard spoken of by anyone in Alba.'

'Okay.' I stand up and gather our dishes. 'I think we need to try and figure out what's going on, but before we even think of doing that, we need you cleaned up and dressed. I'll do the same but in the meantime I'm going to try and get hold of my cousins or my uncles and see what they think we should do.'

I lead Thorn up to Marc's room and open the doors to the wardrobe. 'You'll find stuff to fit you in here. Marc won't mind. I'm not sure about shoes, but we'll find something.' I look at his riding boots and at the torn trousers he's wearing and am relieved that I have several boy cousins and uncles whose wardrobes we can raid. 'Let's have a look at the cut on your arm first. The bathroom is through here.'

Thorn takes a seat on the side of the bath and shrugs out of the button-up shirt. There's definitely been some bleeding but it's not as bad as I thought it would be. The cut looks surprisingly good, with the edges starting to knit together, and my stitches look clean and neat. There's bruising too, along his ribs, but the bruises look a few days old already, not fresh, as if they had happened a few hours ago.

I look away to find those blue eyes watching me closely. I've seen boys look at Megan like that in the past but personally I've never had to deal with anything this intense. And to be honest, I'm not entirely sure I dislike it.

I clear my throat, lean back and attempt to ignore my suddenly pounding heart.

'It looks okay,' I say lamely. 'How fast exactly do you heal?'

'Here, a few hours, maybe a day at the longest. By tomorrow morning the cut will be a pink scar. In the Otherwhere it's faster, depending how close I am to the songlines.'

I'd only read about the Fae's ability to heal rapidly. It is what gives credence to rumours of their immortality. I am also charmed by him using the term 'songlines'. It's another word for the earth's energy, the 'leylines' that criss-cross the world.

'You can definitely die, then?'

His eyebrows shoot up in surprise. 'Why, are you planning something?' When he sees the shock on my face his lips curve into a smile. 'Sorry, that was a stupid joke. But, yes, if the damage done to our physical bodies is severe enough, we can die.'

Now that's really interesting. The magic and energy from the songlines in the Otherwhere must be linked to the Fae's longevity. I wonder what would happen if I ever visited there, how my magic would react. Would my lifespan become longer? Would I become tougher to hurt and kill?

'We have some books in the library at the Citadel that will help explain it,' Thorn says, watching me with curiosity. 'It's clearly something that interests you.'

I smile. 'I promise to look after the books,' I say. 'I won't even drop them in the swimming pool or anything.'

He senses that it's a joke and grins at me, standing up. 'Well, that's good. They are very old books and the librarian is very fierce.'

For a second the awkwardness kills me as he's very close, but then I remember why he's here in Marc's en-suite. 'Shower is right there, clean towels, soaps. If you need anything, just shout.'

He gives me a grateful smile and I click the bathroom door shut behind me. For the briefest second I lean against the door, listening to him moving around behind it.

What have I let myself in for? This is going to be big. I can feel it in my bones. The banshee's words come back to me, the smug way he spoke of darkness and not being able to cope with what's coming my way. I almost regret not hurting him more.

Chapter Nine

My shower takes longer than I would have liked. I felt tired and had trouble getting redcap blood from underneath my nails and resorted to using a spare toothbrush to clean them. Soon enough I find myself in Kyle's room, dressed in jeans, a clean T-shirt, hiking boots and my spare hoodie. The place is as immaculate as a dormitory. The bed is made with hospital corners and looks pristine. An old large floor-to-ceiling bookshelf, triple stacked with well-thumbed paperbacks, is propped up against the one wall. It contains everything from spy novels, political journals to heavy computer coding to contemporary literary fiction. There are also books in Latin and a scroll that looks very fragile, and I wonder if he had to fill in forms to get permission to take it out of the library.

I send off a series of urgent emails to everyone in the Blackhart registry that I know, hoping to get help from anyone and soon. Next I check the database that Kyle's built up to satisfy Aunt Letitia's obsessive record keeping. I find the folders on Alba easily enough and after half an hour of rapid reading I'm not really much wiser. King Aelfric came to power six hundred years ago through a series of wars and deaths in his family. I skim back and my eyes cross over when I see the long line of his lineage. They seem to have always ruled Alba, since a time called the Sundering. Aelfric is a modern king, well thought of, and he's a firm and fair ruler, having managed to prevent out-and-out bloodshed between the Seelie and Unseelie Courts, which are, even at times of peace, forever at each other's throats. He is progressive and has gone out of his way to strengthen ties with the human community, negotiating intricate business deals in both realms. He maintains strong relationships with various politically powerful families known as the Free Fae who have long ago decided to declare themselves ruled by no sovereign.

He entertains lavishly at his Court at winter, inviting the rulers of all the countries of the Otherwhere, and uses the festivities to network and sign new treaties for trade and continued peace. Spring is the time when he strengthens his ties to the human world. I sit back in surprise, remembering Marc, Megan and Kyle's parents coming back from the States to attend the Spring Equinox Ball held in Hyde Park shortly after my nan's funeral. I thought I was adjusting to my new life but when the detachment of Fae bodyguards turned up at the front door to accompany Uncle Andrew and Aunt Jessica to the ball, it felt as if I had been dropped into the middle of the filming of *Lord of the Rings*.

They were dressed in armour that fascinated me. It was made of metal of some sort but it looked more as if the blacksmith had taken large leaves from oak trees and moulded them into protective armour, covering the guards' chests, torsos and backs. Their great helms, shields and even their weapons repeated the leaf design. The horses they rode looked as if they were made from sea foam and moonlight, until you got too close and saw the fire in the depths of their dark eyes and the sparks their hooves struck from the ground. When my aunt and uncle left with the Fae guards I watched them ride into the forest and knew that this was just one more thing signalling the end to my pre-Blackhart life.

I drag myself back to the now and open the folder Kyle created for each of Thorn's siblings. They are all exceptionally attractive specimens. Very Viking-esque with strong shoulders, thick blond hair and handsome faces. I flick through their files but don't see anything interesting. Six of them are married and five of them already have their own kids. I find Thorn's file and open it. The first thing I notice is a photo of Thorn. It must have been taken a few years ago. He looks maybe fourteen and there is an arrogance there that I don't recognize in the boy that's having a shower only a few doors down. In the photo he's wearing a black tunic and loose-fitting black trousers that resemble karate trousers. His hair is tousled and he looks a mess, as if he's just come away from a sparring match. There is blood on his face and he's standing with his fists clenched. The expression in his eyes is one of anger and dislike. I have no idea where the photo is from or how Kyle even has it in his database. There isn't much info about Thorn, except to say when he was born (using our timeline) and so, yes, that makes him nineteen now, with his birthday having been on the summer solstice in June.

I push back from the screens before me and check the main inbox. Nothing. No emails from anyone. Where is everyone?

I close my eyes. What do we do next? Do we stay here, where we are relatively safe and protected by the wards on the house, or do we leave, travel to London to try and find help there? What do we do? I lean back in the chair and prop my ankles up on the desk, knowing Kyle would have a fit if he saw me putting my feet anywhere near his precious computers. I adopt a thinking pose – fingertips steepled together – and close my eyes to think.

There is someone in London who will be able to help; her name is Olga Kassan. She's a friend of the family and I've met her a few times now. Marc calls her a witch, a *bruja*, which is Spanish for witch, but when he says it, he definitely means more than just a witch. At each equinox she travels down to the Manor to help Jamie and Marc (and now me) refresh the warding around the house. In return, they pay her a lot of money. The more I think about it, the more I think that getting to Olga's is definitely our best option and because I can't find any info on her in Kyle's database, and therefore no number, we'll just have to head to London and track her down at the shop she runs for her grandfather. I have the address in my phone so I'll be able to set the satnav to navigate us there.

I hear a noise in the passage and turn to find Thorn standing behind me. He's found a pair of jeans that fit his long legs and he's wearing one of Marc's well-worn surf T-shirts but it sits a bit tight at the shoulders.

'Better?'

He closes his eyes in an expression of bliss. 'Much, thank you.' He looks past me and I'm tempted to swing around and turn the screens off, but it's too late. He's seen the photo of himself on there. 'Research?'

I nod, finding it interesting that he doesn't cross the threshold into Kyle's room to come closer and inspect the computer set-up. 'Yep. Just trying to see if there's anything in our files that can help us.'

'Any luck?'

I swing back to the screen and jab a finger at the photo of him. 'No, but this guy intrigues me. He looks like a bit of trouble.'

I'm favoured with a full smile. My heart actually stutters and my insides all do on-the-spot breakdancing. No one should be allowed to be this dangerously cute!

'Oh, he was. I reckon if you had met him last night, instead of me, you would have left him to be redcap dinner.'

'Seriously?' I look at him doubtfully, then back at the screen. 'He's very young, though.'

'Youth is no excuse for arrogance and stupidity.'

The way he says it makes me think that maybe those aren't his words. They sound as if they've been drilled into him. Maybe by a tutor? Or his father?

'Regardless, I would have saved his butt. No one that cute is allowed to suffer at the hands of redcaps.'

This time I get an actual chuckle. 'I'll remember that. Now, what can we do about shoes?' He points at his bare toes and wiggles them. And even they are attractive. 'My boots are great for riding but not really fit for everyday wear in the human world.'

'Let's see what we can find.'

Because we are such a big extended family, we always have people leaving bits of clothing behind. So, unless it's underwear (*ech*), we tend to dry clean it and hang it in one of the spare bedrooms. This is where I lead Thorn and after a few minutes of rummaging he comes away with a pair of trainers and a pair of solid hiking boots. We also find him a few more T-shirts and a pair of jeans. On our way downstairs, I grab a rucksack from Kyle's room and stuff Thorn's new clothes in there.

'Now you at least own something that's not covered in blood,' I tell him as we head back downstairs to the kitchen. I'm embarrassed to admit this but I am hungry again. I make some toast and smear it with peanut butter and, without asking, I make some for Thorn too. He accepts the plate without commenting and for a moment everything is quiet as we eat.

'Coffee?' I ask, heading for the filter machine, but he shakes his head.

'No, thank you,' he answers politely; I swear he's blushing. 'I'm allergic. I'd prefer some tea instead.'

'Wow, seriously?' I'd heard of this, but had never met someone who was actually allergic to my own personal rocket fuel.

I look over my shoulder at him but he's studiously bent over his plate, lifting crumbs with his finger, not meeting my eyes.

'All Fae must avoid coffee,' he says after a small strained silence. 'It has . . . an effect on us that could spell trouble for humans if they are around us if we somehow imbibe the stuff.'

Imbibe, really? I lift my eyebrows. 'Will you die from it?'

Thorn looks up and colour is blooming on his cheeks. 'Coffee works as a stimulant,' he says, his voice strained. When my look is still clueless he has to spell it out for me. 'It makes us amorous. It works far too well on the Fae, something to do with our higher metabolism. Its use is controlled in Alba. We import the stuff from the Frontier in small quantities only.'

Thankfully I manage to keep control of my face. I just about prevent myself from laughing, but the information that coffee is basically faery Viagra just totally took the wind out of my sails.

'Oh.' I make a show of looking through the cupboard. 'So, erm, herbal tea it is then.'

There's a muffled sound from Thorn and I look over to see his shoulders shaking. And when he looks up I see tears running down his face. And the next thing I know, I'm laughing with him, deep belly laughs that shake me so much I have to hold on to the counter. I certainly felt better as the tension of the last twenty-four hours was finally released.

'Well, that will definitely teach me to pay attention when Jamie gives us lessons about the differences between humans and Fae.'

Thorn wipes the tears of laughter from his face. 'I think it will be beneficial if you do.'

'Phew, now we've got that little problem over with,' I say as I put down his tea and my coffee, keeping it far away from him, 'what do we do?' I ask him, when I sit back down again. We sit facing one another like we did earlier this morning. 'Are we trying to get you back to Alba or are we staying here?'

'I need to get back home, but I don't think I'll be able to. Not from here, anyway.'

'You mean the redcaps?'

'Not just the redcaps. I should have been here days ago. Every gateway we reached had been destroyed. Every single one, for three days' hard ride through Alba. It was pure chance that we tried the gateway we stumbled across in the Otherwhere. One of my bodyguards knew of it . . .'

'Convenient.'

His grimace tells me he has already thought about it too. 'So I'm not sure the gateway that brought me here can send me back.'

Chapter Ten

Magic Mirrors: Staple of the common fairy tale (See:
Snow White, Beauty and the Beast, The Snow Queen).
Logic dictates that magic mirrors should not exist.
There is no scientific way that a mirror can speak
to a person and give advice. Furthermore, using
mirrors for far-seeing or spying on others has never
been proven.

From an archived report filed in HMDSDI HQ, 1988

'Okay,' I say, standing up. 'What weapons can you use?'

'Sword, dagger, bow.' Thorn was frowning at me. 'Why
do you ask?'

'We are going to tool up. You'll like this, I promise.
Come with me.'

I fish a key from the ugly ceramic bowl of keys in the
library and lead Thorn downstairs into the house's basement.
I flick on the lights and can't suppress the shudder that goes
through me as the size of the basement is revealed in the
glare. Too many horror movies have given me the creeps
for our perfectly safe and rather mundane basement. Part

of it is given over to the Manor's garage, where a range of cars, including Lolita, stand gleaming, waiting for Megan's delicate touch.

In the furthest corner, away from the lights, is Uncle Andrew's wine cellar, housed behind iron bars that form a deterrent to mischievous Fae, who have tried to break in several times in the past to steal some of the antique bottles of faery mead he's been given as part payment for work.

I lead Thorn to a part of the wall near the wine cellar. I stand quietly and count the bricks. Seven down, eight across. I press my palm to the brick and it slides back with a grating sound. There's a *thunk* and ratcheting noise and the wall slides cleanly to the side, allowing us access to a high arched wooden door inlaid with heavy steel bars. I show Thorn the key – it's as long as the palm of my hand – and slide it into the keyhole.

The door opens and we step into the armoury. The lights come on automatically and I watch Thorn's face as the darkness steadily gives way to the light, revealing rows of weapons, suits of armour and glass cases housing axes, flintlock pistols, gauntlets and every other bit of armour and man-made weapon for hurting another person, all of the highest workmanship.

Thorn lets out a soft whistle. 'My brother Kieran would go crazy if he ever saw this. He's visited all the Frontier museums where they have exhibits of arms and armour. It's an obsession with him.'

A wave of nausea hits me out of nowhere and the hairs lift at the back of my neck. Before I can even wonder what's going on, the ground shifts beneath my feet and I grab hold of the nearest cabinet. Thorn looks at me in alarm as a loud groaning noise emanates from somewhere far, far below us. Beneath my feet the floor looks normal: large industrial tiles that can withstand heavy loads, and no sign of cracks or anything peculiar, just this terrible moaning sound.

'Earthquake?' Thorn raises his voice over the noise but all I can do for a few seconds is shake my head.

'Earthquakes are rare in the UK,' I tell him, doing my utmost to sound less panicked that I feel. 'I mean, it could be one, but, you know, it's pretty unusual.'

My heart thuds against my ribs and I quickly direct him to collect whatever weapons he'd like to take with him.

I help him measure arrow shafts against his arm and he quickly packs a few into a quiver that he slings over his shoulder.

The noise and the shaking stopped almost as soon as it started but I'm not prepared to take a chance. I collect a brace of throwing knives, plus a spare stab-proof hoodie for Thorn. I agonize for a second over my favourite pair of duelling pistols. I am far more accurate with them than I have ever been with the bow, and there's no way I'm going to break into the gun safe. My magic is too random and unpredictable when it comes to using modern guns but these eighteenth-century Italian pistols work well for me. They are also only one-shot weapons, but whatever I fire at will be guaranteed to go down. I strap the belt Megan helped me fashion around my waist. The holsters are low-slung and comfortable and I check the pistols over before I slide them into the holsters and tie the ammunition and pre-measured ampoules of powder to my belt.

I look up to see Thorn walking towards me. He picks up a Tuareg dagger and flips it in his hand, checking the balance. It goes into his belt, next to another more modern-looking blade.

'We need some modern armour,' I tell him. 'The Kevlar stuff is over there.' I lead him to a tall metal cabinet and pull out two normal-seeming waxed jackets that look like traditional Barbour jackets. I pass the bigger one to Thorn, who, after taking the quiver and longbow off, pulls it on.

'It's bulletproof and stab-proof but looks like normal everyday wear.' I punch him on the chest. 'We don't know what's going on, so we aim to be prepared.'

He nods and hefts his gear onto his shoulder once more. I lock the door behind us and the panel hiding the room slides shut.

A very loud boom shakes the house around us and dust drops down from the ceiling. I duck instinctively and pull Thorn along behind me but he stops halfway up the stairs, a look of concentration on his face.

'We have to go now,' I tell him, watching in alarm as the lights below us in the basement swing wildly from side to side. 'We need to get upstairs and get our stuff so we can leave.'

'There's something here, Kit.' He turns and walks back down the stairs and I consider screaming at him. Now was not the time for him to go on a mini-adventure.

'Yes,' I say. 'Someone is attacking the house.'

'No. Not that. Something very old, very magical.' He smiles apologetically as I tap the banister impatiently. 'I think I know what it is. It's something that can help us.'

I throw my hands up in the air. 'What?'

'Your mirror.'

I feel my mouth form the letters WTF but nothing comes out. He drops all his gear and starts looking rapidly around the basement area.

'Tell me what we're looking for,' I ask him. 'I can help.'

'Your mirror – you must have one. I didn't even think about it until just now. I can feel it. Can't you?'

I shake my head. 'Honestly? No. All I want to do is get back upstairs and check what's going on. What mirror? We have hundreds of mirrors all around the house. Can it be any of them?'

'No. It's here. I can hear its song.'

I'm now wondering if I've brought a crazy boy into the house. He can hear the mirror's *song*? Maybe he had a severe head injury and I didn't know about it. I'm tempted to leave him to it so I can figure out what's going on upstairs and who's attacking the house and how they're doing it.

No one can get past the magic shield protecting the house – that much I've been assured of by Uncle Andrew and Jamie. The spells are part of the house and have been for hundreds of years. It has withstood physical attack in the past and magical attacks too, or so the books in the library say. It all happened a very long time ago now.

'What's in here?' Thorn pushes his shoulder against an old wooden door. 'Any idea?'

'Uhm, I don't know. Old bits of furniture we don't use any more.'

'Help me.'

I go over and together we charge the door with our

shoulders. The door flies open and I grab Thorn by the arm before he goes headfirst into a broken antique sideboard. The place is thick with dust and cobwebs but now I can feel the slipperiness in the air too and I know this is what Thorn meant when he said he could sense the mirror.

I walk into the main garage area and come back with one of the torches that Megan uses when fixing cars. The light isn't the best but Thorn wades into the mess without a backward glance. He shifts some chairs around, pushes a piano with no keys to the side and eventually brings out a large four-foot shape covered in thick black cloth.

'Got it!' He backs out of the room holding onto his prize.

'What is it?'

Thorn frowns at me. 'I told you, it's your mirror.'

'You keep saying that but I have no idea what you're talking about.'

Another boom rattles through the basement and I grab Thorn's arm as the ground beneath us heaves upwards briefly before settling down once more. I push him and his bloody mirror up the stairs, pausing just long enough to collect his bow and arrows. We rush into the room beside the kitchen and I slam the door to the basement shut, locking it and dropping the heavy wooden bar across it.

'Help me put this somewhere,' Thorn says, his voice straining. 'It's heavy.'

I guide him into the main living room and he props it onto one of the sofas. I worry that it's too heavy and might tear the leather but then, really, what do I care? The house is under attack and a tiny tear in a couch is the least of my concerns.

'Listen, I need to go grab some stuff, okay? I'll be right back.'

I leave him faffing with the mirror and run up the stairs to my room. I grab my go-bag, already packed with toiletries, changes of clothes, a spare knife and some of the loose cash we all have in case of emergency.

I ghost up to my window and pull the curtains aside, wondering if I'd see anything from here. The gardens lie serene under a blue sky, basking in the late morning sun. Beyond the gardens and the smooth lawn are the standing stones, and past them is the curve of the forest. It lies verdant and green and quiet, looking for all the world like a scene from a nature programme.

Nausea grips me again and I lean forward, supporting myself against the windowsill. The house rumbles around me, like a giant creature reluctant to get up. From the ground floor I hear glass breaking and the sound of the crystal chandelier hanging in the entrance hall shaking itself loose.

Where are they attacking us from? I run from my room and race across to the east wing of the house where Uncle Andrew's rooms are. The forest is much closer to this side of the house and that's where I spot the probable cause of our problem.

A man dressed casually in jeans, shirt and waistcoat stands just within the shadows of the forest. Lined up behind him I see around a hundred goblins, redcaps and some Fae arrayed for battle. They keep to the forest's shadows and only venture slightly into the harsh sunlight to shout and jeer at the house.

I look around the room and spot a pair of binoculars on the bedside table. I grab them, focusing them on the attacking force. As I watch, the man turns to speak to someone behind him and I take the opportunity to pull my mobile out again.

There is no signal now, none at all. I leap at the telephone on Aunt Jessica's side of the bed and pick it up. There is a dialling tone and I quickly look up Megan's mobile number. To my relief the phone rings.

I hold on until voicemail picks up.

'Megan, it's Kit. The house is under attack. I've got the youngest Prince of Alba here with me. Long story, but it's looking bad. There's a lot of bad guys out in the forest and it looks as if they are preparing for a siege.' I draw a breath. 'We're going to leave soon. Head for London. I'll call again later.'

I ring Marc and Kyle and leave the same message. I have no idea what time it is in New York but I find Uncle Andrew's number and ring that too. It goes straight to voicemail. I swear vehemently and leave an even terser message.

I turn back to the window in time to see the guy at the front of the mob of Fae creatures step into the sunlight. He lights up like a flare when he does. He brings his hands together above his head and in an overly exaggerated movement – it almost looks like a martial arts move – he brings his arms back down and thrusts them towards the house.

I don't need my magic sight to see what he's doing. I

can sense the wave of energy he expels. It races across the lawn and slams into the barrier held up by the standing stones.

The house rumbles and shakes around me and suddenly I wonder how much I want to bet that the wards will hold. I grab my bag and run down the stairs.

Thorn is standing in the living room and looks up when I come in. A worried frown draws his brows together and he gestures at the mirror.

'It's broken. Dangerous to use.'

'What?' I'm completely distracted and trying to think what would be our best way out of the house. In the open we'd be sitting ducks. Do we run or do we drive? The only car in the garage at the moment is Lolita and I have no idea what her capabilities are. Honestly, I'd prefer a tank.

'The mirror, Kit. I can use the mirror to find out what's going on back home, at the Citadel.'

Thorn looms in front of me so that I can't help but stand still and look at him.

'Thorn, at the moment I really don't give a damn about your mirror. The house is under attack. They've got an entire army hidden in the forest behind the house. I don't know how long the wards will last under sustained attack.'

I don't like the panic in my voice. This is not who I am, or how I've been taught to cope with situations. Assess. React. But that's easier said than done.

'It's important, Kit. My parents – I can find out about my brothers.'

'Bring the mirror, then,' I tell him. 'We're leaving.'

'We can't take it with us. The mirrors are keyed to specific locations. This one is locked on to the Manor, to your family.'

I want to shout at him that we need to go but he watches me with an anxious expression.

'Please, it won't take long. Maybe five minutes.'

Chapter Eleven

'If it doesn't work in five minutes, we leave, right?' I say against my better judgement. The lopsided smile he gives me makes my stomach flip-flop but I narrow my eyes. 'What do we do?'

'Are you a full-blooded Blackhart?'

'Pardon?'

'Do you have a parent who carried the name Blackhart?'

'Yes, my mum. Why?'

'Good, this will make things easier.'

I sink down in front of the mirror when he tugs me down next to him. 'Will you cut your finger, not a big cut, so that a drop wells up?'

'Blood magic?' I say, suddenly very uneasy. 'Not quite comfortable with that.'

'It's just to wake it up, to talk to it. It might not even work.'

I curl my lip, knowing that this little parlour trick will end up sucking up the rest of my magic. 'How do we do that?' I ask, not caring that I sound fed-up and irritable.

'We take the blood from your finger and you anoint it

here and here.' He presses his fingers against the petals carved in the north and south positions of the mirror. 'And then you say your name. And I'll do the rest.'

'And what's that?'

'I'll sing it awake.'

Sing? Not what I was expecting and I'm tempted to laugh but I hold myself in check. I lean forward and pull my knife from its sheath. I press the point into my forefinger and watch a droplet of blood well up. I press it slightly more so that the droplet grows in size. I press my finger first to the lily petal to the top of the mirror, then I move my hand to press it against the lower petal.

Thorn nods at me. 'Now say your name and say, I call on you to wake up.'

'This is not some kind of faerie trick, right? I'm not going to be sucked into the mirror or anything?'

He has the decency to look worried for a second but then shakes his head. 'No, it's not that kind of mirror.'

I roll my eyes at him. As I open my mouth to speak my name I remember one of the things Jamie told me never ever to do and that is to gift a supernatural creature with my full name. It would mean that they have full power over me, and will be able to summon me or cast spells on me to do their bidding. So, I clear my throat and say clearly, 'I am Kit Blackhart. I call on you to wake up.'

Thorn slants me a quick look to see if I'm ready; when I nod, he starts humming a melody.

He has a good voice. I don't know much about singing, but I know I like his voice. My nan would have made him sing for his supper. She had a thing for handsome tenors.

As I listen to his voice the tension eases out of my shoulders and the aches in my body lessen.

I close my eyes because I can almost remember hearing this song. Maybe, when I was very small, someone sang this to me. The humming grows a bit louder and I feel the frame shift beneath my fingers, the way a horse flexes its muscles when you sit astride it. My eyes fly open, no longer listening to Thorn's voice. I'm tempted to pull my fingers back, away from the mirror because I can feel a wetness on my fingers where they touch the frame and, as I watch, the frame darkens beneath my fingers like skin flushing with blood. I do my best to suppress a shudder but Thorn sees and drops a calming hand to my shoulder.

The voice, when it comes, is from far away, filled with interference, like static. 'What do you seek, Blackhart? We had a mutual agreement. You leave me be, I leave you be.' The voice is all around me, inside my head. It's not really loud, just very present, but there are odd sounds too: more voices, the sound of nails across a chalkboard.

'I'm sorry,' I say, hating how hesitant and scared I sound. 'I, uhm, I'm not the Blackhart you know. I don't know about the agreement you brokered.' I look at Thorn and whisper at him, 'I'm not comfortable doing this.'

Before Thorn can answer, the mirror speaks again. 'There is only ever one Blackhart,' the voice says, sounding distracted, tired. 'The agreement was Mirabelle's. She paid the price. I need no further recompense, only to rest from now until all eternity, girl. What is your wish?'

'I seek to know of my parents,' Thorn answers in my place. 'I am Thorn, Prince of Alba.'

There's a rustling, like something big shifting its weight around. 'Is this your wish too, Blackhart, to know of the House of Alba?'

I swallow against the tightness in my throat. 'Yes, it is.' What agreement would my nan have made with this weird thing?

A high-pitched whine comes from the mirror and I wince, turning away from it, clapping my hands over my ears. The pitch increases but then fades back into louder static before it is turned off, like a switch. 'I do not see them,' the mirror says. 'I see the Citadel in ruins. A man sits on the throne, but he is not the king. He is a puppet-king, a pretend king.' There comes a scritching noise, like an insect rubbing its legs together. 'But he is of the royal blood.'

I watch Thorn as he reaches out and grabs hold of the mirror. 'What does this man look like?'

'Blackhart, do you desire to know?' The voice is so far off I have to strain to hear it.

'I do.' My whisper is hoarse.

'The man feels great fear. He wears a ring on his right hand. It's a moonstone ring carved into a lion's head. But there is a man in the shadows behind him. This is the man who controls the usurper.'

'Who? Do you know who these men are?' Thorn asks, leaning forward, staring into the blackness of the mirror.

'I want to know too,' I tell the mirror, pre-empting the question. 'We need to know.'

'I do not know either of these men. The sorcerer is born of darkness. I cannot see his face. He's wreathed in layers of mist. The man on the throne does not know he is a pawn in a greater game.' There is a sound of something shattering and I jump back from the mirror. 'It is a pity, Blackhart, that he does not understand the game that's afoot.'

I jerk with fright when the mirror shudders, and the unexpected shadow that falls across its surface bulges towards us, in the shape of a face.

'Who are you?' another voice demands. This time the voice is full of harsh authority and suppressed anger. 'Who are you? Speak!'

The sound of screeching is followed by a long wail that rises and falls. 'Beware, Blackhart, he knows you're watching,' the mirror's whisper is tired, resigned. 'Such anger and hatred.' There's a moaning noise and a howl that lifts the hair at the back of my neck. 'This is finally the end, Blackhart, you had promised to keep me safe, but now, now you bring me to the end of my days.' The voice holds no inflection, merely stating a fact.

I sit forward, gripping the frame of the mirror, my pulse racing.

'I'm sorry, we had no idea,' I gasp, curling my fingers around the frame. 'Please . . . tell me what we can do?'

The answer is a tearing ripping sound, an awful noise so close to me it makes me leap backwards, away from the mirror.

Thorn has his arm around my waist and is pulling me away when a hand bursts through the mirror. It reaches for me, the skin pallid and the fingers curling, sinister. 'You will not escape. I know you. I can smell you, Blackhart.'

I let out a yelp in surprise but before I can do anything else, Thorn opens his hand and sends a blast of pure energy into the mirror. As it strikes the centre of the mirror, he spins himself around so his back is to it and folds me against his chest. It's a sweet gesture but as I'm tall I can see over his shoulder. The energy arcs across the surface of the mirror, running the labyrinth of cracks that has appeared across it, before exploding into a billion flying shards.

Thorn tucks my head beneath his chin and I can feel his heart thudding through the thin fabric of his shirt. My hands rest on his hips and for a few seconds it's nice to just feel comfortable standing pressed up against him like this. I can almost pretend he's hugging me because he likes me, like a real boy would, and wants to protect me and take me away from the madness that's creeping up on us.

'Do you know who he described?' I ask, after a few long moments of listening to his heart. 'The man, the guy with the ring?'

'I think so,' he says, shifting slightly. His eyes, when they meet mine, are troubled. 'If the mirror is to be believed, I think my father's younger brother's decided to overthrow him and make a bid for the throne of Alba.'

'Oh.' I'm blazingly erudite, as always. 'Well then, we'd better try and stop him.'

Chapter Twelve

Lolita roars out of the garage and I swing her left, down the drive towards the side of the house that leads north. I'm not familiar with the secondary road the estate manager uses to get around the massive Manor grounds, but I'm pretty sure that there has to be another entrance at the back of the property.

Thorn is in the passenger seat and looks deeply unhappy. His face is pale, he's buckled himself tightly into his seat and his grip on his sword makes his knuckles stand out white.

'I'm a good driver,' I promise him. 'I did an advanced driving course with Marc a few months ago.'

Thorn rolls his eyes at me. 'It's not that,' he says, his voice hoarse. 'All the metal and iron . . . it makes me feel ill.'

Bah. How stupid of me. I should have remembered how much the Fae, especially the higher-born Sidhe, dislike iron and metal.

'Sorry. We don't stable horses at the Manor any more.' I shoot him a look. 'Can you imagine going all the way to London by horse?'

'Just watch where you're going.' He gestures briefly with one hand before grasping his hilt again. 'How long will it take us to get there?'

I look at the GPS on the dash. 'To London? About six hours?'

He moans under his breath but nods. 'If we can stop now and again, for fresh air, I'm sure I'll make it.'

We speed through the late afternoon air, bouncing along the dirt road. The forest is off to the right and behind us. Flashes of energy are still hitting the wards surrounding the house and to my eyes the flashes seem to be a far less intense green than before, which probably means that the wards are running out of juice.

I spot a tall standing stone coming up. 'We're about to pop through the wards. Are you ready?'

Thorn only nods, swallowing hard. I press my foot down on the accelerator and we shoot past the wards, between two of the standing stones. For a second it feels as if we are airborne, suspended in the air, but then we thunk down solidly onto the road. I gasp and Lolita stalls as I bend forward over the wheel sucking in gulps of air.

I feel as if I've been punched in the gut and my skin raked with sharp nails. When I manage to open my eyes, my vision is blurry. I blink against it but another wave of pain hits me and I cry out, gripping the steering wheel harder.

'What's wrong?' Thorn's harsh voice cuts through the fog in my brain. 'Kit? Look at me.'

My brain is fighting off the pain racking my body and I'm unable to answer him.

'Can you hear me? Nod if you can hear me!' His voice comes from a long way off and I stare at his lips forming the words. I nod my head at him and look away, concentrating on bringing pieces of myself back together again. Slowly, so slowly it feels like a million years passing, the pain dissolves and I can sit up straight in my seat. I lean back and close my eyes in relief, a heavy sigh escaping from my lips.

'Kit? Please speak to me.'

'The magic.' I swallow against the dryness in my throat. 'It's always been difficult for me to leave the Manor. The wards claim us when we come home. It's always so reluctant to let me go. It's been like this since I joined the family. No one else seems to suffer this badly when they leave.'

He blinks at me. 'Was it this bad when you came to fetch me in the forest?'

'No. I wasn't leaving to go, was I? The magic knew that.'

'Sweet Mother Gaia,' he whispers to himself, turning back in his seat. 'I thought you were dying. I could see the bones beneath your skin.'

I get my breathing under control and reach forward to start the car when Thorn speaks again. 'Do you believe in dragons?' he asks me, his voice taut with strain.

'I've never seen one. I've read about them in the library,' I offer. 'They were sent back to the Dragonrealm a few million years ago by one of the gods after taking—'

'I didn't ask for a lecture. I asked if you believed in dragons.' His voice is sharp and impatient. 'I ask because I think we have one flying towards us right now.'

I start smiling feebly, ready to tell him not to be stupid,

but the words die on my lips. A dark shadow is coming straight at us at an incredible speed. A part of me still wants to laugh, to say I was hallucinating, that the pain from leaving the protective circle of the house somehow scrambled my brains. The laughter dies on my lips because another more primitive part of my brain recognizes that silhouette, the upbeat of those huge wings, the massive serpentine body and the giant triangular horned head with its wide protective crest.

'It's not real.' My voice quivers and I clear my throat. 'It's the sorcerer, right? It's sending us this vision, to scare us.'

'It's real. It's as real as you and me. I think you should start driving.' He snaps his fingers impatiently before my eyes, momentarily blocking my view of this improbable, incredible dragon. 'Kit, listen. We need to go. Now.'

I nod and turn the key. Lolita fires on the first go and I throw her in gear and we race forward, towards the on-coming dragon.

'This is mad,' I say, shifting gears as we speed ahead. 'How is it even here?'

The dragon is bigger than I can fully comprehend, perhaps the size of a very large plane. A heavy gust of wind hits us from nowhere and I feel Lolita rock on her chassis. We're going at forty-five miles an hour down a dirt road, yet it feels as if we're standing still. Outside, the wind tears at the park and the trees lining the road whip wildly about like tiny saplings in a breeze.

'I can't tell if it's going to attack us or fly right over,' Thorn tells me as I concentrate on not going onto the verge.

'It's not slowing down at all. I've never seen anything like it.' His voice sounds distant and when I glance at him he's staring at the dragon as if mesmerized. I reach over with my left hand and punch him on the leg, one of Jamie's special punches. Thorn lets out a yelp. 'What was that for?'

'Before you fall under its spell or something, shoot it!'

Thorn gestures at the car, the sword and me in desperation. 'How? The bow is in the back and I can't really menace it with a sword while sitting in your car!'

I hand him one of the pistols that I'd slid into the panel of the door next to me. 'Use that!'

He gives the wooden handle of the antique pistol a cursory glance and shrugs. I open his window and watch him lean his body halfway out of the window like some Bruce Willis wannabe and take aim at the oncoming dragon. The thing is huge! I have no idea what effect a bullet would have on the dragon, but it was worth a shot. I doubted that it would even manage to fire the distance.

Thorn lets out a shout and I hear him fire the pistol. There's a flash from the muzzle just before he falls back into his seat, gasping. The dragon sweeps over us in a rush of wind and the car whines under the unexpected onslaught of heavy wind and rain that follows in the dragon's wake. I struggle to find the windscreen wipers to clear my view. How we went from bright sunshine to hurricane weather in a blink of an eye is beyond me. The clouds above us broil with menace and I lean forward to look out of the windscreen.

The weather has gone crazy. Fat drops of rain fall from the black clouds and obscure everything around us. Thorn struggles but eventually finds the button and the window whirs up. His wet hair is plastered to his face and he is shaking from the cold. His lips are verging on blue.

'Where's the dragon?' he asks, twisting backwards and peering out of the back window. 'I think I shot him, but I don't know.' He wiggles the pistol. 'Do we know what the range is on this thing? Would the bullet have even hit?' When I shrug in reply, too keyed up to wonder about range, wind interference and other things that go into getting off a good shot, he swears and drops the pistol on the floor of the car. He proceeds to wipe ineffectually at his wet hair and face while I try and keep the car on the road.

'I can't see it,' I say, peering out of the windows and using my mirrors. I get Lolita started up again and I pray I don't hit anything as I floor the pedal. 'Let's just get out of here.' I try not to think about a dragon being loose in the countryside. Jamie never thought to teach us how to fight dragons and the only reason I even looked at the books in the library about them was because I thought they were cool and, of course, I didn't really take their existence seriously. Who would?

We race through the rain, our eyes on the road before us, behind us, to the side of us. I can't even begin to think how a dragon came to be at the Manor. Dragons have not flown in this world for hundreds of thousands of years. These days they only exist in movies and fantasy novels.

'It's back,' says Thorn, his voice hoarse. 'Behind us.'

Chapter Thirteen

Dragons: Elemental beings, the First Born, dragons possess free will (similar to djinns). Highly intelligent and cunning, dragons are not to be trifled with. Summoning a dragon into the human realm should only be attempted by a Master Sorcerer. The sorcerer must be in control at all times, especially when performing the dragon's binding ritual. Evidence of a failed binding and its repercussions can be seen in the Great Fire of London in 1666 when Magnus Kirkbright attempted and failed at summoning and binding a dragon. It took Gregory and Aliette Blackhart three days to hunt the dragon and return him to the Dragonrealm.

From *The Blackhart Bestiarum*

I look in the rear-view mirror and I let out a soft moan. I press down harder on the pedal and Lolita answers without coaxing. I throw a prayer of thanks to Megan for doing impossible things to car engines. The rough road ahead of us curves and I see a gate. And beyond the gate I see an actual tarmac road.

'It's gone.' Thorn's right. There's no sign of the dragon near us. Where has it gone? I slow down and we peer in all directions. In our race I'd not noticed it but we had climbed a small hill and our view of the forest and the Manor is unobstructed, with the heavy rain giving the familiar landscape a desolate air.

For a few seconds we sit quietly, peering back through the back window. Thorn grips my arm. 'There!' I follow the line of his pointing finger and then I see it. The dragon must have climbed high into the sky and banked over the forest. Its course is set for Blackhart Manor.

We sit in stunned silence and watch the creature pass over the wards without any harm and head straight for the house. It opens its massive jaws and a sound like the world tearing itself apart emanates from it in waves, rolling over the Manor. For a moment everything looks fine, but then the house starts shaking and trembling, as if the earth itself is trying to dislodge it.

Beside me Thorn is very still and hardly seems to breathe. The wind whips around us, shaking the car from side to side. I unlock my door and struggle out, ignoring my impulse to run, to hide from the big bad thing flying above us. The rain is icy against my skin and I'm drenched within seconds but I only notice it peripherally.

My eyes are riveted to the spectacle below us. A vortex of spinning darkness opens in the middle of the Manor and keeps growing, consuming the house, brick by brick, inch by inch.

A noise reaches me, dampened by the clouds and the rain and wind howling around me. A shriek, sounding very human, lifts from the depths of the house as it continues its slide into the abyss.

The man from the forest strides towards the house, a swirling mass of energy trapped in his hands. He seems completely unconcerned about the dragon circling back towards the house, and as he gets to the edge of the garden, he launches the cone of energy at my home.

Numb with shock, I watch as the dragon drops lower, swooping towards the Manor, chasing the cone of energy. The dragon rears back its triangular head and unhinges its jaw. The pulse of pure blinding power that emanates from it hits the house, in conjunction with the energy from the denim-clad guy, and rips apart the final wards protecting the house.

I feel them tear to shreds like a physical blow to my chest and double over, a moan wrenching itself from me. I drop to my knees and tears stream down my face as the place gives a final jolt before sliding like sludge down a sinkhole.

I catch movement to the side and watch as the dragon flies towards the man who just blasted my house to bits. My breath hitches, fully expecting the dragon to crash to the ground, but instead it curls up into itself somehow as it plummets to earth. It strikes the ground in a flurry of wings and when it straightens up, my world-view of things that can be and that can't be changes once more.

A tall figure rises upwards in its place, dressed in a cloak that whips around his long legs. The newcomer clasps the first aggressor in a brief hug, before turning to survey the achingly empty black pit where the Manor once stood.

I lean against the car, racked by sobs, letting the tears mingle with the driving rain. In just over a year I've lost two homes. First, the home I shared with my nan, burned to the ground because an Unseelie noble hated the Blackharts – even ones who refused to accept their lineage – and now the home Jamie brought me to after Nan's death.

The Manor became a place where I could rest, feel safe and be part of a family I never knew I had but so desperately needed.

The rain keeps coming and I start shivering and grip myself hard for warmth but also comfort. The torn earth where the house stood looks like a raw wound amidst the neat landscaped gardens. Emotions churn inside me as I watch the distant group carousing, counting the loss of the Manor as a major battle won.

Thorn, who must have joined me at some stage, reaches for me and helps me stand. He runs his hand down my forearm and grips my hand. 'I'm so sorry,' he says, his voice hushed. He makes a gesture that expresses the futility of trying to convey his feelings but I do understand. There are no words to express the sadness and anger, so I give him a nod.

'I know,' I say dully. 'Let's get in the car and figure out how to make all these bastards pay.'

Chapter Fourteen

The storm follows us, increasing in strength and anger. Two hours into our journey I've stopped shaking and crying and sit behind the wheel of Lolita tense with concentration as the car is hit by sheets of rain. Thorn sits beside me, rigid in his seat, his face pale. We've propped a towel from one of the backpacks against the door so that his arm doesn't rest against the metal of the car, but even so, he doesn't look well.

'I'm hungry,' I say, slanting a glance at him. 'Are you okay for us to stop and get something to eat?'

He nods mutely and I turn my attention back to the cars ahead of us on the road and when we see signs for the next service station, I indicate and pull in.

Inside, the place is far busier than it should be but we find a free table at the back of the communal eating area. I buy a selection of sandwiches, crisps and drinks and we tuck in without bothering to make small talk.

I feel bleak, empty and worried. I showed Thorn how to use my mobile in the car and he's checked it every few minutes for messages, both texts and emails, but no word from anyone. Anxiety eats at me and I wonder if we are doing the right thing, travelling to London. I don't have Olga's number and the number listed on the shop's website just goes to voicemail.

I look up from eating and notice the TV screens facing the eating area. Several of them hold reports about the unseasonable weather, reporting that Cornwall and Devon seem hardest hit by the freak hurricane winds and rain. There are warnings of local flooding and that motorists should be extra careful driving. Two schools have been shut and there's footage of a giant oak tree torn from the ground and flung across several cars.

'The dragon.'

I jerk with fright and look at Thorn. 'What? Did you see it? Is it here?' Sitting at the back of the restaurant area, there's no way he can see the front of the building. There are no windows, but it doesn't stop me from staring around.

'No. Yes, the dragon is here.' He gestured in a big circle with his hands. 'The dragon is here, in this realm, on your earth, but not here-here.'

'Yes, I know that. We both saw it.' I am tempted to tut at him, but something in his gaze stops me. 'What do you know that you're not telling me?'

'I think I know what it is.'

This time I do tut and make a hand-swirling motion to show him that he has to go on. He shakes his head at my childishness but does continue.

'When I was little, my mother used to tell us stories of the Time Before Time. Her favourite stories were about dragons. She always made them sound noble and interesting. Not this.' He shakes his head and rubs the cut above his eyebrow. 'Having a dragon in this world, in the Frontier, is more dangerous than I can explain. These storms we're seeing are the dragon's presence unbalancing your world. There is a reason the dragons were banished when they were, all that time ago. The world needed to thaw, to learn how to be green again.'

I put the cup of coffee back down on the table.

'Are you talking about an Ice Age?'

He nods. 'Essentially, yes. Dragons are elemental beings and they are powerful. Their essence or rather their life force is fed by the earth's magic. They suck worlds dry and leave destruction in their wake. Do you understand what I'm saying?' His eyes rake my face and I nod vaguely, not really understanding but unable to say otherwise. 'If you or your family or any of my people go up against this dragon when the time comes, they will have to be very close to use their magic.' He pushes a piece of salad around on his plate. 'My mother always said that no sorcerer was ever able to stand against a dragon on a fair fight. Not when using magic at least. It's like fighting fire with fire. Any fight will have to be hand-to-hand combat.'

'That is spectacularly crap.' I stare blankly at my empty mug of coffee. 'How about cannons? Can we shoot it with cannons?'

'Honestly? I have no idea.'

'Who are we going to see?' Thorn asks me after we've driven another hour. I've shown him how to operate the radio and we've gone through talk radio, news, jazz music, classics and then hip hop.

'This lady called Olga. I don't know her very well but she's friends with my uncles Andrew and Jamie. She comes around on the equinox days and helps.' My breath hitches. 'Helped us strengthen the wards on the house. My cousin Kyle says she's a witch, but a real one, one that can curse you or cure you at will.'

'Witches are as powerful in Alba as any sorcerer in my father's academy. I think that the man we saw helping the dragon, uhm, person is a sorcerer.'

'What's the difference between sorcerers, witches and wizards?' I ask him. I have my own suspicions, but hearing it from someone who lives in the Otherwhere, where magic is a part of everyday life, will be interesting. 'Like, when that man tried to come out of the mirror, you threw a ball of fire at it. What are you?'

'Sorcerers and witches use the energies around them, tapping into the songlines, to produce their magics. You call them leylines but the people of Chin call them dragonlines. Wizards and witches use spells, which in turn require ingredients, to produce magic. Sorcerers have no need to learn spells, not in the way you would perhaps read a recipe. They need to know what needs doing and then they will it to happen by using the energy from the leylines around them. Failing that, if there are no leylines to tap into, they will instead use captives and drain them of energy to power their magic.' He rubs his face and drinks some of the water we bought at our second stop. 'I have a little magic only, a bit of skill, mostly for cantrips and bits of glamour. My eldest brother is an adept and even when he was a baby there were rumours of his stunning abilities. I'm definitely a disappointment to my father. The seventh son of the seventh son and all I can do on a good day is float a book around the library on air and then set it on fire.'

'But that ball of fire,' I say, 'and the mirror. That was pretty impressive.'

'Thank you, I was only trying to save the fair lady.' He smiles and pretends to puff out his chest a bit and I laugh.

'Have you got any idea where your parents would have gone?' I ask him. 'We will need to figure out how to get you back to them.'

'They could have gone anywhere in the world,' he replies. 'Either in the Otherwhere or your world. The person I was relying on knowing where they'd be wasn't at the Manor.' When he sees my look, he explains. 'Your Uncle Andrew.'

'No, he's hardly in the UK any more. He works in New York most of the time.'

'Petur didn't know that or he would have had me travel there instead.'

Annoyance plucks at me as I stare out of the windscreen, watching the rain falling and the wipers work double time to keep up with the load. 'I'm sorry that the right people weren't ready to save your arse,' I say, keeping my voice low. 'That you got me instead, the new Blackhart. The clueless one.'

'That is not what I meant,' Thorn says, the regret clear in his voice. 'Had I gone to New York, it's most likely your home would still be standing.'

I consider this in silence for a few seconds and decide he has a point. But I'm still not too happy with what he said or implied.

A frosty silence falls for a while and he fiddles with the radio again, finding yet more talk radio. By the time I've unwound enough to look at him again, he's fallen asleep in his seat.

We stop twice more on our way to London. Traffic is a mess everywhere and it takes us eight hours before we pull up outside Olga's shop, Emm's of Mayfair.

My eyes are burning and I'm more tired than I've been in a long time. Thorn looks wiped out and we both move like much older versions of ourselves when we unfold ourselves from Lolita.

The rain is still pelting down with no sign of stopping and it's cold. Not just a summer evening kind of coolness to the air, but proper cold, like autumn, heading straight for the claws of winter. I shudder and hitch my bag and sword higher and head up the stairs to the front of the shop. The lights are off and the 'Closed' sign in the window would have turned away a casual passer-by. I use the gnarled dragon's head knocker with some reluctance and let it drop against the door. The sound echoes through the building and gives the impression of a much larger space behind the door than indicated by the frontage of the shop.

Thorn seems to cope better with the cold than me, but he looks bedraggled and miserable when he comes to stand next to me on the step. He's reloaded the pistol and it's stuck through a loop in his jeans. His sword gleams dully in the darkness and he has the bow and arrows slung casually over his shoulder. We look like refugees from a historical re-enactment society, only far more battered and tired.

'Is she here, do we think?' he asks, looking up at the

sign. The sign itself gives nothing away. It is maybe a bit old-timey and reads only, 'Emm's of Mayfair – Purveyor of unique items to the establishment' – which in fact means very little – but if you know Emm's, you'll know it means exactly what it says on the sign. I know Olga lives upstairs, above the main shop, so I just nod and huddle under the light and turn slightly away from Thorn to peer upwards again, expecting to see movement or lights coming on upstairs, but instead I hear footsteps nearing the door. A light from one of the table lamps comes on in the shop and I turn sideways to look through the window. A strained pale face looks back at me, and I recognize Olga. Her usually smiling face holds reluctance and a wariness I've not seen before.

'Kit? Who do you have with you?' Her voice sounds muffled and suspicious through the thick door.

I shoot an embarrassed look at Thorn before answering. 'It's Prince Thorn. King Aelfric's youngest son. We need help, Olga.'

I expect the door to swing open immediately but there is a hesitation that worries me. My knife is in my hand before I'm aware of it and I push Thorn out of the way so that I face the door fully.

'Olga? Are you okay?'

There's a muffled noise from behind the door and I can hear voices talking rapidly and urgently, but it eventually opens and Olga stands there. She's dressed in jeans and a cardigan. Her hair's a mess and she looks as if she's been crying. Behind her the shop stretches into darkness and I can just make out cabinets, tables and chairs and a few random *objets d'art* that Emm's sells to 'normal', yet very rich, people.

'Come in, quickly.' She steps aside and I hurry in, aware of the light magical tingle that touches the nape of my neck as I pass over the threshold. Behind me Thorn passes through the wards unharmed, showing that he means her no ill will. He's not wearing his ring and I wonder if he has it on him or if it disappeared with the house. I let out a small puff of breath I didn't realize I'd been holding and try and look tough and competent and in charge.

Olga shuts the door behind us and goes about locking it. I feel the air in the shop move against the skin of my face and I whip my remaining pistol out and level it at the shadows to my right. A young man walks into the light, unfazed by the pistol pointed at him.

As he walks closer, from a patch of shadow into the murky light, I have to blink against the illusion of a wolf's head on his shoulders. I physically shake my head and the image clears instantly. By my side Thorn lets out an exclamation and I realize he's seen the boy's head shift from that of a wolf's too.

There is no scent of magic in the air; my own magic tells me no spell has been triggered. So I know what I just saw was real. I've heard about werewolves but I've never actually seen one in the flesh. Until now.

Thorn's presence is solid behind my back and I catch a glimpse of Olga behind him as I edge my body to track the boy's movement. She's standing very still by the door, her expression tense.

I swing my gaze back to the young man and see that his

hands are up and an amused grin twists his lips. He's attractive in a rugged way. Shaggy dark unkempt hair, blue-green eyes with flecks of gold. Firm jaw, cheekbones all angles and upswept black eyebrows. And tall too, at least six four but he looks no older than eighteen. His build is rangy and I have the impression that he's not yet stopped growing into his shoulders or hands. He reminds me of how the promise of size can be seen in the shape and size of a mastiff puppy's paws and how it takes a while to fulfil the promise of its breed. But there is nothing puppy-ish about the way he looks us over. His gaze is lazy and lightly challenging as he takes us in, assessing our level of threat.

As big as he is, I don't doubt for a second that I can stop him in his tracks with a bullet between the eyes. It might not kill him, but it will give me long enough to get both Olga and Thorn out of the shop before he changes into his more animal form. Nothing I've encountered in the past could dodge a bullet to the head.

'Olga? Who is this guy?' I shoot a quick glance at Olga as she moves up behind me. I notice her favouring her left leg and she's not moving as gracefully as I remember. Thorn is standing easy, watching me for cues, holding his pistol in his right hand and sword in his left. He looks like a modern-day pirate in a scruffy t-shirt and jeans.

'He's a friend, Kit. Put your weapons away. You too, your highness. Today has been a bad day for all of us. Let's not make it worse.'

She brushes past me and walks down the long passage to the back of the shop and up a set of stairs that lead to her living quarters. She doesn't pause, she doesn't offer any other comment and I narrow my eyes at the young man. Just because Olga trusts him doesn't mean that I have to. I gesture with the pistol at him.

'Go on, we'll follow.'

He walks past me, close enough to brush against me.

'You smell very interesting,' he says, his voice low enough for only me to hear. 'Like anger and thunderstorms.'

I stand my ground, not giving a millimetre, knowing that he's doing it on purpose to try and intimidate me. Thorn takes half a step closer to me and growls softly in his throat. The noise brings the boy's head around sharply and his eyes flash a bright blue for a second; I feel my heart stutter and my grip tightens on my gun. My other free hand drops to the knife resting in the sheath behind my back.

'Don't you even dare breathe in the wrong way,' I tell him. 'I will fillet you.'

He gives a snort, one so full of derision that I feel like kicking him, but he walks past us and follows Olga upstairs.

As if we've planned it, Thorn and I fall in side by side, with me a slight step behind, covering our backs.

Olga leads us into a brightly lit modern kitchen and it's only when I walk in and I smell Bolognese sauce cooking that I realize how hungry I am. Wolf boy goes to the counter and starts putting cups out for coffee and tea. The way he moves around the kitchen tells me he's been here before. But that still doesn't make me any less nervous. Olga's strained face and worried eyes make me feel deeply uncomfortable and I hover at the table, torn between staying and trusting her and the werewolf or turning around, leaving and trying to find somewhere else.

'Oh, for heaven's sake, Kit. Relax. Really – just put your stuff down and stop glowering at me like a thug. You Blackharts make everything an issue.' She picks up a wooden spoon and jabs at the bubbling sauce. 'Do you know Aiden Garrett?' She nods with her chin at the young man who is yet to speak. 'He's Jonathan's son.'

I look at the young man again. I've never met any of the Garretts but I know who they are. Why was he here when his dad and the pack were in Scotland helping my cousins sort through the cattle mutilations?

'I'm Kit Blackhart,' I say to him when he turns to look at me. He surveys me frankly and I must meet with his approval because I'm treated to a smile that shows off very sharp white teeth against his tanned skin. 'This is Thorn. From Alba.'

'You guys look like shit,' he says conversationally as he gives us each a nod before gesturing to the kettle. 'Can I get you tea?' His question is directed at Thorn, who doesn't look at all out of place in the cosy kitchen. 'We've got almost everything you people like to drink.'

'Normal tea would be fine, thanks.' There's a tightening of Thorn's mouth at Aiden's term of 'you people' and I wonder what the undercurrent meant.

'I'll have coffee,' I tell him. 'Thanks.'

Olga sits down at the table and I do too, but I keep my bag by my feet and my knife on the table next to me. Thorn seats himself with an obvious sigh of relief.

'You need to tell me everything that's happened,' she says, leaning forward. 'I got attacked by a handful of goblins when I was coming home from the grocery shop. I saw them off but I hurt my leg. And now I'm hearing all kinds of rumours about a coup in Alba, about dragons and other crazy things and now you guys are here looking like death.' She pauses and watches Aiden pass us our drinks. 'And I have no idea what's going on. I've not been able to get hold of Jamie or Andrew, either. Where is everyone?'

I feel the last bit of my hope drain away and stare at her in shock. This is not the reception I expected.

Chapter Fifteen

Emm's: Run by Emory Kassan, Emm's is a renowned antique store in the Frontier. There are several branches of Emm's throughout the human world, with a wide range of very wealthy clientele. The London store of Emm's is run by Kassan's adoptive granddaughter, Olga Kassan. Olga's adopted mother was Emory Kassan's only child.

From an archived report filed in HMDSDI HQ, 1955

It's several hours later. The silence is only broken by the sound of the rain outside. Below us the shop lies in darkness and beyond the shop Mayfair and London huddle miserably beneath a wet cloak. It's not really late by London standards but there are no cars out, no late-night office workers or partygoers. Sitting in the lit kitchen, it suddenly feels as if we are the only people in the world.

'What do we do now?' I ask Olga. 'We don't know anything else that might help us decide on next steps.'

'Have you got any idea where else your family could have gone, Thorn?' Olga asks for the umpteenth time. 'The ruling house of Alba can't just disappear off the face of the planet without someone knowing where they are.'

Thorn looks at the list he wrote out in careful script, translating the place names for us. Between him and Olga they've tried contacting various people around the country but the phones are either going straight to voicemail or are just plain dead. It's not a good sign.

'These are the people who might know,' he says, tapping his fingers on the scrap of paper. 'And if we can't contact them, then I don't know.'

'It is late,' Aiden interrupts. 'They could easily be asleep or out.'

'Or dead.' Olga arches an eyebrow. 'Let's be honest. If it were me staging a coup I'd take out anyone who'd help my enemy.'

I say a bad word that Jamie would have made me pay for with a further five laps of the circuit back home and Aiden gives a surprised huff at my swearing. Olga just looks serious and to my surprise Thorn looks as if he wants to crumple and cry in frustration.

'The Fae Holds are full to overflowing with escapees from Alba,' Olga says. 'There are horror stories of torture and . . .' she gestures. 'Well, you can imagine. Overthrowing a regime is always accompanied by posturing and violence. Our problem is that the Holds aren't made to home a lot of homeless Fae. Their supplies are already running low and some of the smaller Fae are succumbing to Iron Sickness.'

The Fae Holds are five safe-houses created for Fae who visit the Frontier, linked to the Otherwhere through the Hold's owner. That person is usually a powerful Sidhe who can sustain ties to the Otherwhere through his or her own magic, or by linking with an object of power anchored in the Otherwhere. The Holds are rare and unusual, and I've only ever been to one. The connection with the Fae realm was designed to foster a concentration of magic powerful enough to keep the Fae sustained while in the Frontier. The upshot of my visit was that my magic got a high just from walking into the place. It was as if I'd had a massive dose of adrenalin and my own magic had raged in my blood for long afterwards, even making me ill with a wild fever that had me hallucinating some pretty bizarre things.

But if enough Fae creatures gathered in such a place, they would deplete those protective magics, leaving them vulnerable to a sickness some contracted in our world. This had many names, Frontier's Bane being one of them. Iron Sickness another.

'What do we know about the person in charge of the coup?' Aiden asks Thorn, interrupting my thoughts. 'Who would have the guts to take on your family? And win?'

Thorn looks conflicted and I watch him struggling to talk about it. He'd evaded my questions about it earlier, but now, faced with other interested parties – people who could help – he seemed even more reluctant.

'Has anyone coming from Alba mentioned anything?' he counters, looking at Olga questioningly. 'Do they know who it is?'

'Not yet. No one has seen the leader but the rumours are that he is a very powerful sorcerer. And he uses sendings.' She sees my blank look and explains hastily. 'This sorcerer is strong enough to compel people to do what he wants – it's like possessing them and it's called a "sending". So he's strong enough to use sendings and on top of that he has a large army of wild Fae and creatures from the far North to do his bidding. Alba was not prepared for this.' She narrows her eyes as Thorn shifts uncomfortably in his seat. 'You know something?'

'We used the broken mirror at the Manor and scried.'

Olga scowls unhappily. 'Are you both insane? That mirror's not worked since the night your pa—' She stops mid-sentence and draws a steadying breath. 'Using a broken mirror is extremely dangerous. The magics that formed them are unstable. You could have been killed.'

I have the grace to look embarrassed and guilty but Thorn squares up to her, being the brave one. 'I had to know what was going on in my home,' he says. 'It was a risk I was prepared to take.'

'What did you learn?' Aiden asks before Olga can do some more shouting.

'The mirror described a man, it didn't recognize him outright, but it gave enough of a description for me to think that the man in charge is my father's younger brother.'

The room fell silent. Aiden looks worried but confused and Olga looks as if she wants to be ill.

'Eadric? You're saying Eadric did this?'

'You know him?' I ask, unable to keep the surprise out of my voice.

'Of course I know him. Eadric and I grew up together on the continent.' She waves her hand. 'A very long time ago now. He was never a violent man; he was content with his role as Aelfric's younger brother. He loved his books and studying.' Her voice takes on a reminiscent tone I recognize that older people fall into when they remember their golden childhoods. My nan had that exact same tone when she told me wild stories as a small child to get me to sleep, to keep the night terrors at bay.

Thorn watches her intently for a few seconds before replying.

'Even so, even if the description sounds like Eadric, I don't know if it is him. There's a lot of history surrounding my family. One aspect tells of a geas, a spell or curse, on the extended royal family. This prevents them from rising up against the rightful king. The geas I'm talking about is ancient, as old as Alba itself, and it secures the royal family's position within the kingdom. There is a story that once, long ago in the past, a king had been threatened by his uncle. When he rose up against the king, the duke found himself surrounded by the guardians of the Citadel. They cut him down and those who conspired with him were banished and the rebellion was quashed. It is known in our history as the Night of Blood.'

I can't help my mouth twisting in distaste. 'Nice.'

Thorn favours me with a stern look. 'The high king's rule is absolute and unquestioned.'

The way Thorn says it, so matter of fact, makes me realize that although we've spent a few hours together and I like him well enough, I really don't know anything about him at all. I shift in my chair, suddenly uncomfortable.

'So, if it's not your uncle, who is it?' I ask him, triggering more questions from Olga and Aiden.

'Is there a way to break this geas?' Olga is leaning against the counter, wiping her hands on a cloth. 'If the curse can be broken, then the usurper could be your uncle.'

'Do we have any other clues about this guy? Can it be someone else?' Aiden asks in turn.

Thorn shakes his head. 'The ring described by the mirror is unique. My uncle was given that by my grandfather when he came of age. The roaring lion. No other ring like that exists and it's unique to our family. It can't be worn by anyone else.'

'I remember the ring,' Olga says unhappily. 'But can we be sure? Could he have passed it to someone else?' She moves to stand behind Aiden, favouring her good leg. 'We have to be sure, Thorn, before you take matters any further. Accusing the wrong person here can easily destroy alliances . . .' She gestures helplessly. 'It could trigger a catastrophe – even worse than what's going on right now.'

'The ring is an heirloom and is Eadric's alone. As is the ring that my father in turn was given on his coming-of-age day.' He moves in his seat, the stiffness in his arm obvious in the way he holds himself. 'I don't know my uncle all that well. I met him when I was very young, maybe three years old. He had done something to upset my father and was called to Court. When he eventually came to the Citadel he was locked away with my father for several hours. I remember sitting in the courtyard by the stables watching my older brothers and cousins practise sword fighting when Uncle Eadric came out. He was in a foul mood. Pale and shaking with anger. He saw me sitting on a barrel and he heaved me up by the collar. He shook me so hard I bit my lip and he said in this voice, frighteningly quiet and full of menace: "Aelfric will rue the day he refused to take my counsel. The kingdom is lost. Alba will burn. I wash my hands of all of you. Boy, I hope you're worth it.""

I find myself leaning closer to Thorn as he speaks. His handsome features are calm as he recounts the story but his voice sounds strained. 'And then he flung me from him with such force that I went flying into a wall. I knocked my head and I remember hearing a roaring sound and there were flames. And then everything went black. I came to two days later and learned that I had tried to protect myself by casting fire at my uncle but it didn't work very well and I set the stables on fire instead. But what was even worse was that my oldest two brothers had laid into my uncle and that it was only my father's intervention that prevented them from killing him for attacking me. My father banished Eadric and his retainers. As high king he had the right to sentence his brother to death, but he showed him mercy, sending him to the wastes in the North, where he was watched over by my father's chamberlain and his assistants. To show the Courts how serious he was about expelling his brother, my father cut all ties with him and ordered his name struck from the tree of Alba entirely.'

There's an awkward silence. I trade a grim look with Aiden but it's Olga who speaks first after some time.

'Am I right saying that by cutting him from the family tree, your father disowned his own brother, threw him out of the family? And that because he's been disowned, he has no rightful way of attaining the crown?' Olga's voice is soft, measured. Her reasoning is easy to follow.

Thorn nods, frowning. 'Yes. Gods, it could be how he

came to bypass the geas. If he is no longer family . . .' He looks shaken. 'I'm sure it didn't cross my father's mind either.'

'It's a good hunch,' Aiden says. 'It means that your uncle's been planning this for a good, what – fifteen years or more? That is a long time to work on allies and getting people in place to help overrun the Citadel.'

'I wonder what he meant, though, by what he said to you. About you being worth it. Do you have any idea?' I have to ask the question, of course I have to. All of this seems to be focused on Thorn. He is definitely the key to the mess.

'No. My father had his advisers, astronomers and sorcerers search for years to try and find anything that could pertain to the threat Eadric made. But they found nothing conclusive. Even so, because of what happened, word spread and no one wanted anything much to do with me. I became bad luck.'

Scarlet kept low in the shadows as she neared the witch's house – or Olga Kassan as the humans knew her. The rain fell mercilessly and she shivered beneath her cloak. But her rapid flight from Alba had a purpose and the news she carried drove her on.

The buildings she slipped past were in darkness and few people were about. She saw a bearded man talking to a broken child's doll in a shop window, not seeming to realize that the doll couldn't hear him through the thick glass. He looked up at Scarlet's passing and watched her suspiciously before scrabbling off, pulling a metal cage on wheels from beside the building and clattering along the pavement in the opposite direction.

Scarlet shook her head, amazed by the mysteries of the Frontier. She soon neared the park, knowing the witch lived close by. She was about to vault over the fence when the attack came.

The fight was brutal and fierce. She laid into her attackers with feet and fists, striving for a rhythm. She felt bones crack and heard grunts from them and smiled in triumph as one of her attackers let out a howl and collapsed to the ground. She stomped where she thought his throat would be and felt the crunch of larynx under her boot.

Scarlet knew she had to end the fight, and soon. There were five of them, large and muscular, and her reserves were low. She had not slept or really eaten anything since her escape from Alba and she had lost her sword in the ribcage of a mountain ogre sent to bring her back.

One of her assailants grunted something. A flash of steel caught her eye too late and she felt the blade slide home. For the longest time she felt nothing, adrenalin surging through her, but in the blade's wake she felt burning.

The smell of her blood on the rainsoaked air filled her nostrils, but with it, she recognized another scent. Sickly and sweet, it teased her with memories of walking with Kieran through the gardens of the Citadel, the night air heavy with the scent of night-blooming flowers. Recognition came too late. Poison.

She shrieked her anger and somewhere thunder rumbled. As fast as the attack had come they let her go and melted into the night. She fell, blood mingling with the rain on the pavement.

Scarlet forced herself upright and hobbled the remaining

distance to Olga's door and used some hidden reserves to ring the bell.

She sensed movement in the building as she huddled in the doorway, then at last the witch stood before her.

Scarlet looked at her with relief. Finally, someone who would know what to do. But before she could speak, her strength failed and she crumpled into the woman's waiting arms.

Chapter Sixteen

Chimera: The word comes from Greek 'kimaros' and pertains to an animal or creature made up from the parts of three or more other animals. Rumours from the Otherwhere persist that some of the more adept sorcerers have been playing around genetically manipulating volunteers.

From an archived report filed in HMDSDI HQ, 2009

The sound of musical chimes startles all of us. Olga is up and away from Aiden's chair in the blink of an eye. I have no idea where it's come from but she has an ugly serrated combat knife in her hand and she looks alarmingly at ease with it. She gestures for us to stay seated and cat-foots it to the top of the stairs, where she flips open a panel in the wall and keys in a code on a numerical pad there. A small screen lights up and shows the outside front of the shop. There's nothing we can see – apart from parked cars, the street and the park itself – all a bit blurry in the darkness.

'Stay there,' she hisses back over her shoulder. 'Aiden,

if there's an attack, leave the way I showed you. Get them out of here.'

I tense up in annoyance but as I reach for my sword, Aiden's grip holds me back.

'Listen to what she's saying. Keep quiet and wait this out.'

I try to pull my arm from his grip and snap, 'Let me go.'

'No. Stay.' He seems to be enjoying this a bit too much and as I raise my other hand to slap him away, he grabs it and forces it down too. 'Just stop.' His smile has a definite edge to it now and I can hear the growl in his voice.

Thorn looks past us at Olga, who watches the screen intently. I fully expect him to get annoyed with Aiden and tell him to stop manhandling me but he's too preoccupied with what Olga is doing. So much for the prince helping the damsel.

I twist in my seat so I can watch Olga as she moves silently down the stairs. She holds the blade by her side and is moving with stealth, only slightly favouring her good leg. The chimes are silent now, and I wonder if that is what they heard when we turned up earlier. And if they watched us before coming downstairs to open the door. They must have. It's a clever, also safe, way of doing business.

Aiden stops paying me any attention and sits with his head tilted to the side, as if he's following her descent into the dark shop by hearing alone. I feel his grip on both my arms loosen and I'm up and away from him, unsheathing my sword in one smooth move, already moving down the stairs after Olga before either he or Thorn can do anything.

The shop also seems far darker than before and I try not to start when I see figures coalesce from the shadowy recesses. They are humanoid shapes cut from the night itself, a darkness so absolute they seem to swallow any light around them.

My magic rises with them and I play out the tiniest of tendrils, curious and attracted to them against my better judgement. Using magic in another magic user's home is not polite and I shrug off Jamie's warnings in my ear, knowing that I am breaking a serious taboo. Just earlier today I almost chewed off Thorn's ear for flaunting host/guest etiquette and here I am doing the exact same thing.

I watch as they coast up to Olga, solidifying into a dark mass behind her. Their presence seems to bolster her and she pulls her shoulders back and lifts her head. The knife in her hand glints in the darkness.

She's by the door now but, instead of opening it, she puts her palms flat against the door. When she turns her head to look at me, her eyes shine an eerie white and I snap my magic guiltily back in place.

'Get ready,' she says and although she's several metres away, I can hear her voice close by my ear.

Behind me the two boys creep towards me. Movement from Olga draws my attention.

'If anything happens,' she says, looking over her shoulder at Aiden, then at me, 'take Thorn and run. Keep him safe.'

Aiden looks as if he wants to protest but he must see something in her expression that changes his mind. He nods briefly and moves in front of Thorn, effectively blocking the Sidhe's path.

I spin around, not keen to see how Thorn reacts to being handed over to someone else's care like a favourite toy. My attention is drawn back to Olga as she swings the door open.

There's only one person out there and Olga's just in time to catch them as they fall forward. She grunts and quickly pulls the stranger back into the passage as I move past her to look into the wet night.

From somewhere nearby some *thing* starts laughing. It's a high cackling sound and the fine hairs on the back of my neck rise with it. Soon, the single voice is joined by more voices and I'm reminded of a nature show I watched once when I was little. It was the sound of hyena laughter. A full-body shudder goes through me as I peer out into the darkness.

There are maybe ten of them, and even though they are a distance away, on the far side of the road, I can see that they are big, brutish, hulking things. Redcaps? I narrow my eyes and concentrate. I am tired and my magic feels sluggish but it responds to my stubborn insistence.

As I did back at the Manor, I let a strand of my magic flash towards them, but it happens faster than I intend and I'm up close and in their faces far too quickly. It's dizzying and I reach out and lean against the doorjamb in an effort not to fall down.

Eventually I focus my abilities by drawing my power back a bit, getting a wider picture. No, they're not redcaps. Nor are they anything that I do recognize. They look part goblin, part feral dog. Still shorter than me, these creatures are squat and muscular, with deep chests and strong forearms. Their skin looks like rough pelt. As I watch, they circle each other, yipping, making odd barking noises. Like hyenas. I blink. I look at their pelts, at their sly faces and tiny midnight eyes and shudder. They are my nightmares made real.

'Mutations,' I say, drawing my magic away from them and snapping back to myself. I look at Olga as she's crouched next to the trembling figure on the floor. 'What are they even doing here?'

Olga mutters under her breath. 'Chimera.' She says the word like something dirty, with a low snarl in her voice. 'Unclean magic.'

Ice crawls down my spine. I've heard about chimera, about the rumours of them, but didn't know they actually still existed. The rumours we'd heard were that enterprising sorcerers in the Otherwhere had taken it on themselves to play with genetics, creating monster hybrids. They toured them around the Otherwhere, like travelling circuses, putting up these huge hybrid-versus-hybrid fights. The draw was tremendous until one of them broke free and went rampaging into a crowd, killing a handful of Sidhe nobles. The circuses were shut down and the monsters were destroyed. Or so we were told.

When Olga straightens she's holding the figure in her arms. I try not to think about how strong she must be to pick up a dead weight off the floor the way she just did.

'Shut the door,' she tells me as she moves back into the shop towards the kitchen. 'Use all the locks.'

I do as I'm told, sliding all the locks shut, but not before I take a final look at the rain-drenched figures at the other side of the square. They are milling around, like a pack of hungry animals. One of them, the leader, is focused on Emm's, staring unblinkingly at me as I slowly close the door. The howling and laughter starts again and I suppress the urge to run away. Running away makes you look like prey. And if there is one thing I'm not, it is prey.

Olga lays our visitor on the small couch in the tiny living room. She peels back the wet cloak and mutters under her breath.

'It's Scarlet,' she says, her voice low. She shoots a meaningful look at Thorn, who looks poleaxed.

I go to the kitchen and rummage around for a medicine kit as they speak quietly. I find disinfectant and bandages but some instinct tells me that they won't be enough. I grab a load of clean tea towels too and walk back into the lounge.

'She's my brother's bodyguard,' Thorn's telling Aiden. 'If she's here it means he's definitely been taken. Or worse.'

I step closer and look down at the female warrior stretched out on the couch. She's not wearing armour but is instead dressed in unobtrusive greys and browns beneath a dark cloak – all are now soaked in blood.

Olga starts packing the more serious wounds with the tea towels in an attempt to stop the blood.

'Scarlet,' Thorn says, curling a hand around the tiny Fae's slender hand. 'Scar, can you hear me?'

The Fae's impossibly purple eyes flutter open to find Thorn. For a second there is confusion, which clears to reveal a look of relief.

'Thorn . . .' Her voice sounds husky and raw, and I try

not to imagine her screaming in pain. 'What are you doing here?'

Olga motions to me and I hand over the rest of the drying-up cloths without a word. She applies pressure to the seeping cuts across Scarlet's chest and stomach. The smell of blood is so intense it sticks to the back of my throat but I can't look away from the warrior lying prone on the couch.

'I'd rather hear how you came to be here,' Thorn counters with a smile. 'Even if you are making a mess of Olga's couch.'

Scarlet's laugh is a hitch of pain but she shakes her head. 'Funny boy. I've come to warn the witch,' she says, her voice a low whisper. 'To get a message to the Free Fae to keep running. And to try and find you.' She leans back with a groan, in obvious pain. 'I almost made it. But they caught up with me outside. So close.'

'You're safe now,' Thorn assures her. 'Can we get you anything?'

'Water. I'm very thirsty.'

Behind me, Aiden heads to the kitchen without a word.

Olga nudges Thorn so she can tend to Scarlet's cuts but from the way she's frowning I suspect that it really is as bad as it looks.

'Where is the king?' Scarlet struggles to stay focused and her gaze is hot with pain. Every word is laboured when she speaks. 'Have you seen him?' She closes her eyes as Thorn silently shakes his head. 'I had such hope I would find him, or anyone. Thorn.' She gasps and lets out a long ragged breath. 'They took Kieran from his study. I was with Evi in the gardens when the attack came. I had to get her to safety first but when I got to the study Kieran was gone.'

My heart goes out to her. Her distress is genuine. She tries to move but both Olga and Thorn urge her to keep still.

'I lost him,' she says, her voice bereft and filled with tears. 'I let them take him.'

'I doubt it, Scar. I've seen you fight.' Thorn gives a wry laugh. 'You beat me up every time you taught fencing. I know you wouldn't have let them just take my brother.'

Aiden passes Thorn a glass of water and he helps Scarlet sit up and drink.

'Do you know who attacked the Citadel?' Olga asks her once she's settled back down again.

'Eadric.' Scarlet's voice is firmer now, and sharp with dislike as she says his name. 'The attacks were well coordinated. No one knew what was going on at first.'

'But you got Evi away and that's what matters,' Thorn says. 'Kieran would want his wife and unborn child safe. It would give him something to fight for.'

'Exactly what I thought.' She coughs and blood bubbles onto her lips. A punctured lung. Even without any medical training I know that. Her breathing is becoming more laboured, but she is determined to deliver her message. 'Thorn, you have to keep moving. If they know you're here . . .' Her hand flutters. 'They'll come for you. Eadric . . . Eadric is insane. When no one knew where you were, he raged. He threw one of his guards off a balcony in a fit of anger.'

'Why would he even care where I am?' Thorn shakes his head. 'I'm nobody.'

'You are a legitimate heir to the throne. As is your brother. He wants you all where he can control you.'

'My father was right to send him away,' Thorn mutters, looking at Olga, who is sitting on the floor beside the couch with one of Scarlet's hands in hers. Her other hand holds the tea towels in place and she has a look of helplessness on her face that I don't like.

After a long silent moment, Scarlet speaks again. 'There's something else. They found the stone in the caves below the Citadel and they're moving it.'

I look blankly at Aiden but he just shrugs at me and I lean towards Thorn.

'What does that mean?'

'There's a large block of black stone that's been part of the Citadel for a very long time,' Thorn says, not looking away from Scarlet. 'Legend says that the stone is the gateway used in the Dawn Age to send the Elder Gods to their prison.'

'It was all they could talk about,' Scarlet says. 'Bringing them back. Reinstating their rule.'

Her gaze meets mine and she seems to notice me for the first time.

'Blackhart?' Her eyes move between Thorn and me and she lets out a sigh. 'You found safety with the Blackharts. Thank the moon and stars. Girl, swear to me that you will look after him. You will see him to safety.'

I nod, struck by her intensity. 'I swear.'

There's a slight ping of magic and I feel a soft warmth spread through me, as if she has just touched me and left me some of her own power.

'Thank you.' Her smile is bright in her pain-ravaged face. She turns to look at Thorn and her eyes are pleading. 'When you free Kieran, tell him . . .'

Thorn folds her hand to his chest. 'I'll tell him,' he promises.

Scarlet lies back against the cushion and closes her eyes. Then she just slips away.

We stay like that, a frozen tableau, for a few seconds before Thorn stands up, unclasping his hand from Scarlet's.

He looks pale and angry, but determined. 'We need to say our goodbyes to Scarlet. Then . . . we have to find my father. The palace is lost and so is my brother. I can't lose my father too.'

Chapter Seventeen

'I'm surprised I fit in the back of your car,' says Aiden, sounding genuinely astonished. I watch him in the rear-view mirror and grin. What he calls 'fitting' and what I call 'crowding in at a weird angle, twisting your head sideways looking very uncomfortable' are clearly the same thing.

'Maybe you should consider that the world's not quite made to accommodate giants any more.'

'Hah. My brothers and my dad are taller still. Remember, I'm the youngest in the pack.'

I groan dramatically. 'Really? There are people even bigger than you?'

He nods. Well, he tries to nod but his head gets stuck against Lolita's roof. 'Hey, do you think the sunroof opens all the way?'

'No. You aren't opening the sunroof and sitting with your head outside. It's pouring with rain.' I sound like an adult. I really don't like it that much.

'Well, not now, maybe later, you know? When it's not raining.'

I am not usually good with banter but it's surprisingly

easy with Aiden. We left Olga behind and are heading to Aiden's house in Kensington. We held a simple ceremony for Scarlet in the small courtyard garden at the back of Emm's. Olga threw a blanketing spell over us so that we would remain unobserved from any peering eyes. Thorn carried Scarlet and I watched in astonishment as roots broke through the damp soil in the small garden and rapidly grew upwards, twining and entwining themselves into a an elaborate coffin large enough to hold Scar's broken body. Olga wrapped Scar carefully in a piece of snow-white silk before Thorn laid her in the cradle. The three of us stood over the Fae's body as Thorn sang a farewell dirge to his friend. His voice wasn't loud but it climbed into the sky and for a few minutes even the rain seemed to die down to allow us to say goodbye. Thorn laid a large thistle on Scar's chest and stood back as Olga knelt down and pressed her palm into the ground. Slowly the roots started retracting back into the earth, folding shut around the coffin. The earth claimed the faerie and the rain started up again. We went indoors and Olga wished us goodnight.

She had people she needed to talk to and had no place to offer us to sleep. Aiden, with his brothers and dad gone, had more than enough space and so we piled into Lolita and with the lure of hot showers and comfortable beds in the offing, I pointed my little car's nose towards Kensington.

To be honest, I am so tired and keyed up I can't think straight any more. So Aiden's banter keeps me awake and smiling as we drive through London's deserted streets to the Garrett house. The expanse of Hyde Park looms next to us and I catch glimpses of it through the fence.

There are shadows moving within shadows in the park. I slow down to peer in, but right now all I want is to get somewhere warm and safe where we won't be attacked by strange creatures.

Lolita responds to my touch as I speed up again. I don't know what's in the park, but it's keeping pace with us. I try not to let it freak me out as I've managed to keep my eyes on the deserted roads for most of the journey. The traffic lights mostly play along, but I charge through any amber lights, refusing to slow down or stop.

Whatever's keeping pace with us can't leave the confines of the park, I realize. I glance quickly to catch sight of it as it falls behind us. In the faint light I glimpse shiny black flanks, legs and hooves that clip fire from the ground.

While Aiden chats to Thorn about why he was left behind when most of the pack went to Edinburgh, I ponder whether I saw a large black horse loose in Hyde Park or something much more sinister. Night mares are mythical entities that manifest as black horses. They ride storms, distributing bad dreams to the susceptible. I hope I haven't just seen one.

Aiden's neighbourhood is quiet and we drive into an underground garage after he keys us in via an intricate-looking alarm system. He doesn't bother showing us the rest of the house and just leads us to two spare bedrooms opposite each other. Each room has its own bathroom and, after shutting the door, I strip my clothes off without thought and stumble into the shower, where I almost fall asleep leaning against the wall.

The bed is as soft and comfortable as Aiden promised and I get a solid four hours in before Thorn wakes me up with a cup of coffee at half past seven. He looks nauseous at the smell of the stuff and hands it to me as if it's a bomb. I can't help but laugh softly and he flames red.

'The wolf is making breakfast,' he says, looking worried.

'I'm sure he knows how to look after his guests,' I say, pushing my hair out of my face. 'You're looking better.'

And he is. The cut above his brow has faded to a red line and I notice that he moves his arm and shoulder more easily and overall he just looks more awake and alert. His shoulders are square and there's a determined glint to his eyes that I like.

'I slept well.' He touches the cut above his brow gingerly. 'But then I also had a good nurse yesterday, so thank you, again, for helping me.'

I wave my hand. 'Glad you're healing. I was worried Aiden and I would have to carry you into battle.' I smile so he knows I'm teasing and I'm relieved when he smiles back. It's still not up to full wattage, but it's enough to make me aware of the fact that he's in my room and I'm only wearing a very short T-shirt under the duvet.

'Give me ten minutes, then I'll see you in the kitchen,' I say, raising my eyebrows meaningfully at him, waiting for him to move. But he hesitates and, when I follow his gaze, he's staring at my accidentally exposed thigh. I bite down on mortification and brazen it out. I'm sure that he's seen half-naked girls in the past – and seeing a bit of flesh first thing in the morning can't be a bad start to the day, right?

'Thorn? I need you to leave the room now so I can get changed.' I just about manage to keep my voice level and not squeak at him.

'Oh! Of course. I was just . . .' He nods and grabs for the cup. '. . . Waiting for you to finish so I can take this. I'll see you in the kitchen.'

I take the opportunity to have another luxurious shower and this time I even stay awake. I rummage in my backpack and find some wrinkled but clean clothes. My beauty regime is appalling and I've forgotten to pack a brush, so I finger-comb the tangles and I end up looking as if I've been pulled through a bush backwards. Grimacing at myself in the mirror, I pull the uneven strands away from my face and secure them with a hairclip so that they can't bother me during the day. The look does my pale face and freckles no favours. But, to be honest, I don't really care all that much. I just need food and lots of it. I remembered to charge my phone as I fell into bed a few hours ago and I check it for any messages. There is none. I sit on my bed and dial Megan, Marc and Kyle's numbers. They all go straight to voicemail. Next I try Uncle Andrew, then Aunt Letitia. Her phone rings for ages before an answering machine kicks in. That's not happened before so I leave her a rambling message and hang up.

I pick my way through the house, using my nose to lead me to the kitchen.

'You smell lovely this morning. No thunder and no pepper,' Aiden says as he hands me a plate and gestures for me to help myself from the spread on the kitchen counter.

'Thanks,' I say, giving him a smile. 'Some kind soul left some classy shower gels for me to use.'

'Must have been my brother Shaun's girlfriend,' Aiden says. 'Occasionally she attempts to girlify us and dumps cologne and smelly soaps on us.'

He looks so unamused by the thought that smelly soaps are even in his house that I laugh out loud. It's only when I crunch into the toast that I realize how hungry I am. Both boys, our plight, missing families and weird goings-on are forgotten as I duck my head and devour my breakfast. What can I say? I think better on a full stomach.

'It looks like you needed that,' Thorn says after I finish my first plateful of food and another coffee. It's still raining outside and the news reports are all about severe flooding and storm warnings.

'I did. I felt hollow inside.' I lean back in my chair. 'Have you heard from your family?' I ask Aiden as he downs another cup of tea.

His cheerful facade fades. 'Not a word. I rang my mum in Australia and she's not heard from my dad. We both rang around some friends and got nothing.'

'I can't get hold of anyone either.' I hold up my phone. 'This may as well be a brick.'

'If they are in the Otherwhere,' Thorn says, pushing a bit of breakfast pancake around on his plate, 'it's likely that they can't get in touch.'

I sit back in surprise. That didn't even occur to me. 'But all of them?' I ask him dubiously. 'Even my Aunt Letitia, who never goes anywhere?'

Aiden looks intrigued. 'Maybe she has safety protocols in place. She must know the Manor's been attacked – she could've taken steps to keep herself safe.'

I shake my head, not liking the idea. 'It makes no sense. She never leaves her place. Ever. It's like she's agoraphobic, or something. So even with everyone else not answering their phones, she should at least be contactable.'

Jamie, I know, is not available because he's in the jungle somewhere teaching government officials how to track and survive monsters. And you can't do that unless you're completely cut off from civilization. And I don't even know which government officials he's training!

'My mum is getting a flight back to London as soon as the bush plane bringing monthly supplies shows up. She'll catch a lift and get to Sydney so she should be here by the end of the week. Hopefully my dad will have been in touch by then or she'll kill him.'

Thorn looks horrified and I sort of hope that Aiden isn't being literal. He sees our expressions, though, and laughs.

'Not actually kill. Maybe maim a bit.'

'Oh that's much better.' They're joking again but I'm starting to feel sick with anxiety. 'Who else can we talk to about what's going on in Alba?' I ask them both. 'Who besides Olga will know this stuff?'

'The guys who run the Fae Holds, for sure,' Aiden offers.

'Or the trolls.' Thorn looks at me. 'We should speak to the trolls.'

'What do you want to meet trolls for?' Aiden asks him dubiously. 'They like eating humans.'

I'm embarrassed to admit this but I really should have thought of talking to the trolls first. Their information network is large and if you sift through enough rumours, you get a kernel of truth, or so Jamie's told me on more than one occasion.

To cover up for being caught out being dumb, I grimace at Aiden. 'Really? How old are you? Three?'

I don't enjoy the scowl he sends me and I busy myself having more coffee.

'Are there any important bridges in London?' Thorn asks us, unaware of my discomfort or Aiden's annoyance.

'Plenty,' I answer after chewing a piece of toast. 'And we have to find out where they're staying now, because they tend to move. A lot.'

Aiden looks unhappy. 'I don't know much about trolls.'

I shrug, pretending nonchalance. 'Not many people do. I've never met any myself but I know they exist. Some of the legends are true, after all.' I can't help but raise my eyebrows at him in a pointed fashion.

'Finding out about the wolves must've been the highlight of your past year, right?' he says with a grin. 'I mean, how can it not be? We are all super-attractive, we have killer instincts, we are good providers and we know how to fight. Unlike the faeries, who sit in their bowers, composing ballads and singing songs of woe, losing their kingdoms left and right.'

I didn't expect Thorn to have a quick temper, or that he'd take what Aiden said as an insult. A blade, a silver sickle, no more than three inches long, presses delicately against Aiden's throat.

'Be careful, wolf, of how you speak about your betters. There are still places in the Otherwhere where they hunt your kind for sport.'

Aiden's eyes go ice blue and a low rumble starts in his chest. He lifts his hand and pushes the blade away from his throat with some trouble.

'Do not try me, prince. I offered you hospitality for the night. Under my roof no harm can come to you, but once we are out there, you'd better watch your step.'

'Are you both utterly insane?' I'm disgusted with both of them. 'After everything and knowing we are in a world of trouble, this is how you choose to act? Like spoiled children. Let me tell you this: by acting like infants we're not going to get anywhere. We present as weak and I don't like it. You follow my lead for now and if you're not happy, then feel free to leave or, rather, not follow, because I'm not going to worry about keeping your asses in line.'

Chapter Eighteen

The silence in the kitchen is absolute. I can almost hear my own heart pounding. I watch Thorn and Aiden stare at each other across the kitchen table. The tension is so thick I could cut it with a butter knife.

I'm about to stand up and hit them both, but my mobile rings and I jerk with fright. I grab to answer it, not recognizing the number.

'Hello?' I say into the quiet room.

'Are you safe?' It's Olga. She sounds tired but her voice is soft, as if she's trying not to draw attention to herself.

I look at the two guys who have not stopped bristling at each other. 'Sort of,' I say. 'Why do you ask?'

'The Hold in North London has been razed to the ground. There are reports coming in from other Holds about attacks and the Free Fae are on the run. It seems that whatever is happening in Alba has spilled over into the Frontier.'

'Shit.'

My eloquence surprises both boys enough that they stare at me rather than glare at each other. I hold the phone away from my ear and hiss at them. 'You guys get to out-macho each other later. Right now, there's trouble. Put the knife down, Thorn. We don't have time for this.' I put Olga on speakerphone. 'Okay, we're all here now. Talk to us.'

Olga keeps her report brief. Of the five Holds, three were attacked during the night by gangs of chimera goblins. In some cases Fae were let go to spread word of the attacks but several were taken prisoner and, horrifyingly, two Hold host families were murdered before their guests. One Hold was burned to the ground.

'What happens to the Fae that are here now? With no safe Holds, where are they going?' This comes from Aiden, who suddenly looks mature and capable. 'I'm happy to offer them our farm out in Hertfordshire. As my dad's not here, I'll take it on me to extend our hospitality to the Fae until we can figure out how to help them further. There's a big forest that's looked after by our warden. They should be safe there until they can travel back to Alba.'

'That is generous of you, Aiden. Thank you. I'll speak to Lord Elias, who contacted me a few hours ago. I'm due to meet him shortly. All routes back to Alba, even the lesser known paths are blocked, either by redcaps or sorcerers. The farm you're offering may be the only way to keep these Fae safe.'

Thorn mutters something under his breath that sounds close to a curse but then he holds out a hand to Aiden, who shrugs and takes it without a word. They shake hands and I wisely decide to keep my mouth shut.

'I'll tell our warden to expect the kin. There are camping facilities on the farm too and fresh water. Plenty of food. I think they'll be okay.'

'Have any humans been harmed?' I ask Olga. 'That we know of, that is?'

There's noise in the background, someone talking and then the sound of Olga moving away. 'It's all been contained, pretty much. If any humans have been harmed, we've not been told.'

'Does SDI know about this?' I use the abbreviation of the abbreviation for Her Majesty's Department of Supernatural Defence and Intervention, the Spook Squad.

'It's been reported. They've sent a liaison officer who looks younger than you do to help out where he can. They are being cautious at the moment, aware of the various accords between the humans and Fae, and don't want to step on toes.'

Thorn leans towards me as Aiden talks to Olga. 'Who are these government people?'

'I've not met any of them myself but my family really doesn't like them. They seem to like interfering and making things difficult for us.'

Before Thorn can respond, Aiden returns with the phone, and Olga's back on the line, all business. 'Listen, you lot. I need you to tell me what your plans are going forward. I am not going to be able to hang around. I'm needed here, organizing a few things first. Are you guys going to be okay until I can meet up with you again?'

'We'll be fine,' Aiden says. 'Thorn and I are practically dating and Kit's ready to swing that sword of hers.'

'Must you make a joke out of everything, wolf?' Thorn asks, but the disapproval in his voice is only slight. 'Thank you, Olga, for helping. Let Lord Elias know I am grateful for any aid he can give both stranded and the Free Fae.'

'Before you go,' I say to Olga. 'Have you heard any rumours about where the trolls are camping out at the moment?'

'The last time I heard, they were holed up beneath Tower Bridge, north side. You know the ritual to open the doorway, right?'

'Uhm.' I think about it, mentally scrabbling for anything that would help me but when I come up blank I hesitate only for a second. 'No, to be honest. No clue.'

'I know how,' Thorn says at Olga's indrawn breath. 'As long as we have chalk.'

I think back to the emergency supplies kit I have in my backpack upstairs. 'I have chalk,' I assure him.

'Then you'll be safe. The trolls are very specific about who they allow into their caves.'

'Caves?' Aiden looks uncertain. 'No one said anything about caves.'

Chapter Nineteen

'Trolls are the gossip-mongers of the Fae world. They know everything. They hear everything.' I frown at Aiden as we walk down the road towards Tower Bridge. 'How do you not know this?'

Aiden shrugs, shoving his hands into his pockets. 'Usually when we want information we intimidate people. You try saying no to three werewolves dangling you off the side of a building.'

Thorn grunts but I can see him hiding a smile.

'Remind me never to have something your pack wants,' I tell Aiden.

'Are there always this many people in the Frontier?' Thorn asks us as we wind our way between and around several groups of tourists. We're making our way through the old Victorian warehouse district of Shad Thames. With its tiny boutique shops and eateries, its million-pound apartments and stunning views across the river, it still manages to hold on to its charm with names like Vanilla and Sesame Court. I came here often with Nan in the past once we'd moved back to the UK. A friend of hers let us stay with her in her large flat whenever we came into town to watch a musical or theatre show. I cringe now, remembering how very cosmopolitan and grown-up twelve-year-old me felt walking around the area, imagining myself as an adult, wealthy enough to own an apartment here and working as a designer or artist. I would sit sketching by the river for hours and quite happily let my nan hang out with her friend, Emmaline.

Today, though, London is busy. Loads of tourists are around and several river-cruise boats are making their way up and down the river. The weather isn't ideal, but everyone seems to have come prepared for the drizzly British summer.

'It's no busier than usual,' Aiden replies as we walk around, our breath steaming in the cold air. 'It's supposed to be the summer holidays and yet this weather is totally drab. Have you spent a lot of time in the Frontier?' he asks Thorn.

'I spent a year in Canada and we come for the revels in Regent's Park.' Thorn hunches his shoulders deeper into his jacket. 'I was supposed to join a university later this year. To study human law.'

I look at Thorn with surprise. 'Really? You guys go to school here and everything?'

'My brothers have been schooled here, Barcelona, St Petersburg and Stockholm. It is the done thing,' he says. 'If the Fae are to survive in the future we need to know how humans think. What they learn. There are some people at Court who do not agree with my father and his friends' way of thinking. All high-born Sidhe send their children for further schooling in the human world when they are old enough.'

'I never knew that,' Aiden admits. He rubs his jaw.' So, law, huh?'

Thorn looks worried that he's said something wrong but he gives a brief nod. 'Yes. These past few years I've been studying Fae law with a tutor, Istvan. I have many more years to go but human law is easier, I think.'

'Oh? What will you specialize in? Property law? Family law?'

Thorn looks at Aiden in confusion and shrugs. 'All of it, of course.'

Aiden and I look at each other and mouth 'of course' to one another and then burst out laughing.

'What? Is that so difficult to do?'

'My friend, I have no idea, but I'll wish you the best of luck.' Aiden claps him on the shoulder and loops his other arm around my shoulders, squashing me to his side. 'I think we're bonding, here. Do you think we're bonding?'

Before I can answer, Thorn leans forward so he can see me past Aiden.

'I think we're here,' he says. 'Where the trolls are.'

'And how do you reckon that?' Aiden frowns as he peers around. We are alone on this stretch of the riverbank; even though there are lots of tourists about, clutching miserably at their umbrellas, the place feels more deserted than it should.

I follow Thorn's pointing finger and can't help but chuckle. Someone's fixed a sign to the wall next to a gate barring a set of steps that disappears into the river itself. The sign read: *Beware! Trolls! Enter at your own risk!*

'Do you think the water is a glamour? How can the trolls live there and not be drowned by river water?' I ask him, peering over the gate.

'It's a glamour. You can see the way the water looks cleaner than the rest of the river.' He points out the relevant section to me and I have to agree. The water looks less muddy here than it does a few metres into the river.

'So, are we going in?' Aiden asks, looking extremely uncomfortable at the thought.

'In? Yes. And if you mean going underground, then, yes. We have to go all the way inside. To meet the trolls.' I raise my eyebrows at him. 'Unless, of course, you have any other ideas.'

'How about I stay up here and guard the entrance? I can also keep the phones with me in case anyone rings.'

To my surprise Thorn nods in agreement. 'It makes sense to have someone out here to keep watch. We don't want to be ambushed.'

'Yes,' I say, my voice tinged with sarcasm. 'Just let us go into the deep dark underground cave to meet with giant creatures from legend all by ourselves. I'm sure we'll be just fine.'

Aiden claps my shoulder. 'You are so brave, Kit Blackhart. It's astonishing.'

I shove my phone at him. 'Shut up. If we're not back in two hours, come looking for us.'

I turn to Thorn, who is humming under his breath and flexing his fingers. It's cold, with a soft incessant drizzle that makes your clothes cling to you uncomfortably. Aiden looks under-dressed in jeans and a thin longsleeved T-shirt but

Thorn had thought ahead and wears the stab-proof jacket I grabbed from the manor before we left.

'We have to ask permission to enter, right?' Thorn asks me as I zip my hoodie up. 'Do you have any gifts?'

I arch an eyebrow. 'Gifts?'

'Yes, an item of value to show that you are there to trade for information. Otherwise you will be in their debt.' This comes from Aiden, who looks unbearably smug that he knows an intricacy of Fae lore that has passed me by. I suppress the urge to stick my tongue out at him and instead do a mental tally of everything I have on me but shake my head. 'Nope. I have me, my knife, my clothes.' I lift the gym bag we borrowed from Aiden. It holds both our swords. 'And these.'

Aiden sighs and takes a small velvet pouch from his pocket. 'I never leave the house without it,' he says, handing it to me. 'Get in the habit of doing the same. If you're going to be dealing with bigwigs, you do not want to be in their debt because they will make you do a shedload of weird things. Most of them detrimental to your health.'

I nod, ignoring his patronizing teacher-voice. 'Right. Gifts. Never leave the house without them.' I open the velvet pouch and I'm sure my eyes bug out in shock. 'Diamonds?' My voice rises an octave. 'Really?'

'Well, don't give them everything, but some, at least. If the information is worth it.'

'The information will be worth it,' Thorn says. 'Time to go.'

He takes my hand and leads me to the gate. 'Because it's iron, I can't touch it. But you can. I'll show you how to open it.'

He lifts my hand and curls my fingers around the one spar. 'Now say: I command thee, open.'

Cheesy as hell but then, if it's tried and tested, why mess with it? I echo his words and feel a spark of magic shoot through me, my arm and hand, into the gate.

'Well done.'

I grin at him and check my palms. No burn marks, nothing. It feels as if my skin should be charred but there's nothing.

We walk down the stairs for a long way, and the water just keeps receding. I turn to look up and see Aiden chatting with a group of women. Most of them are teens. They look like a school group with their teacher. I can't help but laugh as I watch Aiden gesture with his hands, indicating the impressive suspension bridge spanning the river, then the Tower of London on the other side of the bank. He also points out the warship from the Second World War, HMS *Belfast*, moored further up the river. He seems to have gone into impromptu tour-guide mode.

'Watch out,' says Thorn, steadying me as I step off the last step onto a muddy bank, and walk straight into him.

The traffic juddering above us seems far quieter down here and, looking up, I realize how incredibly tall the bridge is and how very small we are in comparison.

The river laps gently at the small muddy beach we're standing on. I swing my backpack off my shoulder and find my first-aid kit. I rummage around inside it and find the herb-infused piece of chalk Megan gave me a few months ago when we were practising drawing summoning circles.

'What do I do?' I ask Thorn over my shoulder.

'Draw a door, big enough for us both to pass through, side by side.'

I turn to the wall holding up the embankment and start drawing. It's a large door, similar in style and look to the one that graced Blackhart Manor before it got sucked into nothingness. I draw the doorknob and a keyhole.

'Have you heard of the troll runes?' Thorn asks me when I stand back to admire my door.

'Uhm. Should I have?'

In answer he holds out his hand to me and I pass him the piece of chalk, now much reduced. He sets about hastily and with precision sketching sigils on the outside of the doorway. They look similar to Viking runes but, as I watch him sketch, the runes sink into the concrete until there's no sign of them.

He takes out the small sickle knife he threatened Aiden with earlier, nicks his finger and presses it against the final rune. His blood, only a small mark, remains visible for a few seconds longer than the chalk rune, before it too disappears into the concrete with a soft *schloep* sound.

'And now we wait?' I ask, looking out across the river with its barges and tourist boats floating by. Watching the river calms my jangling nerves and I push my hands deep into my pockets and hunch my shoulders against the rain. Thorn reaches out and tucks the hood up over my head.

'Now you'll be a little bit less wet,' he says with a smile.

'Have you ever met the trolls?' I ask him, pretending not to notice that he's trying to shield me from most of the rain by angling me towards the wall.

'A few times, but because they travel so much, you never know who you'll meet. And there are quite a few of them.'

'Oh?' So, ten points to me that I actually knew of the trolls. All the other points to Thorn for knowing far more about them and not being braggy about it.

'There are maybe seven of them, and three of them get to stay in London somewhere and work their spy network. And the others travel or hibernate. No one really knows.'

I grin and shake my head. 'I never thought I'd hear that trolls run a spy network.'

'Well, to be fair, it's not really a spy network. It's more like gossip. Your house brownie will speak to a nixie in the local park, who'll tell a boggart, who'll pass that information on to a dunter and, before you know, the trolls know that you're being particularly mean to visitors by giving them sub-par wine to drink. Reputations are made and broken this way.' His face is serious, except for a faint quirk of his lips but then he's all grave again. 'You really don't have to come along, Kit. It may not be safe.'

'Don't even think it,' I say, keeping my voice even. 'We're a team, you and I. I told your friend Scarlet that I'd look after you and I intend to keep my promise.'

'Scarlet's been Kieran's bodyguard for years. I think I've always been a tiny bit in love with her. Kieran used to tease me mercilessly whenever she left the room and I would just stand there, gaping after her. She taught me to fence.'

'She seemed very fierce.' I can't reconcile the broken Fae creature we buried in Olga's garden with the person he's talking about. 'And loyal.'

'Her family have been bodyguards and soldiers in our army for millennia.' His gaze is bleak. 'We have to stop Eadric before he tears the kingdom apart.'

I jump as someone coughs politely behind us. We turn at the same time and take in the little girl standing in the doorway I'd drawn. Dressed in a summer party dress that has quite a bit of Alice to it, she looks maybe eleven years old. Her arms and feet are bare but she gives no indication that she feels the cold. Her mass of tumbling chestnut-coloured hair matches the rich tones of her skin and eyes.

She favours us with a quick smile and does a tiny curtsy. 'Prince Thorn?' she says, her voice light and friendly. 'They have been expecting you. Please, come with me.' Then her gaze moves past him, to me, and her smile deepens. 'And you brought a tribute. They will be very pleased with your gift.'

Thorn's gaze widens but he holds out a hand. 'No, she is not a tribute. This is Kit Blackhart. A companion and a good friend.'

She looks crestfallen for a few moments and I wonder about the type of gifts people bring the trolls but then I decide not to think about it too much and smile at her nervously. She gives me a brief nod. 'Ah, the Blackhart, of course. Are you one of Jamie's nieces? He always brings me sweets. He is my favourite.' Suddenly, she seems to remember her role and turns to Thorn, arranging her features into a serious expression as befits her status as messenger. 'Please, come with me. You've been expected for some time.'

Scotia – Rook's Keep

Ioric Brightwing flung himself down in his favourite wing-backed chair with a groan. He was tired to the bone. Everything that could ache, ached, even things he didn't know could. The room was small and cosy, a fire blazing in the brazier, in complete contrast to the bastard weather raging across Scotia. Being warm and dry was a relief and he relished it for a few moments before turning to the task at hand. He reached for his writing set and began the painstaking coded missive to his father in the Frontier.

Thorn was still missing and Blackhart Manor was utterly destroyed, with no vestige left of it in either world. The trackers could find no trace of the young prince or any survivors. There were signs of a dragon attack, with the energies of both worlds pulled out of kilter. The weather was worsening in the Frontier, and Alba lay sweltering in unseasonably warm weather. Even the Sun King's Court had registered their discomfort before leaving the realm.

Ioric struggled with the wording. King Aelfric had to be told that his son was feared lost, but the person to do that should have been Ioric's father, the Rook Master. Even so, Ioric felt the responsibility to tell Thorn's father weigh heavily on his shoulders. He had known Thorn all his life. They'd grown up together, been schooled together and learned to fight together against the bigger Sidhe boys in the palace. Just because they were high born hadn't meant they were exempt from being bullied.

Ioric heard a movement behind him and gestured with his hand without looking up.

'Bethany. Can you ask Iko to prepare one of the ravens to send to my father?'

'I have never yet been mistaken for a girl,' an unexpected male voice said, startling the young Sidhe warrior.

Ioric looked up and relaxed back into his chair, smiling in welcome. 'Lord Istvan, what a surprise. No one told me you'd come to visit the Rookery. Is everything well with the king? I am just sending my father a message to let him know . . .'

'Be calm, boy. The king is well, or is as well as a man can be with no kingdom to rule.' Istvan pulled a chair closer and sat down opposite the young noble. 'I have come to ask you a favour. It is a matter of some delicacy and I know no one else I can entrust this task to.'

Ioric flushed with pleasure. 'You flatter me, Istvan, but my men and I are stretched thin as it is, searching for Prince Thorn.'

'Ah, that is unfortunate.' Istvan pursed his lips and leaned forward towards Ioric. 'I really would have liked to keep things amenable between us. I must ask you to take a look at this.' Istvan fanned his fingers open, revealing a small powder compact. He flicked it open and showed Ioric the small mirror.

'I don't understand,' Ioric said in confusion, looking from Istvan to the compact. 'Is it a trick?'

'All will be clear. Look into the mirror.'

A frown drew Ioric's brows together and he bent over the mirror. 'I see nothing except my face, Istvan.'

'Watch.'

Istvan drew his hand across the mirror and it moment-arily went dark before clearing. Ioric sucked in his breath in shock when the image came into focus. His hand went to the curved blade at his side and he lurched at his guest. Istvan raised a hand and a band of black shadow unfurled lightning fast, punching Ioric in the chest, pressing him back into his chair.

'What kind of coward are you?' Ioric ground out, his face flushed in anger. 'That is my mother and sisters. Let them go immediately.'

'I'll let them go if you do what I ask you.' Istvan stood, forcing Ioric to look up at him. 'Stop struggling, boy. You won't get free.'

The black band of darkness tightened across Ioric's arms and chest, pinning him to his chair. No matter how much he writhed, he couldn't get free. He sat back, breathing heavily.

'You will pay for this,' Ioric promised. 'Know that I will come for you . . .'

Istvan shook his head, smiling unpleasantly. 'I have heard so many threats these past weeks, my boy, one more does not frighten me. Now, are you ready to listen or do I tell my men to have some sport with your mother and sisters? They tell me the sluagh is hungry.'

'Yes, damn your maggot-filled heart, I will listen.'

'Outstanding. I've always liked you, Ioric. You seem such a sensible chap.'

Chapter Twenty

Time Slips (London): A young man was found wandering the streets in Greenwich, early hours of the morning, 17 August 1997. Dressed in period clothing dated from 1560, the young man told authorities he was a noble in the court of Elizabeth and that he had been on his way to a meeting with one of the queen's advisers, William Cecil, when he took the wrong turning in the palace and found himself here, out of time. The young man was still in custody when he disappeared without a trace from a locked cell.

From an ongoing introductory report filed
in HMDSDI HQ, 2001

I pass Thorn his sword, take out mine and hastily buckle it on before following him. We pass the little girl as we head into the tunnel leading into the riverbank. I realize that by now things like this should feel normal, but I can't help it. It still gives me a thrill but mostly it freaks me out. I am on my way to meet a bunch of trolls living under Tower Bridge and my companion is a Fae prince. Not even during the wildest fever I had as a small child did I dream anything as insane.

'You may call me Amy,' the girl says as she moves past us down the narrow tunnel. 'I'll look after anything you may need. Please, follow me.'

I'm not sure how long we walk for, but Amy leads us deeper and deeper along the tunnel, seeming to choose random passages leading off the main tunnel. I notice entrances marked 'Elizabeth I' and 'Dickens' and 'Edinburgh 1885' and a few more with either names or dates on them. I wonder if these relate to the urban myths of London that Megan's told me about: hidden pockets of time that you can fall into if you take the wrong set of stairs or lonely road when travelling around the city. It seems likely, bizarrely, but I don't want to stop and ask our little guide as she scoots us along.

We walk for several minutes before the current passage levels out again. I notice a difference in the ground I'm walking on and peer down at my feet. Previously we walked along compacted earth and rock, now we are treading on something else, something that looks like compressed dark crystal. Shortly after that the tunnel opens up, and I gape unashamedly.

The cavern that spreads before us is massive. You could probably lay five rugby fields side by side or have enough space for three jumbo jets to land. But it's not just the scale of the cave that's impressive. There is a lake, trees, birds. It looks like a terrarium. In the centre of the chamber a shaft of light from above illuminates an inky-black pool from which a small island has sprouted. The island itself has a sandy beach and on its shore lies the ruin of a wooden boat with a high prow.

Amy's been talking softly to Thorn while I gawk at the magnificent cave with its underground forest and crystal ceiling. I wonder if we are still beneath London or somewhere altogether different.

'I have tribute,' Thorn assures her in a quiet voice. 'I would not dream to insult the Watchers and not follow etiquette.'

Amy doesn't really sigh in relief but she gives a brief nod that is both acknowledgement and apology. Then she walks over to a small intricately carved table set to one side. A delicate crystal bell the size of my palm rests on a silver platter. She picks this up and rings it. The sound is sharp, high and crystal clear, and as Amy keeps ringing, the sound changes and becomes sonorous and deep. I feel my bones ache at its tone. I hold on to Thorn's arm and lean against him because it feels as if my knees are going to give in. The sound changes once more, becoming so high I can't hear it at all but I can feel it vibrating in the air all around me. Ice crawls down my spine and I'm horrified to find that I can't stop shivering.

From nowhere, three rather large trolls stand before us. Two of them are so tall my neck hurts staring up at them. The other is less tall, maybe only seven feet, and I think he must be the youngest of the three. They are human in shape, with two arms and two legs and a head. But everything else about them is richly earth coloured and they look as if they are fused from earth and rock and marbled stone. One troll has a small tree growing from his shoulder but seems oblivious to its presence. Their features are rough, with prominent brows, large jaws and bulging eyes. Some things I've met in the past year were big but have little presence. These creatures have a presence about them that makes me feel small and insignificant. I resist the urge to step further back, into the shadows. I draw my courage together and stand my ground next to Thorn.

Amy is talking to them in a rapid language that sounds like Greek. She gestures to Thorn and to me, giving our names and, with introductions over, she moves aside to come and stand next to me.

Thorn moves towards them, seemingly unfazed by their impassive gazes. It feels an eternity that they just stand there, the silence only broken by the soft drip, drip of water somewhere in the cave.

Amy gives my hand a little squeeze, before rummaging in her pocket and coming up with a wrapped sweet. 'You're doing really well,' she says, her voice encouraging. 'The first time I met them I fainted. I was sure they were going to eat me.' Her smile is teasing. 'But of course trolls don't often eat people. Only ogres do that.' She made a face, sticking her tongue out, showing me how gross the thought of eating humans was to her.

My answering smile is weak. 'What are they doing?' I ask her. 'They're just standing there, staring at Thorn.'

'They are talking. Watch.'

I don't see a thing. Nothing. But then I try a trick I learned when I was very little and I could just catch glimpses of the tiny faeries flitting about my room. I was desperate to see them for real and eventually I figured it out. If you narrow your eyes, concentrate and then peer steadily from the corner of your eyes, you tend to see things.

At first I don't see anything really, but I sense colours and I become aware of almost imperceptible movements of their faces. Then suddenly, Thorn turns to me and beckons me forward.

Amy's hand slips from mine and we walk forward together.

'This is Kit Blackhart. She is my companion in this quest.'

I don't like the sound of that but I put a smile on my face and, as I stare at the faces of the three trolls, I have a feeling that they know exactly who I am and aren't too impressed.

'We know you rescued the prince, Blackhart. For that brave act we name you troll friend and pledge our honesty and wisdom to your cause.' Their mouths don't move but I hear them speaking in unison in my head. It is an oddly soothing feeling and not at all as intrusive as I thought it would be.

'I have done what any would have done in my place,' I say carefully. 'I accept your friendship and pledge and return it with friendship of my own.' I get the impression they approve of my words and I put on a smile that I hope is charming and sweet, and not at all frightened.

'You have brought us something?'

Thorn looks towards them, facing the largest so probably the eldest. 'I have indeed. A token of our esteem and thanks for seeing us on such short notice. We hope it finds favour with the Watchers.'

Thorn holds out his hand to me and I pass him half the baggie of diamonds Aiden had given me. Amy moves forward and takes the velvet pouch from Thorn. Without looking inside, she juggles it in her hand, feeling the weight of the stones, and gives a brief nod to the trolls.

'You do us a great honour, Prince of Alba.' The voice is different now, female and younger. It also conveys far more emotion and I watch the trolls, wondering which one of them is speaking.

I get the impression that our gift has more than impressed them and they are suddenly more attentive and focused on us. I suspect we've passed some kind of test. Previously their regard has been intense but disinterested; now, however, we are the centre of their attention.

'We have prepared a small repast. Please follow the human child and we will join you shortly. There is much to discuss.'

The larger of the three trolls starts moving off and the scent of fresh-cut grass fills the air in his wake. From above a shadow passes over the gap in the ceiling and the cave darkens and the temperature drops. I shiver and turn to look towards the gap. I rest my hand on the knife tucked into the small of my back and wonder what bad news is coming our way.

Amy disappears the velvet pouch among the folds of her pretty sundress and beckons us to follow her. I fall in beside Thorn.

'That went well,' I say. 'I still have all my limbs.'

He pulls a face. 'My formal manners are rusty,' he says. 'With the old races, like the trolls, you can't ever be sure how things are going to play out until you are at least three days' ride away from their caves.'

'Oh great. I'm nervous all over again.'

'Don't be,' he says. 'You're doing well. They know who you are. As a Blackhart and my friend you're far more than the average supplicant.'

'You make these trolls sound far more . . .' I wave my hand. 'Just more. Who are they really?'

Thorn slows his pace so we drop further behind Amy.

'They are our Watchers, our chroniclers. They write our histories and watch over our past, anticipating the future.'

My eyebrows shoot up. 'So they don't just live in caves, eat goats and humans and worry bridges.'

'No. Not all of them are like that, only the ones that feel up to the task. Most trolls live quiet lives. They've become vilified in various stories and it's hard to convince the world otherwise.'

'Okay. So noted.' I can't help but bristle a bit under the censure in his voice. I also wonder how much of what he said pertains to him and the Fae in general.

I shake my head. I'm starting to feel a bit out of my league here and I find myself wishing dearly for a decent fight. Those I can handle; dangerous subtleties make me feel uncertain and trapped.

Amy eventually stops and gestures us to enter a smaller cave ahead. We do and I gasp involuntarily.

A heavy chandelier is suspended above a vast black table that reflects the light of a thousand diamonds. The entire cave is encrusted with precious stones and the chandelier itself is a dripping cascade of large gems.

We sit and the chairs are large, leaving my feet dangling

in mid-air. It's like something from *Alice in Wonderland* after Alice has drunk the shrinking potion.

The trolls enter and move forward to seat themselves with ponderous grace. Amy is dismissed as they settle themselves.

'The situation in Alba is dire,' one of them utters sonorously.

The acoustics in the cave are superb, the way a cathedral's acoustics amplify a soft sigh, but even so it takes me a second to realize they're talking aloud, not in my head this time. I sigh in relief and relax, crossing my legs on the huge chair, feeling ridiculously at home in this cavern that, although vast, feels cosy and I wonder if it has something to do with the strangely calming presence of the three trolls.

'We have had reports from far and wide, telling of the coup against the House of Alba. It took some time to weigh the value of this knowledge and we will happily now share this with you.'

Thorn looks grateful but composes himself as he sits forward. 'My father will hear of your assistance in this. Do you know where the royal household has retired to?'

'We do not, we are sad to say. We know your brother Kieran is housed in cells beneath the Citadel. He is alive but badly hurt.'

Thorn takes the confirmation of Scarlet's information calmly enough but it must be a big blow. 'Are any of the gateways working?'

'All twelve Sidhe houses have shut their gateways and some of them have lost control of them entirely. The smaller pathways are inaccessible, except for those Fae who are small and very fast.'

There is movement behind the trolls in the shadows but it's gone too quickly to see what it was. I assume there are bats in the caves. The thought alone makes me shudder. I can cope with all kinds of nasties but bats freak me out.

The female troll speaks up and her voice is wonderful aloud, beautiful and rich. 'Powerful sorcery is at work, assisting Eadric against his brother.'

'Any clues as to who it could be? The sorcerer, I mean. He was strong enough to bring a dragon into our realm. Surely that's not something just anyone can do?' My voice gives away my anxiety, it's too loud in the hushed space, and I take a breath, before speaking more quietly. 'There must be some way we can find out.'

Time slows inexplicably and unexpectedly as the shadows behind the trolls coalesce into the shape of a man; all in black leather, his face is hidden behind a black scarf. A stupidly large flintlock pistol is pointed unwavering at my head and in his other hand he grips Amy as he scans the room.

Chapter Twenty-One

Before any of us can move, the stranger utters a guttural sequence of words that makes my ears itch. The lights dim momentarily before brightening again.

The onset of tiredness is so sudden that my head droops forward and hits my chest. Instinctively, my hand moves to grasp my sword, but it feels inappropriate for someone as tired as I am, and I allow my hand to drop.

I want to slump to the table and sleep as I'm sure I've never had a decent sleep in all my life. As the thought lingers in my tired brain, Thorn grabs my wrist and pinches me hard.

The spell breaks as quickly as it fell. I sit up in surprise, this time reaching for my sword in earnest.

'No, not a good idea.' The stranger's voice is soft and intimate and I can hear the sound of teeth in the smile I can't see. A gesture from him with the pistol and energy sparks off my sword pommel. I pull my hand away in shock, my nerve-endings tingling unpleasantly. 'Sit quietly, there's a good girl.'

Whatever spell the newcomer cast as he walked into the

cavern has completely immobilized the trolls. They seem unable to move at all, but I can sense their fury at the intrusion.

The man poses dramatically before us, his actions strangely exaggerated. I even wonder through the adrenalin in my veins if he's drunk. Then he twists Amy's arm savagely and pushes her forward, so that they can move closer towards us. Her eyes are wide but not panicked. No, she looks pissed and I like her just that tiny bit more than before.

'I've been sent to bring you home,' the intruder says to Thorn. 'If you come quietly neither of the humans will get hurt.'

Thorn stares at him, puzzled. 'Who are you?'

The chuckle is friendly, disarming. 'How haven't you guessed?' He pulls the scarf away from his face, revealing beautifully sculpted features with skin as smooth as black marble.

Thorn clearly can't believe his eyes. 'Ioric?'

'Surprised?' Ioric moves closer and I pull my sleeves down over my hands to grip my sword as I stand. No little electric shock will prevent me from grabbing it again.

'What are you doing here? Let the girl go and drop your pistol.'

'No.' I can hear the smugness in his voice. Whoever he is, he seems to be revelling in his moment of power. 'Definitely not. Tell your human girl to put her sword on the table where I can see it. Make her keep her hands visible at all times. You know I am an excellent shot.'

Thorn gives me a reluctant nod and I obey, while wishing looks could kill this Ioric.

'I don't think my father sent you,' Thorn says. 'So who did?'

'Another interested party. I'm shocked that you're even here, not with your family.' He wiggles the pistol and it sways alarmingly between us. 'Oh, I know. You don't know where they've gone, do you? And no one bothered telling you. Could it be that no one remembered you even existed?'

As Thorn moves to square up to Ioric, I feel a sudden burst of alarm for him, despite his Fae powers.

'Ioric, why have you come here? Like this?' He nods to the immobile trolls. 'What have you done to the Watchers?'

'Them? They're fine. You really should be more concerned about yourself, my friend.'

'You still haven't answered me, *my friend*. What are you doing here?'

As Thorn asks this, he gestures widely towards Ioric. The tingle across my skin tells me magic's in play and I'm just in time to see a flash of power hit Ioric in the arm. His pistol goes off and drops to the floor. Something zips past my face, close enough to leave a burning streak along my cheek. I duck and swivel on instinct, grabbing my sword, and spin from the table towards Ioric.

Amy's in my way as he shoves her at me and turns to face an unarmed Thorn. Ioric's hands are bare of weapons and I find it strange that he's not drawn one of the knives that I see strapped to his back.

'Thorn. Let's not play this game. You must know that you're not really facing Ioric.' This time the voice is definitely not that of Ioric. It's older, the tone serious and a bit weary . . . it sounds familiar.

'I know.' Thorn takes a step towards him. 'Who are you? And what have you done to my friend?'

There's a wet wrenching sound and Ioric arches back, letting rip a scream filled with blood and pain.

'Stay where you are, boy. I can do worse.' I stiffen at the danger in the air when he shifts his attention towards me briefly. His gaze narrows before dismissing me as being of little consequence. He focuses on Thorn and the smile he gives is a smile I'm sure Ioric's never given in real life. It just looks nasty, with too much teeth by far. 'Oh, he's here, tucked away. I'm just enjoying the ride. Now, will you come of your own free will – or do I make you?'

'No.' Thorn glances at me, and I nod slightly in support. 'I can't do that. You will surrender and just perhaps my father will extend his mercy.'

Thorn's words are ignored, and Ioric's eyes gleam with borrowed malevolence. 'What if I let Ioric speak to you directly? Perhaps he can convince you outright, without my interference?'

Thorn moves at the same time as the sorcerer withdraws from Ioric. A shiver goes through the possessed Sidhe warrior and he drops to the floor with a grunt, like a puppet whose strings have been severed, a thick stream of blood spilling from his mouth.

'Help him,' I shout without thinking and we both rush towards the fallen Fae. I kneel beside him and pull him towards me as Thorn tilts his head sideways so he doesn't swallow any more of his own blood.

'Gaia's wounds, Ioric. What has he done to you?'

'Don't,' Ioric gasps out. 'Don't go with him.' He bucks

under my hands as if he's having some kind of fit and I have to use all my might to hold him. 'I can't stop him, Thorn. He's everywhere inside me, tearing me apart. He has my mother. He has my sisters . . . You have to stay free and save them.'

'Who?' Thorn demands, 'Tell me who is doing this to you, Ioric.'

'Can't.' Blood bubbles on his lips. 'I'm under a geas and he's too strong.' His body twists violently, there's blood everywhere and he now looks positively insane with pain. 'But your parents . . . He can't stop me telling you where they are. Get back to the Frontier. They are camped in Scotland with an army. Find them at the fairgrounds. In the Cairngorms.'

Ioric lets out a violent cry and I'm sure I hear something wrench in his back. He relaxes so abruptly that I lose my grip on him and am then thrown aside as the sorcerer resumes control.

Ioric snaps upright like a jack-in-the-box. It's a movement so unnatural that I get goosebumps and I feel real fear.

'Enough talk.' The sorcerer is back in charge. He gestures towards Thorn. 'Come. Now is the time to save your friend and do as I command.'

Thorn's sword now points directly at Ioric's throat. 'Never. You won't get away with this, know that. I will make sure you are hunted to the ends of all the worlds.'

'Ioric' smiles. 'I'll take that as a definite "no".'

It happens so quickly I don't have the chance to turn away or rush at Amy to cover her eyes.

The man controlling Ioric reaches for one of his knives

and draws it swiftly across his own throat. The slit is deep and the gush of blood transfixes us all.

My shocked gasp echoes around the room. Thorn is swiftly back by his friend's side, on his knees, cradling Ioric in his arms, his expression heartbreaking. He tries to stem the flow of blood but it runs over his hands like a river, staining them red.

Amy shows us the way out. She's given us new clothes to replace our bloodstained ones but I don't think I'll ever feel clean again. The door she opens for us is on the side of a building and it takes me a few seconds to work out where we are. We've emerged next to Covent Garden piazza. It's dusk and soft incessant drizzle falls from a grey sky. There are still tourists and office workers around, but the rain has kept many away.

Amy gives me a quick fierce hug and I'm touched. When she turns to Thorn she starts to sink into a curtsy, but he shakes his head briefly and she runs to hug him too.

'Kill them all,' she says to him, her voice vibrating with feeling.

She turns back to me and passes me the small velvet pouch.

'My masters are embarrassed about what's happened. They are closing the entrance here and won't be back until they can guarantee the safety of their guests. They've decided to return the gift you brought them. They don't think they deserve it.'

I open my mouth to argue but Thorn gives Amy a quick bow. 'Thank you, Amy. Tell your masters they have honoured their word to us and we look forward to meeting with them again under better circumstances.'

With a final wave, she shuts the door to leave us standing in the middle of the West End, feeling completely disconnected from our surroundings.

'How are you doing?' I ask Thorn, and when he looks at me his expression is thoughtful.

'I'm not sure,' he admits. 'A lot has just happened.'

I nod and sigh, popping my hood back up. 'I'm really sorry about your friend,' I say. 'And things were going so well for about five minutes. At least we know where to go from here.'

His expression is miserable. 'Within a very short space of time, a lot of people I care about have been attacked, turned and killed. Or tried to kill me. Now that we know where my parents are, maybe I should go, leave you and Aiden here. It may be for the best.'

'And what? Do you have money?' I ask him. 'How are you getting to Scotland? Are you going to fly? Have you got super-secret faery wings you've not told me about? I've seen you without your shirt on, matey – there were no wings. So, will you take a bus up? All that metal – it will be like being in a cage for hours on end. Just think about it, all those people pressing close, drinking coffee and talking to you. If you want to do that, just say. I know where the buses leave from.'

'You really are quite dramatic, Kit Blackhart,' he says, a ghost of a smile on his face. 'If you don't want me to go, just say so.'

'Don't be an idiot, Thorn. You're free to leave if you

want. But think about it: without money or a clue, you're not going to get very far.'

'You are, of course, correct,' he admits grudgingly. 'But it doesn't mean I have to like it.'

I grimace. 'And whoever controlled Ioric said he knows where we are. I don't feel safe out here in the open. Let's get moving. There must be somewhere I can phone Aiden from to come and collect us.'

I stay close to Thorn as we make our way through the thinning crowd. Our weapons are wrapped up, courtesy of Amy, so that we look as if we're carrying poster tubes; a bit bulky but perfectly disguised.

Luckily we don't have to wander too far before I spot a red phone box. Once utilitarian, now rare and developing tourist attraction status.

'Why don't you grab us something to drink?' I ask Thorn, gesturing to a cafe. 'I could do with a coffee. Also something to eat – maybe a pastry?' He seems bemused by the money I hand him but heads off to do my bidding.

The streets here are far quieter but in the phone box I turn my back to the world so I can have some privacy. I close my eyes to business cards of partially naked women offering various services in various languages.

The phone rings twice before Aiden comes on the line. 'Er, hi?'

'It's me, wolf boy. We're in Covent Garden. Come find us. Near the Transport Museum.'

'How'd you get there?' he half yells. 'I've been going crazy. The gate and everything just disappeared after you guys went down to that little beach. I've been waiting for hours. I've even got a mate driving me around to see if we can find you.'

'It's magic!' I say like a panto-clown but the smile I'm trying to put in my voice just doesn't make it.

He groans under his breath at my lame attempt at humour. 'I'll see you soon. We're about five minutes away.'

As I'm pushing out of the phone cubicle a massive flat hand hits the glass hard, shutting me in. I open my mouth to yell but my voice dies in my throat when I see the snarling face behind the glass. It looks human, but only for the briefest of seconds, until the badly constructed glamour drops away, leaving me staring at one of the hyena-faced mutant things from the night before.

'Pretty,' it grunts. 'Want.' It slaps its misshapen three-fingered claws against the glass again, the nails trailing down and leaving deep scratch marks behind. Drips of thick drool drop from his mouth as he opens his massive jaws in an open-mouthed laugh at my surprised expression.

Well, I decide, it clearly wants to play. I whip my trusty knife from the sheath at the small of my back, regretting my over-wrapped sword. At the same time I shoulder open the door and watch it take a surprised step back. It always amuses me that creatures both from this world and the Otherwhere never expect a girl to be physically strong or take the initiative in a fight.

I say balls to being eaten.

The street is one of the quieter roads off the main section of the piazza and the people who are around are only too happy not to see anything. And even if someone did stop and look, what they can see wouldn't correspond with what they think they see. It's as if other humans have a circuit in their brains to not see things that don't make sense. A dark-haired girl fighting a hyena-faced creature in the middle of the street, for instance. Not even if she's wielding a knife with a blade as long as her forearm or if the creature is making weird laughing barking noises to attract the attention of its pack.

I duck under swooping claws as it lashes out at me. I remember only too well the deep cuts that laced across poor Scar's body the night before. So I dance out of its way, frustrating it, making it angry, waiting for it to mess up. I launch fake attacks and watch how it moves. It's oddly graceful but it doesn't look comfortable. It's like watching a dog trying to walk on its hind legs; it can do it, but it's not its preferred way of movement.

I dart forward, and in a move Jamie showed me and made me practise over and over, I sort of spin into the chimera, stab the knife into his side, keeping the knife at least three inches in his belly as I speed-pirouette away from him, switching hands as I draw the blade across his stomach.

The knife comes away with a wet sucking sound and I flick my wrist, clearing it of blood. It looks like a polished ballet move and to a certain extent that's exactly what it is. When Jamie taught me to fight, he utilized the tools I came with: my body, my height, my suppleness. And here's where the martial arts and ballet classes my nan had me take really pay off.

I catch movement from the corner of my eye and twist to face the oncoming threat. Two more chimeras are coming at me. Unlike their comrade, they have given up all appearance of being human and are loping towards me on all fours.

I do the only thing I know how to do, even though my mind is screaming for me to exit stage left. I run at the lead monster and leap at it just as it leaps at me. We clash mid-air and, as I feel its massive chest strike mine, I drive the knife deep into the soft bit of his jaw, and up into its brain, as far as my blade can go. The impact as we connect is ruthless and steals my breath from my labouring lungs. I feel its hot breath on my face and then we're falling. I haul out the knife and just start stabbing as hard and fast as I can, anywhere I can find space. Then we hit the ground and I land hard and badly, my leg twisting beneath me. The monster collapses on top of me, gives a very human-sounding whimper and dies. Over its massive hairy shoulder I can see the other one watching in evident surprise.

The chimera takes a far shorter time than I do to recover from its friend dying and stalks towards me where I lie trapped beneath the press of the dead creature. My hand holding onto the knife is slippery and dark with the thing's blood. I grimace and wipe the blade and handle on its pelt before I try and lift its body off me. It's heavy and I'm already breathing hard. I'm worried the other one will come and finish the job the first two started while I'm lying prone. With a massive heave, I lever the dead monster off me and struggle to stand up. My leg gives a twinge and I bite back a howl of pain as it refuses to take my weight.

There's a snorting sound that sounds like husky laughter from the hyena goblin. It licks its fangs and leans closer. 'Lunch.'

It circles me, slowly. Standing on all fours it comes to above my waist. Massive shoulders taper down towards a narrow waist and powerful haunches. Its markings are darker than the other two monsters' and I think that maybe it's older than the others. It is certainly more wary. But also arrogant.

It circles me for a second time and I keep turning, following it, making sure I keep my weight off my leg. It's throbbing like mad and I wonder if it's broken. Unlike my cousins, I've never broken anything before, apart from my nose, so I have no idea what breaking a bone would feel like. I think I would maybe be in more pain than I am now, and in a way I'm relieved I'm in pain that I can handle, rather than wanting to pass out. It's keeping the adrenalin pumping through my veins and I know that when I crash, it's going to be awful.

I watch the chimera carefully, as I've been taught, and see it gathering itself for an attack. It doesn't run at me, it doesn't herd me. Instead it rears up on its hind legs and tries to grab me. My blade flashes and I feel as it cuts deep into the fleshy bit beneath the creature's arm (leg?) and I'm in the process of moving away when one of its claws rips across my arm as it extends its reach. The skin on my upper arm splits like ripe fruit and for the briefest second, there's nothing, then pain engulfs me and it's so severe I scream in shock and anger.

I turn on the creature, regardless of my sore leg and the pain in my arm, but before I can even move someone steps between us. There is a flurry of movement so fast I take an involuntary step back, fully expecting a heavy blow to knock me out. Instead, I see the chimera being lifted in the air and flung bodily into the wall of the building opposite. There's a sound I can barely hear, a distracting droning noise and a wave of nausea washes over me. I blink rapidly to focus because what I'm seeing now is even more surreal than events in the cavern.

Thorn's standing a few metres away. His chest is heaving and his wet hair is plastered to his pale face. His eyes have gone all black and his hands are clenching and unclenching at his sides. For the longest moment he just stands there, looking dangerous, as if he's fighting for control, then he stalks over to the chimera lying in a messy heap against the wall and lifts it with one hand, shoving it hard up against the wall.

'Who sent you?' His voice is low, frightening. 'Tell me or I will break every bone in your body.'

The chimera opens its mouth and grins a bloody grin. 'Do it. He will fix us and we'll keep coming back.' Its gaze flares silver, the same colour as Ioric's eyes when controlled by the sorcerer. It barks in laughter, wrapping its massive paws around Thorn's forearm. Then it chills us with the same voice we heard in the trolls' cave. ' Have you any idea what's coming for you?'

A ball of light arcs from Thorn's open left palm and hits the chimera high in the shoulder. Instead of dispersing, the magic grows into a tightly focused beam and drills into its fur and the flesh beneath it. The creature squirms in his hold, curving those black talons around Thorn's forearm, holding tighter, cutting into his skin. 'No, why don't you tell me?' Thorn says, his teeth clenched.

I'm next to them now and I'm shocked to see how ill Thorn looks. His cheeks are flushed while the rest of his face is sickly pale and his eyes have become otherworldly black; in their depths I see madness. The thrumming noise, like thousands of angry wasps, comes from Thorn in waves, and when I lean my head forward I hear it even more clearly. I glance at him and my eyesight jumps, going fuzzy, like a poorly tuned TV. It's as if he's vibrating at a really high frequency and I find it difficult to see him properly.

'The Elder Gods are coming. Alba will be cast down and we will rule in your place.' The creature's jaw falls open and he laughs, his gaze directed at me. 'Humans will know their rightful place once more. You can't fight their coming.'

'Kit! Thorn! What the hell . . . ?' I spin around at Aiden's voice behind me and as I do I forget about my painful leg and rest my weight on it. I let out a yelp and slowly crumple to the ground but before I reach it, Thorn has a strong arm around my waist.

The fierce predatory look in his eyes scares me and I bite back a sob of surprise and close my eyes briefly against the shock. I've grown to like Thorn, but he suddenly seems like a dangerous stranger.

I'm aware of Aiden nearby now, talking to Thorn, but as he talks there's the sound of something going squelch and snap. It's a sound I recognize, a sound that's haunted my dreams ever since I killed for the first time. It's the sound of bones breaking, of flesh tearing. Thorn is holding me against him, slightly to the side, so that when I open my eyes, I see him drop the chimera with a look of detached distaste on his face. The thing that was once the chimera now looks like a dried husk no larger than a desiccated dog mummy from the Egypt exhibition in the British Museum.

'Come away now, Thorn. They are all dead.' Aiden's voice is low, calming, but I can sense real shock in his tone.

I look up at Thorn and I'm sickened by the wildness I see there. Gone is the civilized handsome prince who bowed to me in the forest as if we were meeting over canapés and champagne. Instead the creature holding on to me looks untamed, resembling a thing from a time far less urbane, with eyes too large and darkly bright. Oddly, his pale skin shows a golden sheen in the rain. I wipe my eyes and decide that I must be seeing things, because there's no way he has snake scales beneath his skin.

'I'm okay,' I tell Thorn, my voice sounding far away, even to me. 'I just hurt my leg. And my arm. But I'm okay.'

Aiden's face appears in my line of sight and he looks really scared. 'Kit, walk to me.'

The steel band resting around my waist loosens and I edge away from Thorn, slowly but surely. Aiden stands loose and open, reaching a hand towards me. I shake my head and instead I step away from Thorn and turn to face him.

He's bigger than he was before: taller, wider. He looks older too, the bones in his face more pronounced. Light plays over his skin, and for a brief moment longer I see an iridescent diamond pattern along his cheeks and jaw, before it's gone.

Thorn watches me intently and unblinkingly from unreadable eyes. It already feels as if I'm living in Alice's Wonderland so the smile I give him is tentative and not just a tiny bit freaked out.

'Hey.' I say to him. 'Are you okay?'

For the longest time Thorn doesn't move and I'm aware of the odd tableau we make, the three of us and three chimera bodies around us. At the back of my mind I register the sound of police sirens in the distance.

'We need to go,' Aiden says. 'I've my friend waiting with a car.' I look at Aiden in surprise but he shrugs. 'We need to get going. Now.'

'Wait.' Thorn's voice is cold, matter of fact. 'We can't leave these for your authorities to find.'

Before either Aiden or I can respond, Thorn stalks to the first two chimera and places his hands on their chests. There is the same wrenching breaking noise as Thorn gathers up their essence. When he stands up there's nothing left of them at all and as a cold breeze races down the road, it lifts the ash the bodies turned into and disperses it into the air. He sways for a few seconds before raising his head and nodding to himself.

I look up at the CCTV cameras. 'What about those?' I ask Aiden. 'They would have filmed everything.'

'They were knocked out the second those things came at you,' Aiden replies confidently. 'Fae glamour makes electronic equipment go wonky.' He hesitates. 'Kit, you should know this.'

I open my mouth but shut it again. He's right. How am I so out of it that I don't remember one of the first things I was taught by the Blackharts?

'Wonky? A technical term, huh?' I say in an attempt to draw attention away from my failure. Aiden's not fooled and his look is worried, on edge. Those sirens are coming closer, so even if the CCTV don't show anything, someone might have reported teenagers fighting some street thugs.

'Are we good?' he asks, looking at us both, concentrating on Thorn, who is standing with his back to us, his mind elsewhere.

'I'm ready,' Thorn says, his voice low. 'Let's go.'

Chapter Twenty-Two

We head past the hardier of the tourists who are gathered in the damp piazza watching a mime dressed as a silent bride do her thing. Thorn walks behind me and I can't help but feel my back itching, pressing back against his magic thrumming against my skin. It's no longer as loud or as forceful as it was in the side street, but it's still grating on my nerves. I risk a glance over my shoulder. His face looks serious and thoughtful and I notice his eyes are their normal blue again. He catches my eye and quirks his lips at me, but it's not a real smile and because I can tell it isn't, it hurts. I look away, leaning against Aiden, whose firm grip around my waist prevents me from falling flat on my face.

'How are you?' he asks. 'How badly are you hurt?'

'My arm will have some sexy new scars. I just need to get it cleaned out quickly. My leg . . . it's not broken, that's for sure. But it hurts like hell.'

'And that's it?' He frowns at me. 'Are you sure?'

'Yes, why?'

'Man, when I got there it looked like Thorn was trying to squash you.'

'No, he was holding on to me. I almost fell and he just picked me up with one arm.' Even to my ears it sounds lame.

'Just picked you up . . . Kit, I know you're as freaked out as I am. Did you see what he did to those things? He flung that thing around like it was a piece of wood. Then he latches on to them and turns them to dust. Who does that? How is that even possible? Since when can he do that? Also, holding up that thing with one hand? Man, even I'd struggle to do that and I'm much stronger than your average muscle-bound human.'

'Aiden, there's a lot of crap going on that we don't know. Thorn's friend Ioric appeared down there with the trolls. He was actually possessed and it was like some kind of bad B-movie. Whoever took control of him is super-strong and his magic is . . .' I gasp as my arm protests at my gesture. 'Nothing I've seen before.' I cast a quick look over my shoulder and watch Thorn dawdling behind us, his head down, hood up. 'He made Thorn's mate kill himself. By slitting his own throat.'

'Holy shit.' Aiden's breath catches in his throat. 'Now what?'

'We get home and we get hold of Olga. Then we go to Scotland.'

'Scotland? Why there?'

'Because that's where Thorn's parents are.'

Aiden's quiet for a moment. 'My dad and the pack went up there.'

'So did my cousins.'

We share a look as we turn past the tiny church of St Paul, putting Covent Garden behind us at last.

'We have to get home,' I say to Aiden. 'We must clean up and head north as soon as we can.'

We seem to be heading for a young guy leaning against a large black Bentley. If he's shocked at the state I'm in he doesn't say anything. Instead, he nods briefly at Aiden, who gently disengages his arm from my waist so that he can open the door for me.

'Leo, this is Kit. Kit, Leo and that's Thorn.'

'Hey,' he says, frowning lightly at Thorn, who isn't looking good, even compared to me – and I look as if I've bathed in blood. 'You guys look rough. I hope whoever you tangled with looks worse.'

I hesitate by the open door and look at Leo.

'They do,' I assure him. 'And I don't want to damage your upholstery . . .'

Leo assesses my stained clothing before shrugging. 'The leather needs replacing anyway. Don't worry about it.' He gives me a charming smile and I return it, too exhausted to read anything into it, just thankful that I can sit down in the relative safety of a rather luxurious interior.

Next Aiden takes Thorn by the arm where he stands swaying by the boot of the car.

'Get in, mate,' he says to the Fae prince. 'You'll be okay, we'll get you some tea and you'll be sorted in no time at all.'

'I'm not sure tea will fix how I'm feeling,' Thorn murmurs but ducks his head into the car and clambers in next to me.

'I'll call you when you can come and get the car,' Aiden says to Leo. 'And thanks for helping out.'

'No worries, bruv. You know all you have to do is ask.'

They shake hands and Leo lifts his hand to me in a light cheery wave, before setting off in the direction of Charing Cross at a jaunty pace. He moves with an easy grace, long legged and casual, easily disappearing in the crowd.

'Who was that?' I ask Aiden as he settles in behind the wheel.

'That was Leo. He, uh, he knows about us.' He looks a bit uncomfortable. 'We went to school together and he saw my first change happen to me during a cross-country race. He didn't run away. He stood his ground and helped.'

'And this is his car?' I ask, looking around the leather interior, at the lit dials. 'A bit fancy for a teenager, don't you think?'

'Yeah. Leo is what I'd like to call a guy who sees opportunities and takes them.' Aiden clicks his seatbelt in place before starting the engine and pulling out. 'His dad's in alternative employment.'

I feel like throwing my hands up in the air in despair, only I ache too much to do it. 'So we're in a stolen car?'

'No, not at all. This is definitely Leo's dad's car. Where *he* got it from is another story.'

I nod and close my eyes, putting Leo and his dad out of my mind. I feel ragged and tired and I hurt all over, plus my mind is buzzing with everything that's happened today. I'm partly relieved to at least suspect where my family is now. If they've all met up with Thorn's parents, it could explain why they've been out of contact. As Fae magic knocks out electronic equipment, that could've stopped them getting or returning my bazillion messages. The same for Aiden's family and his pack. Chances seem good that they are all together.

I do my best to ignore the throb in my arm and the dull ache in my leg. To be fair, I don't think there's a part of me that's not hurting. I slant a look at Thorn where he's slumped with me in the back seat. He looks tense and troubled, but his anger has dissipated.

'What happened?' I ask him. I know he's awake. 'Who was that guy back there?' I don't have to explain to him what I mean. The boy I've come to know these past few days definitely wasn't the one I saw in that side street a few minutes ago.

'I don't know.' For the longest time he doesn't look at me but then he does and his eyes are full of self-loathing. 'I've never in my life done anything like that to another living thing. It is not the kind of magic I've grown up using.'

'Is it normal?' I ask him, genuinely curious. 'What you did back there?'

'No,' he answers firmly. 'I've never displayed any of these abilities before.'

I let that sink in for a few seconds. I'm still a novice to how magic works, mine especially. But seeing what he just did, his eyes turning black and his skin going snake-like, makes me wonder if being in the Frontier is to blame.

'Dude, you scared me shitless back there,' Aiden puts in, looking at us in the rearview mirror. 'I've never seen anyone pull that kind of stunt before.'

'Neither have I,' Thorn says, sounding tired. 'I went looking for Kit when she took so long coming back. When I saw that thing standing over her I just . . .'

'Went berserk?' Aiden prompted, his eyebrows raised.

'I am not a berserker.' Thorn bit the words out. 'I am

not some uncaged wild animal. That, back there, was not who I am.'

'I don't know what a berserker is,' I point out before they can start bickering.

'A berserker is someone who goes into battle so full of adrenalin that even if his limbs get lobbed off, he still keeps fighting. He makes no distinction between friends and foes in battle.'

I raise my eyebrows. 'Ah, that's not someone I'd like to run into.'

'My dad's told me that there's an entire squad of berserkers who fight for Aelfric,' Aiden says. 'Is that true?'

'It is true but they are shunned by the other warriors. The way they fight, giving themselves over to their basest form, is seen as impure.'

I open my mouth to ask more but I spot Aiden's warning look in the mirror and catch myself. I settle back against the leather seat and watch passers-by huddle beneath umbrellas on the pavements as we drive along.

Aiden fiddles with the radio and music swells around us, coming from hidden speakers. It's something classical with lots of violins and a woman's soothing voice. I sigh, letting it wrap around me as I watch the rain throw odd patterns against the skin of my hand as it rests in Thorn's. When did he take my hand? I can't remember. I watch as his thumb traces an intricate pattern along the back of my hand and although it's nice I don't think he even notices that he's doing it. I close my eyes again and bite the inside of my cheek. Today has gone crazy, and more than anything else I want my family around me. I feel genuinely lost and out of my depth with none of my cousins to help me figure this mess out. I check the phone Aiden slipped me. The cracked screen shows full signal, but no messages, no emails, nothing. It might as well be a paperweight for all the good it's done me these past two days.

'Leo's called Olga for us,' Aiden says over his shoulder. 'She should be at the house later.'

'Can he be trusted?' Thorn asks him. 'It seems we're running out of people we can turn to for help.'

'Leo is solid. He won't speak to anyone about what he saw today.'

To my surprise Thorn takes Aiden's word and settles back down again.

Chapter Twenty-Three

Olga Kassan: The granddaughter of Emory Kassan.
There are mentions of Olga Kassan in our files since
the early 1700s. She runs the London branch of
Emm's Antiques and is a regular visitor to the
Blackhart estate.

From an archived report filed in HMDSDI HQ, 1921

Olga walks into my room as I'm pulling off my shoes.

'You stink,' she says with a frown. 'What have you been
doing?'

'Oh, you know, fighting bad things. Getting covered in
blood.'

'Did you beat them?' She heaves her small suitcase onto
the bed and zips it open. 'Where are you hurt?' Her gaze rakes
me. 'Your arm? Get your shirt off, let's look at your arm.'

'I beat two of them.' I pull off my dirty hoodie and look
down at my long-sleeved thermal vest; it's been completely
ruined by blood. My arm has stopped throbbing and is now
just a mass of soreness all the time. 'Then Thorn turned up
and went darkside on me.'

'Can you get your sleeve off?' Olga tuts under her breath when I shake my head and brings out a sharp knife. She slides it up and under my sleeve and smoothly cuts the fabric away. I bite my lip to hold back a squeal as she carefully prises the bits of cloth out of the three gashes. It feels as if she's raking glass over my exposed wounds.

'Lift your arm.' She pulls the vest off me and her dark eyes narrow. 'What is it with you Blackharts trying to stop blows with your body? Ever heard about running?'

I ignore the new bruises that have blossomed everywhere and I stare straight ahead, trying not to shiver in the cooler air, and grimace at her. 'Funny.'

'Go have your shower and then come back out here and I'll do my best to fix up your arm. You can tell me about the fight and what's made Thorn look like he wants to leap off the nearest tall building.'

I nod and yank off my wet jeans and squelch in wet socks to the bathroom. The shower feels great and I wash and rinse my hair, scrubbing hard to get rid of all the blood, especially under my nails. Washing with only one flexible arm isn't easy. When I'm done, I hobble into some clean underwear, shorts and a strappy thermal cami, and go sit on the bed next to Olga, who has laid out various medical bits.

'This is going to hurt,' she says, completely unnecessarily, I think. 'So, what happened? Tell me all of it.'

So I do. I tell her about the visit to the trolls, about Ioric Brightwing's appearance and the immobilizing spell he cast over the trolls and how Thorn questioned him. In telling the story I become aware of the strangeness of it, how surreal it sounds, like a bad fever dream.

Olga takes great care cleaning my arm; the pain becomes dizzying and my story comes in fits and starts. She has to ask me questions to keep me making sense. However, the retelling, especially the part involving Ioric cutting his own throat, distracts me from my arm.

'Thorn took it hard?' she asks.

I nod. 'Of course he did. I took it hard and I didn't even know the guy. Ioric's death set the trolls free, and they had to lift his friend out of his arms before he let him go. Olga, the man who did this is a beast. It made no sense what he did.'

'Showing off.' Olga looked up from tidying her bandages away. 'He was showing off for Thorn's benefit. Like a small child.'

'It's exactly what it felt like. But why was he so desperate?' I ask her. 'Why does he want Thorn so badly?'

Olga pulls her chair closer to examine my leg. 'I don't know. But I do wonder why Eadric went to see Thorn's dad all those years ago. If we can figure out what they spoke about, maybe it would be clearer.'

I let out a howl as Olga does something to my leg and it feels as if she's digging her entire hand into my muscle and pulling at it, hard. I sit up to see what she's doing but she pushes me back down with her free hand.

'You don't want to see this,' she tells me and I gasp for breath and squeeze my eyes shut at the terrible pain she's inflicting on me. 'I'm listening: what else? Tell me about Thorn.'

Between groans and shouting at her, I tell her about Thorn, about him rushing in and saving me from being a chimera snack. That he seemed bigger too, and how his eyes went coal black as he took the life force from the chimeras, turning them to dust.

Olga pauses for a second, a look of surprise on her face. 'He did that?'

'He looked so ill afterwards. I thought he was going to pass out,' I tell the ceiling. 'What kind of magic does that, Olga?'

'I can't even begin to say. My magic is small magics: cantrips, glamours and healing. I've been helping your family look after the Manor for years. But the spells used to keep it safe against magical attack were laid down by far more talented magic users than me. All I ever did was follow the formulae they left behind. Each consecutive layer we added boosted the house's defences – but the dragon that demolished those wards is not of this earth. Dragons absorb the energies around them, channelling them to power their own magic. Sounds like Thorn used the same principle – gathering the energies that exist all around us, and using them against the chimeras. Then he reversed that magic and turned them to dust.'

She's not precisely said it, but she's likening Thorn to the dragon that destroyed my home. I take a deep breath and try and concentrate on the warmth of her hands as she manipulates my leg.

'Do you remember anything else about Thorn's change?' Olga is saying. 'Anything at all?'

I think back and shiver. 'It just wasn't him. He didn't even look like himself. And he smelled funny.' As I say it I realize it's true and my eyes widen in surprise. 'He smelled funny – like, I don't know . . . the air at a bonfire.'

'Hmm.' Olga pushes her finger against my leg. 'How's your leg?'

I open my mouth to tell her it hurts like hell but then I realize it doesn't. It's still a bit achy, but nothing as bad as it was earlier. I stand up and walk around the room with a slight limp.

'Fine,' I say, grinning at her. 'Thanks.'

'You're welcome.' Her smile is sweet but strained. 'Kit, we need to know if Thorn is stable. His family are good people, but strong willed and sometimes difficult to be around. Aelfric likes to see himself as a progressive leader, bringing the Fae slowly into the twenty-first century, but it's hard. For centuries they've lived very secular lives, occasionally stealing a human, spying on us from behind shrubbery. But things are changing faster than Aelfric can cope with. Factions in the Otherwhere are keen to tear down the gateways between our world and theirs. They want free passage in the human world. They want it to be the way it was once before, before the gateways were put in place and our world and the Otherwhere separated forever.'

Dread settles in the pit of my stomach. 'But it won't be safe. Not for anyone.'

She nods wearily. 'Exactly.'

'Are you saying Thorn's uncle is the guy wanting to make these changes?'

'I'm saying he might be behind this. And if he can show the Otherwhere he has the King of Alba's support, then it's likely the Seelie and Unseelie Courts will fall in line. As would the Empress of Russia and Chin's dragon lords.'

'So he wants Thorn so he can blackmail the king?'

'Is what I'm thinking.' She straightens up and surveys me with her hands on her hips. 'Okay, you're done. Get dressed. But, Kit, can I ask you something . . . about what it's like when you're with Thorn and he uses his magic?'

'It's a buzz. I feel it against my skin.' I think for a second. 'Give me your arm.'

I push her sleeve up to her elbow. 'Now close your eyes.'

I lift her arm to my throat so that her skin almost touches mine. Then I start humming. 'Like that, can you feel it? That's what it feels like when I sense him using his magic. Only all of me feels it and I can hear it in my head, this constant buzzing.'

'I've never come across anyone who can feel magic. Or use it the way you do.'

My eyebrows shoot up in surprise. 'Really?'

'Kit, there's something about you and this prince that just—' her voice trails off. 'Something is clicking in ways it's not done before. I need to do far more research before I can even begin to guess what's going on with him.'

'But you suspect something, right? Olga, listen. If it helps him in any way, you have to tell me.'

She just watches me. 'I'll tell you as soon as I have proof, Kit. But in the meantime, stay close to him. Things have been set in motion I don't think any of us have prepared for.'

'Those Elder Gods?'

'Them, yes. And other things. Go on, get dressed. I'll see you downstairs.'

In the kitchen Thorn's sitting in the same place at the table as he did this morning when we were having breakfast. He's also had a shower and looks clean and free of monster blood. He's dressed in a long-sleeved T-shirt that fits him better and I guess it probably belongs to Aiden. I take my place opposite him and lean forward to look at him. I take my time, looking closely at his face, his eyes, the long dark eyelashes, the blue-green of his eyes, the fact that there are gold specks in one (his left) but none in the other. He watches me, his gaze very steady, as I examine him.

'Freak?' he says.

I nod. 'Freak.'

We smile at each other and I sit back. 'Olga's fixed me up,' I say, pointing to my arm. 'How are you doing?'

'We seem to be asking each other that a lot,' he replies but smiles. This time it almost makes it into his eyes. 'I'm better, thank you. Still shaking but it could be all the sugar Aiden's given me in my tea.'

I look at his hand resting on the table and put mine next to it, palm down.

'Any idea what happened back there?' I ask him. 'With the super-strength and everything?'

'No, I have no idea. I can still see it in my mind's eye. I came out of the coffee shop with our drinks and as I rounded the corner . . . Something in here tore loose when I saw that thing standing over you. I panicked and all I could think of was losing you and I just couldn't let that happen.'

I'll admit it: my heart flutters in a very dramatic and girly way hearing those words coming from him. They are unexpected and sweet – and annoying. I feel my anger flare that he put himself needlessly into danger. And he'd only just survived being either killed or kidnapped by his possessed friend.

'You know I can take care of myself, Thorn,' I say levelly. 'Next time, before doing something stupid like that just stop and think. You *are* a prince of Alba. You have to get home safely. Your family need you to help them. Your whole world is at risk.'

'Really? You were almost killed, Kit Blackhart. Do you realize how close you came to that today? One day your luck will run out and you will find yourself in a world of trouble.'

'Of course I realize how dangerous it was, dammit! I was there, remember? And, honestly, I did not save your ass back in the forest and bring you to London to watch you go mental. You have to learn to pick your fights,' I say, aware of movement near the kitchen door. 'You need to get up north, regardless of what happens to me or Aiden or Olga.'

'Oh, and leave you to martyr yourself for a cause that's not got anything to do with you?' Thorn is standing now and looks royally pissed off. 'Have you completely lost your mind? How do you think I'll live with myself knowing that you sacrificed yourself to see me to safety? What is wrong with you?' He leans forward and jabs a finger at me. 'Are you so desperate to get away from all of this that you are willing to die?'

I jump up, equally annoyed now, ignoring the clatter of my falling chair. 'You know nothing about me! Are we clear? Nothing. I helped you because it's what we Blackharts do. I promised your dying friend to look out for you. But, if you don't want my help, just say so.'

Thorn is glaring at me, arms crossed over his body. I mirror his body language and scowl at him.

'You are being a giant idiot about nothing,' I tell him.

'I don't want to fight about any of this,' he says at the same time.

I narrow my eyes at him and he does the same.

'So, do you feel better?' Aiden asks, walking into the room carrying six pizza boxes balanced on his extended arms. 'I heard some noise and thought we were being attacked again. But no, it's only you lovebirds having a bit of a tiff.'

'Shut up, Aiden,' I grind out. 'Or I'll punch you.'

Thorn just looks at us both and shakes his head. 'You humans are impossible and contrary creatures.'

'Enough sounding like an alien,' Aiden says looking unconcerned about the high emotions flying around the kitchen. 'Both of you, sit down and eat while this is still hot. I've never been a fan of cold pizza. Olga!'

A few seconds later Olga strolls in and sits down at the head of the table while Aiden passes out plates and cutlery. We help ourselves to slices of pizza and eat in strained silence. Aiden seems blissfully unconcerned about everything except the food and I must admit that the gooey cheese and crispy crusts do the trick. I wash it down with coffee and feel happiness spread from my tummy outwards.

'I've been thinking,' Olga says. 'We'll all be going to Scotland to help Aelfric. Do we tell the Fae currently staying at your farm what's going on?' She directs the question to Aiden as he stretches out, patting his full belly.

His face is serious as he nods without hesitation. 'I'd

want to fight for my home country if the time ever came,'
Aiden says. 'I'll let the warden at the farm know we'll be
travelling north. The Fae can choose what they'd like to do.
Those staying behind will be safe on the farm. Those who
choose to join their friends in Scotland will be given food
and whatever else we can spare them.'

'How big an army do we think your dad has?' I ask
Thorn, whose face looks shuttered and moody.

'Both the Courts will come when he calls. That aside,
we have a standing army of thirty thousand Fae. The
barracks are north of the Citadel. If the army's survived, it
and its generals will be with my father.'

I can't even imagine what thirty thousand warriors would
look like.

'What about the other lands in the Otherwhere? Would
any of them send help?'

'I think so. He has good ties with everyone, but it would
depend on what my uncle's offering them. Maybe they'll
decide it's more prudent to sit it out until it's clear which
side is winning.'

What Thorn says surprises me. I'd have thought that if
Aelfric, Alba's high king called for help, the Otherwhere's
rulers would do their utmost to help him. Clearly, I know
nothing about politics.

'But why would they think about helping your uncle
when your father is the rightful ruler?'

I'm grateful to Aiden for asking the question, but hide
my smile when I see Olga huff impatiently at him.

'Guys, Thorn's having a tough time. He doesn't have all
the answers.' She directs a look first at Aiden, then at me.

'Does your dad tell you all the pack business he has to deal with? Kit, does your uncle give you the lowdown on his negotiations when he sends you guys on your missions? I didn't think so. It's the same with Thorn. The best we can do is guess and hope for the best. In the circumstances.'

'Thank you, Olga.' Thorn's expression is pained. 'My father is a very private man, keeping a small group of advisers only. I could only guess at his plans. Even if I did, my guesses would be wrong, as he's pretty eccentric. Prone to hasty decisions.'

'Your dad sounds a real treat.'

'He is the king.' Thorn's expression holds a bleakness I don't like. 'You never question the king.'

Chapter Twenty-Four

Elder Gods: A race of ancient beings that ruled over the Earth As It Once Was. Such was the Elder Gods' terrible reign on earth that human, Fae and dragon came together to bind them and ban them from this world for all eternity. In completing the banishment, the world was split in two parts, forever since known as the Frontier (the lands with no magic), where the humans decided to dwell, and the Otherwhere (lands with magic), where the Fae and other creatures dwell to this day. The Elder Gods, or the Old Ones as they are also known, were worshipped by cults who sacrificed to them unquestioningly, succumbing to terrible deprivation and horrors. The majority of those who belonged to the cults were hunted down and killed although rumours persist that some escaped and are biding their time to bring back the return of the Elder Gods.

The Elder Gods were made popular in more modern times and brought into the public eye by the writer H.P. Lovecraft through his Cthulhu mythos.

From an archived report filed in HMDSDI HQ, 1978

I try to sleep, but each time I close my eyes I see Thorn's angry face and hear his words. I throw my duvet off and go stand in front of the window. If I were at home I'd go downstairs to the gym and exhaust myself by hitting the punchbag until I couldn't move for tiredness. There are no such options here.

I excused myself after dinner and came upstairs to think. I spent ages worrying about my cousins, wondering if they were safe. Knowing them, they would rebel against Aelfric's rules and try to contact me or their dad, for sure. If they were caught, Aelfric could have clapped them in chains. I wondered if he was the kind of guy who'd do that to make a point.

I spent about an hour working the phone, ringing people I knew to somehow make contact with my cousins, but no one'd heard from them for days. My only consolation was that we'd be on our way up north by dawn, which was only a few hours away.

I sneak out of my room, careful not to wake the others, and tiptoe downstairs to the kitchen. I make myself a hot chocolate with milk and chilli, the way my nan always made it. I prop myself up on the barstool, curling my legs under myself, and enjoy the peace and half-darkness, listening to the rain drumming against the windows. I am tired, bone tired, but sleep just won't come. Everything just keeps racing through my head and I want nothing more than to – I don't know, have things laid out in a neat diagram. For stuff to make sense.

'Kit?'

I recognize Thorn's silhouette in the doorway and sit up straight.

'Are you going to shout at me some more?' I ask him, my voice wary.

'No. I don't want to fight,' he says. He suddenly sounds young and somehow vulnerable. 'I'm sorry.'

'Good. I don't react well to being shouted at,' I tell him. 'Would you like some hot chocolate?'

'I'm not sure I've had any before.'

My eyebrows shoot up in surprise but he can't see it in the darkened kitchen. 'Here, tell me what you think.'

He moves closer to the table and picks the mug up, takes a sip. 'Nice. I'd like some, thank you.'

I get more milk out of the fridge and pour it into the pan. 'Have you even been to bed?' I ask him. 'We're going to be up in a few hours.'

'Tried, but I can't sleep. Instead I've been in Aiden's dad's study.' He sees my look of surprise. 'They have a decent selection of folklore.' He offers this by way of explanation and looks a bit sheepish. 'I can't resist a good lore book.'

I bite my cheeks to prevent a grin from spreading over my face. He was being very cute right now but I was still annoyed with him.

'Oh? You find anything interesting?'

'Not really.' He rubs his face, frustrated. 'All my life I've known of the Elder Gods. They are our bogeymen, the things our nannies told us about to scare us into behaving. And now suddenly they are a real threat. Ioric told us as much, as did the chimera.'

'The only thing I know about the Elder Gods is that one of my ancestors was sent North in Victorian times to record their mythologies. Helena Blackhart. I had some of her journals.' I feel a pang of loss. Her journals were the only things that I had that mentioned her magic ability, even if she glossed over it most of the time.

'Her name sounds familiar, but then there have been so many Blackharts who've worked with my family.' He shrugs almost apologetically. 'Lore on the Elder Gods is vague and contradictory at the best of times. What most books do agree on is that it took humans and Fae working together to banish them, in the Time Before Time. Power-mad and hungry for human sacrifice, the Elder Gods demanded untold sacrifices from their followers. There is a temple in Russia where the bones of their victims are buried.'

'Do we know how they banished these guys?'

'Not that I've read or heard of. Perhaps the knowledge is there but not readily accessible to us. Sorcerers and priests would control that kind of information.'

I put the hot chocolate down before him and he catches my hand before I manage to sit down.

'I don't want things to be weird,' he says. 'I know things got out of hand earlier today and I'm worried you think there's something wrong with me. I don't know what happened. I've never felt such wild uncontrolled anger in my life. Really, the only thing I saw was you in danger and it was as if suddenly I was someone, some*thing*, else and I wanted to rip the chimera apart and anything else that might want to hurt you.'

I look down at my captured hand and make no move to try and untangle it from his.

'I understand, I really do.' I take a deep breath, not quite believing what I am about to do. 'Let me tell you something.

This is something I've never told anyone before. Not even my cousins know all of this, okay? My uncle Jamie does, but that's because he was there for part of it. The night I found out about my heritage – who I really am – was the same night my nan died in a house fire. Only, it turns out the fire was started by an Unseelie knight who had a grudge against the Blackharts. At the time I didn't even know who or what the Blackharts were. My birthday was coming up and Nan promised she had something big to share with me. I was so excited. I thought she was going to tell me more about my parents, maybe about where they were buried. Stuff like that.' I move back to my seat and pick up my cooling mug. 'The Sidhe knight had seen her at a farmers' market. He recognized her and threatened her. When I got home from school she was on the phone to someone. She told me that my uncle Jamie would be showing up later that evening, that she was going to tell me about my family when he got there.'

'You didn't know anything about your family at all?' he interrupts, lifting his hand in apology.

'I was very small when she took me away. She changed our names, got false passports. I never knew at all. She was trying to protect me, and didn't want me growing up with the violence and craziness. She wanted me to have a life of my own.'

'And the knight took her dream for you away.' His look is astute and I nod, sighing.

'Yes. A neighbour was up to let his cat out when he looked over and saw our house on fire. He raised the street and I woke to find our neighbour climbing through my window to rescue me. He tried to find my nan but it was too late: her room was ablaze and the ceiling was collapsing. My neighbour basically threw me out of my bedroom window and I managed to cling to the tree outside, then climb down. I had inhaled so much smoke I was sick, then an ambulance rushed me to hospital. I woke up in the small hours of the morning and a stranger was sitting next to my bed. It was my uncle Jamie. He told me who I was. He didn't try and pretty it up. He said: "Your family hunts monsters. And I'm going to show you how to do it too." Then he made me dress and we drove back to the village where I used to live. The house was gone, burned right down to the ground. Jamie gave me a knife and told me to follow him.'

It feels weird talking about all of this. I've not ever told Megan or anyone about that night. It was just me and Jamie under the moonless sky. 'We tracked the knight and his bunch of redcap cronies to a hill outside the village. They were bragging about how they set the fire. How the bitches got what they deserved. I got so angry, I couldn't think straight. I walked up that hill with Jamie, armed with my knife and this growing rage.' I touch that same knife through the fabric of my shirt, where it's nestled against my back. 'I didn't even know how to use the knife properly. Jamie spoke to the Unseelie knight, demanding that his unlawful killing of a human, a Blackhart, be taken to the Courts. The knight just laughed at him. All this time, I could feel this white rage building. They ganged up on us and I killed one redcap outright, the knife into his eye. The others . . . I don't remember much of it but Jamie told me afterwards that this wave of energy spilled out of me, this magic that'd been part of my gift since I was born. I had no idea it was even in me, and it tore down the hill, flattening it – destroying trees and rocks and crushing the Unseelie knight and his redcaps. I woke up in the back of Jamie's car with a nose-bleed, and a migraine so bad I couldn't see properly for days.' I smile grimly in the darkness. 'So I think I know what you mean, Thorn, about getting angry. I'm not saying it's a good thing, or a bad thing. I'm saying we have to be careful and watch out for each other but also trust one another. And know that the other person is capable and strong.'

The silence in the kitchen lengthens but then he nods. 'I didn't know about your family. About your grandmother, I mean. I'm truly sorry for your loss.'

It's difficult not to just shrug it off and be glib. Being glib is easier than facing it all over again. I've tried to forget about that night, about the smell of the smoke and the heat of the flames. Of course it's not possible. For months I struggled to sleep properly.

Jamie found me in the Manor's gym, training in the middle of the night, and decided that if I couldn't sleep, he wouldn't sleep either. He helped build my fitness levels and taught me various new katas and self-defence techniques from different fighting styles. But, more importantly, he showed me how to use my knife and sword properly. He utterly failed to teach me how to use a bow, even a crossbow, and was only marginally more successful when it came to gun training.

I'm an old-school girl, apparently. I'm all about physicality and punching and hitting and swinging around bladed weapons. I practised for hours with the bow but none of the arrows went where I wanted it to. He told me I'd inherited my nan's and mother's stubbornness. It hit me hard then, when I realized what he was saying. I was so focused on the loss of my grandmother; I had never stopped to think that he would be mourning his sister, my father and my grandmother, his aunt. It was a big wake-up call.

'Thank you. She was a special lady, very fierce. I think she would have liked you.' And it's the truth. Only, knowing my nan, she would have had him singing all the time.

'She sounds a remarkable person. It must run in the family.'

I flame bright in the darkness and duck my head, uncertain how to answer this. The kitchen suddenly feels far too small and intimate. I finish the last bit of my hot chocolate and walk over to the sink to rinse my mug before wandering back to my chair.

For a few minutes there's only the sound of the rain and wind outside as he watches me.

'Let's not fight again,' he says, holding out his hand. 'It creates too much of a dissonance.' He taps his head. 'In here especially.'

'Agreed.' I can see a flash of his teeth in the darkness.

'Friends?'

I nod and chuckle. 'Friends.'

The kitchen door that leads to the garage suddenly opens and the lights go on. Olga and Aiden burst in, laughing and looking a bit flushed. They both stop to look at us in surprise, me in my overlarge T-shirt and far too much bare leg and

Thorn fully dressed in a T-shirt and jeans but looking dishevelled.

'Are we interrupting?' Aiden asks, looking at us narrowly, taking notice of how close we're standing, that Thorn still holds my hand. That I may or may not have been crying.

'No,' says Thorn, not bothering to unlock his fingers from mine. 'We're just having hot chocolate. It's customary, isn't it? When one can't sleep?'

'So that's what you're calling it,' Aiden says giving me an elaborate wink. 'That's okay with me.'

'Shut up, or I'll hurt you,' I tell him, taking my hand with me when I move away from Thorn. I look at Olga, who's carrying a large backpack. She's wiping her face and hands with kitchen towel and she looks flushed and pretty in the unforgiving light of the kitchen. They are both wet and out of breath. 'And where exactly have you guys been at this time of night?'

'I had to run an errand and took Aiden with me. I think I've got something.' She hefts the backpack onto the table. 'Check it out.'

Chapter Twenty-Five

I'm probably the only one who isn't thrilled to look at the crumbling manuscript. It's not that it's not exciting, it's just that whatever language it's in, I can't read it – unlike my cousins and the rest of my family, who all have an impressive repertoire of ancient and dead and forgotten languages. Growing up normal, away from having to know folklore and legends and weird esoterica, although it did give me a better grasp of how the real everyday world works, did not help me feel that I was contributing when the family sat down and discussed the pros and cons of cornering an ogre in its lair or the proper etiquette in negotiating a crossing of the Cerulean Sea with its mer-keepers.

We are all crowded around the lectern in the Garretts' study. The manuscript Olga brought back from Emm's rests beneath a softly glowing light, spread wide beneath a plate of glass that has a magnifying effect. I don't know what the manuscript is made of, but I know it's not parchment or paper. I refuse to acknowledge that the texture looks like finely worked human skin.

'This is it,' says Olga, looking at Thorn. 'It's in Peri.'

Aiden notices my blank look. 'Old dead name for the Fae language,' he offers in a stage whisper. I scowl at him and lean closer to look at the squiggles, suppressing a yawn.

Thorn gives her a distracted look; as he turns back to the manuscript, his gaze briefly meets mine and in the depths of those dark eyes of his I see worry.

I watch Thorn rub the scar of the cut above his brow in a gesture I've started to associate with him feeling uncomfortable. 'After Eadric attacked me, my father sent our sages and sorcerers combing the combined libraries of the Citadel and those in all of Alba to find any scrap of prophecy or threat about the future. He sent out word to the other high kings in Afrique, the Americas, to the Dragon Lords in the Far East, seeking any bit of prophecy they could find. It took him almost six years to find a copy of this.'

'What does it say?' Aiden is poring over it, a frown drawing his brows together. 'To me it looks like some drunk decided to make up his own language.'

Oh Aiden. You really should keep your mouth shut, I think to myself, but secretly I have to agree. The markings on the manuscript are so vague and delicate that it takes a lot of eyestrain even to make sense of the curly lines and marks.

'In far more flowery language it basically says that the fate of the worlds rests on the shoulders of the youngest son, that his choice will unleash the forces of creation, blah, blah.' Olga gestures with her cup of tea. 'There is nothing in this so-called prophecy that indicates that it relates to Thorn. It can as easily relate to the youngest son of a swineherd in Pax Australasia.'

'And they assumed this was about you?' I ask Thorn.

'It's the only thing they could find after all that time searching. So they made it fit.' He shrugs.

'That's shite.' Aiden's scowl is impressive. He claps Thorn on the shoulder. 'No wonder you're so uptight.'

For a second it looks as if Thorn's going to lose his temper but then he grins and it lightens his features, and once again he's the handsome Fae prince I secretly enjoy checking out when I think he's not looking. 'It's not been too bad. At first it was, I mean. No one wanted anything to do with me, but my brothers stood by me and beat up anyone who said anything about me, behind my back, or called me names to my face. But then, as I grew older and the world did not go up in flames, people started forgetting, or worrying about it less. Even my father seemed to breathe easier. He started paying attention to my training and listened to my opinions about things. He sent me into the Frontier to live for a while and get accustomed to being around humans. But still, this prophecy, this rumour of darkness remained. I didn't have many friends and I learned very quickly how to fight.'

I remember the photo on the computer back at the Manor, the heavily scowling Thorn aged fourteen, the petulant lips and the disdain in those eyes. Things are becoming clearer now.

'You said the manuscript mentions the Elder Gods,' I prompt Olga, letting my hand trail across the glass.

'It's here,' says Thorn, touching the far right-hand bottom corner of the manuscript where it looks as if something, long ago, decided to try and eat the manuscript. 'You can't see it well, but basically it says: "Woe to the prophesied son as the Elder Gods await his coming. Upon his decision to cast aside what has gone before rests the fate of the world and the Elder Gods' return. They will remake the world as it once was, bringing with them the destruction of fire and water and all will be as new." Pretty dire, right?'

Aiden grimaces. 'It's a ball of crap. It could even mean me. I'm my father's youngest son.' When we all turn to look at him in shock he holds up his hands in mock surrender. 'Hey, I'm fine. I'm not going to go all Dark Lord on you, I swear.'

I lean over and swat him on the arm. 'Stop being a smartass.'

But the tension in the room is gone and he gives me a toothy grin. I shake my head and laugh, catching Thorn watching me. When I keep on smiling, he returns it, but it's not the smile I would have liked. It looks sad and pensive.

'Right, time to get going. We have a long old way to travel today.' Olga makes a swirling motion with her hand. 'Let's ride. Or rather, let's drive.'

Chapter Twenty-Six

Iron: Iron is anathema to fairies and creatures from the Otherwhere. No one is sure how this has come to be, but it's been noted in experiments done in the past that iron burns Fae creatures and drives them insane with pain. Tied with this is the old folklore belief that you circle a graveyard with iron spikes to keep the souls of the dead contained within. Similarly, if you nail a horse-shoe to your door it brings you luck while repelling evil spirits.

From an archived report filed in HMDSDI HQ, 1933

I don't have that much to pack. Most of the clothes I had with me are now covered in blood so I dump them in a black bin bag. I'll have to stop and buy more clothes or try not to get covered in too much blood for the rest of the day. With my backpack over my shoulder, I trundle downstairs and find Thorn in the study, poring over the manuscript.

'Are you ready?' I ask him, dumping my bag on a chair. I go and stand next to him and stare at the manuscript. It's still old and creepy.

In answer to my question he kicks his bag resting by his feet. We really do look like orphans getting ready to run away together.

'How long will it take us to get to . . . ?'

'The Cairngorms? I have no idea. It depends on traffic too.' I tap the glass over the manuscript. 'How much of this do you believe?'

'I'm not sure. None of it, if the world's a logical place. All of it, if you believe the craziness that's happening. Do you believe it?'

'The prophecy feels weird.' I mimic him rubbing his brow, realize what I'm doing and drop my hand quickly. 'Like it was written by someone who knew what prophecies were meant to do, mentioning the One but being purposefully vague at the same time. Does that make sense? No, it doesn't. What does being the seventh son of the seventh son have to do with anything?'

Thorn's trying not to laugh at me and unexpected dimples appear in his cheeks. It looks too cute. I stare back down at the manuscript and shift a bit away from him. Now is not the time to make eyes at him, or anyone else for that matter. We don't know what we're walking into when we get up north and we need to stay focused.

'Old legends and faery tales . . .'

I snigger.

'What? We have faery tales too. Only ours have actual faerie creatures in them. The seventh son is supposed to be the magical son, the one with power, of healing or of supreme luck. So far, I think it's a whole load of lies.'

'Hey, I resent that. I think me saving you in the forest was a decent amount of luck.'

'Okay, maybe that one thing then – that was luck.'

'Do you think we're going to find all our missing families there?'

He sighs. 'I would really like to think so. It would make sense if they were all together, wouldn't it? I think I know the place we're going to. I recall going there when I was younger. It was for an equinox feast. But it was a long time ago.'

I wander over to stare out of the windows. It's still dark outside, with a lightening of the skies in the east, but it looks as if it's going to be a grey rubbish day, with lots of rain.

'What do you think's happened to the dragon?' I ask him. 'I've checked the news reports and no dragon sightings were reported at all. Unless regular humans can't retain the memory.'

'I've not even thought about the dragon,' he says, unexpectedly close beside me. I can feel the warmth of his shoulder next to mine. 'My guess is that he's still around. This weather isn't normal, even for your country. With the dragon in the Frontier, the natural balance of your world is upset.'

'You said that before.' I think about it. 'It's just weird, though. You know, if I had a dragon, I'd use it to create complete havoc. Why hide it?'

'It could be that they're keeping it in reserve. For something bigger.'

'Yeah, that really doesn't fill me with excitement, at all. Listen, Thorn, can I ask you something?'

He looks at me warily. But when he nods, I forge ahead. 'Your magic, how does it work? I've never been able to ask anyone about it, about how it works, I mean. Everything I know I've learned through the journals a sometime-great-aunt left behind. We're talking two hundred years ago, and what's in there isn't much help. My uncle Andrew's been sending me old bits of treatise on magic. But mostly I've been doing these yoga breathing exercises that help me connect with this ball of magic inside, which feels just about here.' I press the space above my diaphragm. 'Sometimes it won't respond, other times I reach and it's there so fast my head spins.' I snap my fingers.

'Magic in the Frontier is very difficult to do.' He leans his forehead against the window as we watch the rain together. 'It's tiring and takes a lot of energy. Legend says that when the Elder Gods were banished and the Frontier was locked away from the Otherwhere, magic left the human world. Humans turned their backs on it to become practical beings. Only a few dreamers believed in magic and managed to practise it. But my magic's tied to my voice, to sound. It's like . . .' He thinks about it for a second. 'It's like when you find the right note in music to make you vibrate, right to your bones. That's what unlocks my magic. It sounds great, doesn't it? But my parents had me tested when I first displayed signs that I had magical abilities as a small child, and compared to my siblings, my magic is rather mundane and impractical. I think, if my magic could knock down mountains, my father would have been relieved. All the fuss would have been worth it. He would have something to show. A remarkable son. As it stands, I can barely teleport a vase across a room. I'm a great disappointment. Everything about me is normal, apart from a random prophecy that may or may not even be based on me.'

I scowl. 'Don't be so hard on yourself. And your dad sounds massively unpleasant. How can he not think any ability you have is remarkable? You're his son!' I shake my head. 'Jamie always says that a commander will find the exact thing a soldier is good at and exploit it. To me it sounds like your dad gave up on you before he even knew who you were.'

I don't expect him to laugh at me, but he does and I take heart that it's not an ugly laugh, more like a chuckle. 'You are very sweet, Kit Blackhart, but I don't think my dad is an idiot. I think he's realistic and has to consider at all times what will benefit the kingdom. I'm the youngest son out of seven very accomplished brothers. I will be expected to marry well when I'm older. My marriage will be political and my life will be about serving the kingdom in one capacity or another. Maybe as an ambassador, and I will likely travel between worlds as I am still young enough to be able to cope with the amount of iron and pollution in your world. It's my duty as his son, and my father knows what I'm capable of. It's the way it has always been. I know that, unlike my brothers, who each manage to excel at something, I'm very . . .' He gestured eloquently. 'Boringly normal.'

I open my mouth to tell him I think it's a load of twaddle when he leans forward unexpectedly and actually kisses me. It's not much of a kiss, just a brushing of his lips against mine for literally two or maybe three heart-stopping seconds, but it takes the wind out of my sails and I gape at him.

'What?' I squeak. 'What was that for?'

'For being a bit crazy, for thinking there's more to me than there really is.'

I roll my eyes at him. 'I think that you've been listening to people say negative things about you for far too long. I think you confuse duty and honour with being subservient and following blindly rather than thinking and leading.'

He leans closer again and I shock myself by taking half a step back. 'No. No more kissing to shut me up.'

'Didn't you like my kiss?'

I flame bright red and have to look away. 'I like your kisses but you're being distracting and so I'm being shouty.'

'Did someone say there's kissing going on here?'

I jump with fright as Aiden walks into the room carrying his own backpack.

'Because no one said there was going to be kissing. I signed up for fighting and punching people in the head but no kissing. Unless I have to kiss Kit, but not you, Thorn. I don't think I'd like to kiss you at all. I hope you're not offended.'

Thorn frowns at him, not at all amused. 'I don't think Kit would let you kiss her,' he says stiffly and a little earnestly. 'I think she'd hurt you, though, if you tried.'

Aiden's grin widens. 'Really? You think she'd hurt me? I've been told I kiss very well.' He turns to me and quirks an eyebrow. 'Would you like me to show you, Kit?'

Before Thorn can rise to Aiden's teasing, I hold up my hands. 'Guys, no more talk about kissing.' I scowl and point at Aiden. 'I'm serious.'

He returns my scowl with one of his own, but his eyes are laughing. 'I'm sorry,' he says, sounding not at all sorry. 'I was just messing around.'

'Do you ever take anything seriously?' Thorn cuts in, sounding annoyed.

'I do. Fighting is very serious business. I'm also very good at it.' He winks. 'Even better at it than kissing.'

'Okay, guys. Two cars, right? Aiden and me in my car and you and Thorn in the Mini. Are we all good?' Olga breezes past us, immaculate and kickass in a black ensemble that makes her look part ninja, part manic ballet dancer, and we scramble in her wake and head out to the cars.

Chapter Twenty-Seven

Traditions and Taboos – Fae: Known records exist
of elaborate family trees indicating marriages between
various houses within the Sidhe caste of Fae. It is,
however, taboo for any Fae, of any of the three
Courts, to reproduce with any other race, specifically
humans. The offspring of such unions are invariably
aberrations that are killed at birth. The parties
involved are ostracized from their community. A
known case of intermarriage dates to 1336 BC (see
Akhenaten, Pharaoh).

From an archived report filed in HMDSDI HQ, 1978

Midday finds us past the Borders. I've got my iPod playing
and the music goes from classics to R&B, to disco, to rock
and metal, folk and acoustic. I'm thankful for Marc's obsession with music because it's easier to talk about the bands
than what's happened. I explain the different styles of music
to Thorn, who seems fascinated by all of it. Some songs
he sings along to and makes up rubbish lyrics to make me
smile.

On long quiet stretches of the highway I catch glimpses of loping creatures shadowing us. These are some of the Fae from the Garrett compound who've decided to travel with us to Scotland. Thorn assures me that he recognizes some of the banners they are trailing. There are Fae loyal to Alba but also, unexpectedly, a large contingent of Free Fae – those who do not see Aelfric or anyone else as their ruler, instead choosing to govern themselves.

I watch Thorn watch them as they flow across the land beside the motorway. None come too close but several of them, some astride whimsical creatures (a giant beetle walking on stilts with a company of young sprites strapped to its back), defy the imagination.

It's become progressively colder still, with the temperature outside reading minus two. I know we'll have to stop at some stage to buy warmer clothes because we're not prepared for weather like this at all. There are news reports of snow in July in high-lying areas in Scotland.

Olga rings my mobile and suggests that we stop off in Edinburgh to get supplies before heading further north. Both Thorn and I readily agree to this. We hit Princes Street and practically empty both of its camping stores of warm clothes. With our stuff piled in the cars we look as if we're heading to one of the Poles or climbing Everest.

At lunch, the restaurant staff are particularly friendly. I'm sure it has something to do with Aiden twinkling charmingly at the waitresses and Thorn looking aghast as the other staff flirt outrageously with him. I load up on coffee and sugar, stuffing my face with chips, a burger and a huge chocolate tart topped with whipped cream. Heaven is food.

While we're eating, Olga goes off to see if she can find the city's matriarch but comes back after about an hour to say that all Fae have gone further north to meet with Aelfric and his growing army. Those who chose to stay behind have battened down the hatches and aren't speaking to anyone. She had to bribe one of the hill boggarts up on Arthur's Seat to tell her that much. I don't blame them for staying out of the madness and sort of wish I could do the same.

We get up to the Cairngorms two and a half hours later, as the sun is setting. I am so tired I can barely move but nothing prepared me for the sheer beauty of the nature reserve. Olga slows down ahead of us and we coast along the roads, just looking at the majesty of the rolling forest and the forbidding snow-covered mountains. Behind us, the army of Fae from the south has grown to an impressive number and I can't even guess how many there are. The creatures we can see with the naked eye number about a thousand alone. Even out here, with no humans to see them, some of them keep up their glamour and stream past the cars in their twos and threes. Noble Sidhe Fae, creatures that look almost human except for their wings, tiny skittering beings with too many eyes and legs, selkies, nixies and a group of phookah lope past. I watch it all with big eyes and grin.

'This is incredible,' I tell Thorn. 'Just look at them.'

His smile is wide. 'Not something you'll see every day in London,' he admits. 'The Free Fae never take sides in any of the battles between the Courts. If they did it would mean that they declare fealty to one of the Courts and they are far wiser than that.'

'They've come to fight to stay free,' I say, watching a

group of very pretty Fae girls stride past me. They are classically beautiful, pointy ears, big eyes and all attitude in their punk outfits. They don't seem to feel the cold. 'They're on their own side.'

My phone buzzes and I answer it. 'Olga says she knows where the campsite is,' Aiden tells me, sounding cheerful. 'It's a well-known site for Fae revels.'

I look at Thorn and mouth, 'Fae revels?' but he gives me a carefully blank look that tells me that he knows too but isn't comfortable talking about it. 'Right, we'll follow you guys,' I tell Aiden, but he interrupts me as I start lowering the phone.

'I've been watching carefully.' Aiden's voice is loud enough really without my having to use the speakerphone. 'And I'm sad to say I didn't see any more kissing.'

'Aiden?'

'Yes, Kit?'

'Shut up before I hurt you.'

My only answer is laughter and Olga's questioning voice in the background asking about kissing, before the phone goes dead.

'Why is he so obsessed with kissing?' asks Thorn. 'Do you think there's something wrong with him?'

I laugh at that and shake my head. 'He's doing it on purpose to annoy you.'

'Well, it's working.'

I know it's bad of me but his unhappy scowl makes me want to hug him.

'He knows that it's working, so you just have to pretend to not care.'

'Hmmm.' Thorn watches Olga's car overtake us on the quiet road and I put my foot down on the accelerator to keep up. 'Also, he is very young and silly.'

'Oh, and you're ancient?' I ask flippantly, still smiling. For a second I worry I've somehow offended him, but then he laughs.

'No, I am not ancient but sometimes I feel it. Especially these past few days.'

'How old are your brothers? Are there big gaps between you?'

'My brothers are all far older than me. I came as a surprise to my parents. They thought they were past child-bearing years when I was conceived. The brother just older than me, the one Eadric has captured, has seen sixty-one summers. My eldest brother is two hundred and eighty summers.'

All right then, Kit – ask questions you're not quite prepared to have answered. 'Two hundred and eighty summers? That's old. Old! Like very old.'

'Not really. My father is over eight hundred summers and my mother is just over five hundred. There was some scandal when they decided to get married. The Courts expected my father to take someone nearer his own age to wife but when they met, it was love at first sight.'

'How did they meet?' I ask, expecting to be told of some exquisite Cinderella ball, but Thorn's grin as he turns to me tells me I couldn't be more wrong. 'My mother rode as a competitor in a tourney to celebrate the first centenary of my father's rule over Alba. It was a big festival with knights from all seven realms. The feasting and jousting went on for weeks. And during that time, my mother beat everyone she rode against. She was crowned champion at the end of the event and when my father handed her the winner's crown, she laid down her sword at his feet and declared herself to him.'

'By declare you mean she told him she loved him?' I can't keep the surprise out of my voice. Gutsy lady!

Thorn nods and grins. 'It was a huge risk. They had only met a few times, had never really spent time alone together and yet they had fallen in love so passionately that my mother risked exile from Alba by declaring herself in front of all his subjects.'

'She placed all her trust in him,' I say, feeling sick. 'He could have turned away, told her that he didn't feel the same way.'

'He could have, but he didn't. He accepted her public declaration, went down on one knee and offered her his sword in return. They were married the next summer.'

Thorn's mum sounded insanely cool and frightening. If she rode in a tourney, it meant she was as tough and strong as any of Alba's knights. Not quite the image I had for the High Queen of Alba.

'Was it only the age thing that worried your Courts?'

'No. My mother was the daughter of a poor nobleman from a small island off the coast of Greenland.' Thorn frowned. 'When she came to court, to be with my father, she brought nothing with her except for a handful of storm-swept islands, a group of fierce warriors and their families. The warriors – they are called Stormborn – refused to acknowledge my father and only took orders from my mother. Of course, rumours started at Court. Most of them were that she was going to kill my father and take the throne. Now and again this rumour would start all over again.' He sighs impatiently. 'Any fool with eyes and a heart has only to be in their presence for five minutes to realize how dedicated they are to each other. Shortly after they were married my mother surprised an assassin sent to kill him and almost died when she was stabbed. The blade was poisoned and death kept her company for two weeks before Istvan found the cure and brought her back.'

'You spoke about Istvan before. Who is he?' How long have I known Thorn now, I wonder, keeping my eyes on the road as we drive. Two, three days? The time we've spent together feels sort of meshed into a tangle of conversations, little sleep and fights, so it's hard to be subjective but I still find it strange listening to him talk about his family and his life in the Otherwhere.

'Istvan's been part of our family for many years. His father sent him to be fostered by mine when he was only a baby. He grew up with my brothers and has become one of my father's closest confidants.' He gives a wry smile. 'But whereas my father is all about the future and the Fae presence in both worlds, Istvan is about our glory days and our past. I sometimes think my father forgets about us, that we need his attention, and so Istvan was the one we went to when we fought or got caught raiding the kitchen gardens or when we were observed kissing a girl.' He clears his throat and flushes. 'Not me, obviously, but my brother Kieran, so I'm told.'

Worried that things are turning a bit maudlin, I keep my

voice light. 'All of this sounds officially insane. Your mum sounds amazing. She must not have been happy about the rumours when she married your dad.'

'Oh, about her trying to take over as high king? There are plenty more stories to choose from. The one that's always been my favourite is that my mum is dragon-kin. She has no small ability controlling fire, which of course makes for lots of gossip.'

'And is it bad being dragon-kin?' I try not to think of the golden scales shining beneath his skin or the animal wildness in his eyes I remember from the chimera fight.

'Fae cannot be with other creatures,' he tells me, after a short painful pause. It takes me a few seconds to realize what he means by *be* and my eyebrows climb up in surprise. I shoot him a wild look and his expression is one of discomfort. Something in his voice, apart from the fact that we are talking about sex and procreating, makes me listen carefully. 'It is forbidden. There are records going back thousands of years showing that unions with other races create terrifying monsters. You call them freaks of nature. So of course you can imagine how much fun they had at Court when Eadric chose to pick on me as the downfall of the kingdom. The rumours about dragon-kin were raised once more and my one hereditary title that comes with being the seventh son of the seventh son took on a whole new meaning.'

I lift my hands off the steering wheel. 'You lost me; I don't know any of your titles.'

'Oh.' He waves airily, the gesture contrasting heavily with his serious expression. 'I have a great many – most of them don't mean much. But the one that gives ammunition to those at Court looking for something to cause trouble over is "Voice of the Dragon".'

'Really? It's a bit pompous, isn't it?'

His wry look makes me laugh. 'I'm a Sidhe noble. We thrive on pompous.'

Chapter Twenty-Eight

We've been driving for what seems hours, deeper and deeper into the Cairngorms without it getting darker, when Thorn points out of the window. I know the place is big, with its forests, mountains, lochs and rivers, but I'm pretty sure we've somehow driven into a pocket between the worlds where it seems to be perpetually damp and twilight.

'We're here.'

I look at the direction he points in and I laugh incredulously. An armoured warrior astride a horse the colour of darkest midnight is racing across the valley to intercept Olga's car ahead of us. They spot the rider too and slow down, bringing the car to a halt in the middle of the road. We stop just behind them and Thorn gets out of the car, pulling on his new padded coat. I follow him as I button up my own coat and go stand next to Olga and Aiden, who looks surprisingly subdued in the presence of the giant warrior mounted on one of the biggest horses I've ever seen. The image in my mind of wisp-thin beautiful warriors on ethereal horses prancing in twin columns along a forest road is banished. This warrior is larger than life and his horse is the size of a truck as they loom over us.

My breath plumes white in front of me, as if I'm exhaling cigarette smoke, and I dig my hands deeper into my coat pockets, squishing my shoulders up against the cutting wind. I huddle next to Olga, who's only wearing a light sweater and jeans, and she puts an arm around me, giving me a quick squeeze.

The rider, in full moulded blackened armour, complete with horned great helm, sits unmoving in the middle of the road. He has a red pennant tied to his lance and for a second I see the strong black outline of a lion rampant on the field of red before the wind ruffles the pennant, curling it back on itself.

'Corash, one of my mother's personal guards,' Thorn says over his shoulder. He steps forward, moving to stand before the giant warrior astride his equally monstrous-looking horse. They face each other for the longest moment, just staring at each other, before the mounted warrior shifts in his saddle.

'Your highness?' The voice is muffled but I can hear the surprise in the warrior's voice. 'Thorn?'

Thorn says something that sounds lilting and amused in his language and the warrior chuckles. He raises a gauntleted hand and lifts the visor, revealing a craggy face and dark eyes.

'Your mother will be pleased to have you safely back with her.' He leans down and grips Thorn's wrist, clapping him firmly on the shoulder. I'm impressed that Thorn takes the greeting without falling over. 'Boy, you led us a merry chase.'

'At least I am here now,' Thorn says. 'How are my parents, Corash?'

'They are well, my prince. Your mother is seething, your father is brooding.' His smile is wide, revealing strong white teeth against a shaggy beard and tanned skin. He turns to look at us, his glance brief, definitely dismissive, and I have to admit that as a group we don't look all that impressive. 'These are the companions you brought with you? Then they too are welcome.' His bow is perfunctory, attesting to good manners. Even if he doesn't think much of us, he isn't about to insult Thorn by saying so. 'Your vehicles will be able to travel some of the distance to the camp at least. Follow me.'

'Corash, before we go on, can you tell me if the Blackharts and the wolves are with my father?'

I catch hold of Olga's arm and she puts a comforting arm round me as I await the answer, my heart thudding in my chest.

'They are. Worse for wear in some instances, but then they aren't Fae trained.' His grin indicates a joke and I close my eyes for a second in relief. 'Come. They were told of your arrival some hours ago. We have warm tents and food ready.' Aiden shares my look of relief as we turn and pile back into both cars. Corash leads us off the road and the Fae still arriving to join the camp make way for him, paying deference to the queen's emissary by dipping their heads.

'What do you think he means by them being the worse for wear?' I ask Thorn after a few seconds.

'Corash likes to tease. He is the joker of the Stormborn family.' He surveys the camp speculatively. 'I don't know what he means, though. Maybe they've been in a battle or two?'

'At least they're here,' I say, feeling my shoulders relax for the first time in days. 'I don't know what I would have done if we'd got here and there was no sign of them.'

'I know.' His voice is low. 'And you'll be reunited soon enough. You've come to the end of your journey.'

I grin and nod. 'And you're back with your mum and dad.'

His smile's not as bright as I would have expected, but I put it out of my mind as I concentrate on not overturning Lolita on the bumpy field. Not only is she able to corner like a dream on a tarmac road, but it feels as if she has inbuilt HGV suspension, or maybe that's just Megan's magic mechanic abilities.

The valley below us is the size of around eight football pitches and is packed with neat rows of thousands of tents. There's a parade ground to one side, where armoured soldiers are doing various drills. I watch for a second, mesmerized by their coordination. Even from up here we can hear the clash of weapons against shields as they form an impenetrable wall of armour and steel.

Cooking fires are lit across the field and the scent of baking bread and stew teases my growling stomach. The wind snaps at hundreds of multicoloured pennants. And, with the light coming from the fires, and lanterns along the walkways, the camp exudes a festive air.

Next to me, Thorn points to the middle of the camp and I spot a pavilion that dwarfs the others. The fluttering pennants flying above it display a gryphon outlined on a field of white.

'My parents' tent,' he says needlessly.

Corash gestures that this is as far as we go by car but instead of escorting us further, he canters off – his task fulfilled, I guess.

As I get out of the car I'm unable to look away from the expanse of tents below. It looks like the Roman army encampments I've seen depicted in books, only far, far bigger than anything I could have imagined. The sheer scale is breathtaking and terrifying, as is the thought of so many laying their lives on the line. In the age of the Xbox, I have forgotten how much more personal war involving hand-to-hand combat has to be.

Then a wave of sound echoes down the valley, and my magic surfaces and wraps around me in response. I feel lifted by it, my heart filling with excitement.

'They're using powerful magics,' Olga says. 'If you look, you can see they've forced a portal open in the Veil – the barrier that separates our world and the Otherwhere. Look. You can see the sorcerers over there.'

I eventually spot three cowled figures with their arms raised, standing in the middle of a stone circle. Olga points and I see another circle of stones a few hundred metres away. Three more cowled figures stand in a similar pose. 'Listen.'

I close my eyes and I feel the vibration of magic under my skin and smile. 'Fantastic,' I say to her and she grins, nodding.

A lone figure is heading towards us up the slope. After a few seconds of staring I recognize my cousin Megan and let out a shout and run at her full tilt. We hug and I'm so happy to see her that I can't actually speak properly. She's laughing and crying at the same time, and it freaks me out a bit.

'Oh, God, Kit. We thought you'd gone missing. We heard about the house.' Her eyes well up and I find myself crying right along with her. We talk at one another not making any sense.

'Why do you have phones if you don't use them?' I end up yelling.

She digs in her pocket and hands me her phone. 'It's dead! None of our stuff works here and we've not been allowed to leave.' Then she spots Thorn and stiffens, stunned. 'You found him,' she says. 'You've had the prince with you all this time?'

I look over at Thorn and beckon him closer to link arms.

'I saved him from being a bunch of redcaps' breakfast,' I tell her. 'Thorn, meet Megan, my cousin. Megan, this is Thorn.'

To my utter surprise Megan executes this perfect curtsy as if she's in some Regency drama, dressed in silk and lace, rather than rugged hiking boots and a Barbour jacket.

'Your highness, I am so pleased to meet you.'

Thorn doesn't seem at all surprised at her curtsy. Instead he inclines his head graciously and takes her hand. 'Miss Blackhart. The pleasure is mine.' He bows over it, touching his lips to her hand before straightening.

Honestly? What is this? A Georgette Heyer novel? My look must speak volumes because Megan steps away from Thorn, still smiling, and I can see tiredness mixed in her mischievous expression.

'I'm just remembering my manners,' she tells me. 'It's rare actually to meet one of the high king's brood, you know? They are A-listers in the Fae world.' She rolls her eyes at me to show that she's joking but there's a streak of something beneath her jokiness that tells me there's more to all of this than she's letting on. What worries me too is that we've only been apart a few days but she looks older to me, and weary. I wonder what exactly they've been through here.

Aiden's voice interrupts my thoughts and I turn to look at him with a start of guilt, having completely forgotten about him, if that was even possible.

'Are you going to introduce us or am I just going to smile at her all evening and no doubt die of unrequited love on a battlefield in the next few days?'

Megan's eyes go wide at that and she looks past me, up at Aiden. I know what guys see when they first see Megan: a tall, very attractive blonde girl with masses of curls, big soft grey eyes and a wide smiling mouth. She carries herself well and, like me, she owns her height, giving her decent poise. There's nothing worse than seeing a tall girl not living up to her tallness.

The biggest thing in the Megan arsenal is this sweet expression that hides the wicked sense of humour, intelligence and stubbornness, easily letting people think they can take advantage of her.

'This is my cousin, Megan,' I say to Aiden. 'Megan, this is Aiden Garrett. You know Olga, of course.'

'So you're the mysterious cousin that Kit's been so keen to get to,' Aiden says, his glance raking Megan's lean form, taking in her no-frills outfit and the sword hilt sticking out over her shoulder. 'I now understand why she was so worried. You look like you need all the help you can get. Being around all these Fae must be very tiring. Have they composed many love songs to your beauty yet?'

Megan's laugh is the lightest thing ever and she grins up at him. 'I've had a few proposals even, but fortunately your brother Shaun's been looking after me.'

Aiden lets out a dramatic groan and clutches at his heart. 'Damn his eyes,' he says in a broken voice. 'You're lost to me already. I will have to turn to Kit to console me now.'

Thorn is looking irritable already and keen to get going.

'I think it's time we moved on. I'm sure we'd all like to get dry and maybe get something to eat.'

With that he starts off down the embankment and we follow in his wake.

'Your father will be so pleased to see you. He has been out of his mind with worry,' Megan says to him after a few paces.

'I very much doubt that, but it is kind of you to say so.' Thorn's smile is friendly but vague, as he focuses on a group of soldiers heading straight for us. Their weapons gleam in the dim light and for a second I feel an air of menace. But then they salute smartly; the leader says something to Thorn in their rapid Fae language and stands back.

'My father sent a guard to escort us to his tent,' Thorn translates expressionlessly. 'Apparently there's concern about discipline in the ranks.'

Megan nudges me to prevent me from asking him what he means. Instead, the five of us are boxed in by the guards, four to each side of us, two each to the front and back, and a further two right at the front ostensibly 'making way' for the small retinue.

It feels more like house arrest than protection. And I'm not a small girl, but these guys in their armour and helms look the business, making even Aiden appear a stripling.

Chapter Twenty-Nine

It takes us time to make our way through the encampment. A lot of people stop to catch a glimpse of Thorn and some call out, welcoming him back. But a lot of Fae hang back and watch, their expressions dark and shuttered.

Those who do call out to him seem to like him well enough, calling him 'the young dragon' or more formally, 'your highness'. The guards don't stop for anyone and the path they clear for us is met with scowls. The soldiers' faces are partly covered by their helmets, but their visible features show no emotion.

I can't shake the feeling that there's something very wrong. I casually drop my hand to the hilt of my sword, as if by accident, but Megan spots it.

'Just relax,' she whispers, so close that her breath tickles. 'We're walking through the Unseelie Court's camp. Suola and Aelfric have been arguing since she got here. Tensions are high.'

The guards do their best to prevent people crowding us, but it seems to make people more determined. I feel a tug on my arm and spin around, but the crowd's closed up again.

Walking through the Unseelie Court's camp is like walking through a nightmare. Creatures of all types surround us and my mind whirls in an attempt to categorize them. Ogres, goblins and a smattering of redcaps crowd around a fire, prodding at something in a pot that looks suspiciously still alive. I see a group of stunning women, Sidhe by the look of them, with fine features, large eyes and razor-sharp teeth. Their diaphanous gowns leave little to the imagination and I expect Aiden to ogle them. But he's watching Thorn's back with an intensity I find worrying.

He catches my eye. 'This place gives me the creeps,' he says. 'Something's not right.'

'I know.'

The guards come to a halt and step aside, making space for a newcomer to approach. He's dressed plainly in something like denim, but his presence is effortlessly commanding. He's handsome like most Fae I've seen, but – for want of a better description – he resembles a romanticized version of a Gypsy prince.

'Where've you been, princeling? We were all very concerned when you went missing.'

For a second I'm shocked by his casual rudeness, but then he does an elaborate bow and when he straightens his expression is impish.

Thorn laughs, and seems to release some of his tension.

'At least someone worried, Istvan,' Thorn says, grinning back at the man, leaning in for a loud thumping hug.

'A lot of people worried, your highness. Your father, but especially your mother. It is good to have you back here and safe.' His gaze takes in our bedraggled and damp group and introductions are made. But although he and Olga have met before, she gives him a frosty greeting:

'If only the king had sent a message, we would have known to come here without delay,' Olga says, her eyes cold. 'Instead we were left in the dark, unsure of the next move.'

'He is the king,' Thorn says, his voice warning. 'And the king is always right.'

Istvan's lips tighten but he nods agreement, though I wonder if I imagine a hint of anger in his eyes. But then he looks past Thorn to include the rest of us.

'Yes! Of course he is.' His voice is just a bit too jovial; I'm not sure what to make of him. 'Come, why are you standing here in the muck and mire? The king and queen await your arrival.'

Istvan gestures and the crowd opens a path. He leads the way, seemingly untouched by the rain and mud we're slogging through.

'So that was Istvan,' Thorn says to me as we fall in behind him.

'He seems pleasant. Happy to see you,' I say.

'Istvan was my tutor. He took on the role after the incident with Eadric. Without him I'd have been sent to a monastery for my schooling.'

Megan is quiet and I'm not used to it, so I wonder what exactly I'm walking into. I touch her wrist in Morse code. *Okay?* I ask. She shakes her head and looks bleak.

Our silent communication goes unnoticed by everyone except Aiden. Then we come to the royal pavilion itself. Here a cadre of soldiers with the most ornate armour yet stand guard, facing blankly outwards. Their gazes don't even flicker towards us when we come to a messy huddle in front of them and push into the tent.

Inside, the tent isn't richly furbished and the man and woman waiting for us look as if they've not slept in weeks. Aelfric, High King of Alba, dominates the space. He has a lot of charisma, I decide, but there is a coldness as he looks us over that I do not like.

Thorn's mother, Dina, is taller than me, with striking Nordic features. Like her husband she's dressed casually and she looks every inch the badass warrior I expected to meet. For the longest moment we all stare at each other then Dina smiles, brightening the atmosphere.

'Thorn,' Dina's voice is raw with emotion. 'Thanks to the gods you are safe. We were so worried.' She doesn't give him a chance to speak and wraps her arms around him. 'Dear stupid boy. What were you thinking, running across all of Alba? You could have been killed.'

'It's not like I had much choice,' Thorn says, annoyance tinging his voice. 'None of the gateways belonged to us any more and my men were tired. We kept running to stay alive.'

'That was reckless, boy.' Aelfric's voice, like him, is cultured, rich and lovely to hear. 'Running to the Frontier, of all places. You caused us no small amount of trouble. Dina, let the boy go. You're strangling him.'

Thorn is still while his father inspects him. There is nothing on King Aelfric's face that indicates he's impressed or unimpressed by what he sees. Then he nods and Thorn's shoulders lower marginally.

'You have gathered quite the group,' Aelfric says, examining each of us in turn. 'One of Garrett's pups, a Kassan and you – what exactly are you, my dear?'

I'm startled to realize he's talking to me. 'I'm Kit, your majesty. I'm a Blackhart.'

He looks at Megan. 'Interesting family, these Blackharts. Is there no end to your talents? Be at peace, little fighter. You are among friends here.'

My hand drops from my sword hilt and I smile weakly at him. Dina is still all about Thorn and she's got her arm around his shoulders, speaking softly and rapidly. Megan shifts next to me.

'We need to talk,' she whispers. 'But not here.'

She leans against me, her arm wrapping around my waist, hugging me close. It feels so good having her next to me that for a second I'm so relieved I almost don't care why she's being cagey.

'Istvan? Let the ministers know we are ready for the war council.' Aelfric nods towards Aiden. 'Your father has been informed that you are here. He is on his way.'

Istvan has been watching all and steps forward, bowing quickly before leaving to carry out Aelfric's orders. The queen gestures to one side of the tent, where there are low tables and cushions.

'Please, everyone, sit. The council is scattered across the camp. It may take Istvan some time to locate them all.'

She grasps Thorn's hand as she leads the way and I'm struck by how alike they look. And how close they seem. I feel a pang of loss but suppress it, focusing instead on Megan.

Olga lingers to talk to Aelfric for a moment and from

their manner, I suspect that they know each other from old. Occasionally I forget that Olga is someone to be reckoned with, and has a foot in both the Otherwhere and the Frontier.

Megan nudges me, nodding towards Aiden where he's hovering near the flap, a look of discomfort on his face.

'How did you meet up with him?' she asks me. 'We've been going insane trying to get word to him and you for days now but every messenger we sent was blocked by Aelfric or Istvan. It's like we've been prisoners more than valued guests.'

I look at Aiden, giving him a wink when he notices us looking. 'He was at Olga's, looking for help to find his dad. It's been tough on all of us, not knowing where you guys were.' I lean back against one of the cushions. Fatigue hits me out of the blue. 'I am so tired, Megan. We've been on the run non-stop since the house disappeared. How did we not know that a dragon exists in this world?'

Megan scowls at me. 'Let's not go there,' she says quietly. 'Not here, anyway. Kyle's been going nuts trying to figure out what happened and how they brought the thing over.'

'Where are they?' I ask her. 'I thought they'd be with you.'

'Marc's not great. He got into a bad situation during one of the battles we had with Eadric's lot. His arm's broken and they had to stitch up a cut he took to his leg. He's in our tent and giving everyone hell, refusing to let any of Aelfric's healers anywhere near him. He's freaked out by their magic.'

'But he's fine around me.'

'You're family. They're not. And they are strange, Kit.'

She twirls her finger next to her head. 'They—' She breaks off and smiles as the flap opens and a large man walks in.

'Aiden's dad,' she says. 'I thought he was physically going to tear apart the guards manning the perimeter of the camp when they wouldn't allow us to leave. All on the strict orders of Aelfric.'

'So you guys *have* basically been held captive?'

I turn to watch the tall man fold his son into a bear hug. I can't hear what they're saying but it looks how I'd imagine a reunion with Aiden's dad would be. There's lots of physical contact and punching and slapping in a way that's somehow both macho and parental.

'You could say that, except in everything else we've been treated really well.' She ticks off on her fingers. 'Food, clothing, hospitality. But no contact with the outside world.'

'How did Marc get hurt, then?'

'We joined a scouting party that went into the Otherwhere, thinking we could slip away and find a way home, but we got involved in a running battle with one of Eadric's scouts.' She stares at me intently. 'Between Aelfric and his brother, the gateways between our world and the Otherwhere are sewn up tight. We were lucky to get back here even.'

Chapter Thirty

I try and question Megan more but she shakes her head. 'More later.' She jerks her head in the direction of Thorn and his mum. They've been talking non-stop, and from Thorn's demeanour he looks to have been thoroughly questioned.

'He is really pretty.' Megan's voice is soft and low. 'What's the story there?'

I look at her in surprise and follow her gaze. Thorn notices us staring at him and I grin at him, giving him big eyes. His smile back is happy and relieved.

I give her a brief recap of how we got to the camp. 'And now I'm wondering if we should be here at all,' I say to her. 'Even if I want to help Thorn.'

'Look, Aelfric told us that our dad knows we're here,' she says. 'And if he knows, then it should be okay. I kinda understand why Aelfric's keeping us here. He wants to limit information leaving the camp. The only way you leave the camp is through those gateways his sorcerers control. And, of course, he controls them.' She sighs. 'There is no way out. The guys patrolling the perimeter aren't pleasant and any deserters they come across are fed to the wyverns.'

When she sees my curious look she shrugs. 'Nasty smelling things that are partial to a bit of human meat.' She shudders.

'Why are we sitting here?' I ask her. 'Can't we go see Marc and Kyle?'

'Not until your boyfriend's mum tells us it's okay to go.'

'What?'

'Etiquette, Kit. We can't come and go without Dina or Aelfric's say-so.'

'That's stupid,' I say, annoyed. 'I'd really like to see my cousins and meet Aiden's dad and his brothers.'

I stand up and she follows suit.

'I'm off to go check on my cousins,' I say to Thorn, doing my best to ignore his mum's look of surprise at my intrusion on their talk. 'My cousin Marc's been hurt and I want to make sure he's okay.'

Thorn excuses himself to his mum and walks towards me.

'I'm sorry to hear that. I can arrange an escort for you.'

'Don't be silly,' I say with a laugh. 'We're capable of looking after ourselves.'

'I'll come with you, then, to make sure.' His glance slides to Megan, who's trying not to look worried at my rude behaviour and flouting of etiquette. 'I'll be a moment only.'

He turns and walks back to Queen Dina, ignoring the councillors who have entered the tent and are now in discussion with his father. His mother's looking at me as he speaks and I do my best to keep my face impassive.

'We are in trouble now. Mama is not at all happy with Thorn running off with you again,' Megan breathes. 'She's glaring like she wants to eat you for dinner.'

'Thanks, that makes me feel safe,' I whisper back and jerk with fright when Thorn comes up next to me.

'Come, I'll escort you to your tent.'

The camp here is as busy as the Unseelie camp, but there's less sense of menace. Even so, I keep my hand on my sword hilt and feel eyes assessing me as I walk next to Thorn. I know that compared to some of the warriors we've seen I look less than impressive, but Jamie's fond of saying that image only counts for so much.

Megan leads us to a tent about the size of my bedroom at the Manor, which houses three cots. Marc's standing upright with Kyle's help in the middle of the tent, struggling to put on a clean shirt. They look up when we come in and are clearly delighted to see me.

I admit to squeaking and acting like a real girl. But there is no reason for Marc to let out quite the exaggerated 'oophh' as I connect with his chest. Then I'm in a Kit sandwich, hugged between Megan, Marc and Kyle.

'You got shish-kebabed,' I say to Marc, pulling back and looking at him. 'Jamie won't be impressed.'

Marc's handsome face pulls into a grimace. 'Don't remind me. Megan's already working out a whole new exercise regime for when I'm better.'

I am relieved to see him okay, even if he's bruised and full of holes. It also looks as if he's lost some weight, like Megan. Kyle, on the other hand, is still a hundred per cent himself, even if he looks not to have slept for a while.

'Don't get me wrong, Kyle, I'm happy to see you, but you're not okay, are you?'

The smile he gives me is sweet but anaemic. 'I'm on

logistics detail,' he says, keeping his voice low. 'I'm keeping track of the network ferrying supplies and goods across to the two sides of Aelfric's army. I'm exhausted. I don't think I've slept since we stumbled across everyone here.'

'Are you going to introduce us at some stage?' Marc asks, nodding to something behind me. I turn to find Thorn standing behind me, watching our reunion.

'I'm so sorry. Thorn, meet my cousins. Kyle, only about a month younger than me, but far more clever. Then this is Marc, Megan's twin. He likes to think he's the boss of us. Or we let him think that.'

There's much friendly greeting and the tension hanging over us all lightens for a moment.

Thorn turns back to me and his smile is sweet. 'I've got to go. My mother wants me where she can see me. For a little while at least. My brothers are on their way back from Alba and she wants me there when they get back.'

I nod and walk with him towards the exit.

'Your cousins are very fond of you,' he says, pausing for a moment.

'Family,' I say, shrugging. He huffs out a laugh and nods.

'I know. Can't live with them and can't live without them.'

As I turn to leave he catches my hand and runs his long fingers through mine briefly, before letting my hand drop. 'Stay out of trouble, Blackhart,' he says earnestly. 'Promise me.'

I grin and shove the hand he's just touched, the one that's tingling, deep into my jeans pocket. 'No promises in times of love and war, Thorn, don't you know anything?'

He shakes his head, still smiling, before ducking back out. Four soldiers stand outside the tent flap and form up around him as he leaves.

I waste no time getting back to my cousins. Marc's taken his seat on his bed and he's wearing his shirt, but it sits awkwardly because of the bandages. Overall, though, he looks more steady.

'Really?' I say, raising my eyebrows. 'Forays into Alba? *More* than one?'

Both Megan and Marc have the grace to look uncomfortable.

'They've been going in and coming back with information about Eadric's movements. Carrying dispatches and stuff.' This comes from Kyle, who glares between his siblings in an uncharacteristic display of anger. 'You try and tell them that it's not safe, because they sure as hell don't bother listening to me.'

'Without that information . . .' Marc waves his hand. 'We'll be going in blind when the time comes for attack.'

'But it doesn't mean you have to go, does it?' Kyle says fiercely. 'Aelfric has his foresters and his scouts out doing recon. You guys are just doing it because you're bored.'

'Kyle, we've been through this. We've been trained by Jamie; we know to look for different things. Has anything we've brought back not been golden?'

Kyle looks as if he's struggling not to speak his mind and shakes his head. 'Dude, you aren't listening, are you? Eadric's army is everywhere now in Alba. He has thousands of supporters. You have to stop and listen to what I'm saying here. Our home ground is here, we have the advantage here, not in Alba. Jamie's trained us as well as he can but we are still just kids.'

Marc's scowl shuts Kyle up pretty quickly. It's the first time I've seen Kyle stand up to his elder brother. I'm not entirely sure Marc's appreciating it right now.

Chapter Thirty-One

'Kyle, listen, I know you think we're mad doing this . . .'

'No, Marc, you listen for a change. I sit here and I compile all the data that's coming in. I am seeing a far bigger army in Alba than Aelfric has any hope of beating with his current forces on such short notice. I read the reports coming in from the scouts. I hear about the devastation Eadric's army is causing in Alba. Aren't you worried that neither Suola nor the Sun King have sent their entire combined armed force to Aelfric to use as needed? The two most powerful rulers in Alba, not counting Aelfric, are sitting on the fence. They are going to wait to see how the war goes before they decide who to support.'

'Which is why it's so crucial for us to go out there and to send back as much information as we can about all of this.' Marc grabs his younger brother by the shoulder. 'If Alba falls to Eadric and his cultists, what do you think will happen to us? Eadric has to be defeated or we will all be killed or become slaves to a raving lunatic and the gods he's bringing back.' Marc rakes his fingers through his hair. I've never seen him this unsettled and it puts me on edge. 'This isn't a domestic tiff Aelfric's having with his baby brother. This is all-out war, Kyle. I know you want to keep us safe, but if we don't fight now, to stop this, what are our chances of stopping this madman when he breaks through that gateway with an army of sorcerers and beasts that've not walked this earth for thousands of years?'

Megan draws me away to where a table of refreshments stands. She pours me a goblet of something rich and herby and pours one for herself.

'What exactly is Marc talking about?' I ask Megan, trying not to let my voice rise in panic. 'It sounds like you guys know far more than we do about this whole thing. Fill me in.'

'What we know is this,' she says, keeping her voice low. 'Aelfric's younger brother, Eadric, is the head of a – what do you call it? Like a doomsday cult, okay? They believe Aelfric's brought the kingdom of Alba low, having the Fae hide from humans and not taking their rightful place in the order of things. The Fae are superior to humans in every way, or so they say. The Fae have magic, they have longevity, they are immune to a lot of diseases that humanity has succumbed to over the years. They are the stronger race. This is what they believe completely. They also believe that by bringing back the Elder Gods, who will remake the world into the place it once was, they will once more rule the world.'

'And what happens to the humans? To us?'

'Those few left that they allow to live will work to do their bidding. As slaves.'

I want to laugh. It is absurd, as insane a plan and unfeasible as any Bond villain's mad idea I've seen on TV.

'Are you serious?'

'Like a bad case of death,' she says, taking my goblet away from me and refilling it.

'But it's crazy.'

'That's Eadric for you,' she says, watching her two brothers still arguing. 'They've been at each other's throats since we got here,' she says. 'We tracked the thing killing the livestock in the area. It was a bloody griffin, can you believe it? It got loose from its pen and its caretaker's not been able to lure it back. We came across Aelfric and his lot within hours of getting here and we've not been able to leave. It's been a nightmare. The gateway is controlled by those sorcerers you saw when you were coming in. No one comes or goes without strict checks and permissions. More and more wounded Fae are coming through too with soldiers returning from Alba and Aelfric's letting them all in. We've been getting reports on Eadric's war bands going round Alba. They are trying to convert more of the Fae to their cause.' She looks serious. 'Things aren't good, at all.'

'Has Aelfric considered asking for external help?' I say, watching the two boys do their best to keep their voices low. 'How about getting in touch with the guys from the Spook Squad?'

Megan shakes her head, frustrated. 'No, we've tried to convince him. Aelfric is insisting that he'll be able to contain all of this. He's been in touch with my dad and so Mum and Dad both know that we're here. They're working with Aelfric to get some of the New World Fae ready to assist in Alba.'

'So your dad's okay with you being a prisoner here?' I

challenge her. 'Because no matter how we try to spin it, that's what this is. Even if Aelfric's using you to help him scout Alba.'

'I don't think Dad knows that we're not allowed to leave. Marc was with Aelfric when they spoke. Dad had this mirror on him that connected him to Aelfric so Marc could see and hear what they were saying and doing. Dad is monumentally pissed off that Aelfric kept all of this from him. He sent us here to check out cattle mutilations, thinking one of the local ogre tribes was getting a bit overzealous, but instead we found a deposed king and his army.'

I try to contain my anger. 'Do you know you have a traitor in the camp?'

'What are you talking about?' Marc says, turning to me, somehow managing to argue with Kyle and keep an ear on my conversation with Megan.

I sigh and rub my face. 'When we went to the trolls for information this guy was there, Ioric Brightwing. He tried to kill me and convince Thorn to go away with him.' I hold up my hand for silence under their sudden barrage of questions. 'But he didn't do it on purpose, or rather, not out of free will. Someone with really strong magic got to him.' I tell them what happened in the troll cave and watch them pale. 'Whoever this sorcerer is, he made Ioric kill himself in front of us. It was horrible.'

I sit back and watch them digest this. I sip the awful wine of which Megan seems so fond. I miss coffee and may have to break out of the camp to go and buy some, even if it gets me thrown into whatever prison camp Aelfric has set aside for deserters.

'And no clue who this person is?' Kyle asks me. 'Brightwing couldn't tell you at all?'

'No. He tried.' I gesture to my throat. 'Every time he tried to speak about the guy his throat closed up.'

'But he told you where Aelfric's camp could be found? Just like that?' Marc is scathing. 'He could have been lying through his teeth!'

'But why?' I ask him. 'He – not Ioric, but this other guy – definitely wanted us here otherwise he would have stopped Ioric from telling us that too.'

'If he attacks the camp, he kills everyone.' Kyle walks towards the tent flap and quickly checks we're still unobserved. 'If this guy, whoever he is, knows Thorn is here, along with all of Aelfric's council and his sons, it means they can take out the camp in a massive attack. They can basically win this war right here.'

'But does he want to kill everyone?' I ask Kyle. 'In the caves he tried to make Thorn go with him, but Thorn refused.'

'So it has something to do with your boyfriend?' Megan asks me and I give her dead eyes for calling Thorn that.

'I don't know!' I grind out, annoyed. 'It feels like I know nothing and it's driving me nuts. Can I resign from the family yet?' I ask, feeling miserable.

Kyle walks over to me and folds me into a hug, dropping a kiss on my temple. 'Dude, you look like shit,' he says, ignoring Marc's frown at the swear word. 'When did you last have a decent night's sleep?'

I prod a finger in his chest. 'Look who's talking, *dude*.'

We all take a few seconds to compose ourselves before Marc leans forward, wincing as he jars his arm.

'This is what we know: Eadric's gathered together a huge, and I mean huge, army. He drove Aelfric from the Citadel and captured one of his sons, I think he's called Kieran? So Aelfric escapes here, to safety, and Eadric sends him a message: join with me or Alba will be destroyed in the coming raising of the Elder Gods. Aelfric sends a messenger back and tells his baby brother to go get knotted.' Marc sits up. 'Shenanigans ensue.'

I close my eyes. 'So, these Elder Gods?' My question is addressed to Kyle because if there's anyone who knows, it will be him. He loves myths and legends and has this funky eidetic memory that freaks me out. 'How bad are they, exactly?'

'Pretty bad. You know the flood myths we have the world over?'

'Like in the Bible,' Megan adds helpfully, trying to hide her smile. When Kyle's got the floor explaining something he loves the attention and goes all out.

'Yes, but remember that these stories can be found everywhere, literally all across the world. Every story agrees on the flood – masses of water with lots of people dying. But behind that story is one about humans and Fae working together for the first time in their short history. They come together in an act of desperation and work together to banish the Elder Gods. Thousands of Fae and humans were dying to appease the bloodlust of the gods. Eventually, someone figured out how to banish them through a ritual that would lock these bad boys away for all eternity. But what no one took into consideration was the effect this Sundering would have on our world. We had the physical manifestation of it in the shape of a flood, but far less noticed, at first, was the splitting of the world into the seen and unseen world. When it became apparent what was happening, the Fae chose to move into the Otherwhere and the humans stayed here, in the Frontier.'

'So, in other words, we tore our world apart to get rid of these gods. And they were very bad gods, right?' I say, just to be clear. 'Not just messing around and having funsies with their adoring followers but truly wicked and vile?'

'They were so bad that their own dedicated followers led a revolt against them.' Olga pushes her way into the tent, startling us. She's wet from the constant rain outside but she seems healthier than I've seen her look since we met up a few days ago. Her limp is also far less pronounced. In fact, curiously, I've never seen her look more alive. 'I was worried that I'd managed to miss you guys somehow,' she says, smiling at Marc and Kyle. 'This camp of Aelfric's is huge.' She nods her thanks at Kyle as he hands her a spare stool and drags it so that she forms a circle with us. 'The Elder Gods were truly wicked, demanding more sacrifices, more debauched rituals as time went on. As fear spread, as more people prayed to them, their power grew and grew. Their followers exulted in doing their every bidding. There was a scale of genocide the new world has yet to see. Clans and families were slaughtered to a babe. Tribes and nations fell by the wayside.'

'You speak as if you were there,' Kyle says, reminding me that Olga's not entirely human and far older than she looks. But I somehow doubt that she is old enough to have seen the world be reborn. 'Not that I'm implying anything by it!'

Olga's eyes glint mysteriously as she leans forward, resting her elbows on her knees. 'I know I'm an older woman, Kyle, but how old do you think I am? As a witch I age slowly but not *that* slowly.' Her grin is infectious and I give a short laugh, unable not to laugh a little at Kyle, who looks mortified. 'But, it's a valid question.' She holds her hands open and I swear I can see a mini Earth swirl between her hands for a moment before she flicks her fingers as if she's shaking water from them and the glamour disappears. 'My real grandfather was there, though. So was my great-grandfather and I grew up with them telling me these stories about the gods and the followers who turned their backs on them. When they both died, Adena Kassan adopted me and I was raised by her and her grandfather, Emory Kassan. I've mostly lived on earth and in this plane for the past five hundred years or so.'

I work hard at it and my jaw doesn't drop. I take another look at Olga and wonder how anyone that old can look as young as she does without their eyes betraying them. Even Thorn's mum, as stunning as she is, shows her real age in her eyes.

'So, listen,' Olga says earnestly, dropping her voice, and we lean closer. 'I've been talking to Aelfric about his next step. One of his foresters reported a lot of activity around the Great Sister Lake.' Olga waves her hand. 'That's in Russia, somewhere. Uhm, Lake Baikal, I think? And so in the morning he's taking his army and attacking. From Eadric's movements, we think that whatever is going to happen is happening there. Aelfric's got his sorcerers working their magics now to open a portal to take his army to the shores of the lake. He's preparing to send an emissary to the Perun to ask permission to send his army across.'

I raise my eyebrows in question at the unusual word and Kyle quickly fills me in. 'The Perun is the leader of the Free Fae in Russia.'

'Is there anything special about this lake?' I ask Olga. 'Why is Eadric bothering with it?'

'It is possibly the oldest lake in the world,' Kyle cuts in. 'It means that if they open the portal to bring the Elder Gods through, the lake will be able to absorb the overflow of magic they'll be using. And it's deep – deep enough to hold the Elder Gods as they once again grow accustomed to being here.'

Olga's nodding in agreement. 'Yes, to everything Kyle's just said. Something else to consider, though, is that the lake in the Otherwhere also holds the temple ruins where the Elder Gods were sent to their prison. The place is called Black Island.' When she sees our blank looks she shakes her head mournfully. 'How do you not know this? What do they teach you in school these days?'

'Not obscure mythology, that's for sure,' I mutter under my breath.

'Excuse me?' There's a tapping at the tent flap and a young squire pops his head into the tent. 'Miss Blackhart? The engineer's asking to see you. Something about one of your designs for the repeater crossbow . . . ?' His voice trails off uncertainly.

Megan sighs and stands up, giving me a quick hug. 'Don't disappear,' she tells me. 'I'll be back in a bit.' She grabs her coat. 'Kyle, come with me so you can talk materials and labour at them.'

Surprised, I watch them leave and turn my gaze to Marc. 'What was that?'

'Your cousin,' he says, his voice telling me that he's somehow divorced himself from his twin, 'has been having the time of her life designing weapons. She has the generals eating out of her hand. The engineers are ready to declare her a saint.' He considers his words. 'I'm not sure if there are Fae saints, but if there were, she'd be canonized.' Marc sighs and gingerly moves from sitting to horizontal, stretching out on his bed.

'Are you okay?' I ask him, pushing the dark curls from his forehead. 'You're not looking too sexy.'

His lips twist up in a smile. 'Thanks, I'm not feeling too sexy. My arm is killing me and my leg feels like it's on fire.'

Olga frowns at him. 'Have you had Aelfric's physicians look at you? They are very well trained in healing.'

'I'm not letting any of them touch me with their creepy magic,' he says, sounding far younger than his actual twenty years. 'I've seen what they do to the prisoners they bring back from Alba. I don't want to be subjected to that.'

'I've been given my own tent,' Olga says. 'My pack and all my medicine is there. Do you want me to take a look?'

'She fixed my arm,' I tell him. 'She's good people, Marc.'

He narrows his eyes at us both and nods. 'Okay, I'll come with. But first we go to Aelfric's tent and sit in on his council of war. The guy is a nutjob and he's going to get a lot of his people killed. Then you can fix my arm.'

Olga's eyebrows rise in surprise. 'Fair enough. But remember to be careful what you say about Aelfric, Marc. You can't be sure who's listening.'

I help Marc stand but Olga easily shifts her weight under his arm and supports him. 'Just lean on me,' she says. 'I'm stronger than I look.'

I pull my hoodie over my head and squelch through the rain. Even the wooden boards laid down to prevent feet from getting too wet have warped and sunk into the mud. We're halfway to the main tent when I realize why I feel so vulnerable. I left my sword behind and it's so unlike me, I swear under my breath impatiently at my absentmindedness.

'I left my sword,' I say. 'I'll see you guys in a few seconds.'

I dash back and strap it to my back. I check my knife and wonder about my pistols but it's so wet out, even if I get them loaded with dry powder, the chances are that they wouldn't fire. I tuck them under Megan's bedding before I jog out again.

It's not raining as hard any more and I slow my jog to a brisk walk. There are soldiers in armour everywhere, and I take the chance to observe them. Although it's wet and cold, everyone seems in positive spirits. There are a lot of smiles and nods in my direction which I'm happy to return, but I can't help but wonder who here is the turncoat and why they could possibly want the return of these Elder Gods.

Chapter Thirty-Two

Magic – humans: Very few humans are born with
magic or any type of magical ability. Please note that
by this we exclude people who have the ability to cast
spells – spells are recipes that, if followed correctly,
and with the correct intent, can be made to work by
the most talentless practitioner. Humans who have a
noticeable magical ability are anomalies. Genetic
research shows that somewhere in the human's family
tree there had been congress with a Fae creature,
which is, of course, forbidden by the Fae themselves.
It is advised to treat such humans with great care as
their magic can be benign or flare up and cause great
disaster (see Hindenburg Disaster 1937).

From an archived report filed in HMDSDI HQ, 1978

The guards outside the main tent see me coming and uncross
their spears to allow me to enter. Stepping into Aelfric's
tent makes me shiver in relief. Far warmer than the outside,
it's dry and comfortable, but it's also full to capacity. Marc
looks up from where he's standing with Olga and three

muscular Viking types of extraordinary handsomeness. These have to be Thorn's brothers, I decide. It's not difficult to recognize him in them. They are bent over a pile of maps and look super-intense and serious so I don't walk over to introduce myself.

Olga's in deep conversation with Dina, who is listening intently. I catch Dina's eye and she gives me a brief nod, which I take to mean that although I'm not her favourite person in the world, she's okay with me being here.

I move past groups talking and it's interesting to note that their clothes are a mixture of modern – contemporary jeans and coats – and medieval tunics and hose. They have friendly smiles for me, and I get the impression they all know who I am, yet I have no clue who they are.

I make my way to the pile of cushions and sink down with a grateful sigh. I want nothing more than to curl up on a bed and sleep for a week but I suspect it won't be possible.

Then I spot Thorn and Istvan a few paces away. They're standing close together and Thorn is listening to the older man. Istvan is serious and his gestures emphatic. Thorn's nodding intently and I wonder what exactly they're discussing that's captured their attention so entirely.

The storm outside's grown in force again and the lights cast by the lamps flutter wildly, casting peculiar shadows in the tent. One of the shadows unfurls from the darkness and curls sinuously up and around Istvan, resting across his shoulders. He shrugs and the shadow disappears as quickly as it appeared.

Did I really just see that? My heart jumps in fright.

I shift so I can watch them and my movement draws Istvan's attention. I don't turn towards them directly, instead watching out of the corner of my eye. I'm reluctant to call my magic forth to spy on them, so this will have to do. I catch the look Istvan gives me, which feels like a punch in the gut. It's not friendly or curious or anything normal. It's the look a dog with a bone gives when he wants you to back away if you like having fingers. His eyes are dark in the shifting light of the tent and whereas I had thought him handsome, I now see something almost feral in his features.

Still watching me, he says something to Thorn, and as the words leave his mouth, it's as if he exhales dark black smoke, which hangs in the air, before dissipating around them.

Am I seeing things? I will Thorn to turn and see me, but he doesn't seem to see anyone except Istvan.

He's nodding again and his features look slack, his eyes drowsy. I stand and move towards them but only manage a few steps. Magic blazes across my skin as I walk into an invisible barrier. I let out a gasp and look down at myself. I'm cocooned in fire, flames covering me from head to toe. There's no heat, but I can't move my legs. I hold up my hands to my face and watch in shock as the ghostly flames run up my hands to play between my fingers. Through them I can clearly see Istvan's calculating expression. I'm panicking now, wondering why no one is running to help, but maybe they can't see the flames? He touches Thorn's arm, still murmuring to him.

The furl of blackness reappears on his shoulders and snakes across Istvan onto Thorn, where it briefly hesitates before soaking into Thorn's skin. It's only visible for a second before it's gone and Thorn looks his usual self, if drowsy.

Whatever spell Istvan's cast, the Fae prince seems completely out of it. He can barely keep his eyes open. The men start moving, but it's slow because Thorn can't seem to make his feet move properly.

I open my mouth to shout a warning but my throat is dry and aches badly. I reach out in desperation, swallowing against the band now constricting my throat and try to scream.

The satisfaction on Istvan's face when he looks at me almost chokes me. He lifts a hand towards me in a pulling gesture and I feel the wildness of the magic nestled inside me respond to him. He reaches deep into the secret place where I've worked so hard to keep the tainted magic locked away. This pit is where my real power and magic lie, the stuff I'm so scared of, the stuff I know can destroy. Here, then, is the real well of magic I inherited the night I tore down the hill outside our village, crushing the Unseelie knight and his goblins.

I've not called on it since and it's grown, a large reservoir of dark slick power and it answers Istvan's summons with an eagerness that makes me sick.

I sense his surprise at finding my secret, but his look is triumphant. He gestures extravagantly, as if scattering some-thing into the air. And as he does, my magic rips from me in the form of blinding, searing heat. I scream as it ignites the ghostly flames Istvan summoned, and then pain is all I know.

I'm distantly aware of shouts and screams. I claw at my

chest and throat, thrashing wildly. I'm burning, burning on the inside and the outside. I can't breathe. I'm dying.

As I writhe in agony on the plush carpet beneath me, the last thing I see before my sight goes black is Istvan and Thorn walking out of the tent.

Chapter Thirty-Three

'Thorn!'

The shout is torn from me as I leap across the black abyss yawning at my feet. I have no idea where I am or how I'm leaping across fissures a good eight metres wide. I know that it feels as if I'm on fire, as if every single particle that makes me me is trying to tear its way out of me. But I'm still running.

I can just see them ahead of me. Thorn and his captor. I don't know how they are moving so fast, across rugged volcanic terrain. I remember watching a programme about Iceland after that volcano blew and I recognize the black slabs of rock and the strange apocalyptic scenery. I'm slowing down and my breath is tearing through my lungs.

I stop and fling my arms back and scream my rage into the turmoil of clouds above me. There's a slow roil of thunder and a bolt of electricity slams into me, into my head, splitting me in two.

'Stop fighting! Kit!' Some very rude swear words are dropped and I realize that someone is trying to contain my wild swinging fists. I wrestle loose from a scrum of bodies and stand, chest heaving, heart pounding, staring at everyone staring at me.

I don't see Thorn. I do see everyone else: Aelfric, Dina, the generals, the Fae princes forming a barrier against the open flap behind them, but no Thorn. Olga is there too, watching me with inscrutable hazel eyes.

'Where is he?' I rasp at them. 'Thorn? He was here when I fell. Where is he now?'

There's a shared look that tells me they think I've lost my mind. I clench my fists and do my best to compose myself.

'Kit, you have to sit down, relax for a bit.' Marc's face is pale and he's sporting a livid scratch mark along his cheek-bone. 'You just collapsed, screaming. Your heart stopped beating and you died, Kit. You died.'

'Don't be absurd,' I say, although my voice wavers and I feel actually pretty crappy. 'That man, Istvan, tried to kill me. And now Thorn is gone.'

'Istvan?' Aelfric looks around the group. 'He was here a moment ago.'

'Do you even know what he is?' I ask Aelfric. 'He's the traitor. He must be the one that sent Ioric to kill me and take Thorn.'

'The girl must have knocked her head.' Aelfric waves a hand dismissively. 'She doesn't know what she's talking about. Perhaps ask for one of my physicians to come see to her.' There's movement by the tent flap and I sense someone running off to do their king's bidding.

'No! You don't know what you're talking about.' My

anger has taken me well beyond caring about royal protocols. As I advance on him, I notice one of the guards shadowing my movement to the side, tracking me in case I attack
the High King of Alba. I hold my hands out, to show that
I'm carrying no weapons. 'I saw him, talking to Thorn, I
saw the darkness seep into your son, Aelfric. Did you never
stop and think for a second who the traitor was in your
camp? He was right under your nose all along, listening in
on all your talks, all your plans. How could you not know
this?'

Aelfric's face is pale and I can't be sure if it's shock at
the way I just spoke to him or at what I'm telling him.

'Where is he, do you think? Did he nip out to the loo?
I don't think so. He's managed to take your son, right from
under your nose. He's been hunting Thorn for days and I
kept him safe. Yet he's here for not even two hours and he's
been taken. Not good going, your majesty.' I feel as if I'm
pushing my way through molasses. My limbs are quivering
with fatigue and my head is pounding with the start of a
migraine that I know is going to knock me out for at least
twenty-four hours.

The tableau in the tent remains frozen as I stalk towards
Aelfric. I can spot when my words hit their target and I
actually revel in the shock I see on his face. But it's Dina
who reacts first.

She lets out a moan and spins to two anxious-looking
Fae guards hovering in the background. She says something
to them and they speed out of the tent.

'What did you see?' Her voice is low and measured but
her horror is clear in her dark eyes. 'Girl. What did you see?'

'Istvan, talking to Thorn. And Thorn listening like I've never seen anyone listen to anything before. With everything inside him.' I frown at her and think hard. 'He walked your son out of here and you didn't even see.'

'Do you know where Thorn's been taken?' One of the Vikings moves forward through the crowd and comes to stand in front of me. He looks like Thorn, but older; I don't know how I know it, but I know I'm talking to Petur, Aelfric's eldest son. The entire tent, including my family, is now staring at me as if I've got the answer to the world's biggest riddle.

'I don't . . . I have no idea,' I say. Without my anger to fuel me, I suddenly feel very embarrassed to be the centre of so much attention.

Dina looks visibly shaken and clutches at Aelfric's hand for comfort.

'Find where they've gone,' Dina says, turning to Petur. 'I can't lose him, not again.'

Suddenly everyone is talking, but not to me. Then Marc is by my side, supporting my weight. 'Olga hit you with electricity, to start your heart,' he says softly, in my ear. 'You need rest.'

'I can't rest. He took – that man took Thorn.' But I know I need to rest, because if I don't I'll break.

There's a commotion by the entrance, angry voices and then one of Dina's guards is back inside, stalking towards us. She's soaked through and her face is pale. She drops into a brief bow and clasps her hand to her chest in salute.

'My queen, Lord Istvan has killed three of the sorcerers and incapacitated the others. He also killed their body-guards.'

'What of the gateway?' Aelfric asks, looking genuinely shocked. 'Is that secure?'

The girl looks from Dina to Aelfric. 'I don't . . . we don't know, sir. There is some damage.'

The chaos that hits the tent gives me my chance. With everyone talking and questioning the guard, I slip out without anyone noticing. Or if they do, they don't think anything of me leaving. I duck my head against the driving rain and run along the planks that have been put in place to keep our feet dry. The entire camp is in uproar. Guards and soldiers thunder by; everyone looks armed to the teeth and focused. I stay out of their way as much as I can and try and make my way back to our tent, but darkness has fallen and I get turned around several times.

I eventually stop at a junction between tents to try and get my bearings. I ache inside where Istvan reached in and tore at me, ripping through the wards I had placed there, guarding the darkness only I knew of and didn't like thinking about or even acknowledging. I lean on my sword and try to catch my breath. The world whirls around me and I have to step to the side to be sick, heaving up the godawful wine Megan gave me and whatever food I had left in my stomach.

I stagger upright, my head feeling lighter, and I cling to my sword. I have to concentrate, to think. If Istvan damaged the gateway, how then did he get himself and Thorn to Alba? It makes sense that they'd go there because really, where else? And damaging the gateway meant Aelfric would struggle to follow, plus being massively inconvenienced in getting his forces to Alba to confront his brother.

Three soldiers standing nearby have witnessed my rather

unlady-like throwing-up and are watching me curiously. The middle one, slightly shorter than me, with a wiry build, moves towards me and his smile is friendly, if tentative.

'You are Prince Thorn's friend,' he says, in careful accented English. 'How can we help you, my lady? Are you lost?'

At any other time, it would give me a kick to be called my lady by a guy in full medieval armour – and to be looked at in a way that indicates definite interest. But right now, a sense of urgency is burning through me and I smile weakly.

'I am a bit, thanks for asking.' I rub my wet face and push my tangled hair out of my face. 'What is in the tent?' I ask, suddenly so cold that I don't mind begging a favour for something to protect me against the weather. 'Would you have a spare cloak or something in there? I'm soaked.'

The guard nods to his companion, who ducks in to fetch a neatly folded garment.

I swirl the thing around my shoulders and, even though I'm feeling wretched, once the cloak's settled around me, I feel as if I can walk a hundred miles. I catch the fabric between my fingers and see the spell woven into it.

'Thank you,' I say, nodding gratefully. 'And can you tell me how to get to Lord Istvan's tent? I really need to find Prince Thorn.'

The younger soldier directs me. 'You can't miss it, my lady. Just keep ahead here and where the road forks, take the right fork. The tent will be the only one that looks dry in this infernal weather.'

I leave them quickly, with my thanks. The cloak, I discover, actually has a hood. I throw that up and hurry, feeling marginally better and warmer. The camp is busy and although I see plenty of soldiers, no alarm's been raised.

I wonder why things aren't in more of an uproar. What is Aelfric playing at? Surely he would care enough about his son being kidnapped to launch a full-scale search? I come to the junction, go right as instructed and it's pretty evident which tent belongs to Istvan. It is the only tent that's remained dry under the constant rain.

I unsheathe my sword and walk towards the open tent flap. The interior is simple: just a cot, a table and chair.

I push forward into the tent but an invisible wall halts my progress. I look around and find a small rock, which I throw inside the tent. There's a bright spark from the barrier and the rock drops to the ground, neatly sheared in half.

I ponder if it's worth persevering, then there's noise ahead and I see a group of soldiers moving towards me. In front marches a small, determined-looking man in an odd pointed hat. If a bulldog ate a wasp, it would wear just that expression.

I retreat to a safe distance to watch.

'Get in there and tear it apart,' the pointy-hatted man tells the soldiers. 'Show me everything you find.'

The first two soldiers approach the tent as directed and, just as I call out to them to be careful, there's a blinding flash of light and I'm lifted off my feet.

A passing soldier lets out a surprised yelp as I land in a heap at his feet and he stops to help me up. 'Are you all right, my lady?' he asks, his eyes searching my face. When I nod and look as if I can stand on my own, he leaves me and runs to help his comrades, who are far more in need of assistance than I am. I check to make sure none is seriously hurt before hurrying away.

I have no idea where I am in relation to the main tent or our tent and everything looks wet and dark. I stop and lean against a tree and take a breath, rubbing my hands together. I close my eyes for a second, trying to sort out my head. Leaving the royal tent with no clue what I was doing was possibly stupid, but it was better than staying there watching people argue.

I take some deep breaths to calm myself. If I were a bad guy, where would I be? I ask myself. How would I make my getaway?

It's likely that there is another gateway nearby – how else would Istvan have left without trace? A hidden one. But how would you even find it? Megan always told me that my magic lit up the sky when I used it. It was just a thing she always said, but it now makes me wonder. What if she's right? What if I could track down the gateway by focusing on the leftover glare of the magic used to operate it?

Having never done anything like this before, I lean further back against the tree and look up through the branches. I propel my magic outwards, up the trunk and into the branches. It moves swiftly and I get the impression of curiosity from the tree, a sleepy acknowledgement. Once I'm in the branches I radiate my magic outwards and upwards. I concentrate on the hum and vibration I felt when Thorn used his magic when we were together. I taste the acrid tang of Istvan's magic shielding his tent and feed that into my own magic and tell it to look for the same thing.

I find it, eventually, the signature that the recent magic

left behind and it's near to the royal tent, a few rows over. I pull my magic back and start running, keeping the image of where the tent is in my head.

I only take two wrong turnings but I eventually track it again. There's nothing about this tent that's odd or makes it stand out. The soldier standing guard beside it looks sleepy when I run up to him, but seems to recognize me.

'What is in this tent?' I ask him. 'It's important. The king's sent me.' I drop the hood back and offer a smile. 'I'm sorry, he was so driven by his need to know that he scared me a bit. I didn't have a chance to collect my escort.'

'Mirrors, my lady.' He looks a bit worried. 'Is there some problem?'

'What kind of mirrors?' I ask him, forcing myself to slow down.

He looks at me in confusion. 'The mirrors Lord Istvan had us bring from Alba.'

I nod slowly, trying not to show him how urgently I need to get in there.

'Have you seen Lord Istvan and the prince go in there just now?'

'We've just had a shift change,' he answers me, still very patient, if perturbed by my questions. 'I can call Willamar and ask him. He just left to go and get some food.'

'Would you?' I ask him. 'I'll just wait here. My escort should be on their way too. If you see them, tell them I'm waiting for them.'

He huffs out a breath uncertainly. 'I'm not supposed to leave my post,' he says.

'The king sent me,' I tell him. 'He's with his generals

now, so commanded me to bring Lord Istvan to him before he left for Alba again.'

The guard looks surprised. 'You know about Lord Istvan using the tent to travel?'

It's dark enough for him not to see the triumphant flush creep across my cheeks as I nod. 'Like I said, the king sent me. You know he doesn't like to be kept waiting.'

'Very well. I won't be long.'

I watch him walk smartly along the wooden boards and wait for him to turn a corner before I walk backwards and duck into the tent.

Chapter Thirty-Four

Nine tall cheval mirrors stand in a semi-circle in the tent. Lit lanterns hang off the beams above our heads. There is no other furniture in the place, just the nine mirrors.

How do they work? I remember Thorn singing to the broken mirror. I shut my eyes and try and remember how it went. With my eyes closed, the smell that's been bothering me becomes more pungent and my stomach heaves. I hold on to the delicate scrollwork of the nearest mirror to keep my balance as I dry-heave. I feel the scroll ripple beneath my hand and snatch it back.

An eye stares out at me from the centre of the mirror. It looks human.

'Istvan,' I gasp. 'I need to follow Istvan.'

There's a rustling throughout the tent, the sound of leathery wings, of dark musty places, and an eye opens on every mirror to stare at me. I bite down hard on my terror and my instinctive need to run away from here.

'Complete the spell, human child.'

'I don't know what it is!' I grind out between my teeth. 'Help me.'

'We cannot.'

'We cannot . . .'

The tent becomes an echo chamber as their voices fill the air. The air is hot and I struggle to catch my breath.

'Stop messing around. Prince Thorn is in danger. I have to follow Istvan or all is lost.'

'So dramatic.'

'So anxious.'

'So in love.'

'Love?'

'Love.'

'I never knew love.'

'I knew love once. He declared himself and never returned. I burned his lands.'

'As was your right.'

What was this? Who were these things in the mirrors? I slap my hand against the surface of the nearest one.

'Listen!' I shout in annoyance. 'I don't have the time for this. Just tell me how to find Istvan. Please.'

'She is so young.'

'So determined.'

'So earnest.'

'So in love with the Dragon.'

'Does she know?'

'She can't know.'

'We should help her.'

Terror clutches at my heart as nine figures wreathed in smoke step from the mirrors. Taller than any human or Fae I've ever seen, their aspect is horrific. Contorted death masks made from finely worked gold cover their faces, but it's the peculiar stop-start of their movement towards me that freaks me out. I skitter backwards, to the tent flap, but they surround me now. The air in the tent has gone ice cold, so cold that my breath plumes in front of me and when I try to move it feels as if I'm trying to run through knee-high mud.

'You have asked.' A heavy hand lands on my shoulder, wrenching me backwards so I land hard on my back. 'Now your wish is being granted.'

I'm hauled upright and no matter how much I struggle, the nine pairs of burning cold hands steady me to stand in the middle of the tent, in the circle of the mirrors.

Electric-blue light arcs from the surface of each mirror, through each of them, and hits me squarely in the chest. I throw my head back and scream, but there is no sound. I'm aware of the fact that I've been lifted off my feet and that I'm several feet up in the air, near the roof of the tent.

Me dangling between heaven and earth doesn't last long, no more than five or maybe six seconds before I'm dropped to the ground and I sprawl there, inelegant and senseless for a few moments.

I sit up in surprise, noticing that the floor beneath my hands and knees is no longer muddy grass. It's finely inlaid marble and warm to my touch. I heave myself upright, taking in my surroundings.

I'm in a large round chamber made from stone. The ceiling is high and vaulted and I get the impression that I'm in a tower. Probably top floor (of course). The room itself is unremarkable: a circular chamber with tall narrow windows all around. I can't see any doors and it's worrying me. I walk over to a large wall hanging of a hawk attacking a wolf and lift it. It's heavy and I strain to peer behind it. Nothing. No door. I walk over to the windows and look out.

Unlike Marc, I don't have a problem with heights but the view from the top of the tower is dizzying. I grip the window frame and lean out as far as I can to get a clear view of where I am. What I see doesn't really make me feel any better. The tower is set on a sheer cliff surrounded by forest. There is green as far as the eye can see, and far in the distance maybe there's the blue of the sea.

I've never seen forest like this. The trees look gnarled and ancient. A faery tale forest, I realize with unease. I'm smack bang in the middle of Alba's Dark Forest, the place where monsters live.

Sword, knife, iron baton. At least I'm armed, I decide. I can probably take most things that come my way, as long as they come in single file. I groan and spin around, staring up at the vaulted ceiling. How am I meant to get down? I pull at my hair in annoyance, wondering if there was ever any merit in the story of Rapunzel growing her hair long.

I start a thorough search of the chamber, pressing and knocking against the walls, stamping my feet to make sure I haven't missed a trapdoor. I circle the chamber three times, and stop short when I notice a tiny silver bell on the windowsill. I'm pretty sure it wasn't there before.

It's a small thing, no bigger than the top joint of my little finger, and intricately carved. I peer at it, not touching it. I wonder about ringing it. Would it bring help or something else?

I agonize for a few seconds only. I draw my sword, pick

up the tiny bell and ring it. The sound is surprisingly robust and sweet. It echoes around the room, making me smile. I turn in a circle, listening to it reverberate around me. It seems to build and build and then there's an unexpected knock on the door I managed to not see during my time in the tower.

I open it only slightly and peer out. There is no one there, just a long, very long circular set of stairs going down. Every few paces there's a lit torch. And it is quiet, like the grave.

Before I freak myself out completely, I slip through the door and it locks behind me with a quiet *snick*, smoothing back into the rock and disappearing altogether. I grab one of the lit torches and start my descent.

The stairs curve with the tower and it plays with my depth perception as I look down the side to see how far they actually go. My leg muscles start complaining ten minutes into the descent and I slow down quite a bit. I hold on to my torch with my left hand and use my right hand to steady myself against the wall.

I climb down the stairs for what seems like an eternity. I take breathers and after the first few times refuse to look either up or down. I find myself making better progress this way and, just as I think I am going to collapse in a bundle of quivering legs and spinning head, I get to the bottom of the tower. A massive door bars my exit and I examine it closely. It's at least eight feet high by five feet wide. It's made from dark wood and banded with strips of iron. I can't see a key or a keyhole and am about to burst into tears when I remember walking around the upstairs chamber three times. So I do that again, only there is no chamber to walk around in. Instead I turn three times and on my third and final turn find a keyhole and key waiting for me in the door. I place my lit torch in an empty sconce and turn to the heavy door.

It swings open, letting in a blast of fresh autumn air. I lean forward and take in great big gulps of air. There's a small clearing around the tower, as well as a small picnic table and a well. I crank the wheel and a bucket comes up, filled to the brim with some of the most amazing sweet-smelling water. I take big mouthfuls and drink until I can't take another swallow.

The biggest thing about survival in a forest, Jamie's voice in my head reminds me, is water and shelter. Drink as much as you can when you can and immediately make shelter. Once those two things are seen to, you can worry about food.

I nod, thanking Jamie's voice, and ignore the bit about shelter and food. I have to find Thorn. I walk around the clearing and find the place where Istvan and Thorn entered the forest. I set off in the same direction, grateful to the tracking lessons that Jamie forced on us.

But then, Istvan and Thorn weren't exactly hiding, either. They strode at an energetic pace. Or rather, Istvan did. Thorn's prints look slower, as if he's dragging his feet, and I find blood on a few plants near the start of the trail.

I step carefully, keeping my wits about me. The forest is dense and the trees tower high above me, letting in very little light from above. When I left the camp it was night, here it's day, early morning. But I have no way of telling if it's today or tomorrow or even yesterday. I hate how screwed-up time is between the Frontier and the Otherwhere.

I rub my face, square my shoulders and with utmost care follow the route Istvan's bashed through the undergrowth.

I walk for about an hour and have become used to the greenery around me when the smell of decomposition hits me full in the face. I reel back and press myself up against a tree. I hear voices too, distantly, but I can't make out what they're saying.

I hunker down and creep forward for several metres. There is a group of the goblin chimera and they are talking to Istvan. They seem to defer to him, but only just. Two of them are standing guard over Thorn, who is slumped on a tree stump. I move slightly to get a better view of him and bite my lip in anger when I see how badly he's been beaten. Not only is his eyebrow cut, he's wearing a spectacular black eye and there's a livid bruise visible around his neck.

Lake Baikal – The Frontier, Russia

A hesitant knock on the shield outside his tent tore Duke Eadric's attention away from his most recent dispatches. A young squire, no older than twelve, slipped into the tent looking as if he'd rather face an army of ogres than be in Eadric's presence. The thought twisted the man's thin lips into a wry smile and the boy paled. For a few seconds they regarded one another in silence before Eadric sighed impatiently and gestured for the boy to come forward.

'Sir, my lord? Lord Istvan has the prince.' The boy

swallowed against the dryness in his throat. 'We just had word from our lookout.'

Eadric exclaimed, startling the boy. 'Excellent news. When do we expect them?'

'I don't . . . My lord, he's not coming to the camp. He's taking the prince directly to the island.'

The boy held his breath as he told Eadric this, watching the duke through worried eyes. He slanted a look to his left, to the shadows, using his peripheral vision to make sure he had a clear exit from the tent in case Eadric decided to throw something at him. It'd been known to happen.

Eadric stood up from the chair behind the desk and stretched. His shadow capered behind him on the canvas and for a moment it didn't resemble the shape of a man at all. For the briefest of seconds the shadow-play looked like a gargoyle, a craven hunched figure, spindly with a swollen belly. The boy stared in horror, blinking, and took an unthinking step back. Before he could turn and run, his training took over and he squared his shoulders. None of this was about him, but it was about the honour of his family. He would stay and face whatever the outcome of the duke's anger and annoyance might be. He swallowed against the terror building in his chest and flicked his eyes towards the duke again.

The duke seemed unaware of the boy in the tent with him. His expression was one of deep thought and for a heartbeat the boy thought that he might return unscathed from carrying the message. The boy shifted in his too-warm doublet but froze mid-movement when Eadric looked at him with hot hungry eyes.

'What is your name, boy?'

'Jesse, sir. My grandfather is Lord Belton.'

'Belton has been a loyal supporter from the start. You are his eldest grandson, yes?'

The boy, Jesse, nodded, risking a quick proud smile. 'My father too, sir. We are all happy to serve you in this great time.'

Eadric's smile was as sickly as it was patronizing. He moved to his desk to pick at a small platter of fruit and cheese. For a while the only sound was that of Eadric eating. He cleaned his fingers on his shirt before beckoning Jesse closer.

'Come here, boy.'

The boy didn't hesitate. He strolled confidently up to Eadric. 'Would you like me to pour you some wine, sir?'

'Yes, why don't you do that?' Eadric watched the boy's movements. 'Do you have brothers and sisters?'

'I do, my lord. I have two younger brothers and a sister.' Jesse's smile was one of pride. 'They are all here in the camp with my parents.'

'Good, that is good.' Eadric nodded, his smile slipping, to be replaced by a look of sadness and perhaps regret. 'With more siblings to occupy them, it will be easier for your parents to get over your death.'

'I . . . what?' Jesse's eyes grew huge as Eadric made a lunge for him.

The boy fought valiantly against the older man, but he was slight for his age and the man was wiry and strong.

When Eadric's servant strode into the tent with his master's nightcap he came to an abrupt halt.

Eadric sat in the darkened tent, with only the brazier

and a small tiered candelabrum for light. Even so, it was easy to see the dark red blood of the young child he clutched to him dripping down his face and chest, covering his clothes and robes. He looked at his manservant and the man, not for the first time, realized that his master had irrevocably lost his mind. There was no recognition, no regret, no sadness for the deed done in Eadric's features. Instead he looked satisfied and a bit bemused at the state he was in. He stood and the child's body dropped to the floor at his feet.

'Clean this up,' he instructed. 'Tell Belton we caught him trying to crawl into the cages with the griffins.'

The man nodded. He placed the sleeping draught on the small table with the platter of fruit and bent to pick up the boy. He averted his gaze from the horrific bites on the boy's arms and neck and he kept his face neutral as he walked from the tent.

Behind him he could hear Eadric talking to someone, laughing softly. The man risked a glance over his shoulder and saw a group of monstrous shadows writhing against the tent canvas. He snapped his gaze back, straightened his shoulders and walked into the night with his burden.

Chapter Thirty-Five

'If you do anything now, you'll get yourself killed.'

Because the voice echoes what I'm thinking it takes me a full second to realize that someone is speaking in my ear. Remaining absolutely still takes more effort than I would've thought possible. But jumping up now will definitely alert Istvan and his cronies to my location and, even though I am pretty competent with my sword, taking on twelve of them, and Istvan for good measure, is not something I'd like to try.

'Good girl,' murmurs the voice. 'My name is Crow.'

'Kit,' I whisper back, not taking my eyes off the group in front of me.

'You move with some skill, Kit. But you aren't from here.'

I risk the slightest shake of my head. 'No. I'm from the Frontier.'

'Thought as much. No one here would voluntarily carry iron on their person.'

I frown, wondering what he means, then realize he is talking about the rod strapped to my arm. How would he even know that I'm carrying iron?

'The smell of it,' Crow says. 'It reeks.'

He'd better not be able to read my mind. 'We have to save the prince,' I tell Crow.

'We will, but not yet.' The presence next to me shifts. 'Come with me.'

Taking the utmost care, I move backwards, keeping the foliage and ferns between me and the group in front. Crow places a hand on my back and guides me further back until we are several metres away, shielded by the wide trunks of the trees and more undergrowth.

Crow, like his namesake, has thick black hair and carries a tan that makes me think he's never spent an hour indoors. His eyes are large and dark, the colour of midnight. He's dressed in leathers and pelts and looks feral and unpredictable. He carries an impressive longbow and quiver slung across his back. A large hunting knife rests on his hip.

He is very lean and there is strength in his hands as he moves me slightly further behind the tree trunk.

'I am one of Aelfric's foresters,' Crow says, keeping his voice very quiet. 'You find yourself in the Dark Forest. How did you come to be here?'

'How can I be sure I can trust you?' I counter. 'I don't know you from Adam. All I have is your word that you work for Aelfric.'

'Don't you think that I would have betrayed you to them if I had not been an ally?'

He had a point. 'How do you know I'm not the enemy?' I counter.

'There are rumours going about the forest, about a human girl who has lost her heart to the Dragon.'

I tut irritably and pray that he doesn't notice my heightened colour as my cheeks flame red. 'I don't even know what that means. Also, how can there be rumours in the forest? You are the only person I've seen and I've not told you anything.'

Crow's smile reminds me of Aiden. Here's another cheeky one, I realize. Just what I need.

'You have been watched since you left the tower. We are all very excited to see a human child in the forest. It has been an age since we had someone from the Frontier visit us.' He gestures, looking contrite. 'Voluntarily, that is.'

'I'm not here to have high tea,' I whisper fiercely. 'I'm here to save your prince.'

Crow blinks in surprise at the anger in my voice but nods. 'I know. But there is no reason not to be friendly.'

I yearn to stomp my feet in frustration but I don't. Instead I give him one of my practised level looks à la Nan.

'Listen, are you helping me to figure out where they're taking Thorn or are we going to stand around here all day?'

'I know where Istvan is taking the young prince. I can show you if you like?'

So help me! I clench my fists and nod, taking a few seconds to get my impatience under control.

'How do I know you're taking me to the right place?'

'You don't.' He bends to draw something in the dirt at his feet. 'We will have to go round Duke Eadric's army and conjure a spirit to help you cross the Lake of Sorrows. There is an island in the middle of the lake. That's where they are taking Thorn.'

'That would be just . . . great. How far is it?' The sketch

makes no sense to me. I walk over and stand next to Crow. Ah, now I can see what he means. The lake doesn't seem to be that far. However, between us and the lake is a huge army. He's drawn a wide curve to show our expected journey.

Crow nods and smiles happily. 'Not far, as the crow flies.'

Chapter Thirty-Six

Humans in the Otherwhere: Traditional stories tell of men and women stumbling across fairy revels (usually on hilltops) and, compelled by the music, they join the fairies. Invariably they partake of food and drink and are then trapped in the fairy world for some time. When they manage to outsmart their captors years have gone by in their own world. Due to new treaties signed by the Courts in Alba specifically, there are fewer and fewer human abductions, that we know of.

From an archived report filed in HMDSDI HQ, 1954

We walk for five hundred million miles. Or that's what it feels like. Occasionally we stop to rest, but mostly we just walk at a punishing pace. It doesn't help that I know I'm slowing Crow down.

'You are doing well,' Crow says over his shoulder. 'For a human.'

I grimace. 'Thanks.'

He nods, taking my thanks at face value, completely unaware of the sarcasm. 'We will have to walk most of the way to the lake edge,' he says after a few more minutes. 'Eadric's forces subdued the Perun's tribes, gaining control of the gateway that leads to the island.'

I stop as a branch swings back and almost hits me in the face. Crow sighs heavily and gestures impatiently at the branch and it moves out of my way. I gape as it does. 'The trees are very curious about you,' he says. 'Can you hear them talking?'

I shake my head numbly. 'So how much time will we waste walking to the lake?' I ask him, ducking below another set of reaching branches. 'How much will they gain?'

Crow passes back a skin of water which I gulp, not spilling one drop.

'A few hours only,' he says, waving his hand negligently. 'They don't have a forester with them so their march is slow.'

I nod as if I know exactly what he means. Part of me wonders why I'm even trusting this guy. But, like he said, why would he go through the motions of helping me, if all he had to do was hand me over to Istvan and his pack of chimeras? As we walk he forages and passes nuts and berries back to me to eat. My initial reaction is to decline them but after the first handful of nuts my shakiness dissipates. He fills his water skin in a small stream and passes it back to me. I sit down briefly and drink deeply, relieved that the nausea that accompanies the start of my migraine attack seems to be fading, along with the heaviness in my head.

I thought I'd done pretty well earlier, climbing over obstacles, ducking beneath branches and things, but walking with Crow is like strolling, at a rapid pace, along the high street. He manages to choose the easiest way through the forest, no tree roots to clamber over, no branches to duck. I'm aware too of how noisy I am. I clomp through the forest like a herd of angry buffalo rather than ghost through it as Crow does. I bite my lip in frustration and grudgingly accept that maybe I will have to work on my stealth tactics.

It must be just before midnight when he stops abruptly and I walk into his back. He grabs my arm to steady me. 'Look, you can see the glow of the campfires of Eadric's army.'

I turn to follow his outstretched arm. We're standing on a slight rise and the view is spectacular. For miles around us I see fires burning and with dawning horror I realize exactly how huge Eadric's army is. If Aelfric's army looked big to me, his brother's army is at least four times that, if not more.

Crow adjusts his bow so that it doesn't whip me in the face as he turns to survey the small clearing. He touches my arm to draw my attention. 'There will be patrols about. We must be careful.'

I'm too tired to say anything and only nod. He sets off again, this time slower and even quieter still. I watch the way he moves and try and copy it. I get it right, or I think I do, for most of the time but at one stage when I step on something that squirms under my feet, I suppress a squeal and clutch at him in surprise. He pats my arm and I'm pretty sure I can see him laughing at me but he wisely keeps his mouth shut for the next few minutes.

'We will rest soon, once we are near the lake. I don't know when they're planning to perform the ritual, but my bet is either dawn or sunset.'

'Ritual?' I ask him, keeping my voice low. I wonder if I'll ever not feel dumb. 'How do you know about it?'

He turns his head to look at me. 'I'm one of the foresters,' he says, as if it explains everything.

'You may need to spell this out for me,' I say to Crow. 'I get that you are a forester. Is that like a groundskeeper? You keep things tidy in the forest, check on animals and things?'

'I have been a guardian of the Dark Forest for a long time. For maybe as long as Aelfric's been king, maybe a bit longer. Time is different here.' He helps me over a low rock and I like how his touch doesn't linger. It's there, then gone. Businesslike and brief. 'The forest is at the heart of Alba. We nurture it, make sure it stays healthy. If the forest dies, Alba dies. It is simple, really.'

'And the forest tells you things?'

Crow's dark head nods. 'It tells us when it senses threats, or when something has raised its curiosity. It is very curious about you, as I said. Can you hear it whispering?'

I want to tell him no, not to be absurd, but I can hear the whispering. I can sense it all around me, movement in the air above me, the leaves rustling and a great sense of lots of people watching me.

I draw a deep breath and I reach hesitantly for my magic, feeling the raw edges of it where Istvan tore it from me, and I wonder how much of it has been drained from me. It's difficult to describe quite how strange it felt having another person touch that well of power and mess around with it. The reservoir of power lies there, quietly thrumming, waiting for my attention. Gently, I coax it forwards and upwards and let it surface so that it hovers like a soft film just above my skin.

The touch of my magic as it settles around me is calming and I let out a sigh, realizing suddenly how tense I have been. I look around me carefully. The entire forest pulses with life and energy, a soft luminescence that covers everything. The night is no longer dark.

'Wow,' I say. 'I should have done this earlier.'

'We were wondering about that,' he says. 'You don't use your magic often.'

I shake my head. 'Usually when I use my magic I become ill. Especially when I use a lot of it. And hungry, I'm hungry for days after I use my magic.'

'You are far stronger than you think, Blackhart.' He crouches low and pulls me down next to him. 'You need to realize that your magic isn't separate to who you are. It's part of you. Like your hands or eyes.' He presses a finger to his lips and motions for me to stay quiet.

Three redcaps blunder past us, trampling the undergrowth. One has a stick he's using to swat tall bushes. They don't see us at all. We remain sitting beneath a large fern for a few more minutes. The night around us is quiet and I'm very aware of my pounding heart and Crow's strong fingers on my wrist. It's as if my magic has heightened all my senses tonight, not just my sight, the way it usually does in the Frontier. I hear a dull thrumming noise and turn my head in the direction. An owl sweeps past, something clutched in its claws, and I can feel the air of its passing.

'Let's go,' Crow says, slipping sideways past the fern and waiting for me to do the same. 'Try and keep your magic awake,' he tells me quietly. 'Let it guide you through the forest.'

'I can't,' I say in frustration as I follow him. 'My magic is . . .' I gesture in frustration. 'It works only in short bursts. Anything more than me using my sight and I get sick. If I overdo it, I feel like I've got the flu for several days.'

We've walked a few paces only when Crow says, 'Down.'

I drop into a crouch and a group of chittering goblins run past, carrying something between them.

'They're hunting,' he says. 'An army that size needs a lot of food.'

We wait a few minutes before we're off again. I'm sure it's my imagination but I'm moving as fast as Crow now, and as quietly.

'You have no casting abilities?' he asks over his shoulder and when I shake my head he continues, 'You can't propel magic in some form?'

'Thorn can do that but, no, I can't.'

'Have you ever tried?'

I think about it. No. I've never tried; I wouldn't know how. I tell Crow as much.

He looks at me curiously but doesn't say anything further. It's strange, talking to him about my magic when it's not something I've been comfortable discussing with others. But somehow, walking in this ancient forest, I feel relaxed about it – more relaxed than I've been since it manifested on the night my nan died.

I draw a deep breath and listen to the forest around me shift and creak. As we move on, Crow spends less time watching out for me and more time keeping an eye out for passing patrols. I can smell their cooking fires on the night air and occasionally the sound of music and revelry drifts towards us.

The closer we get to the lake, the more patrols there are. We hurry through the night, one time hiding inside a giant oak tree and stepping out the other side to let a patrol of feral Fae run past us.

I'm finding reserves of energy I had no idea I had, but even so I'm dead on my feet when we eventually stop. Crow instructs me to climb a tree, which I manage without breaking an arm or falling on my back. He shimmies up after I do and once I'm sure of my seat so far up, he shows me the shores of the lake in the distance. It's maybe three in the morning and the sun hasn't risen yet. There is a greyness to the sky, though, and a soft creeping mist covers most of the forest around us.

I fall asleep for a few minutes and when I wake up Crow hands me a cup with a spicy drink that tastes of coconut and chillies. He's cut slices of dried meat for me and I fall on it with gusto. We eat in silence and I like our quiet camaraderie.

'You're one of the people who's been telling Aelfric about Eadric's movements,' I say after a while. 'Have you met my cousins?'

'I have seen a human boy and a human girl clattering

about the forest, playing at spying.' He frowns. 'I had to kill three redcaps who were setting an ambush for them. So, if that's who you are talking about, then yes, I have seen them.'

'Why has Aelfric sent them when he has you?' I ask him. 'And how many of you are there?'

Crow's teeth flash in a smile towards me. 'There are only nine foresters in all of Alba. Our roles are hereditary.' He hands me something else. 'Bread and conserve,' he says. 'I can only guess why Aelfric sent your family into the forest. Maybe it was a way to test their abilities and their loyalty.'

'Huh,' I say. 'Maybe he hoped they'd get killed and he wouldn't have to worry about having humans in his camp.'

'Dangerous talk.' Crow's voice comes from slightly above me now. He's standing against the trunk, looking towards the lake. 'Come, we need to go.'

'How do you get word to the king about Eadric's movements?'

'I send a rook to Petur. He handles all war communications.'

'How do the rooks get to Petur if the gateways don't work?'

'Some creatures, like rooks and crows, don't need gateways. They don't belong to either world and so move freely between them.'

This is the first time I've heard anything like this. 'Maybe you should tell Aelfric where we are and what we are planning to do in the morning.'

'What are we doing in the morning?'

'Saving Thorn, killing Istvan and banishing these Elder Gods back to their prison where they belong.'

Crow's face is thoughtful in the half-light.

'I think I like you,' he says, his tone serious. 'Are you sure you aren't part Sidhe?'

Chapter Thirty-Seven

Ever tried conjuring a spirit? No, me neither. I watch Crow as he builds a very small fire at the edge of the forest. There's about a hundred yards of low shrub, then there's the beach, and beyond the beach is the lake and in the middle of this great lake lies the island. Even from here I can sense the watchfulness of the island. I shiver in my jacket and hunch forward in an attempt to keep warm.

'Have you done this before?' I ask Crow, as I keep watch.

'Once, a very long time ago.'

'Did it end well?'

He holds out his hand and wiggles it from side to side, indicating a little yes, a little no. I groan. 'Why do we need this spirit?'

'It will grant us safe passage across the lake to the island.'

'And we definitely need its guidance?'

'Yes.' He says it so firmly I don't doubt him. 'We're ready.'

From one of his pockets he withdraws a small pouch. He sprinkles the contents into the fire. The smell is strong but not unpleasant. He takes a jagged piece of clear crystal on a leather cord from around his neck. This he dips into a shallow nutshell. It comes out glistening dark.

He holds it over the fire, as you would a pendulum to do scrying. Slowly but surely the crystal starts spinning and, although I watch closely, there is no way to see if Crow's spinning the crystal or if it's spinning of its own accord.

I know, I know, after all I've seen and been through, I still have doubt. Maybe it's a human thing, this not being able to believe in the other world a hundred per cent.

A light breeze stirs, lifting my hair away from my face, and I shiver slightly, moving closer to the fire.

The crystal is a blur above the fire, emitting a pleasant humming noise.

'Shade of time, guardian of the lake, hear our plea. We come humbly before you to ask you to guide our way. A favour given, a favour returned, as it has always been.' He takes out a very small knife and it glints in the firelight. He raises his hand to make a cut across it, but I lean forward and shake my head. No, this is on me, my eyes tell him. I hold out my hand to him and for a second he hesitates, but then nods. He slides the blade across my palm. It's not a big or very deep cut, but the blood pools rapidly. Crow takes my hand and turns it so that the blood drips into the fire. 'We conjure thee, guardian. By earth, air, fire and spirit.'

There's a soft *snick* and I feel a gust of air on my cheek, then tickling my ear, as if someone was whispering to me. Then, without warning, a slender cloaked figure is standing behind Crow. The cowl moves towards me and it raises a skeletal wrist.

'You.'

I swallow against the rising scream in my throat. I know – very stupid of me. What was I expecting? Casper?

'You dare disturb my rest?'

Crow is standing now too. He edges around the fire so he stands next to me. We both face the wraith. I realize it's not actually standing on the ground, but is hovering a few centimetres above it.

'We seek your assistance, spirit. To cross the lake, to the island.'

'It is forbidden,' the spirit counters before Crow's even finished speaking. 'Forbidden.'

'We know it's forbidden, but we have to find a way to cross.'

'The living cannot pass.' There is a sibilant hiss at the end of the last word. 'Lives will be lost.' Lossssst.

I shudder and look at Crow. 'Is there any other way we can get there? Fly?'

'Can you fly?' he asks me and I have to shake my head. 'So this is the only way.'

'Please.' I don't notice it, but I've moved closer to the wraith. 'Please, we need your help. It is a matter of life or death.'

The cowl moves to face me and the shadows within seem to writhe. 'Whose?'

Not what I expected to be asked. 'All of ours.' I gesture out to the lake in the direction of Eadric's army. 'Please, you must know what's going on there, why you have an army camped on your shores. They are planning something bad. Really bad.'

The breeze shifts, fluttering the shade's tattered robes

against its slender figure. The gust toys with my hair, tugging hard. I hear giggling and frown at Crow. He looks pale and awkward in the presence of the spirit he's conjured.

'Say something,' I say to him. 'Help me convince it to help us.'

'Yes, forester, help convince me.' Something in the wraith's voice makes me shift and lean forward. I stare hard at Crow then back at the cloaked figure.

'Please, Eilian, don't do this.' Crow's voice holds a world of pain and misery.

'No, we *will* do this, Crow. Tell me why I should care, why I should help you and the Blackhart, whose quest is being sung of by the West wind itself.'

I move back in surprise. Gone is all pretence of ghostliness or etherealness. The 'wraith' Eilian stops hovering, planting her feet solidly on the ground as she pulls her hood back.

She is frighteningly beautiful. Wild strong features with eyes like ice regard us intensely. The wind dies down and two small children scamper from the undergrowth to cling to her. She presses them against her and angles their faces so Crow and I can both see them.

In my mind they look exactly how I expect Sidhe children to look. Tiny delicate things with golden curls and wide slanting eyes. Pointy ears are just visible above their curls. The girl giggles, shyly trying to hide her face in her mother's robes, and as she does so, she shifts and bright butterfly wings flutter from between her shoulder blades.

The shade Crow addressed as Eilian watches him intently.

'See this man, children? He is one of King Aelfric's

favourite foresters. He could ask any boon from the high king and it will be granted. Don't you think that's amazing?'

I'm watching this, my mouth open. What is going on here? The little boy bravely moves forward to look up at Crow.

'He's fierce, Mother,' he says clearly, pointing a sticky wet finger at him. 'Do we know him?'

'We know him very well, children. His name is Crow and he's your uncle.'

A pin could drop and be heard in the clearing. I feel my eyebrows rise in surprise. Not what I expected to hear at all; I wonder if I actually need to be here for this right now. All I wanted was to cross the lake, not watch this family melodrama, however compelling. Crow and his sister look nothing alike. Although he is all dark, dressed in greens with lively eyes, he has a calm about him that settles my nerves. Whereas Eilian looks mercurial and palely beautiful.

'Don't do this,' Crow pleads of her. 'Now is not the time.'

'Why would you not want your niece and nephew to know, brother Crow, that all you have to do is ask Aelfric the boon you swore you'd take to him?'

The little girl claps her hands together and jumps up and down. 'What boon, Mother? What boon?'

'The thing your uncle Crow promised to ask Aelfric the Wise is a simple thing,' she says, waving her hand airily. 'All I want him to ask is for your mother to be released from the geas.' Her smile as she looks at her children is sweet. But the gaze she directs at Crow is cold. 'This cursed hell of ferrying the souls of the dead.'

'Eilian, you know I cannot do this.' Crow's face is a picture of misery. He moves closer to the woman, his arms wide. 'It is your birthright.'

'Then you won't be ferried across,' she says decisively, moving away from him and turning to me. 'You, human girl. Why do you have to go? If I agree to do this forbidden thing, you must know that you will not be able to come back alive.'

With my heart thudding in my chest at the way all of this is playing out, I nod. 'I understand and I agree.' I look over to the island, wreathed in mists at the centre of the vast lake. 'I need to save someone dear to me from harm, and from being part of something that will destroy our worlds.'

Eilian tilts her head and considers my words. Her nod is swift and sure. 'I will do this.'

'Kit, no! You don't understand what she means. You will die on the island.' Crow's grip on my shoulder hurts.

'I understand clearly enough. I actually died earlier because Istvan attacked me. And I had thought dying would be a final forever thing, but I know I came back because I have to do this – help Thorn and stop the madness. And what I can say is that I'm so scared that I feel ill, but I must see this through. You probably think I'm mad and stupid but I promised to keep him safe and protect him and he was taken right in front of my eyes. I can't not go, Crow. Do you understand? I have to bring him back.'

Eilian's smile is triumphant as she turns to look at her brother. 'See, baby brother? Some people know what to stand up for.'

She hunkers down beside her two children. The boy – no older than seven – is staring at his uncle with a fierce look. 'Stay here with Uncle Crow and Mummy will be back in a bit.' She presses a kiss to each of their foreheads before standing up. 'Look after them for me, Crow. I'll be back shortly.'

I hear a soft rumbling sound and turn to see a small coracle making its way across the smooth surface of the lake. It docks lightly against the sandy shore and cants to one side.

Crow moves forward and gives me a quick hug, placing feather-light kisses on both my cheeks. 'Be safe, Kit. May your blade strike swift and true.'

Chapter Thirty-Eight

The Ferryman: A person or creature who ferries the souls of the dead between the worlds of the living and the dead is not a new or unusual concept across most cultures. In Ancient Greek mythology Charon was Hades' ferryman, carrying newly deceased souls across the river Styx. It is traditional to bury the dead with a coin in the mouth in order to 'pay the ferryman'.

From an archived report filed in HMDSDI HQ, 1946

It feels as if I'm flying across the lake. The surface is mirror smooth. Over my shoulder in the distance I see the thousands of men and beasts Duke Eadric has camped near the lake and yet, if they've seen the coracle, they've not bothered giving chase. They fill my entire horizon, as far as I can see. The scale of the army makes me feel ill. There are roars from caged beasts and the sound of screams and laughter. It sounds as if Eadric's army is made up of monsters rather than soldiers. I think back to Aelfric's army camped in Scotland and I doubt it would be able to dent Eadric's superior force.

Eilian sits facing me, wrapped in her grey robes, with the cowl up over her head so that it casts her face into deep shadows.

'How is it that a human girl is trusted enough on a mission this important?'

'Thorn is my friend. I have to help him.' I shift under her watchfulness. 'I made a promise. A Blackhart never goes back on a promise once it's made.'

'And you're not scared?'

I give a dry laugh. 'I'm scared beyond belief.'

'You are interesting to me, human girl.' She dips her sleeve into the lake. Something large surfaces beside us. It looks like a whale but it's larger than I ever thought a whale could be. It turns an almost human eye on us before sinking below the surface again. I'm amazed that there'd been no ripple of water at all and I wonder if I'm starting to hallucinate. 'Crow too seems enamoured of you.'

'He helped me,' I say to her, wondering what exactly her problem is. 'I didn't have to ask him. Or promise him anything.'

'More fool he,' she says. 'That boy really should learn that the world is bigger than his forest.'

'Boy?' I say, unable to hide my surprise. 'Crow said he's been a forester since King Aelfric's been the ruler of Alba. That must make him over six hundred years old. At least.'

Eilian shrugs. 'He is a boy to me. And he will always be, no matter what great age we attain.'

'What changed your mind?' I ask her, leaning closer, catching her gaze with mine. 'Something made you change your mind about bringing me across.'

She's quiet for a few moments and all I can hear is the sound of the tiny waves slapping the side of the boat but then she answers me in a quiet voice. 'I am bargaining on either you or the prince surviving. In fact, I'm counting on your survival, girl. It means you are in my debt.'

My eyes open wide in surprise. 'You want me to ask Aelfric to lift the curse?'

'It is a small thing, is it not?' she asks in turn.

'You told me that I wouldn't return,' I point out. 'You also said that it was forbidden to take me across.'

'It is forbidden to ferry the living across the lake. It never ends well.' Her smile is wry. 'But then I'm ferrying one human girl across to the Island of the Dead. The sorcerer has been using the island for his unclean deeds for years. One human girl brought back alive is a very small violation compared to everything he has done.'

'Are you talking about Istvan?' I stare at her in disbelief when she inclines her head gracefully. 'Why have you never told anyone?'

'Who could I tell,' she says. 'I ferry the dead. That is all I do.'

'But surely someone could have stopped him – he's evil!'

'Is he?' She watches me closely as my hand moves involuntarily to the hilt of my sword. 'Is he truly evil? What if I tell you that his family once ruled the Otherwhere? Aelfric's family overthrew Lord Istvan's when they banished the Elder Gods. Perhaps he just wants people to remember. Aelfric and his family have been in charge for a very long time, Blackhart. Some Fae feel the need for change.'

'And so what? You agree Istvan the Insane and Aelfric's

brother should bring back the Elder Gods?' I stare at her incredulously and wonder how I'm going to get to the island. At this rate, I'm going to have to swim for my life when she decides I'm being impertinent and drops me overboard.

'I do not,' she says. 'I support no one. What they do has no bearing on me. I serve Lady Death and she endures regardless of who sits on Alba's throne.'

'But they are going to destroy the world,' I say, with emphasis, to make sure she understands.

Her silver eyes flash at me from the depths of her hood. 'I am not of this world,' she says calmly. 'And I do not care for it.'

'But . . . how am I going to ask Aelfric to lift your geas if he's no longer the king?'

'It does not matter if he is king or not; it only matters that he's alive. He has the power to revoke my geas, because I had to swear fealty to him when he took power, like I did for his father, and his father's father.'

I turn away from her, struggling to wrap my mind around how she can seem so apathetic.

'This geas you're under,' I ask her. 'What is it?'

For the longest time she doesn't answer me and stares up at the night sky above us. I look up too and am amazed I've not noticed the heavy star-scattered heavens above us.

'The geas is like a curse, a spell, a promise that belongs to our family. In each generation one is chosen to become the ferryman of souls. The geas can fall on anyone within our family and it is something that is our family's legacy, till the end of our days.' She sighs and turns her liquid gaze on me. 'I am tired, human girl. I have been doing this for a very long time. Can you imagine the toll it takes, wrestling with the souls of our dead, moving them on to the Valleys of Peace? Lady Death is my very close companion these days and I fear my time has become short.' Her voice is sad. 'My children do not know their father and Crow is incapable of caring for them. I would very much like to spend time with them before I pass.'

I peer into her proud face, see the anguish in her eyes and make my decision. 'I will help you, I promise. I will ask Aelfric to lift this if he is able.'

Her smile is sad and she lays an icy hand on mine.

'You have a good heart, human child. I wish you success in your battle against the Old Ones.'

Chapter Thirty-Nine

The coracle smoothly settles on the soft black sand of the island. There's a narrow strip of beach before the verdant undergrowth starts. I look at Eilian and she regards me quietly with big solemn eyes.

'This is it,' I say, desperate not to sound as scared as I feel. 'Well, wish me luck.'

I jump over the side of the boat and my boots sink deep into the black sand. Volcanic sand. I reach down and touch it with my fingertips. It's warm to the touch. I turn and look back at the faraway shore where I can just make out the thousands of soldiers in Eadric's army. I feel the coracle move and Eilian's standing by my side.

'Are they here?' I ask her. 'Istvan and Thorn?'

'They are here. All of them are here.' Her cold eyes hold my gaze. 'Be watchful, girl. Remember, there is more than one way to die.'

Something Aiden said to me comes to mind. I put my hand in my jeans pocket and take out the small velvet pouch. 'A gift,' I say to her, dipping my fingers into the baggie. 'An expression of my thanks and my promise made.'

She accepts the two diamonds I drop into her palm but doesn't look at them. Her nod is brisk but before she gets back into her small boat she leans forward and brushes ice-cold lips across my cheek.

'Your bravery commends you,' she says, sounding truly sad. 'You do not know what you face, and yet you still run towards it. If all humans are like you, the Elder Gods will not rule as easily as they think.'

Her words frighten me but they also give me the boost I need. I turn and swiftly forge a path through the under-growth, which starts a few metres from the beach. The coracle ride gave me time to rest physically, but mentally my mind's buzzing. I'm starting to regret going it alone, but I had to follow Istvan's trail while there still was one. But I want backup more than anything, and walking onto this island with no clue as to what I'm doing is one of the stupidest things I have ever done. And that includes facing down a group of redcaps, by myself, as they attacked a young Sidhe noble.

My pace quickens and I wish I'd thought to take one of Crow's water skins with me. It's hot on the island even if it's still not quite dawn. I fling my cloak off and fasten it to my back with my belt, backpack style. My jacket I leave tucked inside an overgrown tree trunk with a handy cavity. Risk of discovery is low but I don't want to take chances. I do my utmost to move the way Crow moved, leaving little or no sign of my passing, but it's hard going.

The plants here are tropical and the air is thick with humidity. I left behind a damp, cool European-type forest, and merely by crossing a lake, managed to land somewhere that looks more Hawaiian to me. I check the iron rod fastened to my forearm and decide to leave it on. It makes my skin itch because it's so warm but I'd rather have it and not need it than leave it behind. The same goes for my knife. The sheath in the small of my back isn't quite comfortable but I'm not about to mess with it to try and reposition it.

I'm off again at a rapid pace. It's been the most hectic twenty-four hours of my life, and all that excitement and only a few hours' sleep makes for a tired and slightly broken Kit.

The island is beautiful and none of the vegetation looks familiar. I don't know much about plants, I'm the first to admit, but my nan was obsessed with her gardens and I've picked up a bit. Looking around at these giant tropical plants and huge trees, I wonder if the island's lain untouched by evolution since the Elder Gods were banished. A kind of Jurassic Park.

The thought creeps me out as I have a thing about dinosaurs, especially raptors, all thanks to the most successful dinosaur movie franchise ever. Give me redcaps instead any time of day.

I feel dwarfed by the landscape as I climb over large black rocks and jump over rapidly flowing streams with no clear idea where it is that I'm going, except that I need to get towards the centre of the island.

I push through heavy vines and duck beneath overhanging rocks slick with condensation. I'm so caught up with balancing and jumping, I almost fall off the edge of a steep cliff as the air around me opens up unexpectedly. Below me is a deep valley completely at odds with the rest of the island. The walls are sheer black rock and in some places it looks like glass. There is no foliage, trees or greenery in the valley itself.

Instead, I see edifices hewn from slabs of rock. There are several such structures, but the largest at the centre, flanked by two smaller buildings, must surely be my target – another clue being the impressive colonnade topped with snarling, fanged demons leading up to it. All three constructions are smooth-sided pyramids for the most part and look completely incongruous sitting in the crater below me.

The entire complex is built from black rock, polished to a high sheen. And the air is heavy and oppressive, as it is before a thunderstorm. I look upwards and the sky is turning shades of pink and purple; dawn is finally making an appearance.

My gaze drops back to the valley and I wonder how I'm going to get down there. There has to be a way but I'm not sure I have the time to find hidden passages. My sense of urgency spurs me on; I take my bearings and start jogging along the edge of the valley.

I don't get far. A loud crash to my right alerts me to the fact that I'm about to be mincemeat. Even as I'm in the process of drawing my sword something heavy tackles me and there's a confusion of pain, the smell of heavy sweaty fur and I'm tumbling.

I jump to my feet as soon as I hit the ground, shaking my head to clear it. My sword is out, my weight balanced and I face off against one of the goblin chimera. Its jaw drops open, revealing a wide maw and a row of frighteningly sharp teeth. A pink tongue lolls out and I get the impression it's actually laughing at me.

It lifts a pelt-covered paw and lazily scratches its stomach as it walks around me, assessing me. There's cunning behind its black eyes that I've not seen in any of the others that I've met.

I lunge at it with my sword, flicking my wrist, claiming first blood across its chest. It lets out a yelp of surprise at my audacity and drops to all fours. We circle each other and I am wary of those claws. My arm burns just remembering how much it hurt the last time – was it only the day before yesterday?

Suddenly, with a burst of speed, powered by those muscular haunches, the hybrid creature launches itself at me in a straight flying manoeuvre. I drop to my knees and flatten myself backwards, letting it fly straight over me.

I flick myself upwards in a mad acrobatic move Jamie relished making me practice. I grimace at my leg protesting at the stupid move, and run at the creature as it's busy turning. I rugby-tackle it, gagging at the smell of it. I have my arm around its neck and I basically wrestle my way round its body until I'm half astride it. It leans forward and gives me a clear shot so I can stab it with my sword. Adrenalin is pumping through my veins at full blast and I make a complete mess of my attack. The stab I was intending he manages to deflect by running full tilt into a tree. I'm launched high and crash down to the ground in a mess of broken ferns and foliage that, contrary to belief, is not at all comfortable to lie on.

But I'm up again and facing it. It looks a bit dazed as it charges at me, and it's off kilter. I quickly realize that it must have hurt itself by ramming that tree and it's surprisingly easy to sidestep its actual charge but I keep my sword in place and the hybrid's momentum carries it past me. I watch as the blade cuts along its neck, leaving a gaping bloody wound. It makes a soft yelping sound and as I turn to look at it, all four legs collapse beneath it before it rolls over and dies.

I throw up in the ferns and wipe my mouth with the back of my wrist. Then I grab some foliage and wipe the blade of my sword, before sheathing it. I kneel down next to the creature I've killed, forcing myself to look at it. Something glints at its throat – a collar made from leather. The sharp studs are on the inside of the collar, pressing into its flesh. The wounds are rotting, and that's what must be giving it that awful smell. I've heard about people training dogs to fight by using collars like this. The thought disgusts me and I almost feel sorry for the beast.

Chapter Forty

I move steadily in the growing heat, looking for a way down, ignoring the cuts and bruises and the ache in my leg. Occasionally I creep out of the foliage and check the cliff slopes. Three more guard patrols pass me by, they move in twos and threes and I keep low. I peer over the edge of the cliff and suddenly wish that I actually packed a backpack for my little jaunt to the island. The first thing Jamie always made us pack is rope.

I lie down on my stomach and peer further over the edge, anchoring myself by wrapping my hand around the roots of a tree. I reckon it's maybe one hundred feet straight down into the valley itself. The rock walls aren't as smooth as they looked. I can definitely see hand and toe grips.

I close my eyes and take a deep breath. I don't have time to run around this plateau to figure out other ways to get down. I will have to climb down and hope I don't break my neck in the process, thereby fulfilling Eilian's words that I would not leave the island alive. I smile wryly to myself. Wouldn't that be a laugh?

* * *

My descent is slow and painful. The valley is even warmer than the plateau above, and the further I climb down, the hotter it gets. I slip a few times and dangle in the air, hanging off my fingertips, but it's Jamie's voice telling me to pull up my big girl panties and get on with it that lets me swing myself to the next handhold and the next. There is no way that I would be able to face him if I didn't succeed. More than halfway down there's a small ledge and I have the chance to rest for a few minutes. I have no idea what time it is. All I know is that I'm hot, that the rising sun is unpleasantly warm and that rivulets of sweat are running down my body in places I didn't know I had places.

I reach the bottom of the valley and crawl off to lie in the shade of one of the pillars that form the processional avenue. The sand is almost unbearably hot and the air shimmers in the heat, making me feel as if I'm surrounded by hordes of silent people. It's a mirage, I tell myself. There really aren't thousands of people crowding this temple complex, no matter what it may feel like. I pull off my boots, wincing at the pain in my feet. I check them over for cuts before putting them back on. The skin on my hands is torn and cut from the jagged rocks I clung to and my arms are shaking with the strain of hanging on and supporting myself against the cliff face. It takes me some time to get my boots tied but eventually I stand up, leaning against the carved stone.

Squaring my shoulders, I turn to face the main pyramid. The place looks deserted but looks can be deceiving.

I keep to the outside of the columns, moving from shade to shade. The air is still, with no breeze at all. As I near the entrance, with the doorway gaping impossibly black in the brightness of the sun, I become aware of a droning noise rising from within.

I flash from the last column to the doorway, pressing my back against the black stone wall. I close my eyes for a few seconds, shutting out the bright sun, then duck my head around to look into the interior of the building. Shadows pierced by shafts of light. Motes dance in the air. The droning is definitely louder. I get the impression of cool empty space.

The entrance leads to a deserted hall; there's a small plinth in the middle of the floor and behind it there's another doorway. From the angle of it I assume the passage must go down because from the outside the pyramid isn't that large. I gather my courage and slip inside the building, keeping to the shadows. My eyes adjust to the darkness and I can see engravings on the walls. I edge closer. The art is similar in style to the stuff I've seen in my nan's books about the Mayans. I see supplicants on their knees. I see tortured people, hearts ripped out, mouths gaping. Prisoners having their blood drained into a vast flat bowl. An executioner wearing a stylized helmet that looks part armour, part monster. I look closely and let my fingers touch the mask it's wearing. It's a white skull with an impressive feathered headdress. Above the executioner on a large platform are five beings, human in shape, but dominating the entire scene. Thousands of bodies are scattered around, and when I sharpen my gaze, I can make out the supplicants and the crowd beyond them, made up of both human and Fae.

There are several scenes of debauchery, of death, of brutality. And in each set at least one of the giants is in attendance. The Elder Gods? Are these the creatures Istvan and Eadric are aiming to bring back?

The scenes become worse as I move along the friezes. There are battles, awful casualties, and the large figures, which I've decided must be the gods, bathe in the blood of those slaughtered. It goes on and on. I'm deep into the building now, a good hundred metres. I hate it, but I become inured to the deaths depicted on the walls and my pace quickens and I give each panel a cursory glance but even so I notice fewer people sacrificing to the gods and fewer pictures of the gods themselves. Another fifty metres on, I come to the wall blocking my way. A doorway is cut into the rock; above and to the sides of it are the final pictorials.

Above the doorway is the scene that's the paycheque. A ritual is being performed. The gods are in shackles but they do not look penitent. They stand on a platform above a volcano. My heart clutches. There are only four of them – what's happened to the fifth? I walk back to the previous panel that I skimmed and find it. A lone warrior stands over the fallen god, large sword raised above his head in triumph. I go back to the final scenes.

There, before the platform, are two men, one human, one definitely a Sidhe warrior. They are dressed finely and wear impressive headdresses. I wonder if they are priests, representing both human and Fae. On the platform above them stands another lone warrior, wearing a similar breastplate to the warrior who presumably vanquished the fallen god. He carries a sword almost as tall as he is and looks superbly fierce. The next scene shows only slight changes, with the young warrior standing closer to the four gods. He has the sword levelled at them and seems to be speaking to them.

The gods' faces are emotionless as they regard him. The armed warrior holds fast to four chains – one tied to the neck of each of the Elder Gods.

The human and Sidhe Fae face the armed warrior, their faces proud at his deeds. In a daze, my eyes drift to the next panel. The volcano is erupting but in the distance I see towering waves crashing towards the scene. The young man has bound the four gods to him, using the giant sword to twist the heavy chain in a complicated pattern and planting it point first into the ground.

The flames consume the gods and the warrior. The Sidhe and human are shown clambering into a coracle, not dissimilar to the one I used on my own lake crossing. Then the water is there, covering everything in huge cataclysmic stylized waves.

The next relief shows the human and Sidhe in conversation before parting ways; each acknowledges the other before leaving. They are shown sailing away from one another in what look like square boats. I reach out and touch the carved figures, realizing that this is the Sundering, where the Fae and human worlds part. This is where the Frontier and the Otherwhere came into existence.

I lean my forehead against the carved wall, feeling dread spread through me. As bad as the Sundering was, it's the return of the Elder Gods that genuinely scares me. If Eadric and Istvan succeed in bringing them back, these scenes of slaughter will become commonplace once more. It means that none of us, either Fae or human, would be safe again, no matter how we try to run.

Chapter Forty-One

Holding my magic close and sending a slender strand out before me, I venture along the dark tunnel. I'm right and it slopes downwards at a steep gradient. There's an odd smell in the air, not quite damp and not quite sulphurous, but something in between. The droning noise is louder, and it sounds more and more like a huge nest of angry wasps.

I creep forward, carrying my sword, every bit of me listening, watching, alert. I've not gone a hundred metres when there's a noise from behind so slight I almost miss it.

There is nowhere to hide from the oncoming group of soldiers behind me. I slide my sword back into its scabbard and peer upwards. I don't have much of a choice in the matter so I apologize to my aching limbs and cut hands before I close my eyes, throw a prayer to Lady Luck and climb the wall. I press my back against the rough ceiling and hope with all my might that my precarious hand and foot holds don't crumble.

The group of redcaps pass by below me grunting at one another animatedly. I hold my breath, hoping that none of them looks up. None of them do, but even so I wonder if they would have seen me in the shadows, clinging to the ceiling like an ugly spider. I wait up there for a few more minutes until my arms start shaking. Getting down is a little noisy and a little difficult and inelegant but I take it as a win because I've managed not to get myself killed.

Creeping further down the passage is frightening and my heart thuds so loudly in my ears I have to stop now and again to try and calm it down. I'm almost on the lone goblin sentry when I notice him. He's dressed in dark clothes and has his back turned towards me.

I carefully lay my sword down and ghost up behind him. He's not much bigger than I am and I have the element of surprise. My arm whips around his neck then I tighten my hold.

He bucks beneath me in shock and tries to shout out, but with so much pressure on his larynx, nothing comes out. I focus on my training and grit my teeth as he squirms and twists in an attempt to escape. He rams me into the wall and I hit my head, but I refuse to let go.

Eventually his movements still but I hold my grip a bit longer just to make sure I've choked him into unconsciousness. I make quick work of tying him up, using his handy rope belt. I rummage in his pockets, trying not to gag at the stench of him, and find a slimy handkerchief. I stuff that in his mouth and, using my knife, I hastily cut a strip from his shirt to bind his mouth.

Next, I drag him further into the small alcove and leave him trussed up like a turkey, ready for the oven.

With my sword back in my hand, I move painfully slowly

down the passage. The passage widens into a beautifully carved archway and as I edge closer I play out my magic – millimetre by aching millimetre.

I'm shown a natural amphitheatre in a cave. A wide avenue, splitting the seating in half, runs straight down the middle. The stage is at the bottom of the natural slope within the cavern and seats have been carved from the rock in some distant past, so that they face the stage. It looks nice enough, like Shakespeare in the Park if only there weren't chimera patrolling the front of the stage area. The droning noise is coming from the throats of maybe a thousand bound people, neatly arranged in rows before the stage. Everyone is dressed in grey robes and seems to be in some kind of trance. The noise they are making rises and falls in cadence as they sway from side to side. I count maybe fifteen guards dotted around the amphitheatre. They are a mix of redcaps and chimeras and they all look tense. Their movements are quick and vicious when they feel someone's not making enough droning sounds. I watch them kick and lash out at a few bound people and I feel my blood thump against my temples at the cruelty. The people are all bound with rope, and the ropes are tied to metal loops thrust into the ground before them.

Up the slope, towards the back of the cave, is a natural overhang and up there are five ogres in charge of the drums that give the beat the rhythmic swaying. The sound isn't entirely unpleasant and reminds me of the hypnotic rhythm of Celtic drums I've heard at folk festivals with my nan.

But the rest of it, the people tied up, seeming to be in some kind of trance, I never thought I'd actually see anything like this in real life. I hunker down for as long as I dare to watch them through my enhanced sight.

The amphitheatre stretches downwards towards a stage, which in turn is dominated by a curved slab of black basalt maybe two storeys high.

I pull my magic back and consider my next move. The only way to get down into the amphitheatre is to walk down the ramp, in plain view of the guards and whoever else is watching. I don't like that idea at all. There has to be another passage or something at the back of the stage area, or how else will people get up there, without jumping up at the front? I rest my head against the rough wall behind me and think hard.

The seemingly random sentinel I took down, I realize, must have been guarding something, probably a gap leading to a passage I didn't see in the dark. I creep back the way I've just come and find him where I'd left him, still slumped to the side and out cold. A faint whisper of air stirs my damp hair as I run my hands along the wall. I encounter a gap hidden by the folds of the wall, not very wide, but wide enough for me to pass through if I turn sideways. I drag the body behind me as I wind my way along the passage. From the way it curves and wends its way along, I know I'm heading in the right direction, flanking the side of the amphitheatre, meaning that with any luck I should come out behind the stage.

'You will sing them back,' demands a familiar voice.

'Or what?'

Thorn's voice brings me up short. He sounds tired and

hurt and thoroughly pissed off. I grin, relief flooding me. He is alive and channelling his inner brat.

'I may be persuaded to see how many fingers I can remove until you agree,' comes the other voice. Istvan! Hearing his voice now, without being able to see him, I recognize it from the mirror at the Manor and from the troll's cave. Heavy with sinister intent, he's given up any pretence of sounding like the king's chamberlain and friend.

'You think I will bring about the destruction of my world for the loss of my fingers.' There's a harsh tone of derision in Thorn's voice now. 'You are very much mistaken.'

There's a noise, a cracking sound, the smell of flesh burning and a muffled cry. I jerk forward, my anger flaring, and cat-foot it swiftly down the narrow passage, keeping my sword ahead of me so that it doesn't clang against the walls.

My magic pushes into the chamber and I crouch low, letting it be my eyes. The room isn't very big, maybe the size of our conservatory at the Manor. Thorn is shackled with iron manacles to a solid piece of rock jutting from the ground. A strip of metal, probably iron, is cuffed around his throat like a dog collar and his skin looks red and swollen where the iron's chafed it. There are bruises that weren't there before and the cut along his cheekbone looks inflamed. His bottom lip is split and I watch him spit out a stream of blood and saliva.

'How about now?' Istvan says, prowling around before Thorn. He's no longer wearing modern clothes, but instead is dressed in a dramatic carnelian-coloured robe with a high collar. It highlights his tan, making him look like a crazy emperor from a far-off sun-drenched land. His long dark hair's scraped back from his forehead and tied back neatly.

Thorn answers, dropping his voice lower. 'Never, in a million years.'

Istvan extends his hand and a line of darkly alive smoke snakes from his palm. It solidifies, then suddenly lashes out to strike Thorn's chest. There's a smell of burning flesh and Thorn gives a muffled curse but maintains his defiance. 'Torture me all you will, Istvan. None of this convinces me to help you.'

I'm about to move forward into the room when a movement in the gloom at the back of the chamber catches my attention. I recall my magic. I don't want to alert anyone to my presence, however small the risk of detection, so I skulk in the shadows and stare but there is no movement now, just a half-suggested shape of something tall and spindly.

Reluctantly I play a thread of magic out. I send it along the side of the room, creeping slowly, so slowly, so as not to draw Istvan's attention.

My sight creeps past cages with rotting carcasses of half-made things. Aborted experiments, I realize. There's a workbench with all manner of tubes and glass vials. I see a silver tray containing various implements that look like torture tools. I try not to focus on these, or the way the light from the torches on the wall reflects off their rusted blades, or how I can see globules of dried blood and what looks like bone still caught in the teeth of a broken saw. The thread creeps past another opening in the wall, where I saw the movement.

Apparently, not all Istvan's experiments failed.

Chapter Forty-Two

The thing lurking in the shadows is a good six feet tall and for a second my mind is completely blank as I try and take in what I'm seeing. My first thought is scorpion and my second thought is *Oh crap*. I see a carapace, pincers set above a human mouth, a row of four round large black eyes across a human brow. It has four segmented arms on either side of its body, ending in obscenely large hands, but a top pair – the fifth pair – end in claws. And of course there is a tail. The sting is viscous looking with venom glistening on its curved tip.

'I have someone to show you,' Istvan says, and his voice sounds particularly gloating. 'I think you'll be very pleased to see him.'

He makes a gesture to the scorpion creature, who disappears down the dark passage. I hold my breath, watching Thorn. The cuts across his chest aren't bleeding any more, which is good. From the look of hatred on his face he's ready to tear Istvan apart if he could get loose.

Istvan moves a few things around on a small table to the side. 'We were lucky enough to capture him right at the beginning of the campaign. It was all so very exciting.' He looks up at the movement by the door. 'Ah, see? Here is my guest. I have some interesting plans for him, but first I thought I'd show you.'

I bite my lip as the scorpion hauls a man dressed in tatters into the room. He is in very bad shape, with an arm dangling uselessly by his side. His face is a mask of bruises and cuts and his hair is matted with blood and gore. There are cuts across his body, revealed by the filthy torn shirt he's wearing. His feet are bare and his leggings are dirty and full of blood. He's leaning heavily on the scorpion creature, favouring his left leg – the other one looks broken.

'Kieran?' Thorn's voice is hoarse with horror.

Istvan walks to Thorn's older brother and grabs his face, forcing the half-conscious prince to look Thorn in the face. 'Guess who's visiting, Prince Kieran? Your baby brother. Say hello.'

With that he nods to the scorpion chimera, who lifts Kieran in the air and hurls him at Thorn. Kieran hits Thorn's body like a sack of potatoes, head-butting him in the process, and slumps to the ground at his bound feet with a moan. Distantly he must be aware that no one is around him because he vainly tries to get up but Istvan stalks over and kicks him in the side, rolling him over onto his back.

'Aren't you happy to see your brother?' he asks Kieran, bending close. 'It took me some time to find him and bring him here. I know you've missed him so. Are you not grateful?'

'You son of a motherless goat,' Kieran grinds out. 'You

will rot in the lowest of dungeons of the Citadel for all eternity.'

'What is it with Aelfric's sons?' Istvan asks no one in particular. 'You excel at making threats you cannot possibly keep.' He stands up and casually lands another kick to Kieran's unprotected stomach.

Kieran makes a dry retching sound but watches Istvan narrowly.

'You were our confidant,' he grinds out. 'Someone we called a friend.'

Istvan looks pityingly at Kieran. 'Unfortunately, that friendship was merely to serve a grander scheme. From when I first entered the household of King Aelfric the Great, the noble, the illegitimate ruler of Alba, I ostensibly became the perfect servant, the perfect adviser.' He pauses. 'My family sat on the right hand of the Elder Gods and we did their bidding. Why would your father assume I would be happy to serve him?' He rubs his face, the strain starting to show. 'The gods were banished, locked away because of treachery but we kept our long watch. We have worked tirelessly to bring this day about and, without realizing it, Aelfric delivered to us the perfect vessel.' He points at Thorn. 'Your baby brother.'

'You are insane, Istvan.'

Istvan looks surprised. 'No, not insane, Kieran. Realistic. For years I've done your father's bidding. I've seen the way Alba's lost its heart, working with humans, with the likes of the Blackharts, signing treaties. Even Suola, the feared Queen of Air and Darkness herself, dare not steal human children for revels. Now we hide in the dark and humans think of us as stories told at bedtime. No longer. It's time to let the Elder Gods walk again. Human and Fae will once more have living gods to fear.' I glimpse a parody of a smile. 'And fear they shall.'

'How have we never noticed how twisted you are?' Thorn asks him, his voice incredulous. 'All these years . . .'

'Because, little princeling, I only let you see what you wanted to see. As a servant, no one notices us, no one takes us seriously.' He narrows his eyes. 'Do you know how much your family is disliked? It was easy to find supporters for Eadric's little rebellion.' He lays his hand against Thorn's cheek. 'And not just in the Citadel but within the Courts too. Our people are tired of having to skulk, Thorn. Once more we want to walk freely between both worlds. Have humans see us and fear us for what we truly are.'

My mind is reeling. The thought of this happening is horrifying. Hearing this little speech of his, there is no doubt in my mind that Istvan has gone over to the dark side completely.

I wonder how long it will take him to lose his patience and stop his grandstanding in front of the two brothers. I've seen him control Thorn with his powers and I worry that maybe, just maybe, Aelfric's sons could be swayed if the magic used against them is strong enough.

'Let us go,' Thorn says, keeping his voice low, friendly. 'Let us go and my father won't order you into the cages with the griffins.'

Istvan doesn't reply. He strikes Thorn's face, raking his nails across his cheek. 'Shut up,' he says, wiping his hands on his robe. 'Unless, of course, you are prepared to sing the Elder Gods home.'

'Don't . . .' Kieran's managed to crawl a few feet away and is bracing himself against the table leg. 'Thorn, don't do it.'

I've seen enough from a distance. It's time to act. I rein in my magic and move to the other side of the passage and, keeping to the shadows, I enter the room, my back pressed against the wall. Istvan and his familiar's attention is focused on the two princes and I take full advantage of that. I creep around the room and notice Thorn's eyes widen slightly when he sees me, but he concentrates on Istvan.

'There is nothing you can do that will make me be part of this ritual.'

'Not even when I promise I'll keep some of your friends alive, perhaps?' Istvan's voice drips with insincerity and he's standing close to Thorn now, right up in his face, unaware of anything else in the room. His servant's watching too, facing away from me. Kieran's doing his best to try and stand upright but not having much success.

I draw a breath, ground myself and let fly a wild shout that has all my pent-up anger and frustration in it. As I yell I run at the scorpion as it turns to face me. My blade slices air as it neatly pirouettes out of the way and I land heavily. There's a scraping noise behind me and I catch Kieran's eye as he manages to grab hold of something on the table above his head and hurls it at Istvan's head.

I duck beneath the scorpion's pincers and drive a wild cut upwards, catching it beneath one of its arms/legs, whatever. As I withdraw the sword a gush of black blood and goo arcs through the air. I'm too slow and don't manage to duck the solid blow it lands me on the side of the head with one of its giant hands. I reel a few steps but steady myself against Thorn, who is doing his utmost to free himself from his shackles.

'Hi,' I say to him, flashing a smile. 'We should stop meeting like this.'

'What are you doing here?' he gasps out, but he has a smile for me. 'You're crazy, you know.'

I launch myself at the scorpion again, perhaps proving he's right. Its tail is up and it's got its arms (I'll call them arms) spread wide, making it look even bigger. Kieran is wrestling with Istvan but, to be honest, it's more like flailing at him with all the finesse of a wet towel.

My blade leaps forward and I execute a perfect cut across the scorpion chimera's abdomen. More goo spills out and I watch in horror as it sizzles when it hits the floor. Oh great, acidic blood. I whirl aside, conscious of the engorged stinger swaying above its head.

I see Istvan punching Kieran repeatedly in the face until the prince drops to the floor in a crumpled heap. There's a truly ugly expression on Istvan's face as he stalks to Thorn. He rains blows on Thorn's face and unprotected body. Black shadows are everywhere now, all around Istvan, circling Thorn, whispering to them both. I see them climbing Thorn like vines and he writhes in pain.

'I am getting sick of you now,' Istvan grinds out between blows. 'You and your entire family. For once in your disgustingly futile lives, will you just do as you are bid?'

I run from the scorpion and dash at Istvan, my sword

raised. Istvan turns to look at me and lifts a negligent hand and a ball of black light hits me full in the chest. I fly through the air, crashing into the wall in a tumble of legs and arms. The scorpion is there within the blink of an eye and I lift myself up, shaking my head to try and clear it, grasping for the handle of my sword.

Chapter Forty-Three

My sword is gone. It's lying between the scorpion and Istvan. Another blow rocks me as the scorpion punches me in the gut. I double over, using it as cover and trigger the mechanism of the rod strapped to my arm. It whips out with a satisfying *snick* and as I straighten I lash the rod forward in an aimed blow. It catches the scorpion across its face and I hear an eye pop. I follow it up with another swipe, backhanded this time, and am gratified to see a gash opening across its neck as the iron rod connects with its skin. I drive my fist hard into its abdomen and am repaid by being lifted in the air and thrown. As I fly through the air, before I fall, I wonder if the amount of airtime I'm getting during this adventure qualifies me for a pilot's licence.

I hit one of the cages with its mouldering contents hard and for a moment I'm tempted to just lie there and quietly bleed but then I'm up and flinging myself at the scorpion again. This time things go badly wrong. It catches me mid-air, as if I'm a ballerina – a bloody and sore one – and the stinger descends in a rapid arc, delivering a pulse of venom into my upper leg.

I can quite honestly say that I have never in my life felt such pain. I let out a scream that for a moment even stops Istvan in shocked surprise. The poison burns – dear heavens, the pain is surreal. It pounds through my veins, tearing at me as it goes. The scorpion drops me, losing interest, knowing the poison will make short work of me.

I curl into a tight ball and sob as the fire rages through me. I can dimly hear Thorn screaming something but it's Istvan's voice that penetrates the fog clouding my brain.

'Do you swear?'

'Yes, you worthless pig, just let her go.'

Istvan's laughter is ugly. 'You will promise thrice. A thrice-spoken promise is binding, even for a son of Alba.'

'No . . .' My voice is raw. 'Thorn, you idiot. Don't do it.'

'I will sing the Elder Gods awake for you,' Thorn said clearly. 'If you let her and Kieran go. This I promise. I promise, I promise.'

'What will your family say, to know all it took for you to turn on them, is the sight of a pretty . . . oh wait, a dirty, bruised, once-upon-a-time pretty face?'

'Die. Just die,' Thorn grinds out between bloody teeth. And for full effect he spits at Istvan's face. For his trouble he gets a slap that rocks his head back.

'Ah, my time is not yet decreed.' Istvan's unpleasant smile is smug. 'Come, now. I need to go and prepare for the ritual.'

He clicks his fingers at the scorpion and it scuttles forward. 'Just drag them into a cage for now.' He walks over and hunkers down next to me, pressing his face unbearably close to mine. 'You will have a perfect view of your handsome boyfriend calling forth the destruction of humanity. Isn't it exciting?'

I give him the thousand-yard stare I've been practising in the mirror but he seems unfazed by it. He wraps his fingers in my hair and pulls my head back, making me bend backwards to prevent him from snapping my neck. I refuse to cry out and instead I scrape the bottom of the barrel and come up with a laugh that sounds unhinged, even to my ears.

'There is no place you will be able to hide,' I promise him through bloody lips. 'If I don't get you, my family will. Do you know that if a Blackhart swears blood vengeance the entire family is bound by that oath?'

'After today, girl, your family will be lucky to survive. After today we make this decrepit world brand new.' He stands up and nods to the scorpion. 'Lock them up securely. We don't want any more heroics.'

I fight as much as I can against the scorpion's grip as it drags me to the nearest cage. It's mercifully empty of Istvan's failed experiments. I'm tossed inside and a moan escapes from me as my thigh crashes into one of the bars. Kieran is thrown in next and I try and catch him. He's too heavy for me, but at least some of him hits me instead of the hard floor. I hold on to him and check his pulse. It flutters weakly under my fingers and I peel his eyelids back. His pupils react to the light and I almost cry from relief.

The gate rattles and shuts behind me. I spin around and grab the bars, yelling, 'How are you going to survive? If the Elder Gods are destroying the world, how will you survive?'

The scorpion launches a kick at the bars and I whip my hands away. 'And you?' I say to it. 'Do you think that thing will let you live?'

It makes a sound that sounds suspiciously like a fart and leaves the room through the open doorway. I recoil from the stench and sit back against the bars.

The pain in my leg is so bad now I find myself doing puffy-breathing to try and control it. I feel as if I'm on fire on the inside.

'Kit?'

'Yes?' I grind out.

'Are you okay?'

'Not . . . really.' I crawl past Kieran so I can get to the other side of the cage. I can just see Thorn. He's still trying to squirm out of the chains binding him to the rock. I draw in a deep breath and speak again. 'I don't know if the poison is fatal.'

'In a high enough dosage, yes. He stung you only once.' He shakes his head and stares at me through strands of damp hair. 'I am so angry with you. Why did you come here? By yourself? Why not bring the army with you?'

I pant out a laugh and spit out some blood. 'Well, I wanted all the glory for myself,' I tell him. 'I thought I'd walk in, beat up the insane sorcerer, throw you over my shoulder and carry you home.'

That gets a chuckle from him and I grin. 'You are insane,' he says. 'Did you bring anyone else with you?'

'No. They were all more interested in arguing than listening to me, so I left. I'm sure we'll be saved any second now.' I raise my voice, hoping that the scorpion hybrid or Istvan or anyone else is listening and will let us go. 'Any. Second. Now.'

Kieran lets out a groan and moves feebly at my feet. I push myself away from the bars and kneel next to him. 'Kieran? Can you hear me?'

'Who . . . ?' he mutters, trying to get a fix on my face. I move around so he can see me properly.

'I'm Kit,' I say. 'I'm a Blackhart.'

'Great,' he says, his voice raw. 'I'm not dressed to meet pretty girls.' When he coughs, he coughs up blood but he waves me away as I try and wipe his chin. 'Thorn?'

'Is still alive. Tied up like a turkey, though.'

'Help me . . .'

I help him sit upright and he leans back against me.

'Thorn?' he calls roughly.

'Kieran?'

'Don't do this,' he says. 'Don't . . .'

'Kieran!' Thorn leans forward against his chains, peering at us from across the room. 'How are you doing?'

'Give me a moment.' He closes his eyes as he gathers himself. I lean against the bars, letting my breathing get back to normal and watch. There's a soft shimmer in the air and a light brush of magic that rolls gently over me.

He's healing himself, I realize, leaning closer, intrigued by the way his colour returns to normal. His breathing seems less laboured too and he flexes the arm that hung useless only a few moments ago.

'Kieran,' Thorn says, pulling against his bindings. 'You

have to take Kit and get away. When the ritual starts, things will go downhill fast.'

'I'm sorry to tell you this, little brother, but I don't think young Kit here is planning on running. Neither am I.' He draws in a steadying breath. 'I almost feel ready for one of mother's dreadful parties.'

Thorn actually growls at him in frustration. 'It's not safe here, Kieran.'

I edge away from Kieran, making sure he can sit by himself. I'm back by the gate to see if I can figure out how to get the lock open. It's an ugly thing, big and old. It takes a normal, if large, key. I grip it and rattle it against the bars. It seems solid enough.

I push my magic through my fingers and coax it into the lock. The tumblers are a bit rusty, but they look sturdy enough. What did I have on me to help me? I take a catalogue of everything I'm carrying. Shoes, laces, socks, jeans, belt, T-shirt. There has to be . . . I squirm as much as I can and bite back a yelp of pain as I press against the sting in my leg.

'I think your girlfriend is getting undressed,' Kieran tells Thorn. 'Pity you can't see.'

I laugh. 'Sorry to disappoint you. I'm just taking my belt off.'

'Oh?' he says, sounding intrigued.

'What are you doing?' Thorn hisses. 'I can hear more noise from outside.' He's right. I can hear the sound of the huge kettledrums. The volume of droning has also increased. I don't know much about evil magics and spells to bring back ancient gods, but something tells me that whatever is going to happen will be happening soon.

'Ah, that would be the thousands of slaves he's got building energy in the amphitheatre outside.' I brandish my belt in relief and examine the pin. It might just do the trick. Breaking and entering has never been my strong suit and I suddenly wish I had Megan's delicate touch, but if wishes were something . . . horses? What a stupid saying.

I push my arms through the bars and grip the lock tightly. I close my eyes and focus all my attention on my fingertips and guide the pin into the keyhole, using my magic to see where it's going.

Chapter Forty-Four

All of eternity passes and I hardly breathe. My arms burn with strain and my head is pounding from a headache that feels as if I've been to an all-night party and drunk all the alcohol.

I feel Kieran's fingers press warningly against my side as the scorpion scuttles into the room. It doesn't even look at us.

Instead it's there for Thorn. It swiftly removes the set of iron manacles keeping Thorn bound to the plinth. I hold my breath, hoping that Thorn will have his chance to get free, but no such luck. It grips Thorn's arms in one huge hand and clamps the irons back around his wrists. When Thorn tries to pull free, it cuffs him around the head and pushes him past us, and out of the doorway, manhandling him with ease.

The *snick* of the padlock opening is the most beautiful sound in the world, right then. I sag with relief and slowly unhook it, carefully placing it on the floor inside the cage. I press against the door and it creaks open.

'If I can get out of here,' Kieran says softly, 'into the amphitheatre, I think I'll be able to help.'

'In what way?' I ask him as I push the gate open further. 'There are about thirty guards out there.'

'I can draw on the energy they are generating but I have to be in the same place, with them.' He draws a breath. 'There is a spell I can try to cast. It's not something I'd try under normal circumstances.'

'What does this spell do, exactly?' I know I sound wary but it's because I know spells cast by someone who's not in full health can go very badly wrong. Helena's diary mentioned that much at least.

'That lot out there are already pretty wound up. The spell I want to try will redirect their own energy back at themselves. They should start to snap out of whatever trance they're in, see where they are and try to escape. The spell works on their emotions and the stronger the emotions, the wilder the need to get away will be. With luck, it will distract them all enough for you to rescue Thorn.'

'How will I not get these delusions?'

'Illusions,' he corrects me, straightening with difficulty. 'If you stay behind me, you should be fine. I will be projecting it towards them, away from us.'

I'm not sure I'm happy with this but I nod and help him limp further. I grind my teeth as pain flares in my leg and I can actually feel the pain and poison pulse upwards. The pain drives some of my doubt from my mind. I'm not entirely sure whether Kieran's planning will work. The shape of the amphitheatre doesn't really lend itself to projecting in only one direction.

'Allow me to help,' he says, leaning forward before I can stop him. His hands hover just above my thigh, cupping my leg. It's the same kind of heat I remember from when Olga healed my muscle ache. 'I can't do anything about the poison in your system, but this bit of healing will help with the pain.'

'Thank you,' I say with genuine gratitude. I test out my leg and although it's still pretty sore, it's no longer the only thing I can think about.

'Weapons?' Kieran asks after a few painful paces towards the doorway. 'We have none.'

I leave him leaning against the wall and hobble back to find my sword and knife. I hold both out to him and he takes hold of the sword.

'Nice blade,' he says. 'Yours?'

'Yes. Before me it belonged to one of my great-aunts.'

'I'll try not to break it.'

We grin at each other and hobble through the doorway and down the narrow passage. The heat here is incredible and within seconds I have sweat pouring off my face. The voices are loud now and the sound of the drums reverberating through the cavern is ear-achingly loud. I can't see much; the dais is off to our right but I can see the bound slaves and their guards.

I leave Kieran leaning against the wall and creep forwards on my knees.

The huge slab of stone dominates the stage, easily twenty feet high and maybe nine across. From this close, I can see that there are countless runes carved on the stone. I recognize a few: the one that means 'ox' for strength and the weird triangle one with longer points at the bottom that means 'fate'. The others make my eyes hurt the longer I stare at them. The entire centre has the sheen of mercury with the light from the lanterns and braziers placed around the amphitheatre.

Istvan has changed out of his robes and now wears another flowing garment: this one the colour of early-morning mist. It floats around him and I'm horrified to see ghostly faces with open mouths press against the fabric. It roils unpleasantly and changes colour, from a dark grey to black, then grey again.

Thorn is standing before the great stone pillar, his arms and legs stretched wide by an iron chain anchored to two tall wooden pillars so that he's effectively forming an X shape. He's still wearing the weird iron collar. On a raised plinth in front of him there's a wide shallow copper bowl that doesn't look like it's held a bit of salad in all its life. The world's biggest sword rests in a cradle right in front of the stone slab.

I turn back to Kieran to find him kneeling next to me. His colour is better and he gives me an encouraging nod. I help him stand up and while everyone's attention is focused on Istvan as he moves to stand in the centre of the dais, I help Kieran into the amphitheatre, keeping to the pools of shadow created by the staggered positions of the torches.

'Go help my brother,' he says, pressing his lips close to my ear.

I give his arm a squeeze and steal towards the dais, hunkering down, firmly ignoring the pain in my leg. Behind me the chanting has increased in volume but I have no trouble hearing Istvan's thunderous voice. He's speaking in a language that sounds as old as time and it makes my bones ache with fatigue.

When did it get this hot in here? I tug at the neck of my T-shirt and fight the urge to close my eyes. My heart thuds against my aching ribs in time with the cacophony of the drums. Panic wraps itself around me and all I want to do is run and run and never ever stop.

But instead I creep backwards, back towards the doorway that leads to the chamber. If I lock myself back in the cage, I'll be fine, I tell myself. Or maybe even if I leave the complex completely, climb back up the walls and get to the top of the plateau and find the coracle and make my way back across the lake, it will be even better. Safer.

I nod to myself, aware that I'm in danger of whispering anxiously, repeating 'must get away, must get away' just under my breath. I'm in the passage and I turn to run (limp fast) but I'm brought up short in my escape by hobbling full tilt into the scorpion. Holding onto my sanity and pinning down my fear, I shift and duck as it grabs at me. I make it only a few paces away when two redcaps appear at the far end of the corridor. Their expressions of surprise would've been funny had I not been this scared.

I look around the narrow passage, wondering how to evade them, and then how to get outside into the fresh air and away from this place. The scorpion doesn't bother thinking any of this. Instead, it picks me up and throws me bodily at the two redcaps. I manage to twist and curl into a ball, using my momentum to knock one of them down. It bounces, hard, lets out a groan and lies still. I land badly and roll off him, feeling faint with pain. I stand with difficulty and face the remaining creature. I've managed to keep hold of my knife and I reverse the blade against the length of my arm and close with the remaining redcap. Its bulging eyes widen in surprise at my audacity and it throws a low blow that hits me in the lower ribs, just as I slice the blade across its forehead. A gush of blood drops into its eyes and it staggers away, desperately trying to clear its eyes. The pain in my midriff, combined with the throbbing in my leg, brings me back to reality. Kieran's spell has somehow managed to drag me into its net, despite his assurances. With a muttered curse, I spin and hobble towards the scorpion chimera as it makes for the door leading into the amphitheatre.

Chapter Forty-Five

Gateway to the Gods: This is an ancient relic housed in the deepest dungeons of the Citadel, Alba's primary city. The gateway was used during the great banishing of the Elder Gods in the Time Before Time and was thought lost for a few thousand years. An item of extraordinary power, the piece of ancient basalt has a variety of runic symbols carved across its surface. It is unclear how the item is activated and, as far as we understand it, it is unstable and not easy to control. (See Mount Pelée – eruption 1902)

From an archived report filed in HMDSDI HQ, 1919

'Kit!'

The voice behind me startles me and I swing around to see Olga running towards me. She's dressed in light leather armour and looks impossibly at ease carrying a sword. I don't even stop to think how she got to the island and came to be here, looking as fresh as a daisy, ready to kick ass.

'Olga,' I gasp in relief, holding my side. 'Istvan's calling them,' I say to her, pointing down the passage.

'Watch her,' she says as she sweeps by, and as she does, she looks over her shoulder and commands, 'Lock her away.'

I follow her gaze and spot the redcap running towards me. Abstractedly I wonder how Olga expects me to lock her up because really, why wouldn't I just knock her unconscious? Then I realize Olga wasn't talking to me, but *about* me and by then my aggressor is almost on me.

I drop into fighter's stance, my knife low and ready. The redcap dummies left, then comes in right, leaving its entire flank exposed. I step in and sink the blade up to the hilt beneath its armpit. It lets out a surprised yelp and drops to the floor in a rapidly growing pool of blood.

I move hurriedly away from the blood as my brain painstakingly puts things together.

Flashes of a limping Olga helping us at her house, of the chimeras lurking outside her house, attacking Scarlet. I remember Olga telling us of Holds being attacked, the trolls' location, closely followed by Ioric Brightwing's attack on Thorn. She arrived at Aiden's with a manuscript that she 'found' at the shop, our first exposure to the prophecy. She's been shadowing our every move and I recall her passing on her private conversations with Aelfric, actually drawing us to the site of the final confrontation.

Olga is helping Istvan. The thought makes me nauseous.

I try to keep calm as I ghost down the passage and hesitate a few feet from the doorway. I can't screw this up, I tell myself. Regardless of how tired I am and how sore I feel, I have promises to keep.

Slowly, painfully, I move forwards, stopping just inside the doorway, and peer out. I catch sight of Kieran hugging the shadows. The scorpion chimera lies at his feet, its limbs hacked off and its head sitting neatly on its thorax.

Kieran's wearing one of the captives' grey robes, but instead of facing Istvan on the dais, he faces the bound slaves with outstretched palms. The slaves don't look as immersed in their chanting now. Some are clawing at their manacles, desperately trying to escape. Others are openly sobbing in terror. There is no sign of their guards, which is not necessarily a good thing. The drummers above are heedless of the panic below, hammering away, their eyes blank.

Olga is on the dais with Istvan, shadows whirling around her in agitation. She too has her voice raised in supplication, holding the gleaming sword aloft in one hand. It could even be the same sword wielded by the warrior in the frieze.

Movement catches my attention and I lift my eyes to the mirrored surface of the stone and I feel my insides clench. It had been reflecting the packed amphitheatre but now it shows a vast expanse of ink-dark sky. Things are moving in there, just beneath the surface, big things that dwarf this hellish island. I pull my gaze away from it with difficulty, finding the void dangerously hypnotic.

Olga walks forward to stand before Thorn and touches his shoulder. Her face looks different. Older and more mature. Her dark curls move in a soft breeze and there's a lushness to her features that stuns me. She looks more vibrant, more alive and, I hate saying this, like a true demigoddess.

Thorn speaks and she smiles at him. One of her shadows drapes itself around her like a cloak as she runs an almost tender hand down Thorn's face and neck, leaving marks like ink on his skin and I notice she's careful not to touch the iron band around his throat.

'If you don't say the words, Thorn, your little caged pet dies, I promise you. She's right over there, locked away, where she belongs.'

'If you touch her I will kill you.'

Olga shakes her head and tuts. 'How?' she asks. 'Your magic is bound to our cause now.' She turns to Istvan and gestures to him. 'Do it, brother.'

My mind reels. Brother? They're related? Or is it some kind of cultish title?

I stare but I just can't see the similarity, except maybe in their build and a certain slant to their eyes. Olga is wild and vibrant and stunning. Istvan is all about darkness, hidden things, bad things.

Ugly tendrils smoke between the three of them, binding them tight.

Istvan lifts the copper bowl before him and drinks deeply. He passes it to Thorn, who refuses it. Thorn's powerless to withstand when Olga makes an impatient noise and grabs Thorn's jaw, forcing whatever is in the bowl down his throat, which then spills down his bloodstained shirt in a mess of dark liquid.

She takes a delicate sip herself before returning it to the plinth. My fear spikes as Istvan turns back to face the mirror.

'Let us begin.'

He brings his hands together with a loud clap, and a low rumble from above answers him. I peer upwards instinctively, into the roof of the giant cavern. To my surprise, there's a gap in the ceiling, big enough maybe for a large plane to fly through. Smoke from the many braziers streams towards Istvan as a wind whips through the cavern, carrying the scent of heavy tropical flowers and thunderstorms. The smoke swirls hypnotically around the central column of stone and something draws me a step forward before I can help it. Istvan has shed his previous dour demeanour and seems almost manic. He's now hurling streams of energy towards the stone, his movements faster and faster. The entire block of stone lights up like a beacon, the runes on its surface shining vividly in the dim light of the cavern.

Olga runs her hand down Thorn's arm and grips his hand. I expect to see Thorn refuse or do something, but it's clear that whatever he's drunk has dropped him into a stupor. She leans forward, unhooks the iron collar from around his neck and gives him a nod.

For a second he starcs at her blankly but then understanding dawns.

I recognize his voice immediately. It's pitched perfectly to be heard above the drums and the chanting. I don't know the words – it's not in any language that's been spoken for the past several thousands of years – it is both beautiful and frightening, made more so by the depth of feeling and yearning in Thorn's voice.

The tiny hairs on my arms lift in response to his voice. It's filled with rich expression, with need and love. It's the voice of an acolyte kneeling in supplicant prayer to his god. It's private and beautiful in a way I can't actually explain.

I blink against tears forming in my eyes and shoot a glance at Istvan and see that he's as captivated by Thorn's voice as I am. The droning behind me has fallen quiet; the entire amphitheatre is still, except for the drums and Thorn's voice.

I creep up the stairs, praying that Istvan's attention is wholly on Thorn as he performs the summoning. Olga will have to be dealt with separately, I decide, but actually hope that Kieran will take care of her.

I stay as low to the ground as my aching leg allows and edge close to the edge of the dais, keen to stay in Istvan's blind spot. I'm three feet from him when he turns to look at me, his face completely blank, his eyes a dark red, the colour of heart's blood.

I explode to my feet and launch a neat roundhouse kick to Istvan's head. It snaps his head back but he moves with the blow, taking a few steps sideways. He shakes off the kick and looks at me in surprise before coming at me with the blade in his hand. My leg protests as I ready myself.

He's got the sickle raised and brings it down towards my face. I go high, grabbing his wrist with my left hand, holding it as tight and hard as I can, and swivel my hips as I plunge my blade into his neck to the hilt. Istvan drops like a stone and I turn to help Thorn but a blast of magic hits me full in my side and I stagger, falling hard on my knees on the polished black stone. My blade skitters across the floor, spinning out of reach. I smell singed skin and I know it's mine, as is the scream of pain that tears from my throat as my leg spasms painfully beneath me.

Istvan rises slowly, his hand clasped to the wound in his neck. There's very little blood coming from it, I notice in horror. Behind him his sister has turned to watch the commotion and she looks thoroughly pissed off.

Chapter Forty-Six

I scramble up and look over my shoulder at Thorn, who has not looked away from the mirrored surface of the stone at all. His voice is stronger than before, just as beautiful, and he seems mesmerized before the sheen, its limitless depths, seeing something to which none of us is privy.

'Thorn!' I shout at him. 'Now would be a good time to snap out of whatever spell he's put you under!'

Istvan sends another flare of magic at me. I expect this and twirl away, feeling very acrobatic in my head but really it's more like a sideways crab-scrabble. As I spin, another blast, this time from Olga, hits me and I go flying into the base of the large basalt stone. I see movement in the amphitheatre as I struggle to stand up, sobbing with pain. Kieran's been hard at work, releasing the people tied to the floor of the amphitheatre. Everyone is running, helping others get loose. I see three dead redcap guards and wonder how he killed them.

A great groaning sound comes from the column of rock behind me and I look up to see a giant horned head push through the surface of the mirror. The rock's mirrored surface stretches and bulges before tearing with a wet sound, like an egg sack breaking. I look up at the creature towering above me as it opens its maw and trumpets out a sound that flattens me to the ground.

Istvan cries out and falls to his knees, abasing himself before the gigantically terrifying creature pressing its way millimetre by millimetre through the torn gateway. Olga, however, remains standing and looks at the creature with an expression of exultant adoration. A smile spreads across her face and she steps towards it, holding out her hands in a gesture of welcome.

I shoot a look at Thorn. He is still standing there in front of the plinth. His face is no longer a completely blank mask and he looks to be coming back from whatever place Istvan sent him.

'Thorn!' I scream, gasping as my ribs protest at the deep breath I draw to shout. 'Get away from there.'

He gives no sign that he's heard me. Above him the thing is having difficulty getting through the archway. It roars with frustration and pulls its head back. The fissure starts closing but hands the size of two double-decker buses press through and start pulling at the gap, widening it. A massive armoured shoulder levers through and with it part of its horned head. An acidic yellow eye turns to take in everything before it. The pupil narrows and focuses first on Thorn, then on Istvan where he lies in supplication, babbling in a religious fervour.

Olga looks as if she's having a fit of rapture. She's tearing at her hair, her face, her clothes. I watch in horror as her skin starts rippling, revealing her true form beneath the disguise of her human shape. Then she raises her draconic head to stare up at the creature pushing through the portal and I know that, however long I live, I will never be as horrifically surprised as I am right now.

What I'm seeing makes no sense, yet all the sense in all the world. I let out a sob and put aside my shock and terror. Olga destroyed my home. She was the dragon. I don't know how I do it but I stand up, sparing my aching leg as much as I can, and limp to retrieve my knife. I catch Thorn's eye and he looks at me as if I'm a stranger. 'Please,' I say, my voice disappearing in the noise all around us. 'Wake up.'

I will him to see me, to know who I am and get what is happening here. We stand like this for a few moments only, my heart thudding against my ribs so hard I'm worried they'll break. I keep myself between Thorn and the gateway. There are sounds behind me that make me want to turn around and look, but I focus wholly on Thorn, showing him me, making him focus. I see that awful darkness in his eyes clear and he blinks and frowns uncertainly, his brow clearing. 'Kit? What are you doing here? Are you hurt?'

I want to laugh in relief. 'You have to stop the ritual,' I say very clearly. 'Do whatever you can to stop the ritual.'

He blinks, dazed, and nods. Then, as his expression shifts to shock, a huge hand wraps itself around me, enfolding me completely. I'm enclosed in darkness and the pressure around my body increases, slowly squeezing the life out of me. Desperate to stay alive, and fighting to stay conscious against the dizzying pain, I manage to wriggle one hand free. It's just enough for my blade to slice at the massive fingers crushing me. There's a dull roar and suddenly I'm free and I'm moving through the air in a high arc. I flail my limbs wildly, wondering where I'm going to hit and how many bones I'm going to break.

I don't really have time to think and curl into a protective ball – the ground comes up to meet me far too fast. I land at the base of the stage, but I don't have the luxury of time to recover fully, so I drag myself upright and waver on my feet, getting my bearings.

All of me hurts so much I want just to fall back down again and quietly die. There's a shout from the stage above me and I turn to look.

Thorn's struggling with Istvan while the beast is partway through into our world. To the back of the stage Olga's dramatic shapeshifting continues and it looks painful and awkward. It makes for an insane tableau and if I wasn't here to see it myself I would never ever begin to believe it.

'Kit!' Kieran is next to me. 'You have to leave.' He is covered in soot and blood but he looks remarkably okay. Whatever spell he cast, he definitely managed to turn some of that energy towards healing himself. He's holding me gently by the arm, careful of my cuts and scrapes. For a second, just standing there, I feel relief wash over me.

I'm not alone in this, after all. I try to smile but tears threaten instead and I gulp them back. Tears come later, action comes now. I draw a deep breath and face him.

'No,' I say firmly. 'Thorn is still here. He's awake. Look.' I start moving up the sloping pathway towards the dais. 'I have to help him.'

'Let me help you first,' Kieran says. 'Just stand still. This won't hurt a bit.'

And who knew a pretty Fae prince could lie so well? His hands are warm as they touch my bare arms and I feel a jolt of heat through my body before I can pull away. I open my mouth to yell at him. But by the time I do, I realize I'm feeling marginally better, more clearheaded and less sore all over. My leg is still a flaming mess but it's a pain that I can handle, like an ever-present toothache.

I grin in relief. 'Let's screw up their plans,' I say and move towards the dais.

'There is nothing we can do now,' he says, jogging next to me. 'The ritual is practically complete. The Elder Gods are awake and seem pretty keen to come back!' He does a double-take when he looks up. 'Who . . . Is that Olga Kassan changing into a dragon?'

'It's a long story,' I say to him. 'And one I'm trying to figure out too. Kieran, pay attention. We have to reverse the opening of the portal.'

'How?'

I have no idea but I know I'm not going to stand here and let my world be destroyed. And I'm definitely not losing Thorn to a traitorous dragon cow and her insane brother.

Chapter Forty-Seven

'Complete the ritual!' Istvan shouts at Thorn. 'Do as you are told!'

In answer Thorn swings a fist at the chamberlain's face and connects solidly with his jaw. Istvan staggers back, letting out an animal cry, and rushes Thorn, grabbing wildly at him. They crash into the base of the stone with resounding force.

As fast as I can, I limp down the aisle with Kieran by my side. He helps me up onto the dais, then he hesitates.

'What are we doing?' he asks me.

'Can we blow up that piece of stone?' I ask him, gritting my teeth. The ache in my leg intensifies as I stay crouched. 'If we break it, don't we stop the ritual?'

Kieran looks at me in surprise. 'That could work. It's a risk, but it could work.'

He looks up at the balcony, his gaze falling on the drums. 'I have an idea. I don't know if it will work. I've not done anything like this before.' He hesitates. 'It's not like I can make things worse, though, is it?'

'Whatever it is you're thinking of doing, just do it,' I tell him. 'Hurry.'

He grins, suddenly looking so like Thorn. 'I don't think my brother knows how lucky he is to have a girl like you,' he says and then he's gone.

I've never seen anyone move that fast. He scales part of the wall with ease and drops onto the shelf where the drums are situated. There is no sign of the drummers and he picks up a large drumstick. He twirls it around his wrist, as if he's a drummer in a rock band, before he brings it down onto the drum. The sound is loud. Somehow louder than the combined noise of all four drums had been previously.

The sound echoes around the amphitheatre and Thorn and Istvan pause in their fight for a second to look up before resuming their struggle. I take my chance. I pick up Istvan's discarded silver sickle and run at the draconic Olga where she's reared up on her hind legs and singing, in a surprisingly beautiful soprano, the rest of the invocation that Thorn failed to complete. I pray for balance and luck and slam into Olga.

I run up her back, sidestepping the rough spines. I'm on fire with pain and everything around me is a blur but I focus on the massive head in front of me and know that nothing else matters. I wrap my legs around her neck and with a great effort of will I bring the sickle around in a sharp cutting motion. At the same time I dig the last bits of my magic out and on impulse I stretch the energy along the curve of the sickle's edge. The steel glides through her neck like a hot blade through butter and I lean away as her head comes loose from her neck and slides off onto the floor with a thundering squelching thud.

There is a great absence of sound as I watch her head roll across the floor and drop off the dais. I want to punch the air and laugh in shock but I don't have the chance to do it. I'm hit by a stream of pure unbound magic and it rolls over me like a wave, forcing its way into every atom of my being, tearing and ripping. It is both glorious and painful and I think I black out for a moment, because when I look up again, I'm sitting against the small plinth that held the copper bowl, and I have no idea how I got from Olga's back to here.

Thorn heaves Istvan away from him as the man lets outs a wild keening noise when he sees the headless body of his sister on the floor behind him.

'Shut the gateway,' I gasp at Thorn. 'Send them back.'

I push myself upwards and I slam into Istvan's knees and he falls hard. We land in a tangle of limbs in front of the mirror and I let out a scream of pain when Istvan rakes his nails along my arm in an effort to get a grip on me. He's definitely stronger than he looks and he stands up without too much effort and lifts me with him, twisting my arm around then up in a vice-like grip. I slam my head back and feel his nose crunch but he doesn't let go of my arm.

Thorn turns to face the demon in the archway as it struggles to widen the rift. For a moment Thorn stands there, immobile. Then he spreads his arms wide and I feel a blast of energy curve through me, running towards Thorn like a river. I will all the magic I have in me at him and almost collapse as it leaves me in a surge. Thorn's gaze widens in surprise but he pulls all my magic into him un-questioningly, filling himself with the raw energies filling the amphitheatre.

There's a second of complete stillness, save for Kieran's drumming, before Thorn unleashes his magic. It hits the reflective surface of the stone I'm facing in a massive explosion of sound and magic, enhanced by Kieran's drums.

Istvan staggers under the onslaught and I spin out of his grip, grabbing hold of his restraining arm, and I lift my leg up and kick him with all my might, ignoring the pain in my leg and arms. I kick with all the force I have left in my tired limbs and throw the very last dregs of my magic with it.

His face turns red with the effort of holding on to me but then we're both in the air and I see a massive hand wrapped around him, squeezing, holding fast. I scream and flail at him as we rise into the air as the demon on the other side of the doorway lifts us effortlessly.

I remember my iron baton and I jerk my arm forward. It slides out and I start hitting his arm frantically. I smell his burning flesh and my ears are assaulted by his screaming and the bellows from the ancient creature behind him.

Istvan lets go of my arm and I hit the ground hard. I slump to the floor in a messy heap and through slitted eyes I watch Thorn walk up to the almost manifest beast in the gateway.

The beast turns to look at Thorn and a look of recognition crosses its features. It opens its mouth to trumpet at him but Thorn gets there first. Claiming the remaining energy ricocheting around the amphitheatre, working with the sound Kieran is creating with the drum, channelling all that cacophony and chaos, Thorn opens his mouth and shouts all his defiance at the demon. The raw power of the noise flattens me and I struggle to raise myself on my arm.

On the dais Thorn looks bigger, wild and feral, like he did back in Covent Garden. But here now, he's nearly as tall as the beast facing him and the sound just keeps coming from him in waves. With his arms spread wide, he challenges the beast. White swirls of energy gather around Thorn, and I don't need my magic to see this energy. It's in the air, visible and wild and increasing in volume and power. The whole amphitheatre is shaking and I realize that the noise must have triggered an actual earthquake. The rune-carved mass of stone sways dangerously and cracks appear on the surface.

The beast lets out a howl of anguish as a hand even more massive than its own reaches through the rift that it's blocking. The hand is followed by a hugely muscular arm and it winds itself around the beast's neck, choking it, controlling it. It proceeds to move backwards, pulling the creature and a desperately flailing Istvan, back into the dark abyss beyond.

With a final bone-crunching heave, the muscled arm draws the beast fully back into the yawning dark maw behind it and the first beast's howl fades into nothingness. The rift closes slowly over, but not before I see the face of the Sidhe warrior guarding the rift.

Thorn makes a complicated gesture that reminds me of martial arts katas. He draws the wild energies to him, gathering them into a tightly compressed ball, working it into a manageable shape and, with a thrust from both hands, sends the now-combined whorls of energy straight at the gateway.

It explodes in a thunderous roar and I turn and run

(limp) towards the passageway in a bid for safety. Massive slabs of black rock break loose from the stone and smash onto the dais. Over my shoulder I see Thorn's blond head disappearing in a cloud of dust and debris. I let out a yell and skid to a halt.

I hear a shout behind me, from the tunnel. I look back to see a familiar Fae warrior thundering towards me. Behind him, I recognize Dina's anxious features and behind her is Aelfric.

There's the sound of thunder and the earth heaves beneath my feet. I let out a cry and flatten myself against the wall as an avalanche of rock and debris fills the tunnel.

Chapter Forty-Eight

'Kit? Kit, you have to wake up now.' The voice is Thorn's but it sounds raw, stretched tight with worry. 'Come on. You've slept for almost five days. You need to wake up.' The bed moves beneath me. 'Marc is driving everyone insane, threatening my father's physicians with bodily harm if they don't get you to wake up. Megan is designing scarier and scarier weapons and has all the generals following her about. Aiden's managed to seduce all of the young women at the Court, along with a few of their mothers, and whenever he leaves his rooms he has a bevy of followers who attend him. It's embarrassing and annoying my mother.' He sounds pretty annoyed too. 'Kyle's not talking to anyone and has locked himself away in the scholars' study, not allowing anyone in. I think, Kit, that if you wake up now, everything will be fine. And calmer, much calmer.' I hear a heavy sigh. 'Kieran's pacing the hallway outside and takes every chance he gets to tell me how useless I am. I think his wife is worried he's going to run away with you. You'd better wake up and fix this.'

I reluctantly, slowly, surface back to waking from the

deepest pools of sleep I've ever fallen into. I feel lethargic and my limbs are heavy, not my own. My head is weighed down and I manage to open my eyes with the greatest of difficulty.

For a long time there is only light, but then I focus on the dark shape next to my bed. The smile that stretches across his face helps rid my head of a lot of the fuzziness.

'Oh, thank the stars,' he says, closing his eyes for a few seconds. 'I didn't think you were ever waking up again.'

I become aware of my bandaged hand resting in his. I smile at him. He looks rough. There are dark circles beneath his eyes and the bruises and cuts on his face from Istvan's beatings are still visible.

'Your poor face,' I whisper, finding that my own throat feels very dry.

'Have some water,' he says, holding a silver goblet to my lips. 'Careful, not too much or you'll be sick.'

'Is everyone safe?' I ask him. I'm not a vain person but I don't think I look my best lying here with bandages on my arms and hands. I'm tempted to ask for a mirror to see how many bruises and cuts I have on my face, but I hesitate. I'm still hurting almost everywhere, especially the left side of my body, but it feels far less than the first time I vaguely remember waking up.

'We lost a lot of good people in the battle at the lake. Eadric surrendered unconditionally the moment he realized the ritual had failed.'

I nod and close my eyes for a second. The room was very bright. 'What about Kieran? Is he safe?'

'Kieran is safe and his wife has vowed to name their

first-born after you. You have a friend for life in his wife, Evi.'

'They are going to call their daughter Kit? That's a horrible name for a girl.'

Thorn's laughter lifts my spirits and I chuckle weakly. 'No, if it's a boy, they will call it Kit and if it's a girl, Katherine.'

'I'm not sure if I should be flattered or worried.'

'Even my mother approves.'

'Worried, definitely worried.'

'And how are you, Kit Blackhart?' His face is so serious, his voice very deep. 'You did so many stupidly reckless things without thinking about your own life. I almost died from fright when I saw you in that room.'

I try to shrug but pain lances through my shoulder and I gasp. He folds his hands around my fingers and leans close. I stare into those impossible eyes of his and keep on falling. 'I think I'll be okay,' I say earnestly. 'I'm just glad it's all over and you're safe and not broken.'

'That's a matter of opinion,' he says and looks incredibly sad. 'I have to go soon but I wanted to make sure you were . . . you know, okay.'

I smile at him and bridge that tiny gap between our faces and let my lips touch his. I feel the shock reverberate through him and he goes very still and my heart stutters. Did I offend him? Was I being too forward? But then his hands cup my face and he looks down at me through long dark lashes and it feels as if I'm swimming in the golden light all around us and I have to squeeze my eyes tightly shut because it hurts so much.

His lips touch mine, a bit shy, a bit hesitant at first but then when I don't draw back, and I rest my hand lightly on his collar bone, letting my fingers run into the thick tangle of his hair at the back, he gives the softest of sighs and gently teases my lips apart with his. Heat flushes through me and I don't know how I'm not bursting into flames because it feels as if I should. I murmur against his lips and I can feel his mouth curve into a smile against mine in answer to whatever inane thing I said and then he kisses me properly this time and I'm sure if I look down at myself I'll find myself floating a few inches off the mattress. He keeps the one hand against my cheek, his thumb stroking downwards, while his other hands rests against my hip, pulling me towards him. When he finally lifts his head and looks at me his breathing is unsteady and my ears are rushing with the sound of blood.

'Wow,' he says, his smile slow and sweet and far more eloquent than I can even think to articulate.

'Yes,' I manage, swallowing. 'Exactly.'

We smile at each other and I know my face is flaming red because I can feel my ears burning. He lifts my chin and looks down at me and I wonder why he looks so unbearably sad when we've just shared possibly the most amazing kiss of all time.

'What?' I ask him, holding on to his wrist. 'What aren't you telling me?'

'I have to go,' he says. 'And it's really very hard to leave you.'

I want to say something flippant, to make him smile and maybe kiss me again, but there is something serious in his voice, in the intense way he's looking at me, taking in my face and holding on to my hand, that makes me think that this goodbye isn't just a normal goodbye.

'Do I get to know where you're going?' I ask him, careful to keep my voice from thickening up into a sob.

'I don't even know that,' he tells me and I know it's the truth. 'It's an apprenticeship of some sort. I've not been told the whole story. But it means that I'm leaving Alba. It means I'm leaving you.'

'For how long?'

He hesitates for a second, breathing deeply. When he looks at me his expression is one of anger and frustration and resignation. His voice is low, miserable. 'Possibly forever.'

Chapter Forty-Nine

Geas: A geas is an inherited responsibility that allows the person it falls on no choice in the matter. It can be seen as a curse that's been magically laid upon a person or persons, and once laid it is irremovable, regardless of rumours to the contrary.

From an archived report filed in HMDSDI HQ, 1978

'Thorn?'

He presses a kiss to my fingers and I feel his tears against my skin.

'Please understand,' he says, his voice hesitant. 'It's not a choice I've made. It's not a choice I would have made, especially now, having met you.' He tangles his fingers with mine. 'I can't escape this. It's been decreed, it's apparently "my destiny".'

I open my mouth to tell him where they can shove talk of destiny but he presses his lips to mine again and his fingers are buried in my hair.

'Where are you going?' I ask against his lips when he pulls slightly away.

'I can't tell you. And not because I don't want to; it's because I honestly don't know.'

'I don't understand this . . .' I say, my lips pressed against his mouth. 'How can they do this to you?'

'You have come to mean so much to me, Kit Blackhart.' His words actually cause me pain and I trace his jawline with my fingertips, finding it impossible not to touch him. His eyes too are more gold than blue now. 'Remember that, please. I wake up and all I think about is you, your smile, how you can frighten your enemies away merely by shouting at them. But mostly I think about how good it feels to hold you.'

Tears are running down my face as he stands up from the chair beside my bed. I sit up and swing my legs off the bed and stand up too fast. I catch the hand he reaches out to me and steady myself. I curl my arms around him and hold him close, pressing a kiss against his lips. I hold on to him, as I remember him doing once before, as if he never wanted to let me go. I take a breath, remembering Eilian and the story she told me as we raced across the lake in the starlight. I remember about duty, honour and obeying a geas and I still think it's a whole load of crap.

But I turn my face to Thorn's and put on a smile far braver than I feel. 'Travel safely, to wherever it is that you're going,' I say to him. 'Let me know if you ever need more rescuing.'

He gives a half-laugh – or was it a sob? – and walks to the door. 'I may just do that,' he says, raising a hand in farewell.

I sink down on my bed, alone in the beautiful room, stupidly trying not to cry and stupidly failing.

Chapter Fifty

The door opens before Thorn can raise his hand to knock. He hesitates a second before stepping into the room, past Aiden.

'She's awake?' Aiden asks as he shuts and locks the door, pointedly ignoring Thorn's bodyguards as they take up their positions – outside the room.

Thorn nods, heading for the balcony, which overlooks the lush gardens that form part of the Citadel's defences. They've miraculously escaped the attentions of Eadric and his occupying forces. And, as Thorn watches, several gardeners go about their business, tending the carefully laid-out walkways and plants.

'Is she okay?' Aiden demands.

'I don't think so,' admits Thorn. 'I'm far from okay and I've had a few days to get used to the fact that I'm leaving.'

'So did you tell her anything?'

'As much as I could, which isn't much. I can't . . .' He gestures helplessly. 'The words won't come. I tried, believe me.'

'Sucks to be you,' Aiden says without any irony and Thorn grins at him.

'Wolf, someone will knock your teeth out one day.'

'But it won't be you,' Aiden ripostes, but senses the prince's heavy mood. 'Why are you really here, Thorn?'

Thorn heads back into the room and pulls forward one of the chairs, slumping into it, his shoulders bowed.

'I'm worried about her, Aiden. She's never going to be safe, not after what she did on that damn island.'

'She's a tough girl. She has her family.' Aiden pauses. 'But that's not why you're wasting time here, charming as I am. Out with it: what's going on?'

'I am asking you to look out for her,' Thorn says reluctantly, his expression pained. 'I need to know you're keeping an eye on her, for me, for her own good.'

'She's going to be okay, Thorn.'

Thorn's expression is grave. 'It's just . . . I have this feeling I just can't shake – it tells me she's in danger and the harder I try and figure it out, the more it slips away.'

'Are you saying you . . .' Aiden clears his throat and gestures. 'That is, the *you* that's now going to be a "Guardian", as your dad put it, is seeing this?'

'There's only me, Aiden,' Thorn said tightly, 'I'm not two people. But, yes, this new role I'm being forced into is making me more aware of the potential danger Kit's in.'

Aiden assesses the Fae prince for a moment.

'I count Kit as a friend. I respect her abilities and think she's made of tough stuff, but I'll do what you ask, Thorn. I'll look out for her.'

'Thank you.' Thorn gets up to leave. He pauses, then holds out his hand. 'You're a good friend.'

Aiden grips his hand firmly. 'You're not too bad. For a

faerie,' he replies and unlocks the door, a grin on his face. Thorn looks exasperated but a smile creeps onto his face as he stalks back down the passage.

The Citadel, Alba

Aelfric, High King of Alba, crept through his own palace like a thief in the night. He knew the passages so well that he required no light to guide his way. He descended further into the bowels of the Citadel, a shadow within shadows. He moved with a swift assurance those of his close acquaintance would be surprised to see; gone were the slow steady movements he cultivated when among his Court. This was the real Aelfric, swift, tireless, determined, ruthless.

He walked past a dozing guard to the entrance of the dungeons and was satisfied to see that the flask of wine he had sent had been shared by the team on the watch. He strolled past, hooded and cloaked, down the passages and past the cells that usually held the occasional thief or illegal griffin hunter but were now full to brimming with traitors and conspirators.

He found Eadric's cell, the last cell at the end of the passage at the very heart of the dungeon. It was dark here and damp and cold enough for his breath to fog in front of him. He drew his cloak closer and hesitated for a moment only, before placing his hand on the door to the cell. It swung open soundlessly, reacting to his light magical touch.

A bundle of rags lay on the pallet and made no movement to indicate that it knew someone had opened the door. Aelfric was not fooled. He knew his brother was awake: he could tell by the silence in the room, the way the younger man held his breath. Even in the darkness he could smell the stench of Eadric's flesh rotting where the iron circled his wrists and throat, effectively silencing and curbing any latent magics he had.

'You always tried to reach for things that did not belong to you,' Aelfric said, pulling up a small tripod stool and settling himself down. 'Father always knew that you would try something as stupid as this.'

Eadric shifted himself upright, careful not to lean back against the rough stone wall behind him. 'You really are our father's son, Aelfric. Too stubborn to see what's happening in your own kingdom.'

'I see everything. I know everything, Eadric.'

'Yet it would seem that my rebellion took you by surprise.' The man could not keep the satisfaction from his voice.

'Hardly.' Aelfric shook his head. 'I let you play out your little game of insurrection. Did it feel good, while it lasted? Did you enjoy playing the puppet-king to mad Istvan and his foul sister?'

'You knew.' Eadric's voice was hoarse with shock. 'You knew what I was planning and you let it happen.'

'It was a way to consolidate my kingdom and form alliances, Eadric. I now know who I can trust and who I can't. I've had my suspicions for a long time about several of our generals and nobles. Watching you working on them was a very interesting exercise, I have to admit. You revealed a great many flaws in our defences. I should really thank you, dear brother.'

'You let your own sons be captured.'

Aelfric shrugged. 'I have many sons, but I knew you would not harm Thorn. Not when I discovered he was so key to your plans. It took me some time to find the prophecies you took such care to hide. But look how it turned out, Eadric. You woke the voice of the dragon. You brought to light both the prophecy foretelling a guardian for our realm and revealed the guardian himself.' He laughed at the irony. 'Nothing I could have done would have set things up as perfectly. Again, I really should thank you, brother. You have strengthened the House of Alba's rule in a fit of childish jealousy. With the Otherwhere acknowledging Thorn's guardianship, Alba's practically been given the golden key to every kingdom across the Otherwhere. Imagine it, Eadric. Alba's name will once again be on the lips of all the worlds.'

'Dina will destroy you if she ever finds out about any of this.'

'My lady wife is content. She has her grandchildren and her causes to keep her occupied. There is much we have to do to rebuild after the destruction you and your underlings created. It will keep everyone busy for some time.' Aelfric stood. 'Know that I will order your execution within the next few days. I have not come to gloat, but to ask you if there is anyone you would like me to send for, to attend you? A son, perhaps? Anyone?'

Eadric peered into the shadows behind Aelfric and smiled a ghostly smile.

'You will never find him, Aelfric. I won't make it this easy for you.'

The only response was the sound of the cell door closing behind the high king.

Chapter Fifty-One

The night is so late that even bad things have crawled back into their dens, leaving only the stars and a whisper of moon to keep watch over the graveyard.

I climb the fence like a pro and refuse to pay attention to the slight ache in my leg as I set off down the slope towards my nan's grave. It's peaceful here and I draw a deep breath. The scent of night-blooming jasmine fills the air and I'm reminded of sitting out late on the deck with my nan in our last home and smelling it on the air. We speculated where the plants were but couldn't ever find them.

But now she knows, I'm pretty sure, that this graveyard was the one place we never thought to look. Silly us.

I find her grave without trouble, knowing I could navigate my way to it with my eyes closed, and grab my usual spot just in front of it. I lay the tulips I bought her next to me.

'Nan,' I say. 'This world sucks.'

Sadness wells up inside me but more than anything I don't want to cry. I'm made of stronger stuff than this, I tell myself. I hate this feeling of being lost and hopeless. Megan tried to pull me out of my slump by dragging me around Paris in a ridiculous shopping spree for clothes, as practically everything we owned had disappeared with Blackhart Manor. We ended up at a nightclub and got involved in a fight between a bunch of Seelie and Unseelie Fae, all trying to be Beyoncé.

It was insane and amusing for a few minutes. But, as we staggered towards the Seine, after the bouncer threw us out right alongside the Fae, I became uncomfortably aware of them knowing my identity.

Their joking faded and their glamour seeped away, revealing their true faces. The Seelie group apologized for disturbing us on our night out and the Unseelie bunch tried to convince us to continue partying with them. But their eyes were just a bit too wild and feral and their enticements became too sharp, until they started freaking even Megan out.

We flew back to London the next day and Megan hired a car to drive down to Devon. Here, Jamie has a team of architects and builders working on a new Blackhart Manor. But I opted to visit Aiden and his family for a bit before driving back down to visit my nan. I needed just to hang out with her a bit.

'You do know most people think graveyards are creepy?' The voice comes from my right. 'Especially at night.'

I relax the grip on my blade and smile up at my uncle Jamie as he walks towards me from the shadows.

'You almost got a knife in your eye,' I tell him.

'I saw. Very impressive.' He nods. 'Like a ninja.' He sits down next to me on the road, stretching his long legs out in front of him. 'So? Is this going to be a thing now? Each time you finish a case you run here?'

I slant him a wry look. 'What if it is?'

'Just checking, so I know where to find you.'

'I have questions. About me and Nan. Did you know about us?' I ask him. 'Be honest.'

He lights a cigarette and inhales deeply. 'This stuff's going to kill me one day,' he says, blowing at the lit ember. 'And yes, I knew where you were. I helped her run with you. I understood what she was doing. If I had kids of my own I'm not sure I'd want them to be part of this life.'

'Wow,' I breathe. 'That's pretty harsh.'

He smiles at me, but there's no real humour behind it. 'Not really. Your parents were the same. They were working one more case, and had wanted out after you came along. Andrew was happy for them to walk away, to stop working for the family. But your dad had worked for the Spook Squad previously; he wanted to go back, and your mum was thinking of joining him.' He draws on the cigarette. 'Of course that pissed the family off no end.'

'I had no idea.' And I really meant that. I had no idea about any of it – my mum wanting to leave the family cause behind, my dad working for the government.

'Oh yeah. There was a blazing row about it. The whole family: all the aunts and uncles and cousins. It was war, I tell you. But a civilized one. Votes were taken, things were discussed, there was some shouting, but mostly lots of talking. Eventually it was decided that your mum could assist your father in his role but she couldn't join him as a Spook. The family wouldn't stand for it.'

'And then the accident happened?'

'Yeah, just before your first birthday.' He shifts next to me and digs something out of his pocket. 'Here, I thought you'd like this. I found it while I was clearing out my wardrobe at home. I actually meant to give it to you the last time I saw you but I forgot. I thought it would suit you.'

I hold my hand out and he drops something into my palm. I close my fingers around it. It feels like a pendant.

'Your mum gave me that after my first solo job. I thought you'd like it.'

'Thanks.' It's too dark to see so I put it in my pocket and stand up. 'It's almost dawn,' I say. 'Want a lift?'

'You don't even know where I'm going.'

I shrug at him. 'With no Manor to go back to and nowhere else really to stay apart from a hotel, I'm not really heading anywhere myself. Besides, I feel the need to keep busy.'

'How about a trip to Windsor?' Jamie says. 'We've had reports in that the Wild Hunt's been seen in the countryside and we've been asked to investigate.'

'Sounds like fun,' I say. 'But I'm driving.'

'Great, it means I can catch up on some sleep.'

We climb over the fence just as the sun breaks over the horizon. I point Lolita's nose north-west and drive out of the small village just as the milkman rattles down the road on his float.

extracts reading groups
competitions books new
discounts extracts extracts events discounts
competitions extracts extracts
books new reading groups
events books
new extracts discounts
books new titles reading groups
interviews
books events extracts extracts
discounts events new
new books events interviews
events new events new books extracts
discounts extracts discounts books
www.panmacmillan.com
extracts events reading groups
competitions books extracts new books